Praise for Imperfect Bliss

"Fales-Hill channels Jane Austen in a bawdy sendup of today's landed gentry . . . but the hilarious hijinks of the Harcourts hide more poignant truths about these strong-willed women. She whips an old-fashioned comedy of manners into a stylish, sharp-edged satire." —*Publishers Weekly*

"Chick lit with an intellec… —*Library Journal*

"The novel's strength is Bl… —a feminist raising a princess-obsessed … narrator. Issues of racial and economic prejud… the Austenesque social commentary."

—*Booklist*

"*Imperfect Bliss* is the perfect summer read. Susan Fales-Hill, a magnificent storyteller, has written a poignant and piquant comedy of manners that will make Jane Austen fans swoon."

—Adriana Trigiani, bestselling author of *The Shoemaker's Wife*

"*Imperfect Bliss* is a hoot! Featuring a heroine who becomes entangled in the nutty world of reality TV, it's a fast, fun read."

—Sarah Pekkanen, author of *These Girls*

"If Candace Bushnell and Zadie Smith had a literary love child, the result would be *Imperfect Bliss*." —Keli Goff, author of *The GQ Candidate*

"*Imperfect Bliss*'s romantic heroine ultimately finds her epiphany in a journey through family discord, reality TV productions, and a candlelight dinner for two . . . this is reading as alluring as the best French perfume."

—André Leon Talley, editor at large, *Vogue*

Praise for Susan Fales-Hill's One Flight Up

"A chick lit masterpiece that leaves Jackie Collins in the dust."

—*New York Post*

"Frank and funny . . . A wise and wicked peek into the overstuffed closets and medicine cabinets of New York's contemporary gilded set." —*Essence*

"A sassy summer beach read." —*Vogue*

ALSO BY SUSAN FALES-HILL

Always Wear Joy

One Flight Up

Imperfect Bliss

A NOVEL

SUSAN FALES-HILL

WASHINGTON SQUARE PRESS
NEW YORK LONDON TORONTO SYDNEY NEW DELHI

WASHINGTON SQUARE PRESS
A Division of Simon & Schuster, Inc.
1230 Avenue of the Americas
New York, NY 10020

First Washington Square Press trade paperback edition August 2013

Designed by Kyoko Watanabe

Manufactured in the United States of America

10 9 8 7 6 5 4 3 2

The Library of Congress has cataloged the hardcover edition as follows:

Fales-Hill, Susan.
Imperfect bliss : a novel / by Susan Fales-Hill. — 1st Atria Books hardcover ed.
p. cm.
I. Title
PS3606.A4275 167 2012
813.'6—dc22 2011035637

ISBN 978-1-4516-2382-6
ISBN 978-1-4516-2383-3 (pbk)
ISBN 978-1-4516-2384-0 (ebook)

To my parents, Timothy Fales and the late great Josephine Premice, who gave me the knowledge and chutzpah to attempt to follow in their footsteps "to undo the folded lie" of race.

To the late and magnificent Jane White, a woman ahead of her time, who fought that battle with talent, humor, and unfettered femininity.

To Diahann and Carmen, the grandes dames who make a mockery of servile stereotypes.

To my late grandmother, Dorothy Mitchell Fales, who embraced truth in defiance of a society that wouldn't.

To the men whose love, friendship, and example have "in a very unusual way . . . made me whole."

To Nanon without whom I could never have survived the men . . .

To Amy whose tragic loss has taught me to embrace life.

To ACH, my partner, my artistic and spiritual muse.

To my magnificent daughter who embodies all that is best in the human spirit. Continue to "throw your soul through every open door." You are my heart.

No soul can be whole that has not been rent.

—William Butler Yeats

And so you learn, to let go of your ideals
and not confuse them with dreams.

—Stephen Sondheim

Marriage is a great institution, but I'm not ready
for an institution yet.

—Mae West

For myself, I am an optimist—it does not seem to be
much use being anything else.

—Winston Churchill

chapter one

Bliss Harcourt stared down at her daughter who stood with cherubically plump arms tightly crossed to prevent her mother from removing her powder-blue ersatz satin princess dress. *How do you tell a four-year-old you can have the right outfit and the right attitude but it doesn't mean your prince will come? And even if he does show up, he might just ride away, permanently,* mused Bliss as Bella scowled at her through baby bifocals worn beneath a spangled plastic tiara. "Bella, please take off the costume," Bliss pleaded, not wanting to use bodily force, but aware that her stores of patience diminished with every passing minute.

"I'm not Bella, I'm Cinderella," the bespectacled tot shot back, setting her lower lip in a defiant *just try to take it off* pout. Bliss took a deep breath and closed her eyes, counting to ten. When she opened them, she found Bella's expression unchanged: she was frozen in stubborn determination to go to school a princess.

Bliss looked around the room, a wax museum of her adolescence. The four-poster bed with its flowered chintz canopy had stood unaltered since her sweet sixteen. In a corner, on the back wall of the room, hung her pantheon of youthful heroes and sheroes: Nelson Mandela, Mary McLeod Bethune, Bono, Mumbet (the first black woman to sue for liberation), and, incongruously, Queen Elizabeth II in full coronation regalia, included at her mother's insistence. Bliss was thirty-three and a half and this is what her life had come to: moving back in with her parents while she dug herself out of postdivorce debt and having standoffs with her daughter over a princess costume made of fabric so synthetic that it crunched like a cellophane candy wrapper being opened in a darkened movie theater every time she moved. Bliss sighed in frustration at what she perceived to be a conspiracy to turn every little girl in the developed world between the ages of two and ten into an aspiring bridezilla. Surely the film companies were in cahoots with the nefarious wedding industry. They had to be or there would be films about girls founding Internet start-ups, going to medical school, joining Habitat for Humanity, not endless rehashings of the parable of the motherless virgin looking for love in all the royal places. If only little girls knew where happily ever after led.

Bliss looked from the poster of a youthful Che Guevara, a hero she and her ex-husband shared, to the Yale insignia ring he'd given her in lieu of an engagement band three years before they actually wed. Neither of them believed in diamonds since you couldn't really be certain they hadn't been dug out of Sierra Leonian sludge by conscripted child soldiers. In the wake of the divorce, Bliss had moved the ring to her right hand, but she couldn't yet bring herself to remove it entirely, and consign it to a box of keepsakes tucked away on a shelf. Every morning she sprung out of bed hoping it would be the day her divorce suddenly struck her as 100 percent the right decision, in the same way that following her beloved down to Miami soon after college and marrying him had. Countless articles in glossy women's magazines told her she should have felt at peace when she ended her marriage. To her that was like saying, "You should feel entirely at ease about your impending amputation. Did we mention, we're all out of anesthesia?" Who were these bloodless couples who could calmly discuss unraveling their conjoined lives over a steaming cup of international coffee?

She looked down once more at Bella who absentmindedly hummed a waltz from the Cinderella movie. When Bella was of age, would Bliss join the cabal of mothers lying about the glories of matrimony in order to perpetuate the human race? No, she would find a way around that myth, while not dashing all her daughter's romantic dreams the way life and recent events had hers. Was this the moment to disabuse Bella of her illusions given that her own father barely bothered to visit, call, or send a text message? Maybe not. She hadn't finished preschool, and it wasn't even 8:00 AM. Bliss decided to spare her, at least till kindergarten. Fairy tales were like candy: fine if you didn't make a steady diet of them. Besides, she had to admit to herself that somewhere in the depths of her soul, she too was clinging to the hope that her ex would someday return. Failing that, she would happily settle for not feeling like she'd been hit by a Mack truck doing a hundred and twenty on I-95. *Not feeling like road kill, yes, that would be a big improvement,* she thought to herself. But there was no time to sing the "why me?" blues. She had to get Bella to school.

Kneeling down before her, she stroked her baby-bottom soft cheek and calmly said, "If you take if off now, you can wear it all afternoon." Bella demurred, frowning. She wanted specifics, from what time till what time? Could she wear it till she went to bed? "Till bath time," her mother answered. Bella furrowed her brow, weighing the offer, and then dropped her arms in surrender. Bliss lifted her own to indicate *this is how we take it off.* Bella followed suit and Bliss peeled the yards of dime-store tulle off her. As she handed her a short skirt, she looked down at Bella's right leg, which splayed out in its ankle brace. It was probably one of the reasons Bella wanted to wear her long costume to school: to shield herself from the taunts of the other children and forget her disability. Donning the skirt, Bella lost her balance, teetered, and fell. Bliss wanted to kick herself for not catching her in time. She repressed the impulse to pick her up and hold her tight. She smiled instead. "Come on, my little toughie," she said, her eyes beaming strength, encouragement, and heartfelt pride. Bella painstakingly pulled herself up. Bliss inwardly sighed with relief. Every such moment was a little Olympic victory in her child's life. *A challenge is an opportunity. That which does not kill me makes me stronger. . . . If it doesn't land me in the lunatic asylum.* Bliss recited the litany in her head, refusing to dwell on the unfairness of genomic roulette. She wished she could switch places and live with the diplegia on Bella's behalf. *There I go again,* she mentally chided herself, *doing useless wishing.* It was her favorite pastime other than reading history. Really they were of a piece. She could earn her PhD and become a world-renowned expert on French and American race relations in the eighteenth and nineteenth centuries, but all she would ever do was comment with the wisdom of hindsight, not change the outcomes.

From downstairs, she heard her mother scream. The last time she'd heard her mother let out such a howl had been when she'd had the misfortune of visiting during the royal engagement of Prince William to "commoner" Kate Middleton. Her mother had felt robbed, as if that "upstart" "Waity Katie" had stolen the position that rightfully belonged to one of her four beautiful, American daughters. "It should have been us!" she'd wailed at the time. Now Bliss wasn't just visiting, she was stuck listening to these rants. Grabbing her knapsack, books, and Bella's hand, Bliss ventured down the slightly tilted and creaking staircase of the two-and-a-half-story Tudor cottage to discover the source of her mother's latest wrath.

chapter two

Closely trailed by Bella, Bliss entered the wainscoted dining room to find her mother at the breakfast table in one of her trademark poses of soap-operatic grief. She leaned back in her reproduction Hepplewhite chair, one hand poised on a bosom so ample it strained the buttons of a peach chiffon peignoir two sizes too small. In spite of her agony, her Eartha Kitt bouffant wig (1980s vintage) was perfectly pinned in place and her "Very Vixen" lipstick flawlessly applied.

"Another opportunity lost," Forsythia wailed as she handed the receiver to her youngest daughter, seventeen-year-old Charlotte, and grabbed a steaming crumpet from a nearby plate. Harold Harcourt, Bliss's father and Forsythia's husband of thirty-six agonizingly long years, raised his day-old London *Times*—a treasured link to his home country—above his face, a shield against the impending onslaught. Bliss stifled a laugh.

"Hi, grandma," Bella ventured brightly, but her greeting went unheeded.

"Does the girl think fiancés grow on trees?" Forsythia cried out to no one in particular as Charlotte dutifully slathered butter on another crumpet and placed it in her mother's plump brown hand with a reassuring smile.

"She discards them like . . . like . . ." the distraught mother of four unmarried girls searched for a suitably dire image, "Fruit pits! Remember the tobacco lobbyist, the venture capitalist, the 'bean bag baby' tycoon Missy introduced her to? He had his own plane! The burger bun magnate, the heir to the stealth-bomber fortune." She rattled off the list of golden chances lost, sinking deeper into melancholy with each one.

"It's sheer recklessness. And waste!!! Shameful waste!!! Harold, do you hear me?" She shrieked at her better half. From behind his paper fortress came the answer.

"Yes, sadly," he said.

"What do you propose to do? We've lost another one."

"Another what?" Harold sighed wearily.

"Another one of Victoria's potential fiancés, of course. The lawyer, Dean Wong. How are we to get him back?"

Harold lowered his paper for a moment and furrowed his brow, as if deep in thought.

"I suppose we should send for the police. No, we can only do that after he's gone missing for twenty-four hours. Better yet, I shall set out with my harpoon and a net this afternoon." With that, he raised his paper barrier against his wife once again. Forsythia Harcourt's face went from cinnamon brown to woman-scorned crimson.

"Don't you see the gravity of the situation?" She screeched in the lilting cadence of her native Jamaica, an accent that reasserted itself whenever she was angry, out of sorts, or slightly smashed. She shoveled an entire crumpet into her heart-shaped mouth. Charlotte patted her arm soothingly, and pouted in sympathy. The barrier never dropped, the pages merely turned. Forsythia knew she had to wage this battle on her own. Her husband was content merely to see their daughters leave home and earn university degrees. He had no sympathy with her plans to see them married into the best, or at the very least, the wealthiest families in the country. Why had she bothered to fight and scrape her way out of her native Jamaica? Why had he left England if not for the opportunity to raise girls who would marry well, which meant wealthily and hopefully worthily? Feminists and career women could yammer all they wanted about independence and gender equality, but the surest path to financial security for a woman was still through a man. She contemplated her last born, Charlotte, a lithe mocha-hued gazelle in her schoolgirl plaid.

"You won't disappoint me, will you, my Charlotte?"

"No, Mama," Charlotte reassured her in a butter-wouldn't-melt-in-my-mouth voice while shaking her brown ringlets. Bliss rolled her eyes knowing full well the inner slut her baby sister concealed beneath her sweet-as-pie exterior.

Forsythia turned away from Charlotte and finally noticed her second eldest, Bliss, and her only grandchild, Bella, disappointments both. Her light-brown eyes narrowed, her pug nose wrinkled as she surveyed Bliss's grad-student dishevelment: she wore sneakers, sweats, and her dirty-blond locks knotted in a scrunchie atop her head. Forsythia washed down her bitterness with a swig of Earl Grey tea. Bliss, the lightest skinned of all her daughters had squandered her nearly Caucasian good looks on, of all things, a Cuban. A shudder went through her at the memory of the penniless "activist." Every time she thought of it, she cringed. Now here Bliss was: back home, divorced, with a child, and eight pounds overweight. Rather than enrolling at the nearest gym and Weight Watchers, as Forsythia had advised her, the foolish girl insisted on burying herself in the library at Georgetown to earn a PhD, of all things. What would that ever do for her romantic prospects? Nothing. One might as well have an unmentionable disease affecting one's private parts in Forsythia's eyes. Bliss was a lost cause. Forsythia did her best to ignore her.

"Looks like another happy morning in the Harcourt home," Bliss said gamely, sensing her mother's reawakened disapproval and frustration and striving to overcome them.

"Morning," Forsythia sniffed.

Harold dropped his paper and beamed at his pride and joy, the only one of his daughters who inspired in him anything other than perfunctory affection, pity, and dismay. It was he who had coined her nickname though she had been christened Elizabeth.

"Bliss," he crowed, warmly opening his arms to give her a bear hug. Forsythia bristled and looked away. Charlotte stared absentmindedly into space, twirling a brown corkscrew curl around her tapered finger. Bliss had inherited her father's peridot-green eyes and vulpine nose, as well as his sardonic wit. Most importantly, she had his heart and he was her oasis of sanity in the midst of a less than intellectual and sometimes unwelcoming household. Bliss settled Bella into her chair and poured her a bowl of cereal, then grabbed a crumpet and slathered it with jam.

"Should you really be eating that?" Her mother simpered.

"Yes, Blissy, you're looking 'vewy wibby' these days. Moooo!!" Charlotte chimed in, shaking a finger at Bliss.

"Mommy's not a cow," Bella protested, sensing her mother was being insulted.

"I like being wide in the beam," Bliss answered with a smile, while winking at Bella. "It means people leave me alone."

"You're a divorced hermit and Victoria's well on her way to becoming a spinster. Lord, why hast thou forsaken me?" Forsythia lamented.

"What happened to Dean? Thought they were serious?" Bliss asked.

"*Were,* that's the operative word. She's done with him," Forsythia explained, her voice quavering.

"Oh, well," Bliss shrugged. "He was boring anyway. And did we really want to be related to the lawyer for half the Bush administration?"

"So now *you* are a judge of suitable men, since when?" her mother asked in a withering tone. Bliss knew she shouldn't let the dart land, but it did, as usual, even after a lifetime of such insults. Just as she wished her ex-husband would turn up at her doorstep, declare his actions a terrible mistake, and fall adoringly at her feet, she wished her mother would just once look at her with something other than searing disapproval. She felt her mother resented her for some original sin she didn't recall committing. Of course she knew it was cruel and irrational of Forsythia to expect her daughters to fulfill her striver's dreams rather than live their own lives. But like therapy, that rational knowledge couldn't extinguish the longing and the hope that she would see, just once, in her mother's eyes, that spark of pride and approval that lets a person know they deserve to occupy space on the planet. But she never did. And she had to accept that she probably never would. Girding herself in humor, she began to form a response to the barb. Her father shot her an imploring keep-the-armistice-it's-not-worth-it look, so she bit her tongue. She needed her mother that afternoon anyway to pick up Bella at day care. She decided to take advantage of the slight guilt she knew her mother felt in the wake of her attack to make the request.

"Mum, I have to meet with my thesis advisor today at three, can you pick Bella up from Bright Beginnings and watch her for the afternoon, please?"

"Everyone depends on me," Forsythia sighed in a martyred tone.

"I'd ask Dad but he's teaching today."

"So am I. Nothing as exalted as the history of the atom, of course," Forsythia said, in a snide reference to her husband's field, the history of science.

"Ampère and the discovery of electromagnetism," Harold grumbled under his breath.

"What are you saying, dear?" Forsythia asked.

"Nothing," her husband mumbled from behind his paper. Forsythia waited for a moment to see if he would change his mind and explain, but he didn't. She had kept him on the treadmill of fatherhood, unable to look up for a moment from his work, or the bills, in order to prevent him from realizing she bored him to death. Yet she knew, every time he retreated into his reading materials, that she had failed in the endeavor. She continued, mustering her pride.

"It's my etiquette group, 'Little Ladies.' There are those who still think manners matter." *And there are those mothers who just need a place to park their children for the afternoon,* Bliss thought to herself. Then she reminded herself that her own Yale education, and her elder sister Victoria's years at Smith, had been subsidized in large part by her mother's earnings leading these anachronistic classes.

"I forgot," Bliss said.

"No matter, I'll go fetch Bella and rush back here. It'll be good for her; maybe she'll learn something. Perhaps there's hope for her." Bliss stifled a retort. How many afternoons had she spent as an adolescent learning to curtsy before the queen (well, a life-size cardboard cutout of her) the only real queen in her mother's book, Elizabeth of England? One of her mother's prized possessions was an original coronation mug from 1952. It sat in the corner cabinet, above the large menagerie of glass animals. The closest they'd ever gotten to meeting royalty was seeing the backside of Princess Michael of Kent from behind a rope line in the pouring rain when she'd judged a horse show in Middleburg. Bliss understood her mother's royalist leanings, though: they'd been beaten into her during a colonial childhood in British-ruled Jamaica. Forsythia's sense of her own inferiority had been earned ferule lick by ferule lick. Rather than rebel, her mother had chosen the path of many colonial subjects: she lived to out-gentrify the gentry and earn their approval and acceptance, all on her husband's limited professor's salary. Bliss did her best not to try to convince her of the absurdity of worshipping a bunch of inbred tax dodgers in borrowed jewelry, especially since she lived in America, a republic. Even Harold managed to remain silent on the point.

Diana, the second youngest, a ripe peach popping out of her pink polo shirt and khaki skirt, ran in brandishing a glossy magazine. "Look who's in *Town and Country,*" she chanted in a sorority girl singsong, tossing the once kinky locks she'd ironed into sleek submission. Forsythia eagerly grabbed the magazine from her, hoping by some miracle her garden club event had been featured. When she looked at the open page, she swooned in earnest. There for all America, nay the world, to see were Mr. and Mrs. Herman Hellman, her very best frenemy's daughter and her new husband, heir to a condiment fortune. She and Mrs. Herman Hellman's mother had loved and competed against each other for thirty years and now she'd been bested by the plump parvenu.

"Kitty Stump's wedding in *Town and Country.* Lord, take me now," Forsythia cried, tears of anger streaming down her cheeks.

"Mom, this is pathetic. It's way at the back of the magazine. Next to the ads for gently used designer purses, and psychics. This is the looser section," Diana sneered, pushing out her rounded chest. "I brought it down for laughs, not to upset you."

"But it's *Town and Country*!!! I won't hear the end of it."

"Don't worry Mum, Diana's right," Charlotte insisted. "Who reads that part? Who reads?" At the last comment, Harold lowered his paper long enough to share a glance of disbelief with Bliss. He retreated just as quickly to his paper, forcing Bliss to wonder if his abdication was in part to blame for Charlotte's ignorance.

"Besides," Diana said enticingly, her cornflower-blue eyes twinkling, "By tonight, I'll have news that'll knock your socks off and blow the Stump/Hellmans out of the water."

Her mother brightened and leaned forward eagerly.

"Did the Pritzker boy buy you a Diet Coke again?" she asked, practically panting.

"Who needs that geek and his overbite. This is better, much much better. And bigger," Diana declared with a dismissive wave of her perfectly manicured hand.

"You'll see." She kissed her mother's still smooth, rounded brown cheek. "Big morning: student government meeting, constitutional law class, and more," she said in the boastful tone of the intellectually passionless but fiercely driven straight-A student/cheerleader she'd always been. In Bliss's view, Diana had realized at a very young age that she was as bright if not brighter than the children of their far-wealthier suburban neighbors. Innately competitive, she was determined to rectify the accident of fate that had placed her on the less affluent side of life's Monopoly board. She used every tool at her disposal to "advance." A racial opportunist, she claimed her color when it suited her, and allowed people to believe she was white with a deep tan when it didn't. She tantalized young men of all hues with her beauty but never surrendered. Nothing deterred her from her ultimate goal: to outstrip her richest neighbors and enter the exalted ranks of the überwealthy and famous.

"Tootles," she cooed, flouncing out of the room. Forsythia's mind reeled. She racked her brain trying to think of what could possibly top a feature, be it postage-stamp size, in *Town & Country*, the sine qua non of society magazines. Perhaps someone had proposed to Diana. How infuriating not to know. Her Diana was such a tease, but she had raised her to be. It was why she held so many young men in her thrall. She enticed but never gave in; at twenty-one, she was still certifiably virginal. A fact Forsythia knew she couldn't assert about her youngest, but she refused to dwell on that discomfiting thought.

"Going too, Mum. Chapel this afternoon. I'll be late coming back," Charlotte said, also planting a kiss on her mother's ample cheek.

"What time?" Forsythia demanded to know.

"Not sure, lots of prayers," Charlotte shrugged wide-eyed, then walked out.

"Charlotte, your books," her father called after her in exasperation. Charlotte ran back in and grabbed the pile on the table.

"Oops," she giggled as she ran back out. Her father stared after her, shaking his head.

"Don't be so hard on the poor child," Forsythia said, defensively. Harold didn't bother to answer. He'd given up on the girl who in his estimation had all the brainpower of a goose in heat. An uncomfortable silence settled over the table, interrupted only by Bella's occasional slurping of her milk. Forsythia was on the verge of pouncing when Bliss locked eyes with her. She'd allow her mother to make mincemeat of her, but she drew the line at her child. Forsythia sat back in her chair and looked away, knowing to retreat from a mother lion.

"Bella, let's get going. You don't want to miss rug time," Bliss said cheerfully.

"No, I don't," Bella agreed, slipping off of her chair and wiping her little mouth. "Bye, Grandpa," she cried as she and Bliss walked out hand in hand.

Out on the walkway, Bliss took a deep breath. It was a crisp September morning. The trees lining the quiet streets of the genteel Maryland neighborhood were still a resplendent emerald green. Bliss considered the little 1925 Tudor cottage: a pygmy among giants in this wealthy suburban enclave. Her father had wanted to purchase a home in a more modest area, closer to the Georgetown campus. But Forsythia would not hear of it. She wanted to be in the best neighborhood, even if she had to live in a shack surrounded by gabled mansions. If she wasn't wealthy herself, at least she could be "wealth adjacent." Her neighbors had not exactly welcomed her with open arms back in 1975, this black woman with a foreign accent married to a bookish, nondescript Brit who made no effort to ingratiate himself. But Forsythia won them over, or wore them down with her relentless good cheer and willingness to help. Not an epic victory, Bliss mused, but an accomplishment nonetheless. She just hoped to apply her own talents, such as they were, to a more worthy pursuit than the grudging acceptance of suburban society matrons.

Bella and Bliss walked toward Bliss's battered ten-year-old Volvo. It was sorely in need of a wash and a new coat of paint. Bliss smirked at the general shambles of her life. At least she was beautiful inside, she laughed to herself.

"I should get married," Bella announced as Bliss backed the car out of the driveway.

"Why?" Bliss countered.

"Because it would make Grandma happy."

Bliss beamed, her daughter's perceptiveness having reassured her. Stupid the child was not. Perhaps she shouldn't worry so much about her future.

"Finish preschool first, okay?" she suggested.

"Okay," Bella answered earnestly.

As they drove down the peaceful street, they passed Charlotte, rolling up the waist of her skirt to shorten it, and tying her shirttails to reveal her pierced belly button while talking animatedly into her cell phone.

"There's Auntie Charlotte."

"There she is," Bliss echoed with a pang of dismay. She felt Charlotte was headed for a personal train wreck that her mother was too much in denial and her father too weary to prevent.

"What's she doing?"

"Something we shouldn't be watching and I hope you never do."

"But what is it?"

"I'll tell you in . . . ten years."

"I can't do anything." Bella sighed.

"Soon we'll have our own place and there will be plenty of things you can do," Bliss vowed to her. She didn't know how or when, but she knew she must rescue her daughter and herself from the emotional cesspool that was the Harcourt home. If they didn't get out soon, they'd drown in Forsythia's self-loathing aspirations to royalty, Diana's ruthless pursuit of fame at any price, and the profusion of chintz in every shade of pink known to man. *When life kicks you in the ass, you kick back,* Bliss thought as she revved up the engine and drove away from 101 Windsor Lane, the "little house of horrors" she called her childhood home.

chapter three

The bell in the clock tower of Healy Hall tolled the hour as Bliss raced across the quad, its lush green lawns dotted here and there with autumn's first fallen leaves. She felt her hair loosing itself from its scrunchie, the weight of her thick locks straining against the silk until the ornament fell to the ground. She didn't stop to pick it up though she could barely afford the five dollars and ninety-five cents to replace it. She hated being late, and it happened each time the head of the department gathered the teaching assistants for the weekly junior faculty meeting. The schedule of a graduate student, a divorced one at that, did not mesh well with day-care drop-off. Between trying to juggle her child rearing with her academic work and striving to rebuild her nest egg, she estimated that she'd be able to break her postdivorce run of celibacy by 2050. She cast a glance at her watch; the meeting had already been under way for ten minutes.

With undergraduates pushing past her, she took the gray stone steps two by two, like the sprinter she'd once been, before the marriage, the divorce, and her daily consolation boatload of Häagen-Dazs French Vanilla. As she raced around the corner of the landing, she collided directly with a man in a priest's habit, her armload of books tumbling to the ground. She slowly looked up and to her dismay met the drawn, ascetic face of Father Ignatius Cuthbert, dean of the Graduate School of Arts and Sciences, a man whose idea of a well-run society was Spain under the Inquisition. *Of all the faculty members in the world to body slam, why did it have to be him?* She thought to herself. He was one of the assessors of the fellowship applications. She was trying to win a grant to conduct research in England and France. After this literal run-in, she'd probably be lucky to get a Greyhound bus ticket to Hoboken, New Jersey.

"I'm so sorry, Father, I'm running to our junior faculty meeting," she explained breathlessly. His face, a dead ringer for one of El Greco's more unsmiling popes, remained stony. He kneeled down to retrieve her books. As he handed them back to her, he consulted his thirty-year-old Timex.

"You'd better hurry then," he coldly intoned. She nodded, and took off down the hall.

When she arrived at room 308, her lungs were on the verge of exploding. She could hear Professor Jordan McIntosh's booming, life-filled voice riffing, as he often did on subjects ranging from jazz to the guilt or innocence of Mary Surratt, the woman hanged for Lincoln's assassination. Bliss took a deep breath and stumbled through the door, a bedraggled, panting madwoman. Professor McIntosh stopped speaking, and three heads, each one more disapproving than the next, turned to stare at her. They belonged to her less-than-friendly junior faculty colleagues and fellow PhD candidates, a council of crabs each begrudging the other a millimeter's worth of advancement up the side of the barrel. There was Dierdre Detweiler, the medievalist, who with her Rapunzel-length blond frizzy hair and penchant for linen maxi dresses looked like an escaped Valkyrie from an amateur opera company's production of Wagner's *The Ring.* Though a professed feminist, she showed Bliss the least support of anyone in the history department, seeking every opportunity to show her up or embarrass her. On this occasion she grumbled, "Just wander in fifteen minutes late. Some people are so self-authorized." *Self-authorized?* Bliss repeated in her head. Since reentering academe, she'd had to learn its arcane language in which petty jabs often masqueraded as intellectual concepts. As in most aspects of her postmarital life, she felt as though she'd been dispatched to colonize an alien and inhospitable planet.

"Self-authorized?" Jordan laughed, "She's late. In my day, we called it CP time, but that's politically incorrect now. She's late 'cause she has a child and life, so let's move on." To Bliss's relief, he flashed her a warm smile, his teeth blindingly white against his buttery caramel complexion. The wildly popular and exceedingly attractive chairman of the history department, Jordan could talk deconstruction with the Lacanians and hip-hop with Kanye West fans.

"You're just in time to join in our discussion of the midterm exam," he added indicating a seat with a large, immaculately groomed hand. Bliss thought what a fright she must appear as she plopped into a chair, grateful as a vampire that the room had no mirrors. "I apologize," she gasped. Angus Gregory, the gaunt queer theorist, stroked the point of his goatee and sneered. Percival Linton, the expert on Catholic missionaries in South America, was his usual crisp, utterly unruffled self. With his high cheekbones, alabaster skin, jet-black hair, and piercing blue eyes, he looked like he'd just stepped off the pages of a Brooks Brothers catalogue and would be Hollywood's handsomer-than-in-real-life pick to play the boyish Christian Conservative Ralph Reed in a television movie.

Soon the warmth of the room, and of Jordan's voice, settled Bliss's rattled nerves. Everything about the space held the comfort of the familiar: the varnished walnut wainscoting, the royal blue walls, the well-worn armchairs that had seated a century's worth of students, and of course, Jordan himself, a man she'd known since his arrival on campus twenty years before. This university and its historic spaces spoke to the eternal quest for knowledge, a quest which to Bliss's delight bowed but was not broken by the more distressing trends of the new century: cell phones as permanent extensions of the body, fragmented sentences, research conducted solely at laptops, and the dismissal of any event that occurred prior to 2000 as ancient history. Sitting in this high-ceilinged space, she could pretend to have returned to the days of President Healy, the first African American to earn a PhD, become a Jesuit priest, and head a university. She listened with rapt attention to Jordan. His thick, dark locks were lightly flecked with gray, his huge chocolate-brown eyes expressed warmth and the pain of recent loss. She imagined how many pies, willing women, aspirants to his heart, had dropped at his doorstep since his wife, Genevieve, had passed away two years before. It was a wonder he hadn't gone all pudgy and bloated. He'd probably been saved from that blubbery fate by his long, lean Hiawatha genes and his legendary basketball pick-up games. He was commonly referred to as the Rick Fox of the campus. A colleague of her father's she'd known since adolescence, his presence always reassured her, particularly during these meetings.

"So, to jump-start those young minds out of neutral, I'm thinking of doing something unorthodox," Jordan announced. "One essay question on the midterm instead of three short ones."

"So brilliant," Dierdre gushed fawningly, "They need to learn to sustain thought past a text message. I think we should follow the Oxford-entrance-exam model and give them just one word: Vicksburg."

Gregory gave one of his trademark did-someone-just-flatulate? scowls.

"So obvious, so traditionally phallicentric with the battles. Yawn! You might as well just bookend it with Gettysburg if you're going to do that. I think you should ask them to think about the impact of Lincoln's sexual orientation on the conduct of the war," he suggested.

"Are you going to sell them sections from your own thesis?" Jordan teased. Like a striking scorpion who'd been stung back, Gregory retreated from the table and sat back in his chair.

"Bliss, what do you think?" Jordan asked.

"I like Dierdre's idea, because it allows the students to reveal their thought process. I would just make it 1865 because it's such a watershed year with so much to cover. From Reconstruction to—"

Rather than take the compliment, Dierdre seized the opportunity for further self-promotion. Cutting Bliss off she said, "I was going to suggest 1865, and obviously, we're asking people to think about the events of that year that impacted where we are today."

"Obviously," Jordan teased. "Some people think it's irrelevant. I actually think the question should be 'Why study the Civil War?' That sets them on their derrieres. That makes them think about why they're in the class, at this school. We need to help these young people find their way."

Amen, Bliss wanted to shout, but refrained. Why was she studying history? Simply because she'd already started her degree before marrying Manuel and moving to Miami? No, this was no choice of convenience. History was her passion, and she believed it held the keys to the present and the future. Professor Jordan McIntosh embodied all that she admired in an academic: integrity, wit, sweeping knowledge, great hair. She couldn't believe she had added that last, but as much as she tried to suppress it, she'd had a crush on him since her teens. And she'd deeply admired his marriage. He and his wife had met during graduate school at Howard and never left each other. They were intellectual soul mates and equals. Their union had always struck her as the polar opposite of her parents': it had grown richer over the years, they had helped each other develop. Even as a girl of fourteen, she'd marveled at their repartee at her dinner table as she watched them finish each other's sentences, teasingly correct each other, with Genevieve McIntosh usually right, but never flaunting it. Their witty, lightning-fast exchanges had silenced even the endlessly chattering Forsythia, who knew she was in the presence of a very different, spiritually elevated couple. This marriage had been Bliss's gold standard.

In Bliss's mind, Genevieve had possessed the beautiful version of her looks: a Creole lovely with light eyes, sandy hair, and features that, unlike Bliss's irregular nose and prominent chin, did not result from the sudden clash of two disparate gene pools, but rather had been honed by several generations of inbreeding within a certain caste. Her death of ovarian cancer had left Jordan utterly bereft. Yet, over the months, he had regained his bonhomie and it was on full display today.

"Now that we've settled that, I've got to share some gloom and doom from the ever-shrinking budget," he announced, trying to make light of a bad situation. Bliss and the others waited tensely. "I know all four of you are applying for fellowships to conduct research abroad. They had budgeted for three such grants. Now, because of the deficit, it's down to two," Jordan continued. Gregory's jaw dropped, Dierdre turned a shade paler, and Bliss nearly stopped breathing. Paul remained placid, apparently unmoved by the devastating news.

"Please know that I fought this reduction, but in the current climate, we're lucky, as part of the humanities department, not to be relegated to a water closet in the basement. All I can say is take a little extra time and care with those applications." Gregory didn't wait to hear the suggestion, he hurriedly gathered his belongings and shot out of the room. Dierdre exited with Paul, muttering under her breath, "What chance do we have against the minorities? I'm going to have to drag out a Native-American ancestor to get this." Bliss heard her, but chose not to retort. All her life, many a black person had resented the "free pass" they assumed her fair skin and light eyes gave her, and many a white person had accused her of hitching a ride on the affirmative-action omnibus on a dubious claim of "blackness." She refused to feel sorry for herself in either instance.

"Bliss, may I ask a nonacademic question?" Jordan said, leaning in to her as she packed up her belongings. She could feel the warmth of his breath, and his well-worn cashmere sweater was tantalizingly close to her right hand.

"Certainly," she answered, trying to appear unaroused.

"Are you all right?" Jordan asked her.

"Not really, but I hear that's the way with divorce."

"It will get better."

"I believe so."

"With Genevieve, it's one day at a time."

"Indeed," she said with forced cheer and sincere compassion for his loss. Selfishly, she wanted to ask him what her chances were of getting the fellowship, but she didn't dare. She refused to take advantage of their long acquaintance. As she rose to leave he said, "You should let me take you to the Pint and Horseshoe sometime." Bliss was stunned by the invitation and not certain what to make of it.

"What if we're seen there?" she asked. Jordan had always been so careful not to become fodder for the campus gossip mill. He'd never jeopardized his reputation by socializing with female students.

"What if we are? I'm starting not to care. You look like you could use some cheering-up, who better to give it than me. I've known you more than half your life." The last words extinguished Bliss's already-dim romantic hopes. This was one crush that was probably destined to remain unrequited. And yet, she detected the hint of a suggestive twinkle in Jordan's eyes.

"I'll take you up on that invite one night, Professor," she responded. "For now, I'd better get to the library and start working on my application, or I'll be living with my parents till I'm ninety." As she exited, she heard Jordan give off one of his rich, guttural laughs. So what if Manuel never came back? Maybe someone as wonderful as Jordan lay in her future.

chapter four

Forsythia marched proudly back and forth across the floor of her parlor, which, with its paneled ceiling molding and needlepoint unicorn pillows, was a careful Ethan Allen recreation of the Great Room at Kentridge, the country seat of an old family from Surrey whose surname vaguely resembled her husband's. As she strutted to and fro, she surveyed the motley crew of seven little girls, lined up boot-camp style in front of the overstuffed sofa with books balanced on their heads. Bella, the smallest, stood at the end of the row, happily sporting her princess costume.

"Stand straight," Forsythia commanded, a field marshal of finesse in her red St. John's knit jacket with burnished gold buttons, parading before her troops.

"You can always tell a lady by her posture. When you slouch, you let the world know you are a slattern. And mind your tone of voice. A lady's voice should sidle up to you softly, not smack you in the face," Forsythia continued breathily. Looking straight ahead so as not to disturb the tome on her head, Bella asked, "Grandma, what's a slattern?"

"A woman no one will ever want to marry, because she threw away her virtue like a crumpled Kleenex," Forsythia answered with complete certainty.

"What's virtue?" queried Melissa, a six-year old sporting a hot pink T-shirt emblazoned with the words *Juicy Princess* in rhinestones. Forsythia looked at her in dismay. She was a lonely soldier in the battle to uphold standards and decency in a world of aspiring pole dancers and visible derriere cleavage. Only she and Queen Elizabeth II seemed to understand what the world should be. She chose to ignore the clueless child and move on with the lesson. She had limited time to restore a modicum of dignity and propriety to a fallen world.

"Now, we're going to try the curtsy. Bend at the knee, don't let those books fall off your heads," Forsythia commanded. They followed her instructions with varying degrees of success. As the "little ladies" rose out of their curtsies, several volumes tumbled noisily to the ground. Forsythia cringed.

"No, no, no!!! Come on, girls, you can do better than that!" she snapped, utterly abandoning her ladylike whisper. "How are you ever to become 'little ladies,' and shine at a cotillion?" The eldest and the most jaded of the girls, a velour-tracksuit-clad nine-year-old named Jasmine, defiantly tossed her ponytail and smacked her gum. She wore an expression that said, *Look, gramma, I'd rather be watching* American Idol.

"Who wants to be a lady anyway?" she queried in a flat, world-weary tone.

"Gum! Is that gum I see? What is gum, ladies?" Forsythia asked, in a tone of unmitigated horror.

"A crime against manners," the girls recited robotically, including Jasmine who scratched her bottom for emphasis. Forsythia proffered a pink Chinese porcelain ashtray—which she claimed was a family heirloom but had actually been purchased, along with some Buddha figurines of dubious jade, at a Times Square bric-a-brac and electronics shop—for Jasmine to dispose of the offending and world-wrecking item. Jasmine continued her bovine ruminations.

"Ladies, I am trying to make something of you, so that your lives can be beautiful and filled with grace," Forsythia declared earnestly. Her tone was so sincerely impassioned that even Jasmine stopped chewing her gum.

"We can revive the grandeur of yesteryear, in our everyday gestures, the way we stand, walk, hold our tea cups. . . ." Forsythia did not hear the insistent knock at the door, so enthralled was she by her own inspirational speech. The knock grew to a pounding. Her charges interrupted her.

"Mrs. Harcoor!" they cried, using the French pronunciation of the family name Forsythia insisted upon to maintain her pretense that Harold's ancestors were French aristocrats who landed on England's shores with William the Conqueror in 1066, rather than field-laborers-turned-apothecaries after the Second World War. Forsythia went to the coffered mahogany front door and opened it to find a lanky All-American in his late thirties standing with a group that included a swarthy Mediterranean-looking man with the physique of a body builder, a hard boiled middle-aged woman wearing the Los Angeles female executive uniform of boxy Armani pants paired with a white T-shirt, and a sinewy androgynous creature with delicate features and a boyish hair bob.

"Good afternoon, I'm Wyatt Evers. May I see the lady of the house, please?" asked the handsome All-American in a booming stage voice.

"That would be I," Forsythia answered grandly.

"Forsythia Harcourt?" Wyatt responded, somewhat surprised.

"Who else would I be?" Forsythia challenged. More than once, and especially when she and Harold had first wed, she had been mistaken for the housekeeper in her largely Caucasian neighborhood. And in spite of her penchant for overdressing, she'd often been asked if she was her mulatto children's nanny. Wyatt smiled, sensing he'd made a faux pas and not wanting to dig himself farther into a hole.

Forsythia forgot the slight when she noticed, to her great delight, that there was a handheld camera trained upon her, manned by a stocky cameraman in Levi's that sagged about his ample posterior. She smoothed the front of her sweater jacket, stood taller, and flashed a happy hostess smile. *The local news had come calling at last,* she thought to herself with delight, *to hear her views on gardening, no doubt.*

"Well, Forsythia, how does it feel to be the mother of America's favorite virgin?"

"What are you talking about?" Forsythia asked, taken aback.

Diana emerged from behind the cluster, tossing her hair and beaming.

"It's me, Mummy, I've been chosen to be the star of *The Virgin*! A new reality show!!!!"

"The reality show that brings old-fashioned virtue and values back to our country," Wyatt announced directly into the camera in his soap-pitchman baritone.

"Because I'm a doctor-certified virgin," Diana announced proudly.

"Here's the certificate," Wyatt seconded, brandishing a diploma-like piece of paper, more for the cameraman than for Forsythia's benefit.

"Bless you! This was your news?" Forsythia said with emotion, joyously clasping her hands together. Diana nodded, a feral gleam in her eyes.

"Mummy, it's going to be incredible. I get courted by a whole bunch of guys, and I get to pick which one I want to marry!" she squealed, overcome with delight and flashing her pearly whites. Forsythia closed her eyes, as if beatified, and quickly said a prayer of thanks in her head to the very God she'd lambasted in the morning. Every year the girls were growing up, she'd dutifully seated them in front of the television set to watch the Miss America pageant, to instill in them the desire for fame of the non-scandalous variety. And now, her dreams were on the verge of coming true: her next-to-youngest would become a household name *and* select a husband. Her efforts had not been in vain; her sacrifices would all be redeemed by the success of her darling Diana.

"You're going to be on TV? National TV?" Forsythia crowed.

"Yes, for eight months!!!" Forsythia let out a rebel yell of delight and grabbed her daughter in a bear hug as Wyatt continued his narration. "Yes, folks, you're seeing the true, unscripted response to the news. This is the Virgin's mother, Forsythia Harcourt, hearing for the first time that her daughter has beaten out a thousand other contestants in a nationwide search to be the Virgin, the damsel in a dress."

"This is good, so so good," the female executive whispered to the other, swarthier gentleman. "She's perfect: biracial, prim, yet sexy. She's like Obama for the Christian side. No, she's the multi-culti Sarah Palin. This girl is going to make us a mint. Loving the overweight black mom. We can get her a deal with Jenny Craig." Her interlocutor remained stone-faced, and offered no response to this assessment. He focused on the scene before him: the rapture of a stage mother.

Forsythia's students clustered in the doorway, drawn by the commotion.

"What's up?" Jasmine asked.

"Diana is going to be famous!!! She's going to be on television!" Forsythia shrieked. Then, suddenly remembering herself, she turned to the production team and said, "Do come in," in a formal tone. Once inside, they found Bella still at her post, dutifully practicing the curtsy.

"Well, well, well, who is this cutie?" Wyatt asked.

"This is my adorable granddaughter," Forsythia said, grinning at the camera. "Wave to the people, Bella."

"What people?" Bella asked, confused.

"The American people," her grandmother answered, somewhat testily.

"Where are they?" Bella insisted, peering around.

"In television land. Just wave and curtsy." Bella did as she was told, causing the book on her head to fall to the ground.

"I can do it," Jasmine announced, jumping in front of Bella and curtsying perfectly with a wink and hip thrust to the camera. As she waved for emphasis, she inadvertently knocked Bella to the ground. The muscle-bound Mediterranean yelled, "Cut!"

"Cut? This is all great stuff," Wyatt objected.

"Can't you see the little one just fell down," his colleague countered, helping Bella to her feet. "You all right, kiddo?" he asked. Bella looked at his face and her eyes brightened instantly from behind their bifocals. She flashed him her widest smile.

"You look like my daddy!" she exclaimed, throwing her arms around him to give all the hugs she'd been unable to lavish upon her real father. He crouched, and hesitantly patted her on the back. Forsythia rushed over, horrified, and pried Bella away.

"Leave the man alone, Bella, it's not proper to hug strangers."

"It's all right," he assured her in a deep, soothing voice.

"He's used to it," the female executive interjected sarcastically.

"Just from an older group," Wyatt teased.

"Not that much," quipped the woman dryly. "They're getting younger and younger, Dario," the fortysomething executive added.

"Perhaps since you've stopped rolling, we should make proper introductions," Forsythia suggested. "I'm Forsythia Harcourt, Mrs. Harold Harcourt, as you know." The All-American stepped forward, took her hand, and gave a half bow. "Wyatt Evers, I'm hosting the show," he said.

"Lovely, lovely," Forsythia said, smiling coquettishly at him. She always did have a crush on Robert Redford and Wyatt put her in mind of the ageless movie star. She batted her eyes ever so slightly while remembering her queen-of-the-manor dignity. "I'm Sue Minors," the female executive barked, "vice president of MBC. This is our most important new project of the season. We expect this show to bring us the biggest ratings since O.J. tried to skip town in the white Bronco."

"But of course, it's about values," Wyatt interceded. "Not just a cheap bid for ratings."

"Dario Fuentes, executive producer and director, Mrs. Harcourt," the Mediterranean said curtly.

"This was his brainchild, mainly because he hasn't seen a virgin since he was thirteen," Sue Minors laughed. Forsythia was not amused. She indicated her charges with an archly raised eyebrow. The intensity of her scowl took Sue by surprise, wiping the cynical smirk off her face.

"Punch," she yelled and the androgynous creature shuffled to her side. "I need coffee. Is there a Starbucks around here?" she asked Forsythia.

"There's one at the strip mall, I mean, the shopping center around the corner. But I can make some tea. It is nearly that time and it's our tradition here. My husband being English," Forsythia said proudly.

"That's nice. But I'm strictly a java girl. Get me a quadruple espresso with soy foam. No-ow!" she barked, snapping her fingers at the scurrying gamine. Forsythia took a step back and looked to her charges as if to say *Exhibit A: The un-lady you don't want to be.*

"Can we get back to the shoot?" Wyatt asked.

"Yes," Dario answered.

"Let's have Diana and her mom take us on the house tour and Diana can share her memories of growing up and what made her decide to remain a virgin till marriage, blah blah," Sue suggested. Forsythia needed no further encouragement to climb on her soapbox.

"Values, pure and simple. My daughters were raised on them. You see, I instill—"

"Hold it, we're not rolling yet," Dario interjected, holding up a large, powerful hand.

"And what about us?" Jasmine objected, blowing an enormous bubble with her un-surrendered gum.

"Who are you guys, anyway? They aren't all yours?" Sue asked perturbed.

"No, no. I only have four daughters. And that one is definitely not one of mine," Forsythia answered, glaring at Jasmine and motioning to her to toss out the offending wad of Trident.

"This is her etiquette class," Bella said brightly, still smiling wide at Dario.

"Love that!! Let's get her to say that again, this time to camera," Sue insisted. Jasmine rolled her eyes, and several girls grumbled.

"Just 'cause she's handicapped, they think she's cute," Jasmine tossed out.

"Say that once more and you'll never come in this house again,"

Forsythia interjected. She resented her grandchild's disability, and felt certain she could blame her former son-in-law's lowly gene pool for it, but her tribal instincts rose up when the child was attacked by outsiders.

"Okay, roll 'em," Dario ordered the cameraman.

"This is her etiquette class!" Bella said loudly.

"One more time, sweetie pie, but this time add Grandma, Nana, whatever you call her," Sue requested.

"Grandmama," Forsythia suggested.

"But I don't call you that."

"You should," Forsythia snapped, then smiled.

"This is Grandmama's etiquette class," Bella parroted somewhat more stiffly, then executed a graceful curtsy. The front door opened and Bliss stumbled in, her arms full of library books and legal pads.

"Bella, I'm home, baby!" she announced, then looked around in utter confusion at the crowded living room. When she saw Bella executing a pirouette for the camera she yelled, "What the hell is going on?" Her mother signaled to her to remain silent. Diana glared. Dario took in the length of Bliss's hourglass figure, set off to poor advantage in her Georgetown sweatpants and hoodie.

"Cut!" he yelled, exasperated.

"Who gave anyone permission to film my child?"

"Calm down, Bliss, it's wonderful news. Diana is going to star in a reality show. It's called *The Virgin*," Forsythia gushed.

"We all are!" beamed Bella. "Doesn't the man look like Daddy?" Bliss studied Dario from head to toe. He had a strong square jaw; smooth glowing skin of a copper hue usually achieved only in a tanning bed, but which in his case was a gift from the gods; amber eyes with a hint of green; and thick, auburn locks that swirled atop his head like wind-tossed waves. To Bliss's annoyance, she had to admit, he could be her ex's twin brother. Only, her ex would never have been caught dead wearing a white muscle T-shirt and gold chain around his thick neck, like some bodybuilder–boardwalk Romeo. That touch of crass made it easy to forget the resemblance, and remember her fury.

"Are you responsible for all this?" she asked, testily.

"Yes, I'm Dario Fuentes. I'm the executive producer," he said extending a hand that she refused to take.

"And you're proud of that?" she challenged.

"It's a living."

"So is selling crack cocaine on street corners."

"And what do you do, other than pass judgment on everybody else?"

"I'm in grad school and a teaching assistant," she said, pulling her shoulders back and holding her head up high.

"So that's why you live with your folks and haven't managed to move out yet."

"Ouch!" Jasmine commented.

The accurate dig utterly deflated Bliss. For all her chutzpah and gumption, it seemed to her that these days, God or Satan was constantly sending messengers to remind her that so far in the game of life, she was on a major losing streak.

Bliss wanted to respond, but couldn't. He'd hit the nail on the head. She decided to get back to the subject at hand, rather than engage in verbal swordplay with this arrogant, mean, if perceptive, alpha male.

"Aren't you supposed to get permission from the parent to put a child on camera? I want the tape erased. You can't use it."

"Oh, Jesus," groaned Sue. "She probably wants the kid paid."

"How dare you? No, I don't. I want her treated like a human being, not a circus act!"

"Bliss, be reasonable," Diana pleaded, always convinced of her own powers of persuasion.

"I'm a mom. It's not my job to be reasonable," Bliss insisted. Dario turned away at this remark, and went to address the cameraman.

"We'll do it, we can play Bella's part!" several girls volunteered, thrusting their arms in the air.

Wyatt approached Bliss. "Excuse me, I'm Wyatt Evers, the host. Allow me to apologize for this. I'm a parent too. I understand exactly how you feel. I wouldn't let my son do television." Bliss relaxed slightly as she looked into his soulful blue eyes.

"Especially not a reality show," he added sotto voce.

"Thank you," Bliss answered, not certain of his motivation but touched that someone was treating her with respect rather than as the madwoman of suburbia.

"Come on, Bella," she called.

"But I want to stay," the four-year-old protested, near tears.

"You can't."

"Why not?"

"I'll explain upstairs."

"How come you never explain down here?" Bella protested, as Bliss led her away. As she passed Dario, she stared him straight in the eyes, thinking to herself that one day she'd make him eat his words. He stared back, unsettled by her unwavering gaze but determined to stand his ground. As she made her way up the leaning stairs of Harcourt House she overheard him say, "Kid's cute. *She* needs an elephant tranquilizer, and a makeover." Bliss started to head back down the staircase.

She could not defend her economically dependent position, but she could certainly refute sexist commentary about her looks. Suddenly, she caught sight of herself in one of her mother's many gilded faux Chippendale mirrors: her naturally pretty face was not enhanced by the Trevi Fountain of frizzy curls sprouting from the top of her head and dribbling down to her shoulders. To make matters worse, her fountain pen had leaked blue ink on her lips, making her look like she'd spent the afternoon orally pleasuring a band of Smurfs. Why didn't someone in her department point it out? How long had she walked around that way?

She'd made great progress in the last few months exploring the contrasts between France's treatment of mulattoes in the eighteenth century and America's, but she had many miles to go in the looks department, and in several others. She didn't just need a makeover, she needed a life do-over. Perhaps Satan's messenger had done her a favor, letting her know it was time to stop wallowing and make an effort. After all, there was a middle ground between being a vain flibbertigibbet obsessed with her appearance and a hag who'd let herself go completely to the dogs. Much as she claimed not to feel sorry for herself, or to have given up, her appearance told her otherwise. Her neglect of herself was an act of revenge on a man who wasn't even around. Even in divorce, she was still living for Manuel Soto, for his reactions. There had to be a way to forget Bliss Harcourt-Soto and reclaim and resurrect Bliss Harcourt in more than just name.

chapter five

Forsythia had gathered her husband, all four of her girls, and her granddaughter for dinner and one of her "family meetings" to discuss the great good fortune that had befallen them. For Bliss, it was yet another torturous groundhog day in the eternal replay of her youth that her life had become. They all sat at the rectangular dining room table that Forsythia, who believed that linens, like clothing, should be changed in accordance with the time of day, and favored metallic fabrics for evening, had bedecked in a golden cloth. Each Harcourt sat in the place they had occupied since time immemorial. Forsythia and her bouffant wig presided at one end. To her left sat Diana, to her right, her eldest, and to Bliss's mind the true beauty of the family, Victoria. With her medium-cocoa complexion, high cheekbones, delicate, perfectly symmetrical nose, she was a dead ringer for the young Lena Horne. Her gentleness of spirit and manner only magnified her physical splendor in her sister's eyes. Next to Victoria sat Charlotte, fidgeting and surreptitiously texting from the cell phone concealed under her oversized napkin. At the other end of the table, Harold did his best to drown out the women's chatter in the sea of his own thoughts. To mollify him, Forsythia had abandoned her usual Julia Child French culinary repertoire and prepared all the island peasant food he relished: spicy jerk chicken bursting with juices and red beans and rice. Bliss occupied her traditional place to his right.

"So, starting this week, I receive the gentlemen callers, seventeen of them," Diana sputtered gleefully.

"Seventeen gentlemen callers?" Bliss repeated with barely concealed sarcasm.

"I know, it's hard for *you* to imagine," Diana taunted, then barreled on as Victoria listened patiently. "The ones I like, the finalists, I give a garter to, the losers get a miniature chastity belt. And as they leave, Wyatt, the host, says to them, 'You have no hope of getting the hymen.'" Forsythia preened, a proud mother hen. Victoria did her best to conceal her distaste. Any discussion of sex unsettled her. Harold barely stifled a groan. Bliss waited for someone else to comment on the certifiable insanity of the situation but before anyone could, Diana had turned on her powder-pink laptop. Ordinarily Forsythia banned all electronics from her dining table, but she'd made a grand exception in this instance, the prime-time beatification of her gorgeous, chaste daughter.

"And here's the pièce de résistance," Diana, the unsullied, bellowed in her well-pronounced French, "My video portrait for the suitors. This is going out virally tonight to three thousand of the most eligible men between the ages of twenty-five and thirty in the world."

Birds chirped in the background as the image of a neo-Gothic cathedral filled the computer screen. The camera traveled down from the spires, to the gargoyles at the church's base. There stood Diana, bathed in a *Vaseline on the camera lens* glow, wearing a long white chiffon gown last considered fashionable daywear in the thirteenth century. She stared down at the lone perfect rose in her right hand then slowly lifted her steely blue eyes to meet the camera's gaze. Parting her heavily glossed lips in an expression of coy wonder, she held the bloom between her ample 36Cs, rendered all the more melonlike by a push-up bra. Breathily, she said, "I'm Diana Harcourt, but please, call me Didi. I'm twenty-one, a junior at Georgetown majoring in psychology and economics. I'm captain of the pep squad, the French club, and the head fund-raiser for the annual holiday drive for Operation Smile, which makes the reparation of cleft palates possible for thousands of children in the Third World every year. What would we do if we couldn't smile?" she asked, flashing her pearly whites before continuing her personal infomercial. "One day, I plan to be a senator, or the head of the International Red Cross, but my most important job, and my biggest priority, is to be a great wife to that really special guy. I'm proud to say that I'm a virgin, because I think it's important to give something sacred to the man you marry." She cast her eyes down at the bloom between the boobs once again before looking up and saying soulfully, her chest heaving, "Could you be that special someone who takes my rose? You'll never know, if you don't try." With that, she looked down again at the rose as if in prayer and added, "Come make a virgin's dream come true, prove that you are the one worthy of the rose." She extended the flower toward the viewer and the camera panned back up to a cloudless blue sky.

"That's it. Isn't it genius?" Diana gushed, shutting off the computer.

Bliss, Victoria, and Harold sat in stunned horror, as if having been turned to stone by a sighting of Medusa herself.

"As a recruitment tool for a terrorist group," Harold muttered under his breath, unheard by the others. Victoria and Bliss exchanged sympathetic glances, as they had so often over the years, over the antics of their mother and sisters.

Unable to contain herself any longer, Bliss burst out, "This is barbaric! Are they going to hang the bloody sheet out the day after the wedding to prove that you were pure?"

"What's a virgin?" Bella asked innocently.

"What you will remain until marriage, like your Auntie Diana. That's how you end up with a prince," Forsythia pronounced.

"Don't tell my daughter that nonsense," Bliss snapped. "A virgin is a person, male or female, who has not yet had intercourse, you know, what we saw the sea lions having at the zoo."

"When one was on the other's back?"

"Yes, sweetie."

"I will not have this filthy talk at my table!" Forsythia snapped.

"Oh, but we can talk about hymens?" Bliss riposted, incredulous.

"You're forgetting *hymen* also means marriage, Bliss," Diana said scornfully.

"Which you're being sold into!" Bliss countered.

A loud buzz emanated from Charlotte's lap. Forsythia cast her eyes around the room in search of the source of the offending sound.

"What was that?" she demanded to know.

"Got to go to the bathroom, excuse me," Charlotte said, getting up and running out of the room. *Who was she taking calls from now,* Bliss wondered.

"It's 'may I be excused please?' Let's not behave like a pack of wild dogs!" Her mother hollered after her at full-fishwife volume. "This is your doing," she reproached Bliss. "You are lowering the standards of this household."

"Doing this show is lowering the standards. Don't you get it? The joke is on us. 'Seventeen gentlemen callers,' that's a reference to Amanda Wingfield in *The Glass Menagerie,* the most delusional character in the Tennessee Williams canon! Whoever came up with this is making fun of the whole concept."

"Jealousy will age you even more quickly than divorce has," Forsythia warned.

"Jealous? That my sister is basically being auctioned off in marriage for ratings?"

"No one's auctioning anyone. I get to choose my husband and they pay for the wedding. And I'm going to be famous. It's called business."

"It's called 'female trafficking.'"

"You've been reading too much about slavery. And maybe if you took your nose out of the history books for a moment, you'd join us in the twenty-first century. Everyone's doing reality TV," Diana countered.

"This will also be an excellent showcase for you, Victoria, since you've tossed away another fiancé," Forsythia pointed out. Victoria struggled to retain her composure.

"Mother, please," she begged, "you promised we wouldn't discuss Dean any longer."

"I just don't understand why you throw away one perfectly good prospect after the other. As the saying goes, 'If you keep picking picking picking, you end up with the one with one eye,'" Forsythia cautioned.

"Mama, that will all change once she gets on TV. They'll probably write in to propose to her too. She'll find someone. She'll be my Pippa Middleton," Diana said encouragingly.

"You're right. She's much prettier than that weasel-eyed Pippa. This show will expose her to a much larger market. International even," Forsythia concurred.

"Market? What is she, a steak? Listen to yourselves. Papa, help me here, we can't let this happen," Bliss implored her father. He slowly and deliberately chewed his piece of chicken, then swallowed before answering.

"Bliss, you're being too harsh."

Forsythia smiled at Bliss, triumphant. Harold continued.

"I'm looking forward to the sequel, which begins with the scene of the blood-stained sheet you so eloquently described, dear Bliss, then takes the viewer back to the act itself. This slight brush with pornography should make us quite rich. And your mother shall have the suitably large and gaudy house of which she's always dreamed and which my paltry university salary could never provide," Harold deadpanned. Forsythia's self-satisfied grin morphed into a scowl as it dawned on her that her husband was mocking her.

"I have never complained," Forsythia insisted in a martyred tone, "about the inadequate size of this house, my lack of jewels, my ten-year-old vehicle, the fact we couldn't join the country club, wearing the same mink, year after year." Her litany of parvenu's grievances was interrupted by the doorbell, which sounded the first eight notes of Beethoven's "Ode to Joy." Charlotte dashed out of the powder room to run and answer the door.

"You didn't flush!" Her mother yelled.

"Oh," Charlotte, said, ducking back into the powder room and correcting her oversight. The toilet bowl's roar served as fanfare for Wyatt Evers, the show's host, who entered brandishing six different bouquets of flowers.

"May I come in?" he asked, having already walked straight into the house.

"Hope I'm not interrupting anything," he said, strutting into the dining room.

"Not at all, you're just in time," Forsythia intoned, rising from her chair to greet him. "Please, have a seat," she said, pulling an extra chair up to the table. "We were just finishing dinner." She smiled at him in her most magnanimous manner.

"Looks delicious, rice and beans, my favorite."

"Not my usual. Ordinarily, I make coq au vin or *boeuf bourguignon.*"

"No, this is my kind of food," he assured her. "And these are for you ladies," he said, making his way around the table to hand each Harcourt woman a bouquet. There were roses for Forsythia, daisies for Charlotte, bluebells for Victoria, baby roses for Bella, tulips for Diana. As he handed Bliss her orchids, he gave her a quick wink. Bliss wasn't certain whether to be charmed or put off by the gesture, but his surfer boy good looks, though not her usual taste, continued to wear down her guardedness.

"One for each of us, so sweet," Diana purred flashing Wyatt a coquettish smile.

"How did you know how many to bring?" marveled Forsythia. "You hadn't met my eldest, Vic—"

"Victoria, the librarian at the Archives of American Art," he said, completing her sentence.

Forsythia's astonishment was total.

"I do my homework, Mrs. Harcourt, especially with such an interesting family. With so many beautiful women, but with a mother like you, the apples couldn't help but be golden," Wyatt said, rubbing his hands as he took a seat. Forsythia basked in the glow of the compliment, and fluffed a strand of her wig. Harold coughed, and noisily cleared his throat, while flashing a devilish grin at Bliss, who remained torn in her opinion of the newcomer. She had liked his courtesy when she had first met him, but she found the flower stunt slightly manipulative.

"What do you want from us, Mr. Evers?" she asked pointedly.

"Bliss, how rude!" her mother admonished. "Please, do sit down, Wyatt. Bliss, go fetch Mr. Evers a plate from the kitchen."

Bliss reluctantly rose from her seat. Since childhood, she'd been the designated gofer and servant, a tactic her mother had used to remove her, and her annoyingly accurate comments, from the family table.

"We were just talking about the show," Diana explained.

"And how delighted we are to be participating," her mother added.

"How delighted *some* of us are," Bliss corrected pointedly, before disappearing into the kitchen through the swinging door. Wyatt took note of the comment before turning his charm on Victoria.

"So tell me about what you do?"

"Oh, it's not very interesting," she demurred.

"Archives of American Art, not interesting, are you kidding?"

"You're familiar with them?" Victoria asked, surprised.

"Absolutely! I used to go there to look at the Wyeth letters and the Stieglitz photographs." Bliss reemerged from the kitchen and set a heaping plate before him.

"No one captured the light and dark of capitalism like—thank you, Bliss—Stieglitz." Bliss listened intrigued. She hadn't thought a host for a cheesy reality show would have read anything. "He hit the conflict at the heart of the American soul. We're torn between our ideals, the sublime, and our venal desires, the crassly commercial." Forsythia tried to follow his train of thought, but he'd lost her back at the flowers. Diana just wanted to return to the details of the show, impatient with this verbiage.

"It's what Fitzgerald captured so eloquently in his novels; it's frankly why I'm a little torn about doing this show myself," he concluded as he took a bite of his chicken. "Mmmm, this is delicious, Mrs. . . . Forsythia." Forsythia beamed.

"As I said, it's not my usual."

"You're torn about doing the show?" Bliss asked skeptically.

"Absolutely. I mean, this is not what I trained to do. I went to the Yale School of Drama. Shakespeare, Miller, O'Neill, that's my beat. The only reference to theater in this gig is the crack about the 'seventeen gentlemen callers,' and no one involved gets that the writer's making fun of us."

"That's what I just said," Bliss assented, sitting down next to him and taking new interest in this man whose eyes were undeniably lovely and whose hands were large and . . . promising.

"Of course, because you've read a book in your life, unlike our executive producer, Dario, glorified 'Guido' and his network henchwoman, Sue. The writer was nominated for an Oscar back in the nineties, but now this is the only way he gets to keep his insurance and a roof over his head. Honestly, that's why I'm doing this."

Diana was less than pleased with this condemnation of the vehicle that was about to propel her to the celebrity stratosphere occupied by the Real Housewives, the Kardashians, and most inspiringly, the Duchess of Cambridge. His comments struck her as nothing short of treasonous.

"Why are you doing it if you think it's so wrong?" she challenged, pushing out her gravity-defying breasts. He took in the admirable sight and smiled.

"I didn't say it was wrong."

Now Bliss was confused; she leaned in to listen. Bella let out a hiccup. Even Harold looked up from his meal, intrigued by the reasoning of this not unintelligent young man.

"Look, it's a living. And I've got an ex-wife and a child to support. I can't just selfishly follow my own dreams and be a deadbeat dad." Bella looked up at him. He'd just scored another point on Bliss's tote board:

knows his literary references and has gone through a divorce and is trying to be decent about it, check check. Even Victoria considered him with renewed interest. Charlotte continued her surreptitious texting under the tablecloth.

"If I had my druthers, I'd be auditioning for the Public Theater and making scale, or singing my folk songs in a New York subway station. This gig came along. I had to grab it. Besides, if we do it right, if those of us with integrity stand up for the quality, it can be very helpful to all the young women out there struggling to 'just say no' to the guys pressuring them for easy hookups, one-night stands."

"Exactly," Diana assented, her faith in her costar restored. "That's why I started my abstinence video blog last year. To make it cool to be pure," she said, pushing her chest out even farther and licking her pulpy lips.

"Charlotte, you're in high school, wouldn't a show like this help you?" Wyatt asked. Bliss was touched by Wyatt's willingness to give Charlotte the benefit of the doubt. She was quite certain Charlotte's virtue had been trampled by more athletes than the Astroturf at Giants Stadium.

"Huh?" Charlotte asked, not having heard the question.

"He said wouldn't the show help you abstain from sex?" Diana repeated, exasperated by her dim-witted sibling.

"Sure, I guess so. . . ."

"Bliss, I hope you'll participate," Wyatt stated.

"She lives here, she doesn't have a choice," Forsythia insisted.

"Yes, she does," Harold objected and shot his wife a rare look of fury she knew not to countermand.

"I'm trying to get a PhD. I can't be on a reality show," Bliss explained good-naturedly to Wyatt.

"You don't have to be on the show. But you can come on some of the trips—we're going to Vienna for the balls at Christmas, England for the jousting in the spring. It's all expenses paid."

"I don't think so," Bliss demurred, though she did love to travel and had not had the opportunity to take an overseas trip since Bella had been born.

"I'm applying for a fellowship to London and Paris, different class of travel," she explained.

"Hey, why not be on the MBC fellowship, first-class travel and you can train it to those places to do your research." His logic appealed to Bliss, as did his slightly raspy voice. She could think of worse fates than sipping champagne in the first-class cabin of a jetliner bound for Europe, sitting next to this tall, lean specimen. First Jordan, now Wyatt peaked her interest. She was on day 375 of postdivorce celibacy, but there were several glimmers of hope that soon her libido would be let out of captivity.

chapter six

As Jordan unlocked the front door of his classic brick Georgetown townhouse, Bliss cast nervous glances onto the street. She felt a warm, large hand fall on her right palm and pull her firmly inside. Jordan pushed her against the door and his full mouth met hers. He parted his lips gently and waited for hers to yield. Then it began, the deeper his tongue penetrated, the more her body relaxed and melded with his strong six-foot-five athletic frame. He began to remove her sweatpants, sliding them slowly over her hips. She stepped out of them and kicked them to the side, all the while running her hands eagerly through his curls. They slipped like silk threads through her fingers. She felt his warm hands caress her ample buttocks, and thought to herself with delicious anticipation, *We're going to do it right here standing up.*

"Mommy, Mommy!" a voice shrieked. Bliss sat bolt upright in her bed, or rather, on the roll away cot in which she slept so as to give her daughter the more comfortable four-poster. Perspiration drenched her Fruit of the Loom T-shirt, a relic from her marriage she'd stolen from her husband. She looked at the clock: it was midnight. She leapt out of the cot to go comfort Bella, who looked around the room, myopic and terrified. Bliss handed Bella her baby bifocals and wrapped her arms around her.

"I had a scary dream," Bella moaned.

"Tell Mama about it," Bliss said soothingly.

"A monster took Daddy away, a big one," Bella recounted in the halting tones of a child recently awakened from a nightmare.

Not entirely untrue, Bliss thought to herself. *Although the monster in question is a size-two refried blonde, twenty-eight years old.*

"What monster? Where?"

"In the swamps, where Daddy took me on the boat and we saw an alligator, that time."

"Yes."

"But this time a monster came and I was all alone."

"There's no monster. It was all just a bad dream."

"Can we look at Daddy on the computer again?"

Bliss cringed. They'd spent half the evening replaying the JPG video Manuel had sent that day. He emailed weekly dispatches that were more like infomercials to a constituent than loving missives to one's toddler daughter, but Bella lived for them.

"It's late, sweetheart, tomorrow."

"No, Mommy, please now," Bella begged. Bliss resignedly crossed to the desk and turned on the laptop. Bella's eyes grew saucer wide with delight as she expertly manned the mouse and opened the missive. Manuel Soto, love of Bliss's life and ultimate traitor to her heart, appeared on the screen. He stood in front of his campaign headquarters. Behind him hung a sign: SOTO FOR CONGRESS: BECAUSE IT'S TIME. He'd clearly taped the message at the end of a long day, Bliss surmised from the slightly rumpled state of his oxford shirt, rolled up at the cuffs, and his loosened tie. Even in his dishevelment, he was the portrait of male sensuality. The blindingly white shirt set off the rich tones of his deep-olive complexion. A tuft of his slicked-back hair fell over his eyes, which were a translucent cinnamon brown with a rim of emerald green. But it was his hands that always did Bliss in: large and well formed, she could remember their warmth and baby softness when they'd strummed her neck. Bella feverishly clicked on the arrow to start the video.

"Hola, mi vida," Manuel's slightly hoarse voice intoned. Bliss closed

her eyes to mitigate the visceral effect of his baritone. It made her entire body lurch toward him, aching to yield.

"Hi, Daddy," Bella squealed waving wildly at the screen as though he were trapped in the computer and her gestures could release him. He paused before continuing, the perpetual campaigner and orator, used to letting his adoring audience simmer down before he graced them with his speech.

"It's been a long day. Daddy was out meeting with farm workers who make very little money, and illegal immigrants from places like Haiti and Cuba where Daddy's parents escaped from." Bella listened with rapt attention, trying to understand, but clearly baffled at the meaning of these bulletins from the front. The mesmeric spell wrought by his voice and the sight of his hands evaporated for Bliss, giving way to fury, the fury she had felt at his constant absences from home, and neglect of Bella from the time she had been diagnosed at two. Could he talk about nothing but himself? Nonetheless, seeing Bella's thirst for the contact, however cyber limited and artificial, forced her to bite her tongue.

"I'm trying to protect the rights of people who have none, Bella. This is a great country but we have to make it a fair place to live for everyone." Bliss wondered when he would make his heart a fair place to live for his daughter.

"Oh, and one more thing, I told the farmers I had a little girl and they gave me this." He picked a jar up from his desk and lifted it toward the camera. Inside it sat a green frog, its throat throbbing, its bulging eyes staring.

"What do we call these in Spanish?" he asked.

"*Una rana!!!*" Bella hopped up and down, nearly falling in the process. "Mommy, Daddy got me a frog!!!! He got me a frog!!!!" she screeched as though he'd just given her the Hope Diamond.

"I'm going to keep this little guy, for when you come visit me. Have a good night, sweetie. Be good!!! Daddy loves you."

"I love you, Daddy," she cried before lunging for the screen and planting a feverish kiss on his now frozen image. Moments before, Bliss had wanted to do the same. Now, she wanted to take a rock and smash it. Such was the schizophrenia of divorce: one minute you wanted nothing so much as to throw your arms around your ex and say "take me now." The next, you could murder him with your bare hands. Suddenly all those pathetic stories of ex-wives sneaking into their former husbands' homes in the middle of the night and shooting them twelve times at point-blank range made perfect sense. At least if you killed him, you never had to see him and crave him again.

"When am I going to see Daddy?" Bella asked, her little shoulders stooped in sadness at the video's having ended. Bliss scooped her up in her arms and held her against her chest.

"When?" Bella repeated the question. Bliss knew she had to tell her the truth, at least the soft-pedaled version of it.

"I'm not sure," she answered. "Daddy is doing very important work and . . . I know he'll come when he has time."

"I wanna go see him," Bella insisted.

"We can't do that, sweetie."

"Why not?"

"Because you have school, I have work and school, and we don't have the money."

"I have money!" Bella said brightening as she indicated the silver piggy bank by the bed.

"That's not enough, sweetie."

"Can we call him?" Bliss knew Manuel did not welcome calls in the middle of the night, if he answered at all, and that Bella was unlikely to have the conversation for which she hoped. She couldn't tell her the truth: *Your father is uncomfortable dealing with you, and therefore he prefers these one-sided missives you can't answer.* She launched into a classic covering-mother's vamp.

"We could, but would that be nice? It's almost one in the morning and Daddy's very tired."

"Oh," Bella realized, disappointed. Bliss hoped against hope this wouldn't lead where it always did: "When will we live with Daddy again?" The question unleashed Bliss's endless loop of self-flagellation. If she'd only been more attentive as a wife, held it together in spite of Bella's disability, they might still be a family. She'd turned him against herself and their child. Logically she knew it wasn't true, but it was hard not to go down the rabbit hole of guilt. Who said divorce was the new liberation? It left one free to wear a hair shirt of self-doubt for the remainder of one's days. Bella burst into tears, a mixture of fatigue, confusion, and genuine pain. Bliss held her and rocked her back and forth, humming till she fell asleep. She wished she could make her child's life a bit more like the fairy tales she shunned.

chapter seven

Bliss pushed the faded-pink chintz curtain aside, the better to peer out of her second-floor window at the reality-TV circus taking place outside. Dozens of women and children from the neighboring houses had massed across the street to watch the parade of "gentlemen callers" vying for the hand of her baby sister, Diana, soon to be known across the land as "The Virgin." Suitor Number Five, a perfectly pleasant-looking preppy in a Paul Stuart tweed jacket, emerged from the house with his head hanging low, the gleaming silver "chastity belt," badge of shame of the rejected, in his hand. Custom dictated that he brandish it for the camera while submitting to the further humiliation of a post-rejection interview with Wyatt on the front stoop. The gawkers let out a collective groan of disappointment. Bliss couldn't believe how many people cared to watch the spectacle of an innocent—and incidentally rather attractive—stranger's disgrace, and yet she had to admit to herself, she was no better. Much as she was ashamed, she was dying to know what was going on, motivated perhaps by the same ghoulish instinct that caused motorists to slow down when they passed a particularly gory car accident. She opened the leaded glass window, the better to hear.

"Mommy, what are you doing? And why can't we go downstairs?" Bella asked. "I want to go downstairs!" she demanded, stomping her braced foot. At least she hadn't stomped on Bliss's. Given her firm principles, and desire to raise a daughter who harbored no fantasies of being rescued by a wealthy man and riding off into the sunset of connubial bliss, she could not admit to her daughter that the reality soap opera taking place below held far more fascination than the eighteenth-century French slave code. She vamped.

"They're filming and they need us up here. We can go down when they take a break."

"But you want to see, so why can't we go down now?" There were moments in which her daughter's keen perceptions were unwelcome, never more so than now. Bliss had to admit she was guilty as charged. Because she really was tired of focusing on her application for the fellowship, and truly desperate to hear the dialogue in full, she relented slightly.

"Come stand by me, we can watch from here."

From outside, they heard a deafening cheer, they rushed to the window and saw an unprepossessing young man, a pale, thin-lipped chinless wonder of a boy who already showed signs of an incipient paunch, triumphantly waving a sparkling red lamé garter over his head.

"Yes, ladies and gentlemen of the heartland," Wyatt gushed, "after five losers, we finally have a winner. Alistair Grant-Smyth of Sussex, England, son of Sir James and Lady Grant-Smyth, has taken the first, the coveted, red garter. He will compete with two other chivalrous knights for the hand of the fairest maiden in the land." *The only maiden in the land over twelve,* Bliss thought to herself.

"Alistair, congratulations. How does it feel to have a chance to win the hand of the Virgin?"

"Um, well, um it's a dream come true, really. Good fun," Alistair stammered, looking around dumbstruck at the crowd of two hundred onlookers. "Really good fun."

"What attracted you to Diana?" Wyatt asked.

"Well, um, dunno, she's beautiful, o' course. And um ah, she's even more beautiful than she was in the cyber portrait, ya know."

"So when you watched the video portrait, did you think, 'There's the woman for me?'"

"Yeah, yeah, that's what I thought," Alistair yammered, grasping at the proffered conversational straw.

"Who will the other two be? Tune in next week when the parade of gentlemen callers continues on *The Virgin*."

Hearing the chinless wonder's name and pseudonoble origins, Bliss knew exactly why he'd beaten out the others. He was aristocracy adjacent, and thereby fulfilled her mother's royalist fantasies. She'd named all her daughters after members of the Windsor clan in the hope they would one day be at least landed gentry.

"Cut!" A voice yelled. Sue Minors barreled up, chomping her ubiquitous Smoke No More gum and wielding her venti latte like a lethal weapon.

"Hey, hey, hey, where's the hymen line?" she barked.

"What?" Wyatt asked, feigning ignorance.

"You have no hope of getting the hymen," Bella recalled robotically to Bliss's dismay. She clapped her hand over her daughter's little mouth.

"But that's the line," Bella insisted to her mother.

"I didn't want to say that, Sue, it's crude," Wyatt protested.

"It works," Sue insisted. "And last time I checked, you weren't the writer."

"Last time I checked, this wasn't what I called writing," Wyatt shot back. Bliss laughed, inwardly cheering for him. In addition to being really cute, he did have standards.

"Look, pretty boy," Sue snapped, "you're not here to volunteer opinions."

"I've got a kid, and so do many of the people watching this show, and we don't need to go there," Wyatt said, standing his ground.

"Hey, I'm a mom, and I have fuckin' standards and I'm also the network here, so if I say 'do it,' we do it." Dario emerged. Bliss watched him pull Sue aside toward the rosebush on the front lawn. Wyatt left the stoop to enter the house.

Turning to Bella, Bliss asked, "How would you like a snack?"

"Yay! Fruit Roll-Ups, please."

They hurried down the tilted stairs and found Forsythia and Diana excitedly reading a résumé while sitting on the couch.

"Look at this," Forsythia cheered, "Alistair's father owns Penny Wise, the largest discount grocery chain in Britain. In addition to having a title, he's rich!"

"I know, his dad was knighted for inventing Soylogna, it's bologna made of soy. They have a five-thousand-acre estate in Essex. Can you say 'undivided inheritance'?" Diana squealed, high-fiving her mother.

Bliss approached Wyatt, who dialed through messages on his BlackBerry. She placed a hand on his arm, startling him.

"Hi."

"Oh, it's you." He instantly flashed a warm smile.

"That was very cool what you did."

"You mean, you watched the proceedings of the Antichrist?" he teased. She looked down sheepishly. "I still don't approve, but it was kind of irresistible."

"This show is going to be huge," Wyatt predicted. "That's why it's got to have integrity."

"I think it might. Thanks to you," she said.

"Excuse me, Bliss," she heard a deep voice say. She turned and saw Dario.

"I have something for your daughter," he said. Before she could respond, Bella ran up and threw her arms around Dario's waist.

"The man who looks like Daddy!!!!" Mortified, Bliss sought to pry her off. Dario assured her with a wave of his hand that he didn't mind. He knelt before Bella, who beamed under his gaze. Bliss cringed at her child's reaction to the resident Cro-Magnon man. Her inattentive father was setting her up for a lifetime of heartbreaks at the hands of cads. This would be an uphill battle all the way.

"I have something for you," Dario said.

"What? What? What?" Bella asked, jumping up and down with excitement.

"She doesn't need any gifts," Bliss objected.

"Don't be such a killjoy," Dario whispered to her. He pulled a bright-pink shopping bag bedecked with plumes and sparkles out of his worn leather satchel. Bella grabbed it from him, like a puppy jumping at a piece of raw meat, and ripped it open to reveal a magnificent Barbie doll dressed like a flower fairy in a flowing lilac dress with shimmering wings.

"A Barbie!!" The word cut Bliss like a knife. She'd made it four years without purchasing that staple of the American girl's toy chest, objecting to its depiction of women and its original model, a German porn star.

"I also bought her the doctor's uniform," Dario said proudly, proffering another package.

"That's very nice, but we can't accept any of it," Bliss insisted.

"Why not, Mama?" Bella asked, clutching the offending item to her chest.

"Yeah, why not, Mama?" Dario echoed, to Bliss's great irritation.

"Because we don't play with Barbies," she explained.

"Okay, *you* don't have to," he quipped.

"But I want to, she's so pretty," Bella pleaded, almost in tears. Bliss knew she couldn't win. If she took the doll away, her daughter would be scarred for life, remembering her as the Grinch Who Stole Barbie and yet, she really didn't want her idolizing a creature with bodily measurements not found in nature. Maybe she was overreacting, it was hard to keep perspective when you were flying blind, broke, and on your own. Nonetheless, she resented Dario for interfering in an already difficult situation.

"May I see you, for a moment?" she asked. They stepped away from Bella.

"Can I keep my doll?" Bella asked panicked.

"We'll see, sweetie," Bliss answered.

"How dare you bring that to my daughter?"

"What are you campaigning for, Scrooge?"

"You are not a parent."

"I have three baby sisters. They all played with Barbies and none of them became hookers or drug addicts as a result."

"Be that as it may, she's my daughter, not yours, and you have no right to talk to her or bring her anything without clearing it with me first."

Dario stood at attention, as though hearing a command that made sense. He cleared his throat. "Will do in the future," he said. "But in the meantime, please let her have a little fun."

"Given that your idea of fun and entertainment is setting women's rights back about five hundred years, I don't think you're my daughter's go-to guy," Bliss averred. Dario smirked and nodded.

"So that's what this is about. You're still pissed off that you couldn't stop your family being on this show." Bliss bristled. Her inability to stop this particular circus was a source of great frustration, but not the point she sought to make.

"I'm pissed off that people like you, who have no respect for women, define their image in popular culture. Shows like this are the leading cause of death for the American brain."

"You're so busy passing judgment from your ivory tower that you don't bother to even get to know people. I happen to have a lot of respect for women," he said, reddening with indignation.

"Yeah, right, tell it to your mama who's probably at home right now fixing you a plate of pasta," Bliss scoffed.

"She's not actually," Dario said evenly.

"Sorry, right. She's probably darning your socks and knitting you a winter scarf."

"My mother died when I was fourteen," Dario stated, looking Bliss right in the eye. Bliss's heart sank. In spite of the utter disdain she felt for this man, she would never have administered such a direct punch to the gut had she known. Before she could even muster an apology, he'd turned away to address the crew and set up the next shot. She was too embarrassed to follow him. Instead, she watched Bella awkwardly dance around the room with her doll. She didn't have the heart to take it away.

chapter eight

Victoria and Bliss nestled at the table at the bay window of the Pint and Horseshoe, a favorite watering hole of the Georgetown academic set. The pub dated back to the Revolutionary War when it was actually known not only for its libations, but also for its farriers. It held the added attraction for Bliss of being the preferred haunt of Professor Jordan "hottie" McIntosh. She had selected it as a meeting place in the hopes of "running into" him purely by accident, outside the confines of the campus. If she wasn't quite ready for a full-fledged relationship, she was at least prepared to indulge in a heavy-duty flirtation, preferably with someone who, by virtue of their professional connection, was strictly speaking off-limits. It was, as one of the innumerable books she'd read about healing, dealing, and dating after divorce termed it, "emotional and sexual window shopping," which might, in the fullness of time, and once she'd turned in her thesis, actually lead to "making a purchase." Her preternaturally innocent sister had no idea of her motivation but thought she had selected the spot because of its proximity to her place of work. She didn't notice how Bliss would turn to look at the door whenever it swung open. A tall blonde with shoulder-length hair and a square jaw, a dead ringer for Kathleen Turner in her youth, strode toward their table. Missy Howland, Victoria's friend since their days as roommates at The Madeira School for girls, plopped down in a chair beside Victoria and planted a kiss on her cheek.

"God, I love driving," she declared in a throaty voice. "It's amazing how clearly you can hear your own thoughts when they aren't drowned out by five screaming children and six yelping hounds. Or is it the other way around? Victoria, how many kids do I have?" she joked to her old friend who smiled wide. Missy had the irreverence and good humor of one whose family had been landed gentry since Jamestown and never lost their fortune. She wore her wealth with casual insouciance, like the lone strand of pearls she paired with the brightly colored wooden bead necklace her five-year-old had made her. Victoria relaxed and came to life in her presence. They shared the level of comfort of women who'd grown together from pimpled puberty to adulthood, and seen each other in every state from grace (Victoria) to drunken disorderliness (Missy).

"Hi, Missy," Bliss greeted her.

"Bliss, I'm just gonna say it. I am soooo jealous of you."

"Of me? Why?" Bliss replied, honestly baffled by the declaration.

"Because you've done it. You're divorced. You've got the kid and now you're back on track. Me, I've got twenty years of hard time before the last one leaves the nest. I won't have a brain cell left. I'll be lucky to get a job as a greeter at the giant Walmart down the road from the farm."

"Missy, I'm broke, out of shape, and a good six years older than my oldest colleague. If this is what you call being on track, I shudder to think what being off track is," Bliss joked.

Missy turned to Victoria, who silently sipped her Perrier. Elbowing her, she prodded.

"Spill."

"What?"

"Your guts. We're playing *Queen for a Day* here and it's your turn. You just broke up with another guy. You must be feeling some degree of misery."

"I'm fine," Victoria insisted.

"You know what that means. Fucked up, insecure, neurotic, and enervated. Other than that, you're doing great."

Victoria turned crimson and laughed nervously.

"Let's not talk about me," she pleaded, "I'm just no good at romance."

"I'm just teasing you," Missy said, rubbing her shoulder, regretting having made her best friend uncomfortable. "But it just doesn't make any sense," Missy couldn't help but add. Bliss shared Missy's bafflement at Victoria's lack of romantic success. She was the most beautiful and likable of all the Harcourt girls. She couldn't fathom why she lived such a vestal-like existence, interrupted by the occasional suitor whom she always rebuffed. As close as they were, Bliss respected her shyness far too much to pry and thought she would one day open up of her own volition. Since they had now reached their thirties, she had resigned herself to the fact that that day would never come. She accepted her sister as the different drummer, marching to the music she heard. She understood the frustration her admirers must feel in the face of her unyielding beauty. She would not have been surprised to learn that Victoria had never consummated a relationship. In a way, she wished she had a bit of her sister's emotional restraint and apparent indifference to sex. It would certainly make day 383 of celibacy more tolerable. The door opened, and Bliss looked up once again.

"Are you expecting someone?" Missy asked.

"No, not really. Well, someone nice hangs out here," Bliss admitted.

"Good, you're finally putting Guantánamo behind you," Missy quipped.

"Don't call him that," Bliss chided her, with a teasing slap on the thigh.

"Hey, if the denigrating label fits. That guy ripped your heart out of your chest, and left you alone to care for the kid while he cavorted with Peroxide Polly. What was the slut's name?"

"I promised myself never to say it out loud again once the divorce was final." And Bliss had hewed to the promise. She hoped that not speaking the name would erase the memory and eventually help to pry loose the thorn that had lodged itself in her heart. Missy gave a sympathetic squeeze to her hand, and tried to lighten the mood.

"More to the point, why does the asshole always have to be a blonde? We always screw things up, from the Nazis right on through Rachel Uchitel, we are always on the wrong side of the play."

Victoria laughed at her friend's outrageous take on life.

"I'm a blonde," Bliss pointed out.

"You're a mutt. You don't count."

"Well, now you know how black people feel when yet another one of us is being hauled off in handcuffs on the evening news," Bliss deadpanned. She wanted to joke further that they breathed a sigh of relief whenever there was a serial killer, because white people seemed to hold the monopoly on that class of psychopath, but she hadn't the heart. The mention of her ex-husband's paramour took the joy out of the moment. Even without hearing the woman's name, the mere evocation of her brought back the instant, over a year before, that she'd realized her marriage had died. She'd put on her prettiest chiffon party dress, a form-fitting flowered number with ruffles. She'd found a sitter for the evening, and planned to surprise Manuel at his campaign offices where he'd been working late night after night. She had a picnic basket filled with his favorite foods, which she'd prepared herself: southern fried chicken, coleslaw, and cornbread muffins made from scratch. She'd had visions of making love to him right on top of his desk, spontaneously and passionately, as they used to before Bella. She walked in to find another had beaten her to the spot: a young campaign worker, a classic all-American, flat-butted beauty. She'd dropped the basket and run out of the room. As Missy watched the clouds gather over Bliss's face, she realized her gaffe.

"I'm an idiot. Forget I brought any of it up," Missy apologized.

If it hadn't been Missy, something else would have reminded her. The pain was ever present, just beneath the game face she presented to the world. Bliss wondered if her initial encounter with Manuel revealed the seeds of their relationship's destruction. They had met in a history class, arguing over the role of women in the Civil Rights movement, and whether the sexism of the movement's leaders detracted from the nobility of the cause. Bliss had argued that naturally it did. "Are you kidding me?" Manuel had scoffed with a toss of his beautiful dark hair. Her first instincts had told her he was trouble but she had ignored them and allowed her attraction, deep, raw, and atomic to guide her. She would not let that happen again.

"There's someone I wouldn't kick out of bed," Missy commented in an earthy drawl and she leaned back in her seat. Bliss perked up, hoping to see Jordan who turned heads everywhere he went. To her dismay, it was none other than Dario, surrounded by members of the show's crew and a gaggle of women ranging in age from twenty to twenty and a half, she surmised.

"He is cute," Victoria admitted, sipping from her straw. "Not my type, but very handsome."

"He's awful," Bliss insisted.

"You know him?" Missy asked, intrigued.

"I've had the displeasure," Bliss answered. "That's the producer and director of the show."

"He's in the house with you every day? Lucky you," Missy commented, eyeing Dario like a cat contemplating a huge saucer of cream.

"Not if I were on a desert island and he was the last man on earth," Bliss pointed out.

Whatever guilt Bliss had felt about her comments about his mother was obliterated by the sight of him with his powerful arm around a giddy coed who was, naturally, a blonde. *He may have suffered loss,* she thought to herself, *but had been rendered more sexist and superficial by the experience.* Seeing him surrounded by his bimbo squad only depressed her further. He spotted her, and to her confusion and displeasure, disengaged from the coed who'd soldered herself to his arm, and made his way to her table, running a hand through his hair on his way. Missy sat up in her chair and broke into a come-and-get-it smile. Her enthusiasm only annoyed Bliss further.

"Really?" she asked.

"Hey, you'd want to flirt too if you'd been living with the same man for seventeen years. I get more attention from the basset hounds than I do from Harry."

"Hello, Bliss," Dario said as he towered over the table. The scent of his cologne, a masculine combination of sandalwood and fern, filled Bliss's nostrils. She did her best to ignore it.

"Dario," she acknowledged, curtly. He waited a moment for her to make introductions. Missy expectantly cleared her throat. Bliss purposefully turned away, and stared into the depths of her Diet Coke. Dario extended a hand toward Victoria.

"I'm Dario Fuentes. I'm producing the show we're filming at Bliss's folks' house. Starring Bliss's sister." Bliss took the comment as a dig and shot him a look that even if it didn't kill clearly said *Must you be such an unrepentant asshole?*

Victoria rose to take his hand.

"I'm Victoria, Bliss's older sister."

"Ah," he said, looking from one to the other. "I don't see the resemblance, but I'm sure it's there somewhere." Bliss zipped up her Georgetown hoodie, as if to shield her dishevelment from his prying and judgmental gaze. In fact, she couldn't have offered more of a contrast to her tall, angular, café au lait sibling, who was always impeccably turned out in pencil skirts and oxford shirts with sleeves neatly rolled up. Victoria wore her shining mahogany waves tucked into a tidy chignon that showed off her exquisitely chiseled features to perfection. Bliss could see Victoria's beauty was not lost on Dario who actually gave her a slight bow after they shook hands. This evidence of a modicum of taste softened her attitude toward him ever so slightly.

"And I'm Missy," the latter said, unabashedly thrusting her hand into his.

"Welcome to DC. Where are you from?"

"Originally, Brooklyn, Bed-Stuy. But I live in LA now."

"Must be kinda boring for you here in this cow town with the local yokels," Missy commented.

"It's not bad," Dario insisted, glancing over at the bevy of girls at the bar.

Bliss noted that just like her ex, women were drawn to him with the gravitational force of metal to a magnet. Men like him never had to work hard for a date, and never developed the power of saying no, but accepted women's sexual favors like so much manna from Heaven. Young or old, fat or thin, bright or stupid, women fell into these men's laps like overripe fruit. Was there a female equivalent of this breed of effortless seducer? If there was, she didn't belong to it. Her evening of fun and escape with the girls was quickly turning into a trip down a lane of memories she had no desire to revisit, ever again. She wondered why she hadn't just holed up at home in her father's study with a trusty bucket of ice cream, instead of venturing out into the social minefield. Jordan McIntosh, the one decent man she knew, was probably at home, leafing through photo albums of his deceased wife.

"Will you watch the show tomorrow night?" Dario asked. Bliss couldn't decide if he aimed the question at her.

"Probably not," she answered brusquely.

"That's a shame," he responded taking a step away. "Nice meeting you ladies," he added with a quick smile to Missy and Victoria before turning his back and returning to his gaggle of geese who greeted him with squeals of delight.

"He doesn't seem so bad," Victoria commented, as she watched him walk away.

"Please, you're too nice. You think everyone means well because you do. Don't project your good intentions on others. They don't deserve the credit," Bliss scoffed.

"Not only would I not kick him out of bed, I think I'd chain him to mine," Missy said, taking a sip of her soda to cool down.

"Can't you see we all exceed his age limit, and his IQ threshold. As Madame de Staël said about one of her brawny but brainless lovers, 'Speech is not his language,'" Bliss quipped.

"I bet he can make any woman's body speak volumes," Missy countered.

"Ugh, not something I care to find out," Bliss groaned.

"Aren't you going to have a bite?" Victoria asked.

"No, I've lost my appetite."

"You should eat something," Victoria said, concerned.

"I've stored enough for a whole winter," Bliss said, patting her rounded bottom. "Have a great night."

"Please don't tell me this is because of what I said about your ex?" Missy pleaded.

"No," Bliss reassured, "it's because of my life. Enough goofing off for one night. Back to work, back to reality," Bliss declared. She made a point of not looking back at Dario and his fellow revelers.

chapter nine

As Bliss walked down the alley leading to the parking lot, she spotted a tall, slender silhouette she recognized emerging from the back door of the Pint and Horseshoe.

"Jordan," she yelled impulsively. He started, probably embarrassed by her forwardness, she surmised. His wide-eyed expression told her he had not expected to encounter anyone he knew.

"I was just picking up some takeout," Jordan hastened to explain, brandishing a Styrofoam container as proof.

"Oh," Bliss said, bewildered by his apparent need to explain his presence, and noting that it was unusual for patrons to pick up their orders from the kitchen as opposed to the bar. Yet, she dismissed it as a privilege accorded to faculty members, along with their twenty percent discount.

"Feeling prepared for the oral exam?" he inquired.

"All I've done for the past year is read. If I'm not ready now, I should just drop out."

"How's your fellowship proposal coming?" he asked.

"Slowly," she sighed. "But I will get it in soon."

"With fewer fellowships, the earlier the better. You know Father Cuthbert is quite partial to Percival Linton. And of course he loves his topic: How the Catholic Church saved the Indian heathens of South America."

"I know. What a retread. People have covered that topic for the last five hundred years. There must be a thousand books on the subject."

"You know that and I know that, but all Cuthbert knows is he likes Percival's eyes." He slammed a hand on his face in mock horror. "Did I just say that?"

"If Linton gets the fellowship because he's Cuthbert's wet dream . . ."

"What are you going to do? Happens all the time."

"You'd never pick someone that way."

"Maybe not," Jordan said, a devilish twinkle in his eye. Seeing Bliss's incipient dismay and shock at this inkling of human failing, he quickly added, "I'm joking."

"I know, Genevieve would never have stood for it," Bliss insisted with the stubbornness of a child declaring that the tooth fairy is a real figure.

Jordan looked away, as if stung by the comment. *Did you have to say that? You idiot!!!* Bliss chastised herself. *Why don't you just drag out pictures of her in the cancer ward while you're at it? You've got the sensitivity of a rhinoceros in heat.* Afraid she'd pained him by mentioning his deceased wife, Bliss placed her hand on his shoulder.

"I'm so sorry. I didn't mean to bring up difficult memories."

"It's okay," he assured her as he made his way toward his car, a classic Alfa Romeo spider convertible he'd lovingly restored himself. He carefully placed his dinner in the back, then turned to face her.

"Can I give you a lift somewhere?"

"No, thank you," she answered. "I've got my beautiful divorcemobile. A hundred thousand miles of bad road."

"We should have drinks sometime," he added sheepishly.

"I'd like that," she answered blushing, then turned to walk to her own car, hoping her rear view was not as ample as it felt. As she watched him drive away, Marvin Gaye blaring from his stereo, she thought to herself that perhaps the evening had not proved a complete loss after all.

chapter ten

As Bliss turned her car down her street, she saw in the glowing light of a late fall afternoon what looked like an enormous mob of placard-wielding protestors surrounding the Harcourt's home. Had her prayers been answered and her wildest rescue fantasy come true? Had the National Organization for Women, the NAACP, and the Ms. Foundation come to stop her family from participating in a show about a woman trafficking her virtue like a rare commodity? As Bliss drove nearer, she realized to her disappointment that far from sharing her disgust, the world relished the barbaric antics of *The Virgin*. It had premiered that week to stratospheric ratings. Since filming of the series had begun, the camera crews had drawn handfuls of onlookers, but now a crowd of near rock concert proportions besieged the neighborhood. Locals and crazed fans from across the country, some holding up handmade signs that spelled *THE VIRGIN* RULES or VIRGINITY ROCKS in glitter stood outside the house chanting "Vir-gin! Vir-gin!" 101 Windsor Lane had officially become a cheesy twenty-first-century version of Lourdes, attracting latter-day "pilgrims" with fanny packs desperate to catch a glimpse of a TV-network-anointed virgin.

Bliss noticed the madding hordes were blocking the driveway. She parked her car a block away.

"Why are we stopping here, Mama?" Bella asked.

"I just want to figure out what's happening," Bliss reassured her. "Besides, we can't get into our garage. Come on, let's get out."

In front the of the Harcourt garage, news trucks and cameras had set up camp. Taffy Thomas, the local anchor, dressed from head to toe in lemon yellow and teetering on a pair of sky-high platform pumps adorned with large Mini Mouse bows, delivered a report in the same peppy tone she used whether describing the rescue of a kitten stuck in a tree or a grizzly murder.

"We're here in front of the Harcourt Manse," she bubbled.

"Manse? It's barely a toolshed," Bliss muttered under her breath.

"The place where the Virgin grew up. It's a mob scene with neighbors and new fans clamoring to get a glimpse of America's latest sweetheart. Hello, ladies," she boomed, turning to a group of girls wearing pink polo shirts, matching madras skirts, and headbands. They all flashed toothy grins.

"Hi, y'all! Hi Mama," one girl screeched giddily into the camera, waving wildly.

"Where are y'all from?" Taffy asked, mimicking the girl's Dixie-Belle-on-Miller-Lite drawl.

"We're from the great state of Kentucky, and we're members of the Me Pure Me chapter of the Alpha Phi Zeta sorority!"

"Me Pure Me. Sounds interesting. What do y'all do?"

"It's what we don't do that counts. We plan to hang on to our purity till we walk down the aisle," the self-appointed spokesvirgin announced. "Come on, girls, let's give America our cheer."

Her madras-clad cohort of five launched into: "Yo, Prince Charmings, we know you care/ But our bodies we will not bare/ Pure is good, pure is fine/ We say I do 'fore we cross that line/ We'll get busy soon enough/ Bring the carats, if you want our stuff!!/ Wanna say hello to this kitty?/ Boy, take a pledge of eternity/ Gooooo Me Pure Me!" They ended in full splits, with their hands coyly folded over their nether regions.

"Fantastic," Taffy commented, brimming with insincerity. Suddenly, Charlotte made her way through the crowd to Taffy's side. As usual, she showcased what she considered her greatest asset: her enormous gravity-defying breasts.

"There's Aunt Charlotte," Bella cried.

"Unfortunately," Bliss groaned.

Charlotte grabbed hold of Taffy's handheld microphone, tussling with her for it.

"I'm Charlotte Harcourt, the Virgin's sister," she shouted. Several in the crowd cheered, and gathered round to film her with their phones and to snap photos.

"Great," Taffy commented, wresting the mike from Charlotte's grasp. "Are you a virgin too?" Charlotte hesitated a moment till a "brilliant" response popped into her head.

"That's for me to know and America to find out," she said with a hip roll and wink.

"I'm sure we'll be hearing a lot more from you," Taffy snapped, pushing past her. No doubt the trussed and botoxed newscaster felt upstaged by Charlotte's natural breasts, Bliss surmised. Taffy moved to a group of attractive men in tuxes accompanied by young girls ranging in age from thirteen to sixteen wearing white dresses with ample skirts and glittering crowns.

"And who do have we here?" Taffy asked.

"Daddy's Girls for Christ and the Virgin of Edison, New Jersey. We've pledged to be pure and true to our daddies till marriage," one brunette girl with braces answered, beaming.

"Our little girls made a vow to stay virgins till marriage," a beefy father explained. "We, the daddies, give them those crowns and these rings," he held up his daughter's hand to show a ring adorned with a single pearl topped by a miniature sieve. "The pearls and the sieve are classic emblems of virginity. The ancient Vestal Tuccia proved her chastity by carrying water in a sieve. That's what virginity is: air tight and miraculous, like our pact."

"So moving. And what a great idea for a Father's Day gift instead of a tie: 'Daddy, I'll stay your little girl and keep my legs crossed and my panties on!'" Taffy exclaimed, exceedingly pleased with her summary.

"I just want to say this show has given real hope to our movement," the father added, getting verklempt.

"Can I marry my daddy like them one day?" Bella asked, innocently. Bliss covered Bella's ears. Before she had a chance to deliver her diatribe against these antiquated and utterly misogynistic customs, the crowd roared. Wyatt had appeared on the doorstep accompanied by an extremely tall, somewhat gaunt young man who had the stooped posture of an adolescent mortified by a sudden growth spurt. Bliss noticed Dario emerging from one of the crew trucks and directing the cameras to angle on Wyatt and his companion.

"Come on, Beowulf, show the folks at home what you got!" Wyatt prodded. In response to this command, the young man sheepishly held up a coveted red lamé garter. The crowd cheered wildly.

"So, Beowulf Jones, Suitor Number Two. Tell us something about yourself." Beowulf stood frozen in terror, staring helplessly at the crowd.

"Come on, I'm sure they'd like to hear how you made your millions, or is it billions?" Wyatt goaded.

A murmur of astonishment went through the impromptu audience. Then the Me Pure Me sorority girls started chanting.

"Sweet Billy Billionaire, don't be shy! / You've made a fortune, we'd give you a try!"

Hearing the mention of his vast fortune, Bliss suddenly understood how this dark-haired poster boy for geeks had made her sister's cut. She watched him, pained, as he struggled to form a sentence, like the stuttering King George in the opening scene of *The King's Speech*. Clearly this was not a man used to the limelight. However he had earned his fortune, it hadn't been through showboating, Bliss deduced. How on earth had he ended up a jester in this media circus?

"I can't talk about myself," he managed at last. "I just want to say that Diana is the most beautiful woman I've ever seen. And I hope to win her heart."

"Awww, that is so sweet. So tell us what you thought when you saw the video portrait. I hear you were skeptical about participating in this and that friends put you up to it."

"Yes, that's right," the young man admitted.

"So what changed your mind?"

"Diana. Just seeing Diana. Her eyes . . ." He couldn't even finish his sentence. He involuntarily raised his hand to his chest as if salving the wound left by Cupid's arrow. Bliss's heart went out to this, the latest victim of her baby sister's beguiling charms.

"Tonight, you'll get a chance to look into those beautiful blue eyes at our special celebration party. And one lucky member of this crowd is going to come. Whoever catches this rose." Wyatt tossed an oversize silk flower into the awaiting horde. People screamed and scrambled, knocking each other over.

"I wanna catch the rose!" Bella yelled, running away from her mother into the crowd.

To Bliss's horror, Bella disappeared into the swarm. The crowd had massed toward the center, diving for the rose. Bliss battled her way through, yelling "Bella!! Watch out for my daughter!" Suddenly, she spotted Dario hoisting Bella onto his shoulders and cutting a swath through people to make his way to her. She didn't even know where he had come from but felt overwhelming relief at the sight of him. Within moments, he was at Bliss's side. Grabbing her hand, he deftly led her past the crowd to the back entrance of the house.

Once in the kitchen, he gently set Bella down in a chair. Bliss had wanted to thank him till she remembered he had wreaked this havoc upon their lives.

"That was fun!" Bella exclaimed, as Dario set her down. "I could see everything."

"Don't ever run into a crowd like that again," Bliss scolded, frustrated at her own failure to keep her daughter safe. Bella bit her upper lip, chastened and near tears. Bliss regretted the sharpness of her tone and knelt by Bella, caressing her bad leg.

"She's fast," Dario said with some astonishment. Bliss looked at him, still reeling and panicked at the thought of what might have befallen Bella if she hadn't been rescued in time.

"Sorry about all of this," Dario offered soberly.

"Sure you are," Bliss retorted. "The show's a huge hit. Congratulations. You've proved yet again that, 'No one ever lost money underestimating the taste of the American public.'"

Dario's eyes flashed and he seemed poised to shoot back but relented. He set his jaw, and turned away.

"Bye, bye, Mr. Fuentes," Bella uttered forlornly.

He turned back to smile at his tiny supporter.

"Listen to your Mama, sweetheart. Don't go running into crowds. It's very dangerous." Bliss nodded, appreciating at least that acknowledgment of her authority.

"I'd stay inside, if I were you," Dario suggested before exiting through the back door. Bliss picked Bella up and hugged her to her chest.

"Are you all right, Mama?" Bella asked.

"Yes, now I am." She put her down and led her to the dining room.

The table had been transformed into command central for the Harcourt "newfound celebrity press office." As Punch rushed about serving coffee and fetching items for Sue Minors, Forsythia and Diana sat next to each other, each speaking into a separate cell phone. Sue, also umbilically attached to her cell phone, barked out what seemed to be endorsement offers.

"L'Oréal Hair Color?"

"I'm definitely worth it," Diana gushed with a wink and a toss of her tresses. "Yes."

"Sustain Sup Hose?" Sue queried Forsythia.

"I don't wear those! I'm trim," Forsythia objected with a huff, then returned to her call. "Yes, I'd definitely be interested in writing such a book. There is much to say on the subject of how to raise a virgin. And frankly, I'm a leading authority."

Charlotte sulked past, sucking on a Popsicle.

"Does anyone have offers for me? I represent Generation Y."

"No, sweetie," Sue snapped dismissively, practically running her over to get to her sister. "Diana, Spring Morning feminine hygiene products wants you to be the face of their Freshen the V campaign. They're quoting six figures."

"Too tasteless," Forsythia replied.

"Yeah, and too low. See if they'll up the ante," Diana added.

"'Too tasteless,'" Bliss repeated. "And doing a national TV show called *The Virgin* isn't?"

Diana ignored her and powered up the iPad that sat before her on a stand made to look like a medieval carved ivory frame, crowned by a unicorn.

"I'll do the Spring Morning ad. I love feeling fresh," Charlotte offered brightly.

"Char, honey, it's not about you today, okay? Face it, Diana's the Kim in this family, and you're Kourtney. Skedaddle, sweetie. We're working here."

"Charlotte, run along and figure out what you're wearing to the party this evening," Forsythia commanded. "And do your homework first, or you're not coming." Charlotte pouted and stomped off.

"Don't get it. My boobs are much bigger than hers," she mumbled to herself as she exited.

"What's that, Auntie Didi?" Bella asked, intrigued by the iPad while climbing into Diana's lap.

"It's a gift from the network for our historically high ratings. I can see my suitors on it. Want to meet my latest prince?" Diana explained proudly.

"Yes," Bella answered eagerly.

The image of a cloudless sky filled the screen. The camera panned from the expanse of blue to a man galloping toward the camera on a white horse. Bliss rolled her eyes.

"Oh brother. This looks like the corollary to yours," she noted.

"This man went to a *lot* of trouble, that's one of the reasons Aunt Didi picked him," Diana said pointedly to Bella. "And look at how well he handles that horse," she said suggestively, smacking her bee-stung lips. *Though she may never have had sex, she certainly has an appetite,* Bliss noted to herself. The man leapt off the horse and led it directly to camera. The close-up revealed a brown-skinned pretty boy with perfect chiseled features and piercingly blue eyes.

"Greetings, damsel, meet your knight in shining armor," he said in a spine-tingling tenor. Diana froze the image.

"Here's the neatest thing, I can juxtapose my image with his to see how we look together." She moved the cursor around the screen and clicked on an altar icon. Their heads appeared together in a heart as if they were leaning toward each other.

"Wow! Magic!" Bella marveled.

"And I can even see how our babies would look." She clicked on an icon of a stork. A little girl with Diana's eyes, the suitor's symmetrical features, and a crown of ringlets appeared grinning on screen.

"Are you having a baby?" Bella asked.

"No. Not till after I'm married."

"Can you do 'mirror, mirror, on the wall' with this like the mean queen in *Snow White*?" Bella asked. Diana glared at Bliss.

"Don't look at me," Bliss protested, laughing. "She came up with that herself. If the evil Disney character fits . . . Come on Bella, let's go give you your bath."

"Aww, I want to watch Aunt Didi make more fake babies."

"Another time," Bliss suggested, leading her out of the room.

"Oh my gosh, we've hit the mother lode," Sue announced. "Hold on to your hats, Maidenform wants to create a new line of push-up bras named after you. They've even come up with a slogan already: 'The Diana, a princess of a bra, it crowns every woman a D-cup.'"

"You'll be immortalized," Forsythia crowed. "My baby." As Forsythia threw her arms around her pride and joy, Diana began mentally tallying the value of all the endorsements gathered so far. She'd soon be able to drive past all her snooty neighbors in a custom Lamborghini and yell, "Eat my gold dust!" It was a lifelong dream come true.

chapter eleven

Bliss was as close as she could come to terrestrial paradise, curled up on the brown tufted velvet settee in her father's cozy wood-paneled study, rereading her fellowship proposal with a gallon of Häagen-Dazs on hand. Had Forsythia been home, she could not have eaten the ice cream without facing the wrath of a hectoring mother scorned. Alone with her father in his sanctuary, she could do as she pleased. With its roaring fireplace, frayed and faded oriental rug, and brass shaded lamps casting an amber glow, it was the one room in the house that really did look plucked out of an English country manor, if a slightly threadbare and modest one.

Worn, leatherbound volumes lined the bookshelves, the comforting friends of Bliss's youth. This was the room to which she had repaired to escape her mother's harangues on good grooming ("If God wanted us to have curly/frizzy/kinky hair, he wouldn't have invented Dark and Lovely relaxer!" The Gospel according to Forsythia Harcourt). It was here her father had introduced her to the magic of C. S. Lewis (*The Lion, the Witch and the Wardrobe*), that she had raised a sword with the three musketeers, that she had litigated against racial injustice with Atticus Finch. It was in this room every evening that her father had told her of the exploits of Hannibal, introduced her to the poetry of Phyllis Wheatley, and made history come alive. Night after night, Harold had inspired a passion for learning. Though her mother gave only the scantest details of her childhood in Jamaica, Bliss knew instinctively no one had ever taken the time to correct the racist teachings imposed by her colonial school masters. Forsythia's island youth remained shrouded in shame and secrecy. There were hints of her having been born illegitimate, and raised in the depths of poverty. Yet, she'd managed to pick an Anglo-Saxon man who could instill in his children a sense of pride in their black heritage. Bliss had to give Forsythia some credit.

There were worse fates than spending the rest of her life living under her beloved father's roof, eschewing live men in favor of dead historic heroes. Her mistake had been in not picking someone like her father in the first place, an academic whose passions were directed toward books, another point in Jordan McIntosh's favor. But for tonight, her heart belonged to Daddy and to the main subject of her thesis: the Chevalier de Saint-Georges. Now, as her father wrote his latest book on Ampère, the eighteenth-century French physicist, Bliss traveled the ballrooms of Paris with her true love, the Chevalier, mulatto, championship fencer, composer, and musician hailed by all of Europe as the "Black Mozart." She and her father shared the platter of fresh scones Bliss had whipped up from scratch in the kitchen. The family had gone out to the party in celebration of the show's stratospheric opening ratings. Because the event wasn't to be filmed, Harold had been able to escape. He and Bliss clicked scones as she turned her attentions from her proposal to a nineteenth-century novel on the Chevalier.

"Saint-George strode into the salon and spotted across the room a pale brunette; this was the Marquise de Montalembert, who would become the love of his life." Suddenly, the first few notes of the *Masterpiece Theatre* trumpet fanfare sounded. Bliss realized to her dismay that someone had arrived at the door. She and Harold sighed.

"Shall we ignore it?" he suggested devilishly. It was such a tempting thought. Bliss dreaded the intrusion of a nosy neighbor, eager to glean information about their newfound celebrity status, and hear tales of the contenders for the Virgin's hand. Perhaps it was some tacky member of the electronic press sent by Sue Minors to interview them on their reaction to the show's successful premiere. If it was, Bliss resolved to slam the door in the interloper's grinning face, ratings be damned. She hadn't signed up for this and neither had her father, and yet, there they sat, prisoners in their own home. The chime sounded again. The persistence of the caller was alarming.

"I'll go up to the second floor and see who it is," Harold offered, getting up from his flat top desk.

"No," Bliss countered, "I'll go. It would help me let off some steam to slam the door shut in someone's face."

"Splendid idea," Harold assented. "Shall I go fetch eggs from the pantry? The better to pelt them?"

Bliss laughed and kissed his jowly cheek. Her father had been so handsome in his youth, in a pale British sort of way. His features and his hopes had sagged together into the pudginess of middle age. Bliss could still see the intense life in his eyes. They danced with mischief whenever he had a naughty thought and Bliss recognized the man she had known when she was four. *Can't let life wear you down,* she thought to herself as she shuffled to the door in her giant Elmo slippers, purchased at an airport to amuse her daughter (who lay peacefully slumbering upstairs). She opened the door and was stunned to find Wyatt, looking ever so dashing in a sky-blue French cuff shirt that set off his eyes, eyes as lively as Harold's, and a charcoal gray suit that fit his V-shaped physique to perfection. Bliss shuddered to think what a shipwreck she must appear to this dreamboat. A lone stray frizzy curl fell from the Trevi Fountain atop her head. She blew it out of the way and felt certain she saw a crumb fly through the air, no doubt propelled from a perch on her upper lip, which, she concluded, was covered in them. Wyatt smiled warmly, and brushed another stray "fruzzy" out of the way, tucking it gently behind her ear. His mouth, though thin lipped, was very pleasant, Bliss noted. She couldn't talk. Unlike her sisters, she'd inherited her father's scant lips rather than her mother's plush mounds. "May I come in?" Wyatt asked, inclining his torso in a slight bow.

"Sure," Bliss answered, pulling her cashmere "boyfriend sweater" down around her generous posterior.

Harold rounded the corner and was as surprised as Bliss to see Wyatt.

"Good evening. Why aren't you at the party, with the others?"

"I was wondering the same about you two," Wyatt responded.

"My daughter is asleep upstairs, and I don't belong at that party," Bliss answered.

"I think you do," Wyatt countered, staring hard.

"No, really, I can't. I have work to do—"

"And your life is passing you by. What if I told you that I would be disappointed not to have you there?"

He asked, caressing her chin in a gesture of intimacy that took her aback. It wasn't unpleasant, just a bit forward. Bliss thought to herself that whatever article it was she'd read that said divorced women regressed to the behavior of their last dating year was right. Much of what she had read was wrong, such as martial arts will heal the hurt more than endless bowls of ice cream, but this was accurate. She felt as awkward and inept as she had at sixteen. She pondered what to make of this particular pretty boy, who wasn't her type. Her type, to her dismay, could be summed up in one word: Manuel. He was the only man she had ever slept with and the only man she had ever loved.

"I think Mr. Evers is right," Harold interjected. "You've done quite enough work for one evening. Go shake a tail feather. I'll watch the little one," he said preempting all possible objections.

"Look at me," Bliss commented dismayed.

"I'll wait while you change," Wyatt suggested. The kindness of the offer stunned her.

"Don't you have to be there for interviews? You'll miss all the action."

"I did all the interviews. What do you say?" Bliss's mind went to another article, *Ebony* magazine's "Twenty-Five Steps to Finding a Man After Divorce." Step Number Fourteen: get out of the house. She raced upstairs, hoping her one good dress wasn't wrinkled and still fit. Well, if it was wrinkled, the tautness would smooth out the effect. She did feel sixteen again, a good sixteen on her way out with a man she'd actually like to kiss.

chapter twelve

Wyatt drove his convertible to a stop in front of the Willard Hotel. Bliss looked up at the imposing façade of that high Victorian grande dame of Washington's luxury hotels. As Wyatt led her up the carpeted steps and into the vaulted-ceilinged foyer, it was not lost on her that a dozen sitting presidents had made the same progress. In spite of her impatience with her mother's obsession with pomp, she had to admit, it was effective in the right circumstances. For the first time in a long time, she felt pretty, nearly as pretty as her surroundings. Her bias-cut purple chiffon dress with a ruffle snaking its way around her voluptuous figure contrasted the ampleness of her hips with the minuteness of her waist. Her perfectly arched feet were poised like cats about to pounce in her favorite pair of mid-heeled character shoes. Her long dirty-blond curls cascaded down her back, and framed her oval face. As she and Wyatt made their way to the elevators, more than one male head turned to admire this latter-day Sophia Loren. The elevator glided noiselessly up to the twenty-third floor, the doors slid open, and a wall of noise and flashing bulbs assaulted them.

"Maybe I should go first," Wyatt offered protectively. The Crystal Room, an ornate turn-of-the-century confection that boasted twenty glistening crystal chandeliers, was crowded with masses of well-dressed young people, women in flirty dresses, and young men who'd barely loosened their ties. Charlotte, clad in a hot-pink taffeta dress reserved enough to satisfy her mother and tight enough to entice the boys, flitted about the room introducing herself and offering her autograph to anyone who would listen. At the center of it all, underneath a bower of white silk roses erected for the occasion, stood the gleaming Diana, resplendent in a tulle confection dotted with rhinestones and paillettes that perfectly captured and refracted the light from the chandeliers above. Bliss could have sworn she even saw Diana's teeth shoot off a beam when she smiled. Diana's sculptural torso, cinched into a ruched strapless bodice, rose out of the cloud of tulle. She was flanked, Scarlett-O'Hara-at-the-barbecue style, by three tuxedo-clad young men. One of them Bliss recognized as the chinless wonder of a Brit from the day of the gentlemen callers. The other two also brandished ruby-red lamé garters, the emblem of the "winners."

"So tell me about the guys," Bliss inquired of Wyatt.

"The one on the left is Alistair."

"I know, the heir to the British supermarket and Soylogna fortune."

"That's right. He's meant to be a close personal friend of Prince Harry's, so we're hoping for a cameo from His Royal Highness."

"Whoopee! Will he wear his swastika? And the others? I saw you interview the skinny one back at the house earlier today."

"Yes, Beowulf Jones, budding Internet billionaire. He invented an antiviral system called Beowulf Bays, guaranteed to protect your files."

"He looks about twelve," Bliss commented as she surveyed his reed-like form and black hair that stood up in Dennis-the-Menace spikes.

"He's twenty-six," Wyatt explained. *And stands no chance of winning Diana's hand,* Bliss surmised, as Diana nearly knocked him over with her gossamer ball skirt.

"To her right," Wyatt continued, "is Paul Daniels the Fourth."

"He looks insincere," Bliss commented of the sleek, mocha-hued Adonis with the perfectly groomed close-cropped afro whom she recognized from the video portrait she'd seen of him on Diana's iPad.

"He's a politician," Wyatt assented with a chuckle, "junior state senator from Tennessee, youngest mayor ever of the bustling metropolis of Wyahoochee."

"Why a hoochie indeed," Bliss commented wryly.

"They're calling him the Christian Obama."

"Obama is a Christian," Bliss objected. Shaking her head at the benightedness of the world.

"You know that, and I know that, but he doesn't sound like one. 'Barack Hussein.' Paul's middle name is Peter."

"Oh, how many apostles can you pack into one child?" Bliss deadpanned.

"Jesus!"

"His parents skipped that one. That would sound too Hispanic," Wyatt quipped. Bliss laughed out loud. She was beginning to like Wyatt's sardonic take on the absurd events unfolding around them. Under the bower, Diana and her suitors posed for one more shot. The men held up their garters in heart shaped formation to frame her head.

"Great, great, loving it!" Sue Minors barked. "We just need one more." Charlotte popped up beside her sister, drawn by the photo opportunity like a moth to a 100-watt bulb.

"I'll pose for one," she proposed, grinning eagerly.

"Not now. Maybe later," Sue waved her off. Deflated, Charlotte slunk away, but brightened instantly at the sight of a tall young man with a basketball player's build and carriage. She sidled up to him with a flirtatious, "Hi, I'm Charlotte, the Virgin's sister."

"Where the fuck is Wyatt?" Sue Minors yelled, like a fishmonger hawking her carp on the dock at five AM.

"His master's voice," Wyatt commented, pained. "Excuse me, will you? Have to go earn my pay." He rushed over to the bower, tousling his hair ever so slightly and spraying breath freshener in his mouth from a diminutive vial. Bliss looked about the crowded room. Underneath another glistening chandelier, her mother answered questions from a local interviewer.

"Yes, I'm proud to say I'm going to start appearing on *Wake Up*

America, as the etiquette and dignity expert," she said preening in a red sequined knit dress that rightfully belonged on Joan Collins in a long ago episode of *Dynasty*, or *Di-nasty* as she insisted on pronouncing it in an accent that only grew more affectedly British by the year. Bliss tried to be patient with her mother's antics, reminding herself that because Forsythia didn't know who she was, mimicry was her refuge. Bliss became aware of someone staring at her and to her shock saw Dario standing alone across the room, gaping. His gaze was so intense it held her on her spot for several moments. Then the unwavering attention began to unnerve her. She looked down at her dress. Did it have a stain of which she was unaware? Then she abruptly stopped her inspection. What did she care what Cro-Magnon Mario, that refugee from the cast of *Jersey Shore*, thought anyway? She was here to enjoy herself, for once. She looked about the room for rescue and to her relief, she spotted Victoria seated at a table. She approached and found her in conversation with Punch, the oddly pretty/handsome girl usually found fetching coffee for the growling Sue.

"So, tell me more about the library," the kneeling creature asked, totally captivated by Victoria's beauty. The latter was utterly oblivious to her effect on the girl and prattled on pleasantly. Bliss approached them. Victoria beamed and turned to introduce her.

"Yes, you're the sister we're always shooting from the rear, as she runs out of the room," Punch teased pleasantly. "Sorry we're so intrusive."

"Not your fault," Bliss said, feeling sorry for this obviously kind soul trapped in an entry-level job Hell.

"Have you done other productions with these guys?" Bliss asked in a tone that implied, "How long have you done hard time in this gulag?"

"Just two, *Around the World in Eighty Ways*, and *Last Chance Corral*."

"What was that one?" Bliss asked.

"It was about women about to turn thirty-five who weren't married and hadn't had a baby, vying for eligible guys at a dude ranch," Punch admitted in embarrassment. Victoria and Bliss looked at each other in mock dismay.

"Well, I guess that means we should throw in the towel. What did they do, rope them and ride them?" Bliss asked.

"I suppose this means I'm doomed. I'm turning thirty-five in a few weeks," Victoria added, laughing nervously.

"You're gorgeous. You'll always be wanted," Punch blurted. Bliss smiled at her sympathetically. Punch blushed, knowing she had revealed her hand.

"Can I get you something to drink?" Punch offered, mortified.

"No thank you," Victoria responded, still completely unaware of Punch's motives in offering. Bliss marveled at her sister's innocence. At nearly thirty-five and some nine boyfriends later, she was the true *virgin* of the family.

"Where's the bar?" a husky voice asked. Bliss turned to see Missy, looking much the worse for wear after an hour's drive from her home in Middleburg, Virginia.

"What happened to your husband?"

"Lost him along the way. You know him, he never wants to leave home. Hello, who are you?"

"I'm Punch Davie. I was just heading to the bar."

"Davie, Davie, of the Santa Barbara Davies?" Missy asked, twisting her family crest pinkie ring.

"Montecito, actually," Punch corrected.

"You must be Huntley's girl."

"Bradley's," Punch corrected again. "Will you excuse me," she said, beating a hasty retreat.

"Ran off like a rabbit staring down the barrel of a Purdey Special. Can't say I blame her. She's from a big Southern California clan and they frown on their own being of the sapphic persuasion. Ridiculous! Okay, I really need a drink!" she bellowed. A salsa number began to play. Bliss's feet started to form the familiar eight-count pattern almost of their own volition. Her hips swayed as her upper body remained motionless. Someone grabbed her hand and whipped her around. It was Wyatt, leading her out onto the floor. He executed a clumsy move, a sort of pseudo cha-cha. Bliss stifled a laugh.

"Okay, so show me," he dared her. She took the lead, advancing toward him, hips moving in double time.

"The hips and feet move, the torso remains still," she commanded.

He obediently followed. A clapping crowd gathered around them. Bliss didn't care. She let the music take her.

"May I cut in," she turned to face Dario, who didn't wait for a reply but swept her out of Wyatt's arms and into his own. Before she could object, his huge hand warmed the small of her back. He reestablished the proper male-leads-woman-follows roles, and Bliss knew instantly she was at the mercy of a master of the art. He indicated, but never pushed. She could anticipate the direction in which he would move her, and happily took the backward stepping role. He kept his eyes steady on hers, as he glided her quickly, crisply but smoothly across the floor to the insistent rhythm. He spun her around and, with their arms entwined in a figure-of-eight, rocked her left and right. Her buttocks collided with his pelvis for a moment but he delicately stepped aside, then whipped her back around to face him. The pelvic brush had titillated her. She almost wished he'd turn her back around and let their bodies meet but instead he slowly let go. They drifted apart. They circled each other like matador and bull, eyes locking. He placed his hand around her waist once again, led her backward and forward in the step, then slowly dipped her till her head nearly touched the dance floor. Then and only then did she realize the entire ballroom full of people was watching them, including Diana who was not the least bit pleased that she and her shimmering cloud of tulle had been upstaged.

Diana looked about her, assessing her prospects and deciding that Paul was probably the least awkward dancer, grabbed him and sauntered out to the middle of the floor. Seeing her advance, Bliss and Dario both knew it was time to relinquish the stage. Dario gently lifted Bliss up to a standing position and led her off the floor. Not to be outdone, Diana began spinning like a whirling dervish, making it clear to the crowd it was her show again. They cheered wildly, and chanted, "Go Virgin!!! Go Virgin!!!"

Dario led Bliss through the crowd to a bar in the corner.

"Champagne?" he offered.

"Yes, please," she answered, thirsty and exhilarated from her turn on the floor.

Dario proffered a flute. He raised his own to her.

"*Salute,*" he said, before taking a sip and rolling it around his tongue. "Not bad," he opined. "I told them not to skimp on the liquor."

"How much is all of this costing anyway?" Bliss marveled.

"Too much," Dario joked. "Price of doing business."

"Listen I—" they both said in unison.

"You first," Bliss offered.

"No, you," Dario insisted.

"I wanted to thank you for rescuing Bella, and apologize for that insensitive reference to your mother," Bliss blurted. She hated apologizing as much as any man did, and she particularly hated apologizing to men since Manuel's betrayal.

"No worries. You didn't know."

"I could see I really hurt you. She must have been very special to you."

"She was everything," Dario said, his face lighting up at the memory. "Patient, funny, always there, always taking care of all of us . . . no matter what," he added wistfully.

"It's nice when you can be that close," Bliss commented, staring across the room at Forsythia, who had taken to the floor in her one-shouldered sequined confection with Alistair, winner of the two-left-feet award. He struggled to lift her out of a low dip while she waved to the crowd. Dario's eyes followed Bliss's.

"I can see why you're not," he sympathized. She smiled back in appreciation of the understanding, without offering any complaints. She was a firm believer in the Katharine Hepburn motto: "Before thirty it's your parents' fault. After thirty, it's your fault."

"Those are the breaks," she said, un-self-pityingly.

"You're zero for two though."

"What do you mean?" she asked, her mistrust of him on high alert once again.

"I mean your dad's no picnic either. He's tough. And indifferent."

Bliss's fury ramped up from zero to sixty in a nanosecond. She stared at Dario incredulous and seething. How dare a man who cared about no one but himself and making millions by capitalizing on the bad taste of the American public criticize her brilliant, beloved father?

"What?" he asked, utterly thrown by the obvious change in her mood.

"Don't talk about people you don't know!" she snapped, looking around her in a frenzy of wanting to get away from this boorish, presumptuous idiot.

"I call it as I see it. I don't edit. Sorry if that offends you."

"Everything about you offends me," Bliss blurted, nearly spitting with fury. "You are a walking, talking offense!" she stammered, wishing she had come up with something pithier and less ridiculous.

"You know, people might actually listen to you from time to time if you weren't always breathing fire," Dario shot back, irritated. Mortified by her own ineptitude and the entire exchange, Bliss stormed away. Wyatt stopped her by the doors.

"Hey, hey, I've been looking all over for you, beautiful, where've you been?"

"Getting offended by your executive producer."

"Dario the Tactless Wonder? Sweetie, what do you expect from a pig but an oink? Forget about him. Let's go have a seat."

Wyatt led Bliss to a table in a corner, far from the dance floor on which Diana and Forsythia were leading a conga line as "I've Got a Feeling" blared through the sound system. Charlotte danced behind them, her athletic swain's large hands firmly planted on her rounded rump. They sang along, changing the lyric "We're going to smash it," to "No, you can't snatch it, not her hymen." "I got a feeling," became "I got a Virgin!!!" Wyatt stood to join in.

"Let's have some fun," he proposed.

"I can't. I'm going home. Don't bother driving me, I'll grab a cab," Bliss said as she exited the room. Wyatt watched her go for a moment, then joyously joined the line of revelers.

chapter thirteen

Harold's eyes were at half-mast as he nursed his Taylor Fladgate 20 Year Old Tawny Porto and watched his wife's ample bottom sway to the rhythms of the calypso music blaring in the living room. Her quick side-to-side swipes mesmerized him like the pendulum swings of a clock. Bliss could see her father's faintly reawakened lust for the woman he'd married exactly nine months before Victoria, who turned thirty-five on that day, had been born. Though Forsythia had always decreed that to be unwed at thirty-five was a fate more unwelcome than contracting the bubonic plague, she had mustered her good humor (or her rum punch had) to give her eldest a proper celebration. Since her birthday fell near Thanksgiving, it had always been an important family occasion. The two youngest Harcourt girls had joined their mother and Victoria to dance in the middle of the living room. Even Diana had dropped her budding star pretensions to abandon herself to the joys of the island sounds. Of course, she'd been disappointed by Victoria's refusal to hold a dinner to be filmed for the show at one of the best restaurants in DC, but reminding herself that it really had no place in a show about these men's chivalrous pursuit of her, she contented herself with this night at home.

"Mama, out de light and give me what you give my daddy last night," Forsythia belted out in full island accent. It was in these moments, most of them alcohol induced, that Bliss liked her mother best.

She became the earthy Jamaican girl she must once have been, luxuriating in the sights and sounds of her distant island home. Watching Diana and Charlotte break into the meringue reminded her she did actually share genetic material with these women. Victoria held Bella's two hands and carefully broke down the steps for her. With her brace, Bella was particularly adept at dragging her right foot across the floor. Bella's gaze traveled from her feet to her aunt's beautiful face. She stared up adoringly. In that worshipful gaze, Bliss recognized her own amazement with Forsythia when she was four and her mother led her around the living room as Victoria now led Bella. Like her marriage, her family life had not been utterly bereft of beautiful memories. That sometimes made the current state of affairs more painful: she couldn't reject her family or her ex-husband out of hand; they both had their good points.

The girls pulled a reluctant Harold up to his feet to draw him into their rhythmic circle. He was hopeless at following their movements, and wanted to give up when Bliss jumped in and encouraged him to remain. Holding hands, all the Harcourt women, including Bella, danced in a circle around Harold who finally abandoned his rhythmically challenged Anglo-Saxon inhibitions and let the alcohol content lead him. Soon the whole clan was singing in unison.

"Yellow bird/ Up high in banana tree." They sang so loud, it drowned out the trumpet fanfare of the electric doorbell. Harold was the last one belting out the song when his wife pulled on his sleeve to stop. In their foyer, holding a dozen long-stemmed red roses, stood a stunning six-foot-two Eurasian with jet-black wavy hair and sapphire-blue slanted eyes that bespoke the clash of heritages.

"Dean?" Victoria said, shocked to see her former boyfriend standing in her parents' home.

"What are you doing here?"

"Your mother said I could come by to wish you happy birthday." Forsythia smiled triumphantly and pulled herself up to her full five-foot-four-inch height. She assumed her air of dame-of-the-manor dignity, utterly unaware that her exertions had left her wig askew.

Charlotte signaled to her to straighten it out. Harold, still literally reeling from the dance, tried to steady himself. Bliss stepped in to support him before he fell. Forsythia began ushering them all out of the room.

"Let's leave the lovebirds alone!" she commanded, resuming her faux British accent.

"Lovebirds? She dumped him," Diana corrected. Forsythia pinched her.

"Ouch, it's true, Mum."

"You were crying about him, weren't you, Glamma?" Bella inquired, to Bliss's great amusement.

"Come, come, excuse us, will you," said Forsythia, summoning enough force to drive a team of cattle, as she dragged everyone but Victoria out of the room.

Dean stood staring at Victoria and awkwardly holding the unwieldy bouquet. Her face glistening with perspiration, her silk charmeuse blouse untucked from her skirt, she struck him as more beautiful than ever. She looked about the room, panicked, trying to decide what tack to take, desperate for this forced rendezvous to end. Too polite to kick him out, she said, "Please sit down." Offering the opposite of what she wanted—to show him the door and just keep dancing in the cocoon of her family—she added, "May I get you something to drink?"

"Nothing, thank you."

He proffered the flowers.

"These are for you. Thirty-six of them, one for good luck," he said in a gentle manner that belied his sharklike ways in the courtrooms of Washington, DC.

"Why are you here, Dean?" Victoria asked.

He dropped to one knee.

"Because I want you to marry me." From behind the French doors leading to the dining room, Forsythia let out an audible cry of "Yes!!!!" One could imagine her pumping the air with her fist and doing a victory dance. Victoria turned beet red with mortification. Dean placed a large reassuring hand on hers. She recoiled from his touch. He nodded to let her know he understood her reticence.

"I know you like me more than you love me," he began. "And that's all right. At first I thought it wasn't, but then I realized that was ego and impatience. My mother didn't love my father when she married him, but now she can't live without him. We Wong men are persuasive. And if it takes a lifetime, that's what I'm prepared to give it." Victoria swallowed hard as she took in his words. She had beguiled many a man in her time, but none had ever made such a declaration. It gave her pause.

"I know you don't like sex, or at least sex with me," Dean continued, looking down embarrassed at the admission. Victoria admired the nape of his neck and wondered what was wrong with her that she didn't enjoy sex with him. But she never had, with anyone, from her first experience at twenty-three. She avoided the act whenever possible. In the brave new pantyless and orgasmic world, it was mortifying to admit that one didn't want to join the "orgy," so she never dared share with anyone, not even Bliss, her indifference to an activity so central to the human experience. Women were bolder and bolder these days, and more than once she'd found herself trapped in a coffee klatch of women swapping stories of the "great swordsmen" they had bedded. It was her worst nightmare.

Rising from his kneeling position, Dean went to caress her cheek, but thought better of it. He cupped her face in the palm of his hand instead. Looking deeply into the large, warm, black eyes that stirred him to heights of adoration he said, "You don't have to answer me now. Think about it over the holidays."

Christmas was approaching and the clan, minus Bliss and Bella, was due to follow the Virgin and her crew to Vienna to film the suitors' waltzing competition at a ball. Victoria imagined herself lying awake in her hotel room weighing the pros and cons of being Dean's wife. She desperately wanted children. She adored their company and their innocence. She just could never imagine herself married and didn't dare seek the counsel of a psychiatrist to probe into the reasons why.

"Promise me you'll think about it," Dean urged.

"Why do you love me?" Victoria asked simply.

The question took Dean aback. He had never really pondered it. His love for her was a phenomenon like those that occur organically in nature. There was no logic behind it. His litigator's prowess failed him and he declared with a shrug, "Just because. I like who I am around you."

Victoria accepted this answer for its honesty. Unlike some who had wanted her because she fit a checklist—five feet seven inches and one hundred and twenty pounds, long hair, able to hold her fork correctly, intelligent enough to be entertaining but not so bright as to overwhelm, no credit card debt—Dean's affections sprang from a pure and innocent place. He truly didn't seem to have an agenda, just real feeling.

"So you'll think about it, please?" he implored.

"I'll think about it," she answered sincerely, thinking to herself, *How could I not?*

He gave her a peck on the cheek, ever so quickly, and rushed out the door. Instinctively, she wiped her cheek with her hand.

No sooner had he left the premises than Forsythia threw open the French doors behind which she'd been eavesdropping to shake some sense into Victoria.

"Now, look here, my girl," she began, "don't think too long about this. You're no spring chicken. Pretty you may be, but looks fade, reproductive organs dry up, it's time to get a move on. Diana can afford to let the boys twist in the wind, she's twenty-one. You can't. Did you count the candles on your birthday cake, my girl? There nearly wasn't space to hold them." Forsythia had purposely ordered a smaller cake to make the point.

"By the time I was your age, I already had you and Bliss with another on the way! Now, tomorrow morning, I want you to ring him up and tell him you accept!" Victoria, Forsythia's oldest and most obedient child, stared at her horrified.

"Nonsense, Forsythia," Harold intervened, feeling very sorry indeed for his eldest. "Victoria shall marry whomever she chooses."

"Look where that got your precious Bliss," Forsythia snapped. Even

Diana and Charlotte winced at the cruelty of the comment. Bliss looked her mother dead in the eye. Unable to face her, Forsythia looked away.

"I'm sorry I'm such a disappointment, Mum," she said, "I'm doing my best to move out of here as soon as possible so you no longer have to look at your greatest failure."

"Mommy," Bella hugged Bliss.

"Mommy's okay," Bliss reassured her.

"Yes, she is," Harold echoed. Victoria swept Bella up in her arms.

"Come on, big girl, let's go finish the cake in the kitchen." Bliss led the way. Forsythia tried to stop them.

"I didn't mean it," she cried unheard. "I didn't mean it that way," she muttered to herself. Harold turned away in disgust and retreated to his study. Diana and Charlotte put comforting arms around their mother. Forsythia wondered why her greatest acts of love got lost in translation with half her clan.

chapter fourteen

On a bleak December afternoon, Bliss waited on a narrow wooden chair in the lugubrious anteroom of Father Cuthbert's office. With its vaulted gothic ceiling, dark wood paneling, and wall hanging of the crucified Jesus, it was calculated to make visitors feel small and sinful. Bliss half expected to hear the sobering chords of a Bach funeral march, played on a massive organ. As she fretted her turn with the oral examiners, her tension was punctuated with metronome-like precision by the tapping of metallic typewriter keys. Sister Perry, Cuthbert's assistant since the dawn of time, a wizened nun who shared his ascetic principles and joylessness de vivre, sat at her desk preparing a letter on a steel typewriter of 1930s vintage. The instrument was a fitting symbol of Father Cuthbert's antediluvian worldview. It would not have surprised Bliss if Sister Perry were typing a petition asking the Vatican to rescind its 2008 pardon of Galileo, the sixteenth-century astronomer, for asserting that the world revolved around the sun.

She consulted the clock above Sister Perry's head. It was 3:05 PM. Whoever preceded her in the examination room had exceeded the time limit. This would certainly put all the examiners in a foul mood. Contemplating the statue of the crucified Jesus, Bliss prayed his gaping wounds were not a metaphor for her impending fate.

She reminded herself that she knew her subject matter cold. She could answer nearly any question spanning three hundred years of

French and American history. There was nothing left to review in these final moments. The past nine months had served as a long study session. The mahogany door, black from three decades of varnish, creaked open at last, and perfectly put together Percival Linton strode out. Bliss surmised from his beatific expression that his examination had gone swimmingly. Or had it? Percival always wore a look of perfect serenity, like a wax rendering of a celebrity at Madame Tussauds. Bliss sometimes felt he could be whipped about by a tornado and still emerge without a hair or shred of clothing out of place. Percival shut the door behind him.

"They're very nice," he assured Bliss.

"Thanks. Congratulations for making it through," she responded. Of all the gradlings, she found him the least petty and vindictive. Bliss looked to Sister Perry for permission. The latter ceased her typing and gestured to her to enter.

Father Cuthbert's study was so somber, it made the antechamber look like a sunroom. Portraits of martyred saints hung on every wall, a heavenly host of the tormented presiding over the gloom. The examiners, Bliss's judge and jury, sat in a row at a long refectory table on the far side of the room. As she surveyed their faces, she felt as though she had landed before the Inquisition. To the left of Cuthbert sat Professor Marian Biddle Barrows, resident expert on the Founding Fathers and eminent biographer of Abigail Adams. Thirteen years after the fact, she was still reeling from the DNA results that had established Jefferson's paternity of Sally Hemings's slave children. She had written several scholarly articles questioning the findings, and maintaining the "moral impossibility" of Jefferson fathering children with a mulatto slave, even though such offspring were the reality on every antebellum plantation from Maryland to Mississippi. Upon seeing her, Bliss almost turned tail to run out of the room. She might as well be asked to defend the theory of evolution to a staunch creationist. Next to the Sally Hemings denier was Dr. Roberto Somosa, Latin American history expert and eminent sexual harasser. He'd spent the previous semester on "academic leave," but had been pardoned and reinstated as a result of his brilliance and popularity with the media. Finally, at the end of this executioner's row, and to Bliss's great relief, sat Jordan, who managed to convey his encouragement while maintaining the proper poker face.

"Welcome, Miss Harcourt," Cuthbert intoned in a voice that could make anyone believe he would bring the wrath of God down upon them.

"Thank you," Bliss said brightly, determined not to let the forces of doom unmoor her. This "tribunal" would judge her not only on this oral examination, but also on her fellowship proposal. Her future depended on making a good first official impression.

"Your thesis is about the relationship of Jefferson to his slaves, and Monsieur de Saint-Georges's to his illegitimate son?" he asked.

"Yes, but if I may be more precise, it contrasts Jefferson's treatment of his slave family and progeny with Monsieur Bologne de Saint-Georges's of his son by the slave Nanon." Professor Marian Biddle Barrows coughed violently, as though having an allergic reaction to the topic.

"Interesting," Cuthbert noted. "Has much been written on the subject?" Barrows coughed louder still. Bliss avoided making eye contact with her intellectual nemesis.

"Very little, Father. Annette Gordon-Reed has written extensively about the Hemings family and their life at Monticello, but to my knowledge, no one has done an in-depth study comparing the two, and by implication their societies, both at that time forging new democracies."

"I see. Well, I look forward to reading it. On to the first question. Professor Barrows, we'll begin with you."

Bliss's heart stopped. Couldn't she have done a warm-up lap with Jordan or even Somosa who seemed to appreciate her curves? *Calm down and focus,* she told herself as the seconds dragged by. *You will not be defeated by this narrow-minded hagiographer of the Founding Fathers!* Barrows smiled at her with sadistic delight, or so it seemed to Bliss. Barrows considered her notes on the yellow pad before her. At long last she looked up.

"Let us begin with Saint Catherine of Siena," she stated, crossing her arms. *Saint Catherine of Siena?* Bliss repeated in her head, panicking. *What the . . .* She remembered that though it was recommended that the examiners question the candidates about their area of expertise, it was not a requirement. Cuthbert had attempted to guide his colleagues toward Bliss's subject matter, but Barrows was deliberately disregarding him. Saint Catherine of Siena was her competitor Dierdre Detweiler's, the medievalist's, bailiwick. Bliss's terror turned to simmering resentment. Barrows stared at her expectantly.

"Well, Ms. Harcourt-Soto? I should think you'd be well versed in all things medieval given your family's participation in that chivalric game show," she added.

Bliss imagined running across the room, grabbing her by her gray chignon, and decking her. This would not improve her prospects for advancement within her field, however, and would, at the very least, land her in jail for assault. She considered lambasting her for mentioning *The Virgin,* which had no relevance to the proceedings. It occurred to her that that would only make her seem defensive. Her other nemesis Dario's statement of a few nights before sprang to mind: *People might actually listen to you if you weren't always breathing fire.* She would rise above this petty ambush. *Catherine of Siena,* she racked her brain and suddenly remembered looking her up in the wake of the royal wedding. Thank goodness her mother had forced her to watch. The Bishop of London had quoted the saint in his sermon, "Be who God meant you to be and you will set the world on fire." She had liked the sentiment and researched the saint to share her story with Bella as part of her pantheon of women who made history.

"Would you like us to go to the next question, Ms. Harcourt?" Father Cuthbert suggested as a result of her silence.

"No, I'm delighted to answer this one," Bliss said, regaining her confidence. "Saint Catherine of Siena, the nun who in the fourteenth century helped bring the papacy back to Rome from Avignon, is most significant for the role she played in the Western Schism of thirteen . . .

seventy eight. She is also remembered as one of Europe's first anorexics," she joked, eliciting a chuckle from Somosa and an approving nod from Father Cuthbert. Emboldened, Bliss continued.

"Saint Catherine belongs to a unique group of women including Eleanor of Aquitaine, Sor Juana of Mexico, and Teresa of Ávila who managed to make significant intellectual contributions to their societies, as well as influence policy at a time when women occupied a place of second class citizenship," she paused for a moment to read the faces. Cuthbert looked intrigued, Jordan repressed a smile, Somosa leered at her with delight. Barrows frowned, no doubt unhappy at having failed to derail her. *Revenge is a dish best served cold,* Bliss thought, then continued aloud.

"Looking at these women, one cannot help but side with the Barbara Tuchman theory, which posits that individuals of will rather than blind forces beyond our control shape the course of history." Whether or not Bliss completely believed this philosophy, she knew it was a worldview that would score points with Cuthbert.

"Mankind is enriched by the people who overcome the limitations of their time to propel their societies forward. This is why the Chevalier de Saint-Georges and his father deserve our attention."

"I'm glad you brought that up," Somosa interjected. "Explain to us please the relevance of the Chevalier, and of Jefferson and his mestizos, to the eighteenth century debate on the natural rights of man."

Bliss wanted to do a victory dance. She had managed to bring them squarely back into her territory. There was no stopping her now.

"You've hit on the question at the heart of the slavery debate. How does one define the rights of man? How does one define a man? For the slaves in France, it was the best of times and the worst of times. . . ." As she continued to speak, she knew she had everyone but Barrows in the palm of her hand. Bigoted though she might be, Marian Biddle Barrows would bow to the democratic process and follow the will of the majority in giving Bliss a high mark. She was one step closer to her goal of earning a PhD and becoming a full-fledged professor herself. As she spoke, Jordan beamed with pride.

chapter fifteen

Bliss stepped into the shower and the warm spray of pin-thin drops caressed her body. Slowly, he stepped in behind her, his butter-soft skin merging with hers as he enveloped her with his muscular arms. Her body fit so perfectly in all the crevices of his, they were as puzzle pieces made of flesh, melding into a coherent whole. He brushed his ripe lips ever so slightly across the nape of her neck then began to nuzzle it with a feathering motion that sent a current of pleasure down her spine. He ran his large hands down her ample but firm thighs. Slowly, she turned to face him, brushing his chest gently with her back. She kept her eyes closed as drops of water poured through her mane, transforming it into a cascade of soaking ringlets. She slowly opened her eyes and cast her gaze upward. She jumped back, startled by the sight of Manuel instead of Jordan. He inclined his head to lower his mouth onto hers. She heard a loud thud and let out a slight cry.

Bliss sat up in bed and surveyed the dark room. Bella lay fast asleep, her chest rising and falling with the steady rhythm of peaceful slumber. She spotted a leg coming through the bedroom window. Bliss reached around in vain for a blunt instrument. Her hand fell on Bella's Elmo doll instead. She hurled it at the intruder, choosing not to scream so as not to awaken her daughter. She leapt to her feet, fully prepared to use the moves she'd learned in a self-defense class in Miami. Her fight-or-flight instincts subsided and she relaxed her stance when she spotted a familiar midriff, and Charlotte stood up to her full height after twisting herself in through the window. At least Charlotte was blessed with "athletic intelligence," the ability to solve physical problems even if she didn't have the common sense God gave a chicken, Bliss surmised. Her terror having subsided, she felt the chill winter air gusting through the open window.

"Shut the window. What are you doing?" she snapped at Charlotte in a hoarse whisper. Before Charlotte could answer, she grabbed her by the hand and led her out into the hall.

In the light, she took in the full effect of her sister's ho-wear for the modern woman. She had managed to achieve new lows in tartishness. Apparently mistaking the title of the book of Revelation for a fashion tip, she had crammed her D-cup breasts into a cropped T-shirt that spelled out EAT ME in rhinestones. This tasteless top was paired with hot-pink spangled tap pants worn underneath a cheerleader-style pleated skirt. Charlotte crossed her arms defiantly with a you're-not-the-boss-of-me pout.

"You must be freezing. Where did you come from?" Bliss asked.

"The window."

"Answer me," Bliss demanded, almost ready to strike her.

"Shush. Keep your voice down. You'll get me in trouble."

"You are in trouble. And you'll be in worse trouble if I wake up Mom and Dad."

"Please, don't," Charlotte pleaded. "I'll tell you everything."

"So?"

"I was just partying with my friends. You know how Mother is. My curfew is eight-thirty, but I'm almost eighteen."

Bliss leaned in to see if she smelled liquor on her sister's breath. There was not a trace of alcohol or marijuana. She did, however, notice white streaks on her sister's chest. She wasn't so mired in celibacy as not to recognize traces of dried semen.

"Are you practicing safe sex?" she challenged Charlotte, who was shocked to be found out.

"I'm not stupid," Charlotte answered defiantly.

"You really shouldn't be having sex at all," Bliss scolded.

"Why not? Everybody else is, well everybody but Didi, that's just because she wants to get more out of guys, and you because you live here." Bliss's heart sank at the partial accuracy of the assessment. She wondered for a moment if her sternness stemmed from envy, but knew in her heart it didn't. No doubt Charlotte's escapades had nothing to do with lovemaking. She felt sorry for her sister. She'd already had sex but had clearly never known the glory of feeling her soul merge with another's through touch, that utter sense of trust and connection that is the basis of true ecstasy. Still, she was nearing day 442 of celibacy. How long would her libido be held hostage to her living situation and her inability to move on from her ex? "I still think I should wake up Mum and Papa," she warned.

"You'll just make them unhappy. It'll be a nightmare for Daddy. Mom will never let him hear the end of it," Charlotte warned, knowing she'd found the right argument. Bliss relented. She hadn't the heart to subject Harold to Forsythia's rants.

"Okay, this time. But you have to promise to stop running around," Bliss demanded sternly.

"What?"

"No more nights like tonight, or I tell all."

"You wouldn't!"

"Don't test me. And if I tell them, they probably won't let you go to Vienna with the show for the holidays." This threat struck terror in Charlotte's heart. She could forfeit hookups, but not her time on camera, and the chance to travel.

"Cross my heart and hope to die," Charlotte pledged. As she watched her saunter to her room, Bliss had the sinking feeling she would break the promise before long.

chapter sixteen

A clothing rack with ball gowns whose skirts ballooned out in a rainbow array of colors dominated the center of the Harcourt living room, like a giant multicolored caterpillar from one of Bella's children's books brought to gargantuan life. As Diana swooped down the lopsided stairs wearing a wasp-waisted white *peau de soie* confection with black velvet bows on the shoulders, Sue Minors and Wyatt nodded their approval. Forsythia ambled down the same stairs, sausaged into a red taffeta bonbon, tugging at the zipper at the back and demanding, "Are you sure this is a size six? Because I'm a six, a six petite and it's not fitting."

From their perch in the dining room, outside of the camera's range, Harold and Bliss exchanged chuckles of amusement. Forsythia hadn't been a size six since the nation's bicentennial, the year before she gave birth to her second child. And yet, over the decades, she clung to the number, going so far as to stitch size six labels into her tens and twelves in the belief that if her husband was rifling through her closet—something he had about as much interest in doing as in joining a quilting bee—he would be reminded that he'd married a woman who in her words "had sacrificed greatly to keep her girlish figure."

Charlotte surveyed the rack listlessly, utterly dismayed at the lack of anything in spandex, velours, spangled, or formfitting.

"These are all so BIG," she moaned, "I'll look like Two Ton Tessie."

"You'll look like a virgin and a lady," her mother corrected, still struggling to close the zipper that gaped chasmlike across her back.

"Besides, you're my lady in waiting, it doesn't matter what you wear," Diana snapped. Charlotte stuck out her tongue at her sister. Sue motioned to the cameraman to zoom in.

"No, don't get that," Dario insisted. "Cut, and let's take a break."

"Those are the moments that make this reality show real: sibling rivalry, petty jealousies," Sue insisted. "This is what the network wants. Otherwise it's not interesting."

"We don't need to make clowns of these people," Dario countered. From their perch in the dining room, Bliss and her father heard him and nodded their approval. Harold offered Dario an encouraging smile of gratitude. Dario took it in stride.

There was a rustling among the skirts and petticoats, Bella's head popped up from under a magenta creation, its tulle petticoats framing her face like a bonnet, and let out a playful, "Boo!"

"How long have you been down there?" Bliss scolded. "I thought you were upstairs."

"I want to go to Vienna," Bella pleaded.

"Sorry, sweetie, we're not going," Bliss explained, as she pulled her out of the rack.

"Why not?" Bella insisted.

"Because we have things to do here."

"But it's vacation and Christmas. And I want to go to the ball and see the pretty dresses. You could wear one," Bella implored.

"Bella, let me teach you to waltz," Dario interjected, with a wink to Bliss. Bliss reacted in shock to the offer. She couldn't decide what surprised her more, his consistent interest in her child or the fact that he, the missing link, could waltz. With his ubiquitous muscle sweaters and uncouth manner, he certainly didn't strike her as someone who'd been to dancing school. Bliss hesitated to let go of her child's hand, but relented. Dario sank to his knees to be at an equal height with the four-year-old. Gently, he placed one arm around her waist and held the other out. She placed a diminutive hand on his shoulder.

"The rhythm is one, two, three, one, two, three, and when I come forward, you step back. Got it?"

"Got it," Bella announced confidently. "One," Bella bellowed as Dario moved forward, on his knees. "Two," she stumbled. Dario instantly caught her. Looking up at Bliss he assured her, "I won't let her fall. Sometimes, if you give a man a chance to step up, he will." He continued to lead her around in a small circle on the carpet. Within a few repetitions, their movements became smoother and more synchronized. Bella held her head up high and looked right into Dario's amber-colored eyes. She beamed with joy, and as she moved, was slowly transformed from an awkward child lugging around a brace, to a graceful, light-footed girl.

"Where did you learn to waltz?" Bliss marveled.

"My mom taught me," Dario answered gruffly, never taking his eyes off of Bella. "She loved to dance. She couldn't afford to go to clubs or fancy parties, so we danced at home."

The trumpet fanfare sounded the arrival of someone at the door. Diana swooped to open it and offered a stagy, "I wonder who it could be," in case any camera was still rolling. She opened the door to reveal a tall, well-built man of thirty-four, with wavy hair, olive skin, and eyes that pierced the soul. It was Manuel Soto, Bliss's ex. The color drained from Bliss's face and her heart literally skipped a beat when her eyes met his. He instantly looked away from her and toward their child. Harold put a protective arm around Bliss, as much to steady her as to comfort her.

"What is he doing here?" Forsythia asked majestically, her haughty demeanor completely at odds with her still gaping zipper. With a harrumph she turned and swept out of the room, like a latter-day Mary Queen of Scots turning her back on her kinswoman and enemy, Elizabeth. Bliss slowly rose from her chair. Dario and Bella were still focused on their dance. It took a moment for Bella to become aware of her father's presence. As Dario spun her around, she spotted him and let out a lung-bursting cry of "Daddy!" She ran toward him, tripped over the stray tulle of the magenta gown, and fell flat on her face with a loud thump. Bliss and Dario instantly lunged for her, Bliss reaching her first and hoisting her to her feet. But Bella, like a raging bull seeing her target, loosed herself from her mother's grasp and ran, dragging her braced foot to meet the father she hadn't seen in nearly four months, except on her computer screen.

"Daddy! You're here!" the child cried, as she threw her little rounded arms around his neck and squeezed with all her might. He embraced her, still not daring to look up and face Bliss.

Bliss bit her lower lip and struggled to contain and comprehend the maelstrom of her emotions. What had brought him here unannounced? It was just like him to be so mercurial and unpredictable. It was part of what had held her, still held her, in thrall, the eternal emotional roller coaster ride, the dizzying highs, usually followed by gut-wrenching lows. *What did he want?*

"Hola, mi princesa," Manuel greeted Bella, disengaging from her strangling hug. He proffered a wrapped gift.

"This is for you!"

"A present! What is it?" Bella cried, eyes gleaming with delight, as though he'd just brought a sleigh full of toys.

"Open it and see," Manuel encouraged her.

"This is great drama," Sue Minors whispered to Wyatt who had emerged from the kitchen, munching on a piece of toast. "The return of the prodigal baby daddy!" Sue chomped her gum avidly as she watched the scene unfold. Bliss was clearly torn between fury and relief, resentment and the deepest soul-felt attraction to the man who'd broken her heart.

"Too bad we can't get it on camera," Wyatt whispered back. "America would eat this up."

"It would bring in the Latino demographic. He's like a young Antonio Banderas," Sue assented.

"Banderas is Spanish," Wyatt pointed out.

"Spanish, Hispanish, who cares? It's numbers and advertisers. Dario, we should be filming," Sue snapped in a stage whisper. He ignored her and walked toward the dining room to give Bella and her father space and time for their reunion. Bella furiously ripped the wrapping paper festooned with balloons to reveal a Barbie, not even a Barbie equipped with a professional uniform, like the one Dario had given her, but a princess Barbie in a bubble-gum pink ball gown.

"Sleeping Beauty Barbie!!!!" Bella screeched. "I always wanted this. Mommy, can I keep her? Can I keep her?" Unable to speak, Bliss simply nodded, then turned and walked out of the room. All eyes fell upon Manuel who finally took in all the incongruous elements: the clothing rack, the two cameras, and the five strangers. Ever the politician, he fixed his gaze on the one person in the room whose support mattered: Harold Harcourt. He crossed toward him and attempted a cordial smile.

"How are you, Harold? It's been a while," he said, masking his nerves with brazen cheer. Harold refused to make the slightest effort to diminish the young man's obvious discomfort. He merely stared in response to the greeting. Then after a moment he said, "Bella, let us go play with your new doll in my study. No doubt your father wants to have a word with your mother." He led Bella out, leaving Manuel to the stares of Sue, Wyatt, Diana, and Charlotte. Mortified at having been snubbed in the presence of all the strangers, Manuel followed the direction Bliss had taken, toward the garden, a spot in the house he knew well.

chapter seventeen

Bliss sat in one of the wrought-iron chairs in her mother's denuded garden, staring at the Queen Elizabeth rosebushes, everything but their stems and thorns shrouded in burlap against the winter frost. In this garden, during summer breaks in college, she and Manuel would meet in the middle of the night to make passionate love when he came to stay with her family. There was a memory of a honey-sweet kiss associated with each wall, and even with the fountain in the center, with its diminutive mannequin piss. It was there that he had proposed to her impulsively one hot August night. Falling to one knee and ripping his Yale insignia ring off his finger to bestow it upon her. Though they'd only officially wed three years later, she'd scotched her plans to attend graduate school in order to follow him to Miami. "Wither thou goest, I will go, and your people shall be my people." She'd proudly selected that section of the Bible as the scriptural reading at the proper Anglican wedding her mother had insisted she have, whether or not she approved of her spouse. She marveled at the naive self-sacrifice she'd blithely undertaken, without an ounce of hesitation or fear. But that was first love, uncompromising, unrestrained, unthinking. She would never love that way again. Her heart was now as guarded as her mother's Queen Elizabeths.

Manuel appeared at the garden's entrance, a bower of climbing roses in summer, now an assemblage of twining sticks that looked like dendrites. He had to stoop to enter, Hyacinth having designed everything to suit Harold's height rather than anyone else's. Bliss looked at the man who'd had her heart since the age of nineteen. She felt she should erect a tombstone somewhere in the garden: "Here lieth our love, 1996–2010. RIP." It occurred to her a pile of guts wrenched from her stomach and bronzed would make a fitting monument. The thought made her laugh inwardly and gave her the courage to face him.

"So, here you are," she said with false bravado. "What's shaking?" He walked slowly toward her and took the wrought-iron seat beside her. It had a heart-shaped back and featured the coat of arms Forsythia had designed for the family: a stag climbing a rocky cliff.

"You look good," Manuel commented, after a moment.

"No, I don't," Bliss corrected. "I look like Hell."

"Not to me," Manuel said gently, looking away.

"See, you're averting your gaze, for fear of being turned to stone," Bliss teased, desperate to stop the dull, insistent ache in her heart. "Body language never lies," she added wistfully as she pulled her arms around her, a barrier against the cold and the confluence of emotions Manuel evoked.

"What you have is more than beauty," he said softly. They stared at each other as she slowly absorbed the comment, the kindest thing he'd said to her in over a year. *Perhaps all was not lost,* she dared to hope. Unbidden, he removed his coat and placed it around her shoulders. She pulled it close around her, caressing the lapel with her cheek.

"Sorry not to have called first," he offered, suddenly formal again, "but this all came together very last minute. I have to see the folks from the DNC."

"Good. Campaign going well?" she inquired, trying to resume "business as usual."

"Yes, yes, very much so. We've got the base behind us," he said brightening at the talk of an area in which he felt utter mastery, his career. "You wouldn't believe how many people we've managed to register. Haitians, everyone in the barrio, you'd love it." As he spoke, Bliss remembered days of going door to door with him to help people register to vote, or enroll in health care programs to which they were entitled. He'd been tireless and fearless and had inspired the same determination in her. She thought she'd married Che Guevara and had been prepared to live a life of poverty and dedication to the greater good. Though the passing years and his vaulting ambition had transformed Manuel from a scruffy community activist into a slick politician campaigning for a vacant congressional seat in a redrawn district, she could still hear the echoes of his youthful idealism. Looking at him so close and face-to-face, she realized the last eighteen months had been an enormous mistake. It didn't matter that he'd had an affair, such things happened. She probably would have had one herself if she'd had the time. Listening to his voice, and watching him pace the garden, passionately describing all that he would do for his constituents, the most invisible people in Miami, she could let go of all the pain he'd caused her. She knew unequivocally she'd never love as deeply or as passionately again. A feeling so precious could not be ignored; it was worth any price, any sacrifice.

Suddenly she called out, "Manuel!" He stopped in mid-speech and resumed his seat beside her. She took his hands in hers. She ran her long fingers over his soft palms. They were warm and welcoming. Just this touch brought back memories of cleaving to each other in the middle of the night on their narrow bed.

"Manuel," she said, "I know this will sound crazy," she hesitated but then decided she had nothing to lose. *Didn't Clare Boothe Luce say that a woman truly in love had no room for pride?*

"What if we started again?" she blurted.

Manuel withdrew his hands and stood up to turn away. This did not deter Bliss; she was as determined as little Bella charging for the person she loved.

"It wasn't all your fault. I made a lot of mistakes too. I can see that now. But if we started again, we could be a family. And you and I can rebuild some of what we had. Because at one point, it was good," she insisted.

"It was," Manuel assented. "At one point. Please, don't do this to me, Bliss."

"What, what am I doing? I'm telling you I love you and that I'd be willing to start over. New life, new terms."

"That's not possible," Manuel said quietly, staring at one of the naked bushes.

"Why? Where there's love, it's never too late."

"There is love, Bliss, there always will be," he said quietly, his back still turned to her. She soaked in his words. They fell on her like soft rain after wandering the desert.

"So?" she asked hopefully.

"I'm engaged to Cindy," Manuel said hoarsely, his back still to Bliss. Sucker punch, the expression suddenly resonated with Bliss who could have thrown up on the spot. She doubled over. He turned to face her. She remained motionless, staring at the ground. Suddenly, she lunged for him, pummeling his chest like a Fury. He grabbed her wrists to arrest her frenzied movements. She pulled away.

"I'm sorry," he said, true despair in his voice.

"No, I'm sorry," she mumbled, embarrassed that she'd replayed a scene from the disintegration of their marriage. On the night she'd found him in flagrante in the office, she smacked him across the face in the parking lot and whipped him with her satchel.

"What I meant to say is, 'congratulations,'" she added, summoning her mother's sense of Emily Post oblige.

"I'm sorry, Bliss," he repeated, his voice breaking.

"Are you in love with her?"

"Please don't ask me that," he answered in a low tone. Bliss struggled to find the meaning: that his feelings were so strong that he didn't dare pour salt on the wound by telling her, or what she'd always suspected, that this woman fit the mold of the political wife better than she, and was the Ruth she'd tried to be but never could. He clearly had no plans to put her out of her misery with an answer.

"I wish you the best," she managed to say, while stifling tears. She removed his coat from around her shoulders and handed it back to him.

"Thank you," he answered, relieved. Now she just wanted him to go and leave her with the wound he'd inflicted, but he lingered.

"I'd like to tell Bella," he said, hesitantly.

"No, not today, you'll crush her," Bliss insisted, her pain turning to fear and blind rage.

"I'm her father," he insisted, with desperation.

"Then act like it!" Bliss yelled. "Are you here when she wakes up crying in the middle of the night wondering where you are? Are you there to console her when some kid makes fun of her brace and the way she walks?"

"She's my daughter too," he protested, knowing he was losing ground.

"Not today. You don't get to decide when to waltz in and be a dad. I'll tell her, when it's the . . . right time," Bliss said, barely holding it together. Manuel turned away, a man defeated.

"We'll do it your way. Again." He relented. Bliss wanted to take back what she'd said, but it was too late. Now it was she who couldn't look at him.

"Kiss the baby for me. I do love her, you know, whether you believe it or not," he said, as he turned to walk away and out of her life. Bliss crumbled to the ground. As her forehead met the flagstones, her survival instincts reawakened. *Get up,* she told herself. No one had brought her to this low pass. She'd done it to herself. When would she tell Bella? Was it protectiveness or revenge not to have let him tell her himself? She couldn't quite fathom in that moment. All she knew was that any remaining hope for a future with Manuel was dead. She was freed from the torment of wishing that he would ever ride back into her life. She ripped his Yale insignia ring off of her finger and threw it into the rosebushes.

She looked up and to her horror noticed Dario, staring at her from under the bower. Embarrassed at having been seen, he turned away, and walked back into the house.

chapter eighteen

Bliss didn't know how many hours had passed since her Garden of Gethsemane moment, suburban edition. She had moved from agony to Emily Dickinson's "formal feeling." Her "nerves [sat] ceremonious like tombs," aided no doubt by the three glasses of excellent California Merlot Jordan had bought her. She stared straight at the print of the election of 1784 on the wall of the Pint and Horseshoe, not even seeing it, blinded by the shock of what had transpired.

"What was I thinking?" she asked dazed.

"You weren't. You were feeling," Jordan said in his soothing baritone. "As the saying goes, 'The heart has reasons that reason cannot fathom.'"

"The heart's a fucking maniac," Bliss deadpanned. "Certifiable, and an imbecile. What do I tell Bella?" She came out of her haze and focused her gaze on Jordan. She found his cocoa-brown eyes filled with empathetic sorrow. His clear compassion was a welcome balm in this soap-operatic Gilead.

"The kids. That's always the worst part. Stops you in your tracks," he said pained. Bliss suddenly felt very self-centered, and myopic. Her co-parent was still alive. In addition to losing the woman of his life, Jordan had been left with a sixteen-year-old son who'd spend the rest of his days grieving an adoring mother taken too soon. She placed a sympathetic hand on his.

"Sorry to dump all of this silliness," she said. "You didn't need to hear all this crap."

"It's not silly," he reassured her, placing a large beautifully manicured hand on hers. "Life, love, it's all . . . fucked up," he said, abandoning his usual eloquence.

"Not just fucked up, fucked up beyond all recognition," Bliss insisted, with the brio of the slightly tipsy. Another sip of Merlot had pushed her over the edge from maudlin to belligerently cheerful. Jordan smiled at her, his beautiful teeth gleaming in the candlelight. They clasped hands. His grasp was comforting and, she had to admit, mildly arousing though she tried hard to banish sexual thoughts of him as incestuous. But he wasn't a relative and at fifty-five, he wasn't *that* much older. Perhaps the moment had come for a fling. If you could drown out sorrow with a glass of distilled grape juice, or several, why not do it with a well-earned roll in the proverbial hay? She was now on day 465 of self-imposed celibacy and her willpower was reaching the breaking point. She felt her unspent energy could power several small cities, for days if not weeks. She shifted in her seat. Jordan looked down at her generous hips, noticing the movement, then looked back up at her. There it was: the flash of mutual attraction in the eyes. Bliss could tell he'd read her illicit thought and shared it. Neither dared speak and Bliss didn't dare rise from the table. She knew that if she did, he'd follow her out and they'd end up in flagrante in the parking lot, like pre–sex rehab Tiger Woods and one of his International House of Pancakes booty calls. No, if she was to have a fling with Jordan, or a relationship, this was not the way to start, but it would be one way to forget the day. The nostrils of Jordan's aquiline nose flared as if he could smell her desires. He began to lean toward her. She couldn't tell if he was going to whisper something in her ear or kiss her, but a voice stopped him in mid-motion.

"Hope I'm not interrupting anything," Wyatt bellowed, beaming his Robert Redford all-American-boy smile. Feeling caught, Bliss and Jordan both leaned back in the high-backed bench of their booth.

"No," they both insisted. "Of course not." Bliss realized the intensity of the spell only after it had been broken by this not entirely welcome intrusion. She liked Wyatt but his blindness to the erotic tension that could have powered the lights of Las Vegas was annoying. She mustered a smile.

"Mind if I have a seat?" Wyatt asked. Bliss shook her head no. Wyatt extended a hand to Jordan.

"We haven't met. But I've seen you on Charlie Rose. You're Jordan McIntosh, author of *No Overcoming Without Them: Black Women in the Civil Rights Movement*. Great book."

"Thank you," Jordan said, seeking to regain his professorial demeanor toward Bliss.

"Well, Bliss, I followed you here because I have a proposition."

"I'm not doing the show," Bliss insisted.

"That's not the proposition," Wyatt said flatly.

"Oh," Bliss said, embarrassed. How could she think they wanted her on screen, with her mop of hair and now fifteen extra pounds and counting? Second grand delusion of the day. She probably had imagined Jordan's attraction to her a moment ago. Why would any man look at her with desire in this moment?

"We want you to come away."

"Who's 'we,' and where?"

"The Virgin, the show, . . . me," Wyatt said sheepishly. "I know you were planning to hang out with Bella, but come on, it's Christmas. Do you really want to hang out alone at home with her? Why not give her the trip of a lifetime?"

What had been completely unappealing and out of the question only three hours ago suddenly struck her as the answer to a prayer. She would break Bella's heart with the news her father was set to marry a woman she didn't even know, but she'd lift her spirits with a fairy-tale trip. Still, it went against her principles and fairy tales were what she was striving to avoid instilling in her child. No, they had to remain and face reality, however grim. There were worse places to spend Christmas than Chuck E. Cheese's.

As if reading her thoughts, Wyatt sought to convince her.

"I know this whole show goes against everything you stand for:

feminism, intellectualism, integrity. Hey, it's hard for me too. But, I'm divorced and I never get to see my son and I'd do anything to be able to take him on a trip like this."

Bliss looked to Jordan for guidance, seeing him again as a surrogate father, rather than her near tumble in the hay.

"I can't argue with the man's reasoning," Jordan assured her.

"So you'd go, in my shoes?"

"In your shoes, I'd go on every trip they offered. Aren't you all headed to England at some point?"

"How do you know?" Bliss asked.

"I read my TV guide online," Jordan laughed. "Got to know what's going on in the world my students live in. The student I'm looking at should go home and pack her bags."

Bliss was embarrassed to admit it to herself, but the prospect of a luxurious trip to a remarkable city was quite delicious in this moment. It didn't hurt either that the offer came from someone who bore more than a passing resemblance to a classic Prince Charming.

Jordan rose from his seat.

"Hope you're not leaving on my account," Wyatt commented.

"No," Jordan insisted, "I was heading out anyway." Bliss knew from this lie that she hadn't imagined the attraction: it had been potent and mutual. Yet in the presence of a more age-appropriate man, Jordan, with his usual chivalry, was bowing out. He put her in mind of a latter-day Chevalier de Saint-Georges, the ultimate elegant true heart. She vowed to herself that if she ever let anyone into her life again, he would be of Jordan's caliber and character, whether or not he were Jordan himself. Much as she admired and lusted after him, she admitted to herself she would not like to live her life playing second fiddle to his late wife's ghost, in a humorless version of *Blithe Spirit*.

"What are you drinking?" Wyatt asked, having seized Bliss's glass, swirling the wine around and inhaling its aroma. "Smells good," he said, then took a swig without asking permission. He winked at her. She didn't know whether to feel cheered or perturbed.

chapter nineteen

Having opted to take a town car, rather than the horse-drawn carriage required by the network, Bliss and Bella arrived before the rest of the party at the majestic Hotel Imperial. As their car drew up before the former palace, even Bliss found herself astonished by its imposing neoclassical beauty. Doormen in red and gold livery bowed as they opened the gleaming glass, brass-handled portals.

"It's a real castle, Mommy!" Bella exclaimed, nearly jumping for joy. Her movements mirrored her mother's true emotions. Bliss loved Europe with a passion and hadn't been in ten years. She and Manuel had poured what little money they had had into the cause of registering voters and attacking illiteracy in Overtown, the most dangerous neighborhood in Miami. There hadn't been much disposable income left to go off gallivanting on the Continent. It wasn't until she'd smelled the Mercedes's diesel fuel and driven the Ringstrasse, Vienna's elegant main boulevard, that it hit Bliss how much she'd missed the insurmountable beauty of an ancient European capital.

She'd never stayed in a hotel of such a caliber. Even when her mother had insisted on a "first-class-all-the-way" trip to Paris and London in her teens, they'd had to content themselves with bargain not-so-grand palaces. Bliss imagined her mother entering the double-height-ceiling marble hall and swooning on the spot. Sue Minors and the network would love it: a pudgy black woman making an utter fool of herself, a true ratings bonanza. Before Bliss could even make it to the registration desk, Bella had boldly approached. Her unbridled chutzpah reassured Bliss. She was at least raising a child who was undeterred by her infirmities. Perhaps this holiday would give Bliss the courage to follow in her daughter's intrepid footsteps. Whatever other choices she regretted in her life, she would never regret having Bella with Manuel.

"Hello," Bliss said cheerfully to the elegant sexagenarian at the desk with metal-rimmed glasses and slicked back salt-and-pepper hair. "I'm with the Harcourt party."

"You are ze Virgin?" the man asked puzzled as he looked from Bliss to Bella and back to Bliss again as if to say, *Am I to deduce that this was an immaculate conception?*

"No, she's coming in a horse-drawn carriage, if they don't get run over by a lorry on the Ringstrasse. I'm her sister, Bliss Harcourt-Soto."

"Oh," the man said, relieved. "Harcourt-Harcourt." He scrolled through the names on the computer screen. With his morning suit and formal demeanor, Bliss could imagine him turning the pages of the handwritten guest log in an earlier century. He mumbled names.

"Imperial Suite, Franz Joseph Suite, Maria Theresia, oh here you are!" he announced at last. "Allow Hannes, our bellboy, to help you with your . . . luggage," he said in a tone of disdain for the battered and beaten black plastic suitcase that Bliss had dragged along. Bliss smiled wide, happy that status symbols had never mattered to her.

Hannes, a handsome young boy, not more than eighteen or nineteen, escorted them to the lift. Bliss wondered how many guests Adolf Hitler had escorted to the same elevator when he'd worked at the hotel as an impoverished young man in the 1920s. Well, if Holocaust survivor Simon Wiesenthal could forgive the Hotel Imperial and hold his ninetieth birthday there, who was she to hold a grudge? The young bellman pressed the last floor. Through the elevator's glass doors, the various luxury floors flashed before them. With each mounting level, the ceilings dropped a foot or two. At last they reached a level that clearly at one time had housed the maids' quarters. Bliss laughed at the appropriateness of her room's location: as the Cinderella or madwoman of her family, she was relegated to the attic.

"Mommy, this is superpretty," Bella squealed, squeezing the Sleeping Beauty Barbie—which had not been out of her hands since her father's visit—tight in her arms. The bellman opened the door to reveal a charming split-level suite with walls elegantly covered in gold Regency-striped silk and a perfect view of the Karlskirche from a large picture window. A flat-screen plasma TV on a white credenza served as the only reminder of the twenty-first century in the time capsule of a space. A large bed, surmounted with a crown and draped with sumptuous damask, dominated the room. Over the headboard hung the obligatory reproduction portrait of an unknown pale and plump eighteenth-century noblewoman with powdered hair piled sky high, clasping a camellia to her bosom.

"A princess bed," Bella exclaimed delighted.

After giving them a perfunctory tour of the room, and handing Bliss the keys to the minibar, Hannes hoisted the hideous suitcase on a collapsible campaign chair and withdrew with a bow.

"Here we are, princess of my heart," Bliss gushed, sweeping Bella up in a hug. She took her to the window and they peered out at the winter morning.

"We're in a snow globe," Bella marveled.

Bliss picked up a little pine box on the bed and opened it. The aroma of dark chocolate filled her nostrils and she surrendered to temptation, popping one of the Imperial Delights into her mouth. The truffle melted on her tongue, awakening her taste buds to the deep cocoa flavor.

She heard a knock at the door. She went to open it and there stood Dario, wearing a parka. He began to smile at her, then caught himself, she thought, and assumed his usual jadedness. Bella ran toward him, hugging his massive legs. He gently caressed her diminutive back then knelt to look her in the eye.

"Did you like being on the airplane?" he asked.

"Yes, the seats were so big. Like sofas! And I watched movies!" Bella exclaimed. Dario chuckled then stood back up and nervously ran a hand through his hair.

"Everything okay? You like it?" he asked, indicating the surroundings.

"Yes," Bliss answered, taken aback by his solicitousness.

"I thought you'd be at the airport," she added.

"No, I wanted to be here to greet you and Bella. The others are making their way here. Problem with the horses. So is this room okay?"

"It's beautiful," Bella answered.

"I have to agree," Bliss added in spite of herself.

"Good, figured you might like something away from the hubbub downstairs." Bliss found herself puzzled. He seemed to be taking credit for the selection of her room when it was Wyatt who'd insisted she come in the first place.

"So now you're playing concierge," she taunted.

He started to answer but thought better of it, clearly put off by her sarcasm.

"You got a cell phone?" he asked, changing the subject.

"Yes."

"Pull it out."

"Why?" Bliss demanded to know. Dario sighed.

"Could you just do it?" he insisted with exasperation.

"Remember, I'm not part of your cast or crew," Bliss bristled.

"Thank God for that," he mumbled to himself. Bliss pulled out her phone and he pulled out his, aimed it at hers, and pressed a button.

"Okay, now you have my number."

"I've had that for some time," she said half to herself.

"No, you really haven't," he corrected. She looked up, slightly embarrassed that he'd heard. He stared back, daring her to take another jab. She refrained. Bella watched them as if they were engaged in a ping-pong match. She was surprised to see her mother put an end to the volley. Bliss felt somehow she'd gone too far. Though Dario had little to recommend him, least of all his short neck and clearly sexist attitude, she didn't want to slide down the slippery slope of the embittered woman who treated every single man as a born enemy. That and never building the financial wherewithal to leave her parents' abode were the twin terrors that plagued her.

"Call me if you need anything. I mean it . . ." he added, "anything." Then he withdrew, closing the door behind him.

"I like Mr. Fuentes," Bella declared. Bliss admitted to herself that in that moment, she rather liked him too. Though she found it hard to believe he had passed up the shoot to greet her and Bella. There was a knock at the door once again. Bliss flung it open.

"Dario, I'm sorry, I was rude—" she blurted to a housekeeper in a black-and-white uniform from the turn of the nineteenth century who stared at her puzzled. She held up a porcelain vase containing a dozen pink tea roses the size of thimbles, their petals just beginning to open.

"For Madame," the lady announced as she entered.

"Oh, from whom?" Bliss asked, hoping perhaps Wyatt had sent them. The housekeeper shrugged as she went to place them on the Biedermeier *guéridon* by the window. Probably from the management, Bliss surmised. No one had sent her flowers in a decade. Who on earth would do so now? She mentally cautioned herself to be careful. The trip and first-class travel were leading her to have delusions of attractiveness at a time when most of the world's men seemed to find her eminently resistible.

"Mommy, Mommy, come look. Aunt Didi looks like a princess!!"

Bella called as she peered out of the open window. Bliss joined her in the casement. Eight flights below, she spotted Diana, who'd worn sweats on the plane, fitted out in a riding habit suitable for the young Queen Victoria, complete with bustled skirt, top hat, and fur muff. She alighted from a large landau as her three suitors, the "knights," proffered helping hands. In their striped pants and cutaways, all three men looked like extras from a crowd scene at the London Stock Exchange in a BBC Edwardian costume drama.

"Here they are arriving at the world-famous Hotel Imperial," Wyatt announced to the camera. First in line stood the chinless Englishman, his slight paunch straining the buttons and seams of his waistcoat and giving him a slight early-pregnancy appearance. Beside him, wearing the smug grin of the southern, light-skinned pretty boy stood Paul Daniels the Fourth, snow falling lightly on his close-cropped curls. Last and most awkward was Beowulf Jones whose bowed posture shaved two inches off of his imposing six-foot-five height. Whereas Paul seemed to angle his face, the better to be flattered by the camera, and Alistair stared aimlessly about, Beowulf's gaze never left Didi. *Another man mesmerized,* Bliss thought to herself. Her sister had held a Svengali-like power over the opposite sex since toddlerhood and had usually used it for the bad. She'd turned countless willing and pimply victims into slavish minions, carrying her books, doing her homework for her, even subbing to complete her household chores. Didi had believed since the cradle that men and life owed her everything and she planned to collect. Bliss had no doubt one day she'd get everything she'd ever coveted in her little Casio calculator of a heart. Diana knew the exact market value of her perky beauty and planned to exchange it at the highest rate.

"I want to go see closer, I want to pet the horses," Bella squealed. Bliss heard Dario yell, "Cut!" She saw Sue Minors, bundled up in white down from head to toe, barrel up to the three suitors.

"We need that again. You!" she yelled pointing at Alistair, "Prince William, Focus!!! Look at her, the horse, something! Join us on planet Earth! You look like you're at a fucking séance. You, Beowulf, angle for camera, please! Your profile is for shit. Once this is over, two words: nose job!" Beowulf stooped another inch lower, devastated by the cruel remark. Punch cringed at her boss's insensitivity, and gave him a thumbs-up in sympathy. Utterly indifferent to the damage she'd done, Sue rattled off the rest of her demands. "You, Paul, you're perfect.

Okay, once again, like it's the first time and you're all virgins." The crew groaned. Bliss wondered how this qualified as real when it had been rehearsed and restaged.

"Why don't we just have cocoa up here?" She suggested to Bella.

"With marshmallows?" Bella asked, eyes wide as saucers.

"With anything you want." As she dialed room service she wondered how to say *marshmallows* in German. Did they even exist?

chapter twenty

As the bright, crystalline light of a winter sun poured through the silk gauze curtains, Bliss sat up in the bed, her arm around Bella, both of them savoring a large basket of breakfast pastries. Bella worked her way through a swirling peak of whipped cream to guzzle her hot cocoa. Bliss sank her teeth into her third Danish topped with custard-smooth cheese. This certainly did beat the life of self-abnegation she had led with Manuel in their four-room cottage in Miami. Embracing her inner sybarite might not be the worst course to take in the future. She had denied herself luxury for so long, she'd convinced herself she didn't care for it. She now realized this was the greatest lie she had ever told herself. Certainly, she'd never marry for it, like Diana, obsess over it like her mother, but striving for it, just a bit, suddenly no longer struck her as a mortal sin for a person of substance.

"I like this, Mommy," Bella declared, sinking her teeth into an almond croissant, glazed golden with melted butter and sugar.

"Me too," Bliss said happily, as she peered out of the window at the majestic green dome of the Karlskirche, Emperor Charles VI's Baroque monument to his namesake, the patron saint of the plague. Architectural atonements for war and pestilence, like this one and the Sacré-Coeur Basilica in Paris, seemed to fill the world's Christian capitals, marble monuments to guilt. Bliss felt none today. She vowed to relish every decadent moment. She laughed to herself thinking of how envious her fellow graduate students would be if they could see her sitting in the lap of luxury. They would resent her, not out of any true spirit of self-denial or concern for the world's less fortunate, but because of a miserly inability to rejoice in anyone else's good fortune. Bliss looked over at the church's dome once again and though far from religious, thanked God for sparing her the envy gene. She was almost congenitally incapable of the emotion. Even when Manuel left her for his campaign worker, she didn't begrudge the woman her gain, she merely mourned her own loss. She caressed Bella's curly auburn locks, grateful to see her so carefree and still dreading the moment when she'd have to tell her about the wedding. She'd do it in her own time and find a way to soften the blow. Until she had a date firm, there was no reason to burst the child's bubble, she reasoned.

Jumping out of the super comfortable bed, she opened a window and let the crisp air fill her nostrils and lungs.

"Come on, baby, let's get dressed and go explore the city!" Bella did not wait to be asked, she slid off the bed.

"Let's go, Mama," she said, heading for the door.

"I think maybe we should dress first," Bliss suggested. Bella fell into fits of laughter.

"I wanna go out in my pajamas," she teased. Bliss closed her eyes to savor the moment of pure, carefree joy.

chapter twenty-one

Bundled up against the winter chill, Bella had walked with Bliss for blocks and not tired. Everything fascinated her: the low buildings crowned with friezes, the cobbled streets, the abundance of horse-drawn carriages, the sounds of the language.

"Auf Wiedersehen! Auf Wiedersehen," she had chanted all the way from the Imperial to the Maria-Theresien-Platz where they now arrived. They paused in front of the statue of Empress Marie-Theresa with its four horses rearing, prepared to gallop away to the four corners of the Austro-Hungarian Empire.

"They erected this statue to commemorate the changing of the laws so a woman could inherit the throne," Bliss explained.

"So she was a queen?" Bella asked.

"Yes, in her own right, not just because she married a king. That's an important lesson to remember. A woman must define herself, not be defined by a ma—"

"Come on, Mommy, let's go inside," Bella interrupted. Bliss realized that for a four-year-old, dinosaur skeletons and the Natural History Museum gift shop trumped lectures on female self-empowerment. She would have to find another opportunity to instill the importance of independence. Perhaps in another decade.

They arrived at the imposing entrance of the late-nineteenth-century limestone edifice. Bella pointed across the snow-covered plaza.

"Mommy, this building is that one's twin," she exclaimed pointing to the Kunsthistorisches Museum.

"Yes, they were built by the same architect. We'll go there after we finish here," Bliss explained, delighted at her daughter's powers of observation.

"They both look like castles. When Aunt Didi gets married, will she live in a castle like this?"

"No," Bliss responded, tempering her exasperation at the nefarious influence of Diana's celebrity.

"But Grandma said she would."

"Well, sometimes Grandma is wrong," Bliss responded, refraining out of respect from saying *Grandma is* always *wrong. Don't listen to her.*

They entered the building and were delighted to be greeted by the massive skeleton of a T. rex.

"Guten Tag!" Bella shouted in greeting. Following a marble maze of corridors led them to the Venus of Willendorf, the twenty-four-thousand-year-old statue of a fertility goddess with a protruding belly and pendulous breasts. Bliss was dismayed to contemplate how much her own physique might one day resemble the goddess's if she failed to curb her Häagen-Dazs habit.

"Hello," she heard a familiar voice say. She turned to see Dario, his hair still wet and slicked back from the shower, a pair of skates slung over his shoulder.

"Good morning . . ." he said, looking her over.

"Mr. Fuentes!" Bella cheered, popping up between them and looking at him with stars in her eyes.

He knelt to her level, smiling broadly.

"How's the princes—" seeing the daggers forming in Bliss's eyes he corrected himself. "How's the future nuclear disarmament expert doing?"

"I walked ten blocks!" Bella announced proudly.

"What are you doing here?" Bliss asked, hoping he wasn't noting her resemblance to the ample-hipped ancient fertility statuette.

"Looking for you," he answered. "And my favorite girl."

"How did you know we'd be here?" Bliss asked.

"I asked the concierge which way you were headed. When he said here, I guessed you'd be in the most educational part of the building. Training the little one to be an archaeologist or paleontologist, not a princess."

Bliss was at once amused and unnerved by his powers of deduction. She sensed in him someone who had a detective's capacity for sizing up people and situations based on the minutest of clues. She was certain he'd noticed her fingernails gnawed down to nubs, the telltale sign of an epically horny woman, deprived of a proper outlet. She hid her hands behind her back.

"Can we spend the day with you?" Bella asked. Bliss knew it was hopeless, her daughter was completely and utterly smitten. At least she was only four and it was a surrogate-father crush. She just had to pray it didn't last past the filming of the series or, heaven forbid, puberty, and turn into a darling-buds-of-May-barren-trees-of-January romance. She had enough real problems without inventing nightmare scenarios. She forced herself to focus on the present.

"I'd like to. I came to see if my favorite little pal wanted to go ice-skating. That is, if it's okay with your mom."

"Mommy, Mommy pleeease, can I? Can I? Can I?" Bella begged like a forlorn puppy coveting a bone. An out clause occurred to Bliss.

"Don't you have to shoot today? Don't the Virgin's suitors have a jousting contest?"

"That's twelve weeks from now. In England. Today, the boys are being fitted for their white tie and those that don't know how, are being taught to waltz. Your sister and mother are having a day of beauty. I'm free till two."

"Mommy, let's go!!! Pleeaase, I don't want to look at the statue of the fat lady anymore. I want to go skating," Bella insisted, pulling Bliss toward the exit.

"Just a minute, sweetie," Bliss responded. "I need to speak to Mr. Fuentes privately."

Bliss stepped out of earshot with Dario.

"Do you really think skating is the right activity for Bella? What if she can't?"

"Are you more scared that maybe she can?"

"Of course not," Bliss bristled. "I want her to be independent."

"Then let her take a chance. I'll be right there. Remember, I don't let her fall." Bliss couldn't argue that point. Still, she hesitated.

"Sometimes, Bliss, you gotta trust someone else, give someone else a chance. You're her mother, and you're great at it, but maybe if you'd let someone, they'd help you." The truth of his words struck her hard. If there was one massive regret she had vis-à-vis Manuel, it was never trusting him to take care of Bella. Though he had shied away from the responsibility in the beginning, when he did try to step up, she'd dismissed him. She feared that mistrust had alienated him from his own child. In the name of protecting Bella, she had done her and her father a disservice. Now, it was perhaps too late. Bella appeared at their side.

"Are we going? Are we going?" she asked eagerly. Bliss knew she was beaten.

"You'll need me to come with you," she insisted.

"That's what I was hoping for," Dario said without a hint of irony.

Bliss was taken aback. She couldn't imagine his wanting to be in her company; she embodied everything he seemed to abhor in women, principally a big mouth and a functioning brain.

"Do you skate?" he asked.

"Not really . . . no, I haven't in a long time, but I'll try."

"This should be interesting," Dario said, smiling broadly. "Okay, let's go."

"Yay," Bella cheered, eagerly placing her tiny hand in his.

Bliss let them walk ahead of her as she tried to make sense of what had just transpired. She had accepted an outing with someone she could barely stand. Adding to her confusion was his undeniable ability to charm children, and his genuine interest in Bella. His attentiveness toward her did not mesh with his chest-beating George-of-the-Jungle approach to everything else. Bliss would have preferred it if he had maintained consistency in his obnoxiousness. This glimmer of heart and humanity was most unsettling.

chapter twenty-two

Bella bounded out onto the snow-covered street. Bliss stifled all negative thoughts and neurotic concerns for how crushed her child would be once the shoot ended and she found herself without a father figure once again. The sun glistening on the freshly fallen snow lent a magical glimmer to the street. Bliss was relieved she had picked her favorite aquamarine turtleneck, the one that set off her green eyes to full advantage. As he looked at her, Dario seemed to like what he saw. Not that it mattered to her, Bliss told herself, as she tossed her curly mane out of her face. Falling around her shoulders in its fullness, it gave her a true leonine appearance.

"Let's hit it," Dario announced as he pointed to a gleaming black carriage pulled by two chestnut steeds.

"We're not going in that," Bliss demurred.

"Yes, it's only a few blocks," Dario explained.

"Yippee, a carriage, just like a princess!" Bella cheered.

"They're called *fiakers* here," Bliss corrected.

"Really?" Dario asked.

"Yes, after *fiacre*, the French term for open carriages."

"If you say so, Professor," he teased.

Dario held open the door of the carriage and stared at Bliss, daring her to reject the magical conveyance and burst her daughter's fairy bubble. Bliss nodded her assent and Dario hoisted Bella onto the backseat. He then extended a hand to help Bliss. As she placed a palm in his, she was struck by its softness and warmth. It was no wonder so many women landed between his sheets. He had been kissed by the gods of sensuality. It was thoroughly annoying and completely undeniable.

Bliss was grateful for the gust of cold air that hit her once the carriage took off, and she and Dario settled beneath the car rug, an uncontrollably giggling Bella between them. The horses trotted down the avenue, the snow beneath their hooves smoothing the ride. Finally, they pulled up in front of the Rathaus, the ancient stone town hall where a skating rink was erected every winter.

"Shouldn't Bella have a helmet," Bliss said, uttering a thought that had just occurred to her.

Dario patted his backpack.

"It's right in here," he assured her. Again, Bliss was stunned by his thoughtfulness, his attention to details usually lost on the childless. *When and where had he even had the time to get Bella a helmet,* she wondered.

While Bliss went to rent her skates, Dario helped Bella into hers. When she returned, they walked out toward the rink, holding Bella between them. The rink was the size of a large lake. The town hall with its clock tower loomed over it, a reassuring symbol of permanence and tradition.

"Why don't I head out first, do a little demonstration, then I'll come back and get you two," Dario suggested.

"Good idea," Bliss assented, feeling somewhat apprehensive about her first foray on the ice since she was fifteen and nearly broke her arm. Few would ever accuse her of having an excess of coordination and she abhorred all sports in which her feet could not touch the ground. Nonetheless, she resolved to screw her courage to the sticking-place, or at least Velcro it. Another unwelcome casualty of divorce had been her damn-the-torpedoes courage. Over the last five torturous years of her dying marriage, her confidence in her abilities had eroded like a beach-front shoreline, Manuel's abandonment the final tsunami. She had to admit to herself that she approached even simple tasks with trepidation, and questioned her instincts at every step. She had believed her marriage and her love would last forever, like the stone monument before her, but it had crumbled under the weight of parenting a young, challenged child, and Manuel's and her divergent ambitions. It was difficult to be confident in her decision-making abilities when she'd bungled one of the most basic: *Whom should I spend my life with?*

"Mommy, look at him," Bella's voice called, rousing her from her navel-gazing. She looked up at the rink to see Dario weaving through the skaters, his hands behind his back, his strong torso leaning forward, his muscular thighs carrying him, making it look as effortless as flight for a bird.

"I want to do that!" Bella exclaimed.

"That's what we're here to learn," Bliss reassured her. She mentally contrasted her own plodding movements, remembering the feeling of trying to move blades through wax. In another instant, Dario had spun around and was wending his way to them backward. Bella let off peels of laughter.

"Ready, ladies?" Dario asked. He led them out on the ice. Bliss moved like a twelve-month-old toddler just finding her balance on her feet. Bella exhibited more confidence, though the inclination of her right leg toward her left made it difficult for her to balance. Dario had purposely positioned himself on her left to compensate. Meanwhile, Bliss dragged on his left side, leaning in without realizing it. He gently prodded her upright.

"I can do it," she insisted letting go of his hand. She took a step or two, then landed flat on her bottom.

"Thank goodness it's well padded," she commented cheerfully.

"Mama, are you okay?" Bella asked, her brow furrowed with worry.

"Just fine, baby, just fine," her mother assured her. Dario leaned over to help her up.

"I've got it," she said, "you two go ahead."

"We're not just going to leave you here," Dario objected.

"This is Bella's lesson, not mine. Go for it." Dario waited a moment.

"I won't have it any other way," Bliss said. "Go, go." She rose up to her feet. "See, I can manage." She instantly stumbled backward. Without waiting for permission, Dario hoisted her to her feet.

"It's okay to fall sometimes to see who will pick you up," Dario reminded her as he moved off with Bella. Bliss stood for a moment watching him as he positioned himself behind Bella, demonstrating how to cut through the ice with the blade. He held her up by the torso, shielding her from the other skaters racing past. A dancing pair whipped past Bliss, reminding her she might want to move. She cautiously pushed forward with one foot, then the other. It was difficult at first, but after ten steps, she began to feel she was getting some traction. Several yards ahead, she saw Bella nearly stumble and Dario catch her just in time. He looked over to Bliss and gave her an okay sign. She responded in kind, then continued, with renewed confidence. Perhaps it was true and that which did not kill us did make us stronger. She watched Dario demonstrate the shifting of weight, and found herself copying his movements from a distance. Stroke after stroke, focusing on his lead, she found she, he, and Bella were moving in unison. Bella never looked back at her but looked ahead, and occasionally cast an adoring glance up at her self-appointed instructor. Bliss inhaled the crisp cold air, let the strains of the techno pop music fill her ears, and admired the variety of people skating around her. There were young, athletic speed racers with powerful thighs, older couples waltzing in spite of the music, teenage girls rehearsing for a hoped-for moment of figure skating glory. Suddenly, a tall, well-built young man, poster boy for cougar prey, smoothly sidled up, flashing a brilliant smile. Bliss smiled back, more than a little intrigued by the handsome stranger.

"*Sprechen sie Deutsch?*" he asked cordially.

"*Nein,*" she answered, smiling back coquettishly, in spite of herself.

"English?"

"*Ja,*" she responded, cheekily.

"Where are you from?"

"Maryland, in the United States." He nodded, clearly uncertain as to the location of this place called *Maryland.* She felt a gaze boring through her and noticed that Dario had planted himself and Bella ten or so yards away. He looked at her questioningly as if to ask, *Is everything all right?* Bliss smiled back, and waved him on, indicating the young hottie with an inclination of her head and smugly thinking to herself, *I've still got it.* Dario reluctantly moved on, but not without casting a backward glance. *He clearly wondered who the handsome stranger was,* Bliss thought to herself with satisfaction. Ah, well, maybe she'd found her "Lolito," out here on the Austrian ice. The young man put a hand on her shoulder. *Would he invite me to stop for a hot cocoa and warm waffle by the side of the rink,* she wondered.

"You haven't skated very much?"

"No," Bliss answered coyly. "But I'm open to learning," she heard herself saying before she could stop herself.

"Good, then you should go over there," the young man said pointing to a pen in which plodding adults and tiny children struggled to find their footing. "It's too dangerous out here and against the rules," he said apologetically. Bliss noticed for the first time since he'd approached her the official Rathaus badge on his jacket. No doubt his beauty had blinded her to it. Now Bliss wished she could vanish in a cloud of ice vapor. Worse than the walk of shame, she had to execute the "skate of submission" to the kiddie rink.

"May I," the young man asked, seeking permission to put his arm around her waist and guide her all the more quickly to the pen. Bliss assented. Once there, she found herself surrounded by octogenarians, overweight women who clearly had never learned, and toddlers. She felt a kinship with alcoholics who kept hitting various "bottoms" before finally rebounding. *How low would I have to sink before bouncing back to the winner's circle of life,* she wondered, chuckling to herself.

Having spotted her, Dario began to make his way over with Bella. Bliss tried to wave them off but they came closer and closer.

"What are you doing here?" Dario asked.

"I've been exiled. To the land of remedial skaters," Bliss said, self-deprecatingly. "I can't skate and that young hottie you saw me with said 'Hey, Grandma, get off the ice before you kill someone.'"

"I know how to skate now, Mama," Bella announced proudly. Before even Dario could stop her, she executed one, then two, then three glides all on her own.

"And I'm not scared one bit," she added. Bliss stared, stunned at the progress she'd made in a mere hour on the ice. She imagined what Bella could do with regular practice. And it wasn't just the skating. Her self-confidence was clearly soaring. Looking Dario in the eyes she quietly said, "Thank you."

chapter twenty-three

The Hotel Imperial's piano bar was nearly empty, save for a few tables occupied by businessmen, Japanese at one and heavily cologned, cigar-smoking Qataris in Saville Row suits at another. Bliss sat with her father, nursing a Viennese coffee and cringing as Forsythia, squeezed into a red cocktail dress and teetering on a pair of spangled pumps, belted out the third stanza of "Santa Baby," the Eartha Kitt come-hither holiday classic. Running a manicured hand through the stunned middle-aged pianist's comb-over she purred, "Boodoobeedoo/ Santa Baby, I wanna yacht/And really that's not a lot," accenting her delivery with a suggestive roll of her well-padded hips. The Qataris let out amused wolf whistles, egging her on. The pianist did his best not to stumble on the keys as a result of her erotic offensive. This sexual teasing was the flip side of her mother's stiff-upper-lip propriety, the Ms. Hoochie to her Our Lady of Perpetual Primness persona. Bliss had come downstairs to enjoy a moment's peace while her sister Victoria watched Bella, and instead she'd stumbled upon one of her mother's one-woman freak shows. And Charlotte sat nearby, impatiently tapping the tabletop as she awaited her turn to shine on stage. Bliss reflected that regrettably, the exhibitionist gene had not skipped a generation. She didn't have the heart to walk out.

Growing up, as she gleaned bits and pieces of her mother's painful personal history from the comments she would let drop in unguarded moments, she came to understand that posturing and aspiring to grandeur were Forsythia's refuge from the harrowing reality of her childhood. Still, when her mother took the proverbial show on the road, Bliss wanted to die of embarrassment. And other than suffering the usual neglect of the youngest child in a large family, she felt Charlotte had little excuse for making a spectacle of herself.

"Papa, you've got to get her to stop," Bliss pleaded. Her anxiety heightened when she saw Sue Minors enter the bar, toting her ever-present BlackBerry, and Charlotte perk up at the sight of her. It would only be a moment, Bliss feared, before Sue summoned the crew to put Forsythia on camera, or worse yet, had Charlotte join her in a mother-daughter duet. These antics were disturbing enough in the confines of their home, but they didn't need to go viral. She could see the *TV Guide* headline now: VIRGIN MOTHER AND CHILD DO KARAOKE, accompanied by a shot of Forsythia shimmying for the shell-shocked piano man and Charlotte exposing her cleavage to the salivating businessmen. To Bliss's astonishment though, she realized her father's embarrassment was superseded by a high degree of arousal at his wife's ghoulish display. The one hold Forsythia still had over Harold was the sexual, and as their nest emptied, her coquettish antics increased in frequency. It was a depressing window into long-term marriage. *Did it all boil down to this,* Bliss thought, *becoming a caricature of yourself?* Her horror redoubled when Dario appeared at the entrance.

"Shit," she said under her breath, then chided herself that it didn't matter what he thought. His jaw dropped at the sight of Forsythia draping herself over the piano and writhing on it like a Jurassic version of Michelle Pfeiffer's torch singer in *The Fabulous Baker Boys.* He wore the expression of a man who, though he had seen a lot in his time, had never quite experienced anything quite like this. Bliss could read a combination of shock and sheer amazement that any sane human being could put on such a circus-worthy display.

"Papa!" Bliss pleaded.

"All right," Harold said, coming out of his erotic reverie and realizing the inappropriateness of the behavior. "Let her finish the song." Spotting Dario he added, "And I thought you didn't care a whit about certain people's opinions."

"I don't," Bliss said reddening. "But Sue Minors is here. I don't want her to decide to put this on camera. That's not good for any of us. It certainly won't help me with the fellowship if she does."

"Sue seems rather consumed with other things," Harold commented, indicating the producer with his chin. Sue's face glowed in the light of her BlackBerry, which she stared at with the intensity of one consulting an oracle as she manically typed messages, and paused only occasionally to sip her cocktail. She spoke or rather snapped comments into her headpiece.

Dario approached their table. Bliss hated to admit that she was mortified that he'd witnessed her mother's display.

"May I?" he asked, indicating the empty chair. Bliss nodded and did her best to maintain a straight-backed air of dignity as her mother wriggled on the piano top and punctuated the song's end by thrusting her right leg in the air as she laid back, her head mere inches above the keyboard.

"Santa Baby, so hurry down the chimney tooo-niiight!"

"Bravo, bravo," Harold cried, clapping as he crossed toward her. "Come my dear," he said, hoisting her up, rather creakily, from her reclining position.

"I'm not done. I was going to sing 'J'ai deux amours,'" Forsythia objected with a Perrier-Jouët-laced hiccup.

"And I was going to sing 'Firework'!" Charlotte objected, jumping out of her seat. "Boom boom boom, even brighter than the moon, moon, moon—" she belted out off-key, shaking her hips Shakira style, double-time from left to right.

"Bravo, my dear, but it's very late," Harold insisted, taking Charlotte by the hand and leading her away from the piano.

"And I think you've delighted them quite enough," Harold whispered in Forsythia's ear. He put a protective arm around her as the Qatari businessmen snickered.

"Encore! Encore!" they chanted and their Japanese counterparts chimed in.

"You see," Forsythia pointed out grandly, oblivious to the taunting nature of the request. Bliss avoided eye contact with Dario. Her heart sank at the entire scene. It wasn't the first time her mother had taken over a piano bar. She'd been barred from the lounge at the Ritz-Carlton, Tysons Corner after a few too many rum-and-coke-laced encores of the Peggy Lee torch song "Fever." Bliss's embarrassment came in part from a protective sense of not wanting others to judge her lunatic clan.

"I think we should go upstairs, my dear," Harold said, raising an eyebrow suggestively.

"Ooh, I see," Forsythia cooed, rubbing her back against him. Harold flushed instantly and a shudder went up his spine. It wasn't the two glasses of champagne, Bliss noted, it was the vestiges of attraction to the woman who'd lured him into marriage.

"That's how you keep a man," Forsythia tossed out at Bliss before knocking back the last drops of champagne in Harold's flute and slapping the glass down on the table. Grabbing Harold's tie, she led him out of the bar. Bliss watched them go noting to herself that her crazy, half drunken mother had a point. Her mother wasn't facing day 476 of divorce-imposed celibacy. However imperfect, she and her parents still had a union. Charlotte stood for a moment forlorn and glum as her parents left her behind yet again.

"Who needs this crowd anyway!" she declared to no one in particular as she flounced out of the room.

"Where's Bella?"

"Upstairs, asleep. Victoria's watching her so I can have a moment to myself. Rare thing these days." Dario started to get up.

"I should let you have your moment."

"No, it's okay. Please."

He sat back down.

"Thank you for all you did for Bella today. She was still talking about it when I put her down."

"You're raising a great kid."

"I'm trying," Bliss said, sincerely moved. She spent so much of her free time mentally cataloging all the ways in which she was failing Bella, beginning with her inability to get Manuel to pay attention to her, that she never stopped to recognize what she was doing well. Her enjoyment of the compliment was instantly overshadowed by the thought of the unhappy task that still lay before her: breaking the news to Bella of her father's impending marriage.

"I don't know how to tell her that her dad's getting remarried," she blurted, to her own surprise. Now that she'd made the statement, there was no taking it back. She looked to Dario for a response. He was unfazed but seemed to mull the thought before asking, "So that's why he showed up the other day and just left?"

"Yes," Bliss said, the pain of the memory shooting through her, like a sudden jab from a sharp pin.

Dario bit his upper lip, as if preventing a comment from stumbling forth.

"I keep trying to find the right moment, but it's never the right moment to break your child's heart," Bliss added.

"I can see that," Dario assented evenly. "But Bella's pretty tough. And with kids, the sooner they get bad news, the better. They can smell when something's not right. Makes them feel better when they know for sure."

Bliss couldn't argue with his empathetic logic.

"How do you know so much about kids? Don't tell me you have some yourself."

"I kind of raised my baby sisters, from when I was fourteen. You learn stuff . . ." he answered, trailing off. Bliss wanted to know more. Was it after his mother passed away? Where was his father? She could tell from the way he shifted uneasily in his seat that he would welcome such queries as eagerly as a high colonic. If marriage had taught her nothing else, it had at least trained her when to sally forth with questions (very rarely), and when to retreat and resign oneself to silence (most of the time). After a pause, Dario continued.

"Can I ask you something? It may be out of line but . . ." He didn't finish the sentence, waiting for permission to continue. This uncharacteristic circumspection intrigued her.

"Please do," she encouraged him.

"Is the hard part about telling Bella her dad's getting remarried that it makes it more real for you?" He paused, before adding gently, "There's no denying it then." The insight utterly disarmed Bliss. It was so obvious, yet such a relief for someone to give voice to her truth. She felt unburdened of an ugly secret. And it moved her beyond words that someone she thought took no notice of her had understood. In that moment, she was immeasurably grateful to him. For the first time in many months, she felt seen and not judged. Overwhelmed, she couldn't move. After a moment she said, "Your sisters were lucky they had you."

"Wow," he answered with a smile, "two compliments in one conversation, I'm doing well." It never occurred to Bliss that her good opinion would matter to him and yet, he sat up, visibly pleased at having won her approval. He no longer fit neatly into her Cro-Magnon-cad classification. His nuances, while intriguing, were beginning to disturb her. She wasn't certain she could trust her own judgment anymore, marriage and its vicissitudes having undermined her profound faith in her own infallible instincts. She'd replaced them with a general wariness of all men who reminded her in any way of her husband. Dario was such a man. With his palpable sensuality and magnetism, he inspired the same mistrust and desire to escape. If she'd been honest with herself, she would have admitted that he scared her.

"Can I refresh your drink?" he offered.

"No, no. Any more and I'll be up there belting out 'I Will Survive.' I do a mean karaoke version."

"I think I'd like to see that," Dario commented with a chuckle.

"Haven't you seen enough of the *Harcourt Horror Show*?" she joked, seeing if he'd take the bait, but he didn't. Instead, he stared at Bliss. She wondered if perhaps there was something unseemly protruding from her nose. Realizing he'd made her uncomfortable, he stopped staring and looked around the room as if searching for the next topic of conversation.

"So, tell me about what you do," he said at last.

"You don't want to hear about that," Bliss deflected.

"Why would I ask?"

"Just to be nice?"

"I'm not nice. I thought you'd figured that out by now." Bliss scrutinized him, then dove in.

"My area is history, specifically France and America in the eighteenth century. I'm comparing racial attitudes and race laws in the two countries at that time. In my thesis, I contrast the situation of Eston Hemings, Jefferson's slave son, with the Chevalier de Saint-Georges who was the son of a noble French planter. I'm focused on the irony in the fact that the French slave code, the *Code Noir,* was actually far more stringent than American codes at the time but that individuals treated their offspring differently, and usually much better. And now, you probably wish you were having a root canal as opposed to listening to this," she joked.

"No, no, it's interesting. . . . I have no idea what you're talking about, but it's interesting," he joked. "Tell me about this Saint-Georges. What was so cool about him?"

"Talk about chivalry? This was *the* guy. Brilliant Renaissance man: composer, conductor, violinist, championship athlete. They called him the black Mozart. Best fencer in Europe. He was just an all-around genius, succeeding at a time when all the odds were against him."

"You talk like you have the hots for him," he commented.

"I do. How's that for going for unattainable men, falling in love with someone who's been dead for two hundred years? A shrink would have a field day with me." Dario laughed out loud at the self-deprecating joke.

"You're giving me ideas for a new dating service: your-dream-dead-guy.com," he jested.

"People could come out of the woodworks: Churchill fetishists, policy wonks with the hots for Woodrow Wilson, women who would have wanted to be a Kennedy concubine."

"I'm seeing it."

"The sad thing is, more people would visit that site in one day than will ever read my thesis in fifty years."

"So why do you bother?"

"Because truth matters. Our history matters," she insisted.

"Why? It's over," he said with a provocative shrug, egging her on.

"We need to come to terms with who we are as a nation. There is no moving forward in the present until we study, understand, and heal the past. All of our current problems are rooted in those eras. We also need to get away from victimology, and study the lives of those who achieved against impossible odds. When it comes to black people, we're not just a nation of rappers, criminals, and maids."

"But how do you get people to come to terms with the past and learn about these heroes if only three eggheads who already know everything read your stuff?"

"You have a point. I guess I should ask Kim Kardashian to hold a press conference about it."

"I know Kim, I could hook it up."

"Haven't you ever worked on something almost for nothing, because you believed in it?" she asked. He paused, intrigued by the notion, then answered. "Nope. Never. I grew up poor. You learn quick and the hard way that money matters."

So engaged were they in their exchange that neither had noticed the entrance of a tall, long-legged brunette with the full lips, endless lashes, and high cheekbones of a supermodel. She approached the table, draped her arms around Dario, and nuzzled his neck. Slightly startled, he looked around, then stood up to greet the apparition.

"I was looking all over the hotel for you. We said nine, no?" she asked in a bedroom voice as she traced the outline of his face with her delicate, tapered finger.

"Yeah," he looked distractedly at his watch. "So let's hit it," then turning awkwardly to Bliss he said, "This is—" Bliss stood up, interrupting him.

"I'm Bliss, you're gorgeous, and you guys are out of here." Clearly embarrassed, Dario sought words that didn't come and led his young and beautiful companion out of the bar.

"Who was that?" Bliss overheard the glamazon ask.

"A friend," he explained. Bliss plopped back in her chair. Perhaps now she could savor her coveted moment alone. She found herself straining to get a look of Dario and the glamazon through the window as they made their way down the street. She watched the girl toss her head back in ecstasy as he caressed her ear. Why had he been so embarrassed when his date showed up? She told herself to stop analyzing his actions. Though he wasn't quite the Cro-Magnon man she'd first thought, he was still just a guy with a raging libido and endless opportunities. Unlike every character Hugh Grant played in movies, he would not wake up one bright morning a reformed lothario desperate for domesticity. When it came to women, his reach would probably never exceed his easy grasp. He had given her one insight that helped. She should content herself with that and focus on more potentially suitable men like Jordan or perhaps Wyatt.

"Bliss, hey!" she heard a voice calling from a corner. She looked up to see Sue beckoning her over.

"Word of advice, woman to woman," Sue cautioned, leaning in confidentially. "Don't sleep with Dario. He'll only break your heart."

"He hasn't asked me, and I hadn't planned to. As you know, he has other offers," Bliss declared, turning away. Sue grabbed her hand and whipped her around.

"I mean it. I can see it in your eyes, you've fallen."

"No, I haven't. And he certainly has no interest. Did you see who he just walked out with?"

"Today's apple strudel. Road kill. Don't sell yourself short. You could get him, but he'll only leave you."

"I've already been road kill, you can't be killed twice," Bliss noted.

"They're all schmucks. Not one is worth anything. Oh, yeah, sorry, the dweebs you don't want to fuck are!" Sue sputtered. Bliss could hear the vodka talking. Sue appeared to her like a terrifying harbinger of singlehood future. She thought to herself that she'd better escape now before the acrimony infected her and she found herself spouting bitter platitudes to near strangers in darkened bars around the world.

"It's been a long day. I'm going to pack it in," Bliss said.

"Lucky you. I've got to watch my adopted daughter Ming Lee's piano concert on Skype," Sue grumbled as she turned to her ever-present device.

As Bliss walked away, she felt grateful for all of her experiences, however heartbreaking. She had known true love with a man and had a magnificent child to show for it. It occurred to her she should write Manuel an email extending the olive branch. Riding up the elevator though, she remembered the difficult task that still lay ahead: breaking the news of his impending marriage with . . . She couldn't even say her name in her head. Her peace offering to Manuel would have to wait.

chapter twenty-four

Bella could barely contain her excitement as she slipped into a daffodil-yellow ball gown with a crinoline that made the skirt stand out like a bell. The dress had arrived that morning, delivered in a box tied with an oversized pink ribbon. There had been a ball gown for Bliss as well, but she dreaded the moment of truth: trying it on. She envisioned herself standing up all night, unable to go to the ladies' room because she could neither remove it, nor sit down. As she zipped Bella into her dress, she decided perhaps it was the moment to tell her about Manuel and . . . She-Whose-Name-Could-Not-Be-Mentioned. Bella was in excellent spirits and if the news saddened her, going to the ball would soon help her forget. The time had come. Dario's words of wisdom echoed in her ears: *Are you afraid to tell her because it makes it real for you?*

"Bella, there's great news!!!" *A mother's lie,* she thought to herself, *essential to the child's survival, akin to insisting,* Nothing can happen to us in this bomb shelter! *during the London Blitz in the Second World War.*

"Daddy is getting married again."

"He is?" Bella said, turning away from the mirror to look at her.

"Yes."

"To you?" Bella asked, a pleading look in her eye. Bliss fought to control her own sadness. She had to smile through this loss to lessen it for Bella.

"Not to me."

"Oh," Bella hung her head in disappointment.

"He already did that once." Bliss searched in vain for a comforting thought to offer. *Look on the bright side. Now you'll have two mothers, like your friend Casey, the lesbians' child!* sprang to mind, but she quickly dismissed it as beyond pathetic. After a moment's silent consideration, Bella piped up, "But I thought when you got married it was forever and ever."

"Sometimes that's the case. It's the hope, always. But life doesn't necessarily work out the way we hope." As Bella searched her mother's eyes again for signs of sadness, Bliss smiled brightly.

"But it works out for the best," she added as much to convince herself as to uplift her child.

"So who is he marrying?"

"A lady that he loves very much. She works on the campaign," she added with difficulty.

"Is she nice?" Bella asked, fingering her mother's wrist.

"Oh, she must be or Daddy wouldn't marry her."

"What's her name?"

Bliss struggled to speak the name, like Helen Keller forming speech for the first time.

"Cindy," she said at last.

Bella turned away, then brightened at the sight of her own reflection in the mirror.

"My dress is *pretty*!" she gushed.

"Yes, it is," Bliss assented. She wanted to add another philosophical musing on the nature of life, but as she watched Bella sway from side to side, mesmerized by the swishing of her skirt, she knew she had escaped back into the fantasy world of childhood, far from divorces, remarriages, and demolished dreams. Children had a schizophrenic's ability to switch moods that she envied. There was a knock at the door and she heard a male voice bellow, "You princesses nearly ready?" Without begging leave to enter, Wyatt strolled in. He cut an elegant yet strange figure in his white tie with a cowl of paper towels framing his face. Seeing Bliss's puzzled expression he explained.

"It's to keep the makeup off the collar."

"Got it," Bliss affirmed.

"So you got the dresses," he said, pleased. Bliss had assumed Dario had sent them in his capacity as executive producer. She was at once disappointed and pleased to realize Wyatt had been responsible.

"You sent them?"

He looked down at his feet with a bashful expression.

"I just haven't seen you since we arrived so I didn't even think we were on your radar screen," she chided.

"Oh, you are," he said with a wink. "Save me a dance," he whispered in Bliss's ear.

"Carriages leave in fifteen minutes. See you downstairs," he announced before popping out.

"Mommy, Mommy, hurry, get dressed," Bella insisted. Bliss was relieved at her reaction, and proud of herself. She had spoken Cindy's name and it hadn't killed her. Now she could abandon herself to the joys of the evening, and the exhilaration she felt at the promise of flirtation to come.

The phone rang, Bliss picked up, and Forsythia's voice assaulted her ears.

"Why do we have to come now? We have to finish dressing and the carriages leave soon. . . . Okay."

"What does Grandmama want?"

"We are summoned to Aunt Didi's room."

"Okay," Bella said gamely.

Bliss decided to take a page from her irrepressibly cheerful daughter's book and treat the entire evening as an adventure.

chapter twenty-five

Bliss and Bella emerged from the elevator on the first floor and looked up. The ceiling loomed miles above them, four times as high as the one on their floor. A triumph of rococo excess, it was painted to look like a sky dotted with fluffy pink clouds, and trumpet-and-lyre-wielding cherubs. The effect was that of landing in a five-star hotel's version of overdecorated Heaven. The contrast to their garret-like section of the Imperial was not lost on Bella.

"Mommy, how come we live in the attic?" she inquired. This was not the time to explain life's unfairness, and the cruel pecking order of fate and families, Bliss decided.

"Sort of, at least we're in the same hotel. If Mommy had to pay for this herself, we would be in a motel by the airport," Bliss explained cheerfully. "And you have to admit it's a really nice and expensive attic."

"Oh, yes," Bella concurred. They arrived at stately cream-colored double doors, with enormous carved gold handles. Punch, wearing headphones, sat perched on a tiny gilded chair with cabriole legs.

"Hey, you guys. Here for the Virgin-gets-dressed-for-the-ball shoot?"

"Uh, no, my mother just wanted us to see something." Bliss answered, her heart sinking. Had Forsythia drafted them into service to be fawning handmaidens in some ludicrous tableau starring her sister as a latter-day Venus? She put nothing past her.

"Go on in. Bliss, do you know where Victoria is?"

"Probably hiding. Lucky her," Bliss joked. "Why?"

"Nothing," Punch shrugged, turning scarlet. "Just don't want her to miss the ride to the ball," she stammered. Bliss listened, nodding. There was an awkward silence as Punch stared down at her own feet, as if caught in an act trespassing. Bliss thought it fair to put her out of her misery.

"Once again into the breach," she declared as she pushed open the door.

Just as she was shutting it behind them, Bella blurted, "That lady looks kind of like a boy," in the booming tone four-year-olds reserve for their most embarrassing declarations. Bliss didn't dare turn around to see if Punch had heard. She was about to chastise Bella, but was instantly awed by the surroundings. She couldn't help but gasp at the sight of the interior of the Imperial Suite. It lived up to its name in all its gaudy magnificence. Everywhere she looked, Bliss's eyes fell upon a profusion of crystal, gilding, and gold damask. The apartment was of a size and an opulence to inspire peasants to revolution.

"Wow," Bella exclaimed, expressing the amazement Bliss did her best to keep in check. "This is a real princess room!!"

"Yes, it is," Bliss agreed with a sigh of resignation. Not that she aspired to such luxury but it certainly was seductive. Sue had stationed herself at the desk in the massive parlor.

"Couldn't be better. Dream dates, arrival at the hotel, we're getting gold here. *The Bachelorette*'s got nothin' on us," she gloated into her phone. "Hold on, hold on, another call coming through, could be my kid. Hello. . . . No, Ming Lee, Mommy told you no more Starburst. They get stuck in your braces and we can't afford another replacement pair. . . . Ming!! Ming!!! . . . Because I said so, that's why! Hey, if you don't listen to me, I'm shipping you off to that Tiger Mom. Ming, I'm putting you in time-out. Ming! Ming . . . . She hung up on me," she said, stunned. "What?" she barked suddenly noticing Bliss and Bella.

"Just here to see Diana and my mum," Bliss explained.

"In there," Sue motioned with her chin, then went back to her call. "Sorry about that, Bob. Yeah, we're gonna clean up here. I'm trying to get her to do the Spring Morning feminine hygiene campaign but it's a tough sell. I know they're a big advertiser. Maybe I can do a product placement. . . ."

Bliss and Bella opened the next set of massive double doors and entered Diana's boudoir. Everything from the wall panels to the bed to the chairs was upholstered in pink damask. Diana, clad in an ice-pink chiffon peignoir with a huge satin bow fastened just below her cleavage, sat at her vanity as the makeup artist applied the finishing touches.

"Lovely, lovely," Forsythia commented of the man's work.

"Can I get a touch up? I think I look too plain," Charlotte whined, thrusting her face in Diana's mirror. Diana shoved her away with the rapidity and force of a Roller Derby contestant bodychecking a competitor.

"Nonsense, you look fine," Forsythia snapped. "And go get dressed."

"Why can't I dress on-screen too?" Charlotte protested.

"Nobody cares to watch you, silly girl. It's your sister's show," Forsythia chided, sending her off. Even Bliss winced as she saw Charlotte wither under the comment. Growing up, they had all been subjected to the revolving door of their mother's favor. When a child brought home an A, or in the case of Diana, won a beauty pageant, she enjoyed endless praise and privileges. Bliss had long ago forfeited her spot in the game of musical chairs of maternal love.

"So nobody cares about me?" Charlotte pouted.

"Of course they do," Forsythia hastened to answer, realizing her gaffe. "You'll get lots of coverage at the ball. We all will. Run along and make sure Victoria is ready. Silly cow, she won't even agree to makeup, imagine?" she said batting unusually long false eyelashes even for her, which Bliss noticed, were tipped and rimmed in rhinestones.

"Don't you look pretty, Bella," Diana commented, finally noticing her sister and child. "You on the other hand, Bliss, I hope you're not planning to wear those at the ball," she said, sneering at Bliss's sweat suit.

"No, I've got the ones with the big hole at the ass for that," Bliss joked.

"Not in front of the child!" Forsythia admonished.

"Want some makeup," Diana offered Bella, tantalizingly.

"Oh, yes. Mommy, can I, can I, can I?" Bella pleaded. Bliss cringed. She envisioned Bella ghoulishly made up like the apple-cheeked, bouffant-haired little girls in baby beauty pageants, pint-size caricatures of their overdone mothers. Yet she was tired of being the naysayer and perpetual Dr. No, killing all the frivolous childhood joys.

"Okay, but not too much, please. Maybe just some lip gloss," she begged the makeup artist. The man nodded with a smile. "And what's this I hear about dressing on camera?" she pursued, dreading the explanation.

"It's a stroke of genius Sue Minors had. A front-row seat to Diana's preparations for the ball. The audience will love it, just like courtiers at Versailles coming to watch the king and queen of France dress in the morning," Forsythia crowed.

"And we know how well that saga ended. 'Hey, Marie Antoinette, say "bye-bye" to your head. You didn't need one anyway.' And now Diana is going to strip for the camera. That's classy."

"She'll do nothing of the sort. They will catch a glimpse of her in her undergarments from behind a diaphanous screen. She'll be in silhouette. It will be exquisite. And we don't need you and your negativity this evening, Bliss. I wanted the baby to see what she can aspire to. Bella, isn't this room pretty?" Forsythia asked, looking to Bliss very much like the witch who convinces Snow White to bite the deadly apple.

"Oh, yes, Grandmama," Bella concurred with saucer-wide eyes.

"Five minutes," Sue Minors barked, poking her head through the double doors.

"Okay, okay, just a moment. I've got to decide who won the Dream Date Contest," Diana demurred.

"Well, make it snappy, your Hymen-ness. There's a whole ballroom full of people waiting for you to show up and we've got to shoot you in the lingerie presto. Maidenform wants these pictures to launch the Diana Bra."

"Okay, okay. This is a big decision," Diana said, turning on her fake-ivory-framed iPad. She appeared on screen, being led into a wood-paneled dining room blindfolded. The camera panned up from a hand to Paul Daniels's face. He smiled a self-satisfied smile as he pulled out her chair and whispered in her ear, "Welcome to the best meal of your life, a feast for the senses, to tempt my lady." Diana bit into an oyster, still blindfolded, a smile of delight spreading across her face. She paused the film.

"Bella, help me decide which suitor won the Dream Date Contest. The one on screen, Paul, from Tennessee, or the one who gave me this," she pulled a diamond-and-sapphire encrusted evening watch out of a black velvet box.

"That's pretty!" Bella exclaimed, her eyes wide behind her bifocals at the sight of the glistening gems. Now Bliss truly wanted to snatch her from this den of temptations. She felt suddenly like the hysterical wife in *The Devil's Advocate,* sinking slowly into madness as everyone denied she was seeing Satan's minions all around her.

"Isn't it obvious?" Forsythia quipped. "Alistair won when he took you to select that bracelet watch. He must have spent a fortune, there's a man," she concluded pointedly, dangling the bracelet watch in front of a mesmerized Bella.

"A man with no imagination who thinks his money is enough to make him wonderful. Does Diana even like sapphires? Did he even bother to find out?" Bliss interjected. Diana sat up taller and nodded.

"That's a good point," she concurred.

"It certainly is not!" Forsythia objected, narrowing her eyes at Bliss, the family Cassandra, forever trumpeting uncomfortable truths and ruining her pretty picture and plans.

"Actually, Mum, it is. Shockingly. Truth be told, I like rubies," Diana insisted, grabbing the watch from her mother and tossing it onto the vanity.

"Don't be so cavalier," Forsythia warned. "You've never been poor, that's the problem. Not that I would wish that on any of you. But you don't show the proper respect for the Almighty Dollar. There's a reason it's inscribed with the words *In God We Trust.*"

"You're so wrong, Mummy. I worship the Almighty Dollar. Though Euros are better," Diana teased.

"Who gave you the saddle?" Bliss asked, pointing to a saddle perched on the dumb valet. She crossed over to it and ran her hands over the smooth calfskin of an English saddle delicately embossed with DWH, Diana's initials, in an elegant font.

"Oh, that. Beowulf," Diana tossed off, utterly unenthused. "After he took me to the Spanish Riding School."

"You love to ride. What a thoughtful gesture," Bliss commented.

"I guess," Diana said flatly, returning to her viewing of Paul. "I have nothing to offer you but my ambition and my passion," he had said to her on-screen as he fed her a strawberry, which she tore into with the gusto of a baby lion feasting on the thigh of an unfortunate gazelle. Bliss wanted to retch. Paul's shtick was worthy of a soap opera, but Diana was clearly titillated. She'd eventually find herself torn between her animal appetites and her financial aspirations, Bliss surmised. Perhaps she'd end up marrying the Brit and amusing herself with brainless muscle-bound boy toys on the side.

"I won't even hear of this. It's Alistair. Bella, remember, it's just as easy to love a rich man as a poor one," Forsythia instructed.

"I will," Bella acquiesced.

"No, you will forget that immediately. We are going back upstairs, see you at the ball," Bliss countered with such force her mother took a step back, as though buffeted by a wind of righteousness.

"I'm only trying to help," Forsythia insisted, hurt, it seemed to Bliss.

"Thanks, Mom. I'll manage without help like that," Bliss countered. "Come on, sweetie," she said, not liking the sight of Bella's furrowed brow. She'd clearly sensed the tension in the room.

"We're going to have a great night," she reassured her.

"Yes, Mama."

As they emerged into the ballroom-size parlor, they found Sue still on the phone.

"Ming, Ming, I told you hanging up on mommy is ru—Ming? She did it again," Sue said to no one in particular, removing the headphone from her ear. She slouched in the desk's carved armchair and buried her head in her hands. Suddenly, Bliss felt a kinship with her parental helplessness. Even Bella looked at her with concern. Bliss wanted to go over but realized she was a woman who'd rather be caught stark naked in the street than in an emotionally vulnerable state. Before she could lead Bella out, the latter blurted, "Mrs. Minors, why are you sad?"

Sue looked up, her eyes rimmed in red. "I'm fine," she insisted hoarsely. "Just tired. Thanks for waking me." She stood up and headed toward Diana's lair.

"You're stupid not to put her on camera," she told Bliss. "She could make you serious dough."

"Thanks for the suggestion. We're fine as we are," Bliss answered. Sue shrugged and disappeared into the bedroom.

chapter twenty-six

Bliss heard the strains of Strauss's "Blue Danube Waltz" as she and Bella mounted the expansive marble staircase of the Hofburg, the imperial palace dating back to the 1750s. Lush, fragrant garlands of pink, red, and white roses festooned the cream-colored balustrades. The music grew louder and Bliss's heartbeat quickened with each step. As soon as she and Bella entered the ballroom, all of their senses were swept up in a whirl of light refracted by crystal, gilding, and the sounds of string instruments. Hundreds of couples swirled around the gleaming parquet dance floor. The women's skirts spun past, a dizzying merry-go-round of taffeta and satin in lush tones of magenta, sapphire blue, and emerald green. Victoria, exquisite in an off-the-shoulder black *peau de soie* gown, her hair in a Gibson Girl updo, stood watching the dancers. *My sister, the world's most beautiful wallflower,* Bliss thought to herself. Charlotte, her décolletage spilling out of her hot-pink corset top, her hair a riot of brown corkscrew curls restrained by a rhinestone mini-tiara, rushed toward them.

"They're about to start the waltzing competition!" she bellowed excitedly.

"I wanna see, I wanna see," Bella demanded, bouncing up and down. Bliss hoisted her up in her arms. They joined Harold and Forsythia who stood with Victoria by an ornate paneled wall on the right side of the room. Forsythia looked every inch the proud mother hen, particularly since an enormous spray of red and purple plumes emanated from the jeweled comb tucked into the side of her wig. The effect was more aging Vegas show girl than the elegant society-mother-of-the-bride-to-be look she'd no doubt hoped to achieve. Forsythia surveyed the room, practically licking her lips at the bounty of eligible men and the array of society grandees gathered under one coffered ceiling.

"Everyone who's anyone is here," she gloated.

"No athletes though," Charlotte sighed.

Harold, red faced in a high collar that strangled his jowly neck, groaned. He couldn't wait for the evening's torments to end. Forsythia, delighted to have finally arrived on the world's social stage, remained utterly oblivious to her husband's irritation. She stabbed Harold's side with her elbow and smacked his arm with her fan as trumpets sounded, the dance floor cleared, and Diana—an eighteen-inch waist, D-cup Barbie prototype in pale-pink satin—appeared at the head of a column of couples. The crowd let out gasps of wonder and approval. Charlotte stood taller, sticking her chest out as far as possible in her perpetual quest to be more than the family also-ran.

One by one, Diana's suitors stepped forward and knelt before her, extending their hands and bowing their heads, except Paul, who preened, showing off his profile. He scanned the room, it seemed to Bliss, for opportunities to find a "wife for the evening." She pegged him as the one who would fail the chastity test in the course of the contest, and certainly in the course of a marriage. His eyes, when they weren't furtively darting about in search of potential supporters, telegraphed *Want to take a rocket to paradise? Slip me your room key, baby.* He simply reeked of dime-store sexiness.

Wyatt, looking every inch the matinee idol, stepped up beside Diana, microphone in hand.

"Good evening, ladies and gentlemen. *Guten Abend, meine Damen und Herren.* And welcome to the waltzing competition at this, one of Vienna's oldest and most prestigious balls. Diana, our maiden fair, will lead the dance with the winner of the Dream Date Competition, after which the other pretenders to her hand will have a chance to strut their stuff and break out their best waltz moves. Diana, whom dost thou pick?" he said in what struck Bliss as a voice reminiscent of a game-show host announcing the winner of the washer and dryer. Diana demurred, feigning maidenly befuddlement.

"Dost thou pick?" Bliss mimicked. "Now we're speaking Elizabethan English?"

"Hush," Forsythia commanded.

"It's been awfully hard to choose," Diana sighed.

She surveyed her options once more: gangly Beowulf, whose hand trembled with anticipation; stolid Alistair, whose incipient bald patch shone like a moonlit lake under the chandeliers; and proud Paul, whose steely blue eyes matched hers. He raised his chin defiantly when she looked at him. Her eyes glinted with arousal and delight and she pointed at him with her fan. He rose, a cocky smirk on his face and took her by the hand.

"So it's Paul!" Wyatt said, egging the crowd to enthusiasm. They applauded on cue. "How did the state senator win? I hear there was some pretty stiff competition, a trip to a world-famous royal stable and souvenir saddle, some serious bling . . ." Wyatt pursued.

"Paul understood that money and bling are not everything," Diana explained coyly. "He knows that sometimes the very simplest pleasures are the best." The crowd let out a collective sigh of "Awww."

Bliss and Victoria exchanged glances of disgust and disbelief.

"Don't say it," Victoria cautioned. "Let's be kind."

"Why?" Bliss riposted. She noticed Beowulf smarting from Diana's comment. Alistair however stood gape mouthed, oblivious to the slight.

"Why did she pick him?" Forsythia barked, smacking Harold with her fan again.

"Why not Alistair?"

"Perhaps because the boy has no chin," Harold answered, wincing from the pain of the fan assault.

"Stupidness!" Forsythia cried. "With his millions, he can buy a chin! The girl has no sense of priorities."

"Or proper prejudice," Bliss commented wryly, thinking of her mother's unspoken rule against marrying men of color, a rule only slightly softened by the election of President Barack Obama. Forsythia glared at her. Of all the sins she'd committed as a daughter that she couldn't fathom, Bliss knew marrying a Latin had been the deadliest.

"Okay you two, damsel and crusader for your heart," Wyatt commanded, stepping away from center stage, "it's time to ROCK THIS WALTZ!"

The guests cheered and applauded and the pair began their dance. Paul expertly guided the graceful Diana around the floor, taking its full sweep, spinning her with a flourish.

"Aunt Didi looks like a princess!" Bella cooed. Bliss smiled, delighted to see that at least one of their party was truly enjoying the festivities and caught up in the manufactured magic.

"This place is full of real princesses," Forsythia declared, standing proud.

"And a few paupers," Harold quipped. "Isn't that the Duchess of York peddling her American Express bill? And look, over there is the pole-dancing prostitute Berlusconi paid to partake of her charms," he said, indicating a young lady in a skin-tight spaghetti-strap satin dress who cackled and tossed her hair with abandon as her escort, a man so old and wrinkled he could have played Yoda without makeup, greedily eyed her ample bosom.

"How did *she* get in here?" Forsythia sniffed with the haughtiness of one who'd been coming since the time of the Hapsburgs.

"But, my dear, she's famous," Harold explained.

"Infamous," Forsythia corrected. "She's a tart. Worse than a tart."

"Well then, she's destined for greatness. Tart one minute, übercelebrity the next," Harold quipped.

Bliss laughed. Forsythia turned away, highly offended. Two men, one dark haired, the other blond, made their way across the floor toward them. Bliss smiled, recognizing Wyatt and Dario, both resplendent in their formal attire. Dario's hair was slicked back with gel. Its seal-like sleekness made her long to tousle it. Their eyes met. The glowing lighting brought out the rim of green around his amber pupils. They were the eyes of a seducer, intense, unblinking, and brimming with the promise of erotic possibility. Bliss looked away; when she looked back he was still staring. She looked down at her violet dress and felt the zipper in the back to make certain it hadn't popped. He actually appeared to be admiring her.

Wyatt grabbed her around the waist.

"Dance with me," he whispered in her ear, his lips grazing her cheek. She started to object but before she could, he had her out on the floor. His waltz was smoother than his salsa, but he forced too much. Nonetheless, Bliss abandoned herself to the joy of the moment, being in the arms of a very handsome man. From the corner of her eyes, she saw Diana glaring at her. By this time, the Virgin had exchanged Paul for Alistair. Wyatt abruptly dropped Bliss from his arms.

"I think I'm on, got to comment on the dances," he said with a half-hearted bow and withdrew to be closer to Diana and her partner. Bliss thought to herself that the commentary on the actual dancing would be done later, via voice-over. Nonetheless, she withdrew, happy to be an observer and join her child and sister.

"Alistair is dancing beautifully," Forsythia commented, utterly ignoring the Englishman's less than graceful turns and frequent crushing of his partner's toes. Diana visibly winced with agony.

"Pay attention to him," Forsythia mouthed, signaling to Diana to smile at the chinless wonder. Beowulf stepped up to take his turn with her.

"He'll be a disaster," Forsythia sniped. To Bliss and Victoria's surprise, Beowulf proved the opposite, deftly whirling Diana around the room to the applause of the other guests. Across the room, she watched Dario give Beowulf a fist pump and a hearty nod.

As the waltz ended, all three suitors kneeled before Diana. She looked from one to the other.

Speaking into the camera, Wyatt asked, "Which one shall it be? The English nobleman? The rising political star? Or the Internet billionaire baby?" Bliss felt she might as well be at a cattle auction. Since when were people reduced to their professions and implied net worth? Still it wasn't Wyatt's fault. The crowd gathered around Diana, and remained motionless, awaiting her decision. While looking in Paul's direction and smiling at him, she pointed her fan at Beowulf. The latter could hardly believe he had won. He jumped up with unbridled joy and excitement, throwing his arms around Diana who, no doubt fearing the bear hug would wrinkle her gown, pushed him away. He fell to his knees and kissed her hand, holding it against his forehead. Again, Bliss watched Dario nod with approval, clearly moved by the underdog's victory.

Suddenly, the clarions sounded.

"Mr. Dean Wong," the majordomo proclaimed. Victoria blanched.

"What's he doing here?" she asked.

Looking like a multicultural prince from a late-issue Disney film, Dean made his way to Victoria. Falling to one knee, he took her hand.

"Victoria Harcourt, I love you, will you marry me?" The crowd applauded. Sue Minors barked, "Get the cameras over here." Forsythia's jaw trembled with emotion and her eyes danced with glee. Bliss wanted to rush over and punch Dean for pressuring her sister so publicly. She could see abject terror in Victoria's eyes. She hated attention and making scenes. She would probably say yes just to put an end to this unbearable moment of scrutiny.

Wyatt hustled over, as did Diana, who did not intend to be left out of a moment on camera. She stared at the pair, like a bad soap-opera actress feigning interest in her costar's story line. Charlotte appeared at her side, equally eager to be included though thoroughly indifferent to the progress of her older sister's romance and, unlike her sister, unable to feign it. She stared directly into the camera with bovine apathy.

Victoria stood panicked, not knowing where to turn. Dean pulled a velvet box from his lapel pocket. He opened it to reveal a gleaming five-karat diamond.

"There's a rock," Wyatt commented crassly. Bliss shot him a look. He mouthed an apology.

The diamond was so large and gleaming even Victoria took a step back, blinded by its brightness under the lights of the multiple chandeliers. Dean whipped the ring out of the box and slid it on Victoria's ring finger. Her eyes grew wide not with wonder but with fear.

"Please," Dean pleaded.

"Say yes, say yes," Forsythia repeated under her breath. "Think of what they can do, have a double wedding, two for one," she gushed to Harold.

"Two loveless matches we needn't pay for. Delightful," he rebutted. Forsythia ignored him. Bliss wondered what had possessed Dean to make such a move. Perhaps in his desperation to win her, he was willing to try anything, including public pressuring and humiliation.

"Yes," Victoria relented at last, saying the word in a near whisper.

"She said YES," Wyatt explained to the crowd who erupted in applause. Diana knocked Charlotte aside, made her way to Victoria, and hugged her, making certain both of their faces were to camera. As the crowd massed around the happy pair, Bliss and Bella were pushed farther and farther to the outside. Bliss wanted to tear through them and tell Victoria she could take it back, but it was too late.

chapter twenty-seven

The black stretch limousine turned onto Windsor Lane with its barren winter trees. Bliss, Diana, Forsythia, Bella, Harold, and Victoria sat in the backseat. On the carpeted floor lay a stack of glossy gossip magazines, several featuring pictures of Diana on the cover. Forsythia and Diana pored over the spread on the Vienna ball featured in *Hola!*

"I can't believe they included a photograph of the Moroccan stripper!" Forsythia exclaimed. "Just because she slept with a prime minister when she was underage, now she's famous. Are there no standards left in this fallen world?" she sniffed.

"Apparently not," Harold said with a sardonic smirk.

"Never mind that tramp," Diana commented. "I got the cover." Charlotte, fed up with her sister's constant litany of self-congratulation, mimed a gagging motion.

"Yes, you did, my baby," Forsythia gushed. "And well deserved it is. I am glad the cameras aren't with us tonight. I'm exhausted from the glamour."

"Yeah, it can really wear you out," Bliss quipped.

"Mommy, do I have to go to school tomorrow?" Bella asked drowsily.

"No, sweetie, you have a couple more days of Christmas vacation."

"Good," Bella commented, laying her head down in her mother's ample lap and closing her eyes.

"Perhaps when Victoria gets married, you can both be on the cover of *People*," Forsythia suggested to Diana.

"Maybe," the latter said, clearly not pleased with the idea of sharing the spotlight.

"I don't think so," Victoria said gently. "It's Diana they want."

"So true," Diana gushed, scrolling through emails on her iPad. "Mum, this list of sponsorships and appearances coming up for the Chastity Tour is endless!"

"Chastity Tour? So you're hitting the road with Cher's transgender son?" Bliss joked.

"For your information, we have a little hiatus and during that time, Mum and I will be traveling the country promoting the show. Listen to this, Mum, they're planning an all-star rally for virginity at the Astrodome in Houston!"

"Whoo, don't want to miss that. Only, what celebrities are they going to get? I don't think anyone in Hollywood knows how to spell virginity," Bliss quipped. Harold laughed out loud.

"It's all well and good for the two of you to make a mockery of this show, but Diana has single-handedly brought purity back into fashion."

"Bliss, shall we observe a moment of silence? Please note that in the history books. Not since Joan of Arc has anyone done more," Harold joked.

"Indeed not," Forsythia concurred, his sarcasm eluding her as it often did.

The limousine pulled up in front of the house. Forsythia peered out of the limousine window. The street was devoid of its usual gawkers and curious neighbors.

"Good, a bit of peace at last. Victoria, the car can take you home. Victoria Wong. Nice ring to it and given that those little Chinese people are taking over the world, I'm thrilled to have one in the family," Forsythia declared. Victoria winced at the comment and balled her fist to avoid looking at the stone adorning her finger, blazingly reminding her of her promise.

"I'll head home in a little bit. I'm going to help Bliss with Bella," she demurred.

Bella lay slumbering in her mother's arms. They walked up to the front door, where Charlotte spotted a polished wooden box.

"Look," she said excitedly, "someone's left us a present!"

"Oh, perhaps it's an engagement gift for Victoria," Forsythia conjectured.

"How would anyone know about me?" Victoria demurred.

"Through the Internet. It was the all the buzz, PopEater, People .com," Forsythia explained as if it should have been obvious. "You will have to get used to being a celebrity, my dear."

Victoria looked pained. She stared down at the enormous rock that weighed her finger down. Bliss shot her a sympathetic glance. She feared Victoria's sense of duty would lead her down the aisle with a man she clearly didn't love so her mother could go out in a blaze of Technicolor glory. In spite of her own marital debacle, she could not bring herself to believe that "sensible choices" and the slavish pursuit of fame were the high road to a fulfilling and happy life.

Charlotte ripped open the card taped to the cherry wood box.

"'To the Harcourt family: Today you, tomorrow America. Happy viewing.' Hmm, that's interesting." She opened the box and saw that it contained a DVD.

"I'll bet it's suggestions for your wedding gowns, girls," Forsythia guessed.

"I don't want to look at those," Victoria said, involuntarily taking a step away from the box.

"Nonsense," Forsythia insisted. "It will be great fun, of course you want to see it."

Victoria knew better than to protest. As Harold opened the door, Forsythia nearly ran him over to get to the television set in the living room hidden inside a faux-Chippendale-style highboy. She popped in the disk. Immediately, the sounds of a man groaning with sexual pleasure filled the room. Forsythia's eyes grew wide as a bush baby's. She gasped in horror and averted her gaze from the screen. Harold, Bliss, Victoria, and Diana rushed to look. They were all dumbfounded at the sight of Charlotte, naked and on all fours, as an athletic man pounded away at her from behind. For several minutes, they all stood frozen in stupor, watching as the moans of pleasure grew louder, and the copulation more frantic.

"Turn it off, please," Harold begged at last as he realized he was looking at his own child. He turned away, cupping his hand to his mouth as if to prevent himself from vomiting. Bliss grabbed the remote control and switched off the television. She'd read countless stories of adolescents getting caught having sex on camera in the brave new world of ubiquitous digital equipment. She never thought her own sister would fall victim to the trend. Bella began to awaken from her slumber.

"What was that noise, Mama?"

"Nothing," Bliss answered, covering.

"Why don't I take her upstairs," Victoria offered.

"Yes, please," Bliss assented, grateful and wanting to see events unfold since she of all the family knew most about Charlotte's extracurricular activities. She blamed herself for not turning her in the night she caught her sneaking into her room. Perhaps she could have prevented this disaster. Victoria gently pried Bella from her arms and exited. Charlotte stood with hunched shoulders, as if trying to shrink, or vanish as she awaited the verbal onslaught. Forsythia sank into the sofa in a daze. Harold sat down beside her, placing an arm around her shoulder, but Forsythia remained as motionless as a statue. Diana seethed and lunged for Charlotte.

"You stupid tramp!!!" she yelled, literally attempting to strangle her.

Harold and Bliss jumped in to tear her away from Charlotte.

"Stop it!" Bliss yelled at Diana.

"She's trying to ruin everything!" the latter cried, her icy blue eyes spewing tears of rage.

"I didn't do it on purpose!" Charlotte protested.

"You shouldn't have done it at all, you idiot! How's Mum supposed to go on *Wake Up, America* and promote her book, *How to Raise a Virgin*?" Diana screeched.

"Clearly we shall have to cancel that appearance," Harold suggested with a calm that came from pure shock.

"And how'm I supposed to go on a Chastity Tour and lead a hundred-thousand-person rally for virginity when my very own sister is a big fat scarlet-letter ho?"

Charlotte retreated farther into her hunchback-of-shame pose.

"He said it was just for him, just for him," she whispered meekly.

Bliss couldn't help but feel sorry for Charlotte who'd never been blessed with common sense.

"Who is he anyway?" Diana asked.

"He plays for the Lakers," Charlotte said, slightly proud of the fact.

"No, he doesn't. I know that team, he's not on it. He lied to you to get you to do this. You're not even an NBA ho, you're a random-loser ho!!" Diana lambasted her.

"I think you'd better go to bed . . . to your room," Harold suggested, unable to look at his youngest after having seen footage of her in flagrante.

"Yes, Papa," Charlotte said. She started toward her mother who still sat as if in a coma. Harold gently stopped her and indicated the stairs with his chin.

"I'm going to go do damage control. I'm calling my agent and publicist now," Diana said, whipping out her pearl-encrusted cell phone.

"When the going gets tough," Bliss commented under her breath.

The door's trumpet fanfare sounded and they all froze in their tracks. It sounded again.

"Great, the press is here already," Diana said. "Don't answer it!"

Harold went to the door. As he opened it, Wyatt entered, looking frazzled. He grabbed Diana by the arms.

"Are you all right?" he asked.

"You know?" she asked, terrified. He nodded.

"Does the network know?" she pursued.

"Afraid so. We were all sent copies. But don't worry, the network's on your side."

He knelt before Forsythia.

"Mrs. Harcourt, I know this must be devastating, but it's all going to be all right. Slowly, Forsythia raised her huge cinnamon-brown eyes to meet his. The light had completely gone out of them and her false eyelashes hung over them like shades.

"How could it possibly be all right? You'll have to excuse me, Mr. Evers," she said with dead calm, slowly rising to her feet. She made her way to the staircase. In all her life, Bliss had never seen her mother beyond words, coquetry, and histrionics. She walked like a zombie. Even Diana was moved for a moment by the sight of her, but then instantly remembered her own interests.

"What if they cancel the show?" she asked, panicked.

"They won't. Not if I have anything to do with it," Wyatt assured her, embracing her.

"I can't just sit here, I've got to call my team," she insisted, knocking his arms out of the way.

"I'll help you," he offered and they went off into the kitchen.

Harold just stood, dejected, in the middle of his little living room.

"Are you all right, Papa?" Bliss asked.

Harold didn't respond. At long last he looked out the window into the night and said, "I'm to blame. A nasty business."

"We'll get Charlotte some help. The Student Health Center can point us to the right psychiatrist, and—" Harold's look of despair stopped Bliss in mid-speech.

"What's the point of all that now? It's too late," he said, patting Bliss on the arm before retreating to his study. Bliss watched him go and remembered Dario's assessment: *Your father's tough and indifferent.* She'd been so insulted by his words, but tonight, their accuracy was hard to deny. Her father had written off all of her siblings from a young age. Much as she could blame her mother's frivolity and misplaced priorities for their problems, her father's abdication of responsibility had helped seal Diana's and Charlotte's fates.

chapter twenty-eight

A mere twelve hours after the discovery of the DVD, Sue had called Diana and Forsythia, warning them her sources at the network news department had told her the scandal was breaking that night. Forsythia had summoned everyone for an emergency family meeting to watch together, and then discuss plans for damage control. She had insisted to Bliss that as a resident of the house, she had no choice but to participate. Only Victoria had been excused as a result of a work conflict. Sue and Wyatt had arrived and were already ensconced in the family room with the rest of the Harcourt clan.

"And when we come back, scandal on the set of *The Virgin*, America's highest-rated reality show," the busty newscaster announced in a come-hither voice. Diana, who sat closest to the set, kicked her baby sister with the point of her now ubiquitous platform heels, which, combined with her high-collared yet skintight dress created a virgin-cum-stripper effect.

"Ouch!" Charlotte exclaimed.

"You put us in this mess," Diana spat.

"Relax, Didi," Sue assured her, ruminating her habitual wad of gum. "It's going to be fine."

"How can you say that?" Diana shrieked. "I'll be tarred as a ho by association, let alone blood."

"All we dreamed of," wailed Forsythia, who up until that point sat gnawing a handkerchief, "up in smoke. I haven't been able to eat a morsel all day." She gave Charlotte's arm a whack with the back of her hand.

"That's enough," Harold protested. The trumpet fanfare announced the arrival of a guest.

"That'll be Dario," Sue commented.

"Half an hour late. Yeah, he's concerned about our futures," Wyatt said sarcastically.

"Go let him in," Forsythia ordered Bliss, who complied, happy to leave the den of insanity, if only briefly. She opened the door and found Dario leaning casually against the jamb. In his butter-soft brown leather jacket, sea-foam-green cashmere boatneck sweater and jeans, he looked the picture of relaxation.

"Can I come in?" he requested after a moment. Bliss stepped away from the door.

"Where is everyone?"

"Glued to the television in the family room," she answered.

"And Bella?"

"Upstairs sleeping. I was not about to let her watch this circus."

"Good call." Dario followed Bliss through the living room. She had the uncomfortable feeling he was staring at her behind. She turned to look at him and he immediately lifted his eyes toward her face. She didn't know whether to be titillated or insulted. She didn't understand why he hadn't come rushing over the night before, when the DVDs were discovered. Now he seemed disturbingly nonchalant.

They entered the family room, an alcove off the kitchen covered in floral wallpaper. It was less a room than a nook, but Forsythia could never admit to the tiny dimensions of her dwelling. As Dario and Bliss entered, they heard the newscaster announce, "Protesters were subdued with tear gas and fifty were killed by army gunmen. In other news, we take you to San Francisco with a breaking development on the set of *The Virgin.*" The newscaster's tone remained equally grave as she transitioned from a massacre in the Middle East to "news from the set of *The Virgin.*" Bliss marveled at living in a world in which loss of human life meant less than reality-series gossip.

"San Francisco? Why San Francisco?" Diana repeated, puzzled.

"Shush!" her mother admonished.

Beowulf Jones appeared on the screen, nervously fidgeting as the entertainment reporter leaned in.

"Beowulf, you are one of the finalists for the hand of the Virgin and according to the show's rules, you took a vow of celibacy and chastity. Last night, you were caught in this amateur video having a little fun at the Hungry Pussycat club." They showed grainy cell phone footage of Beowulf with a thong-clad woman gyrating on his thigh, the nipples of her huge breasts blacked out by rectangular bands. Diana clasped her mouth to her hand in mock horror and let out a gasp. In spite of her performance, Bliss could see pure glee in her eyes.

"What do you have to say to America and to Diana, the woman you're trying to win?"

Beowulf looked like the proverbial deer in the headlights on an unlit country road. Bliss felt for him. Of all the people involved in this circus, other than perhaps Wyatt, he was the only innocent.

After moving his lips soundlessly like a trapped animal, he finally managed to come out with, "I'm just sorry, really sorry, and I hope America and especially Diana can forgive me."

"As in the case of Tiger Woods, why does he owe America an apology?" Bliss said under her breath. She looked over and caught Dario nodding and chuckling at her comment. They shared a look of mutual understanding.

"I'm not sure I can forgive, or that I should. What do you think, Sue, Wyatt?" Diana asked.

"Well, I say we've got a kick-ass groveling apology scene. In fact I think we can come up with another chivalric feat he has to complete to win your forgiveness. Dario?"

"I was thinking a walk across hot coals, or a bed of nails, or maybe we change his wardrobe to a hair shirt. Heck, what about a hair suit?"

he answered with a straight face. Forsythia, Sue, Charlotte, and Diana all looked at him to see if he was serious. Harold guffawed. Wyatt's eyes narrowed.

"Do you really think this is a time for sarcasm, Dario? This family's just been through an ordeal," he said.

"Yeah, I forgot," Dario responded acidly.

"In other news," the newscaster prattled on.

"Wait, that's it. They didn't talk about the tapes," Diana realized, elated.

"Nope, that's it, you guys are off the hot seat," Sue commented.

"How can you be certain? The note said 'Today you, tomorrow America'?" Bliss asked suspiciously.

"Somebody must have quashed them," Wyatt explained.

"But who?" Diana asked.

"The network has its ways," Sue commented cryptically. "This is a much better scandal, less tawdry. The network wanted extra episodes. We can stretch out Beowulf's repentance to an episode and a half."

"Well, it's late and we work tomorrow," Dario said, heading toward the door.

"What's your hurry?" Wyatt asked, following him to the door.

Bliss overheard Dario say, "Watch it," in a menacing tone. Wyatt backed away. In Dario's manner, she read danger and genuine threat, the violence lurking beneath his controlled exterior. Wyatt would be no match for him. For that reason, her sympathies lay squarely with Wyatt. She reverted to her initial opinion of Dario: his kindnesses to her daughter notwithstanding, he was just a brute in badly worn expensive clothing. Forsythia stood up completely revived.

"We've been blessed and spared. Dinner anyone?" she offered, buoyant.

"I'm starving," Sue answered, jumping up.

"I'm not very hungry. You'll excuse me, my dear, I've work to do," Harold said quietly as he retreated toward his study. The quick dismissal of such a cataclysmic event left Bliss speechless. She realized though that her father's retreat, and her mother's refusal to accept the darker implications of Charlotte's behavior, were all par for the course. Denial was a way of life for the Harcourt clan.

"Mum," she said sotto voce to Forsythia, "this isn't over. Aren't you going to get Charlotte some help?"

"What sort of help?" Forsythia inquired.

"Send her to a psychiatrist? Go with her?"

"Tell our problems to a stranger? Madness! Absolutely not!! We will go to church, we will pray, and we will forget this ever happened," Forsythia announced imperiously, her chin high in the air. Bliss knew to press no further.

"What do I wear for Beowulf's groveling scene?" Diana wondered aloud, trailing Sue and Forsythia out of the room.

"Excellent question. You must look very feminine and innocent, to contrast with Beowulf, the sinner. Never liked that boy," Forsythia advised.

"I say go virgin dominatrix. I'm seeing a white-leather bustier and skirt with some strappy sandals. We want to make every guy in America wish he could be 'the one' and wish he could be punished by her," Sue proposed.

Charlotte remained frozen in front of the television. Her lower lip began to tremble, and she burst into tears. Bliss put her arms around her.

"Must be a relief," she said gently. "It's over. But it's still scary."

"That's not it," Charlotte said, looking at her as if she were the world's most clueless imbecile. "I was going to be famous. Now no one cares about me!" Bliss stared at her, horrified.

"Is that why you did it? To be famous?" she asked, incredulous.

"No!" Charlotte answered in a tone of exasperation. "I did it 'cause he was hot and it was fun, and everybody films their hookups these days. But last night, I got to thinking this could really be big, like Paris Hilton big. Bigger even," she added, a distant look in her eyes. Bliss thanked God she was part of the pre-home-porn-movie generation.

She wondered what the future held for little Bella. Would all distinctions between public and private disappear? Would every neighborhood be equipped with a Jumbotron on which people vied to upload "home movies" of themselves copulating, going to the bathroom, masturbating? Terrifyingly, it all seemed in the realm of possibility.

chapter twenty-nine

In a sleek beige marble heat room in Washington's Mandarin Oriental spa, with floor-to-ceiling picture windows overlooking the shimmering Potomac, Bliss and Missy sat luxuriating in the soothing waters of a Jacuzzi. Bliss, her abundant curls piled atop her head in their traditional scrunchy spout, took deep, grateful breaths of the steam-imbued eighty-degree air as she savored this moment of calm and luxury.

"Let's face it, this is better than sex," Missy quipped.

"Let's not get carried away," Bliss countered with a wry smile.

"I forgot, you actually *liked* sex with your ex-husband, Bliss. Sexually satisfied American wife, party of one."

"That's part of what made my divorce so hard. Other people fight over money. We didn't have any. I want my orgasms back," Bliss assented.

"It shouldn't be that painful for me then," Missy muttered under her breath.

"What did you say?" Bliss asked, concerned.

"Nothing," Missy waved away her question. The glass door opened and a cool draft hit them as Victoria entered, a turbaned towel framing her Nefertiti-perfect face, her robe tightly fastened around her reedlike figure. She walked to the pegs at a clip, and removed her robe. Underneath, she wore a black Speedo that came up to her neck. She looked like a nun prepared to swim her daily laps in a frigid pool.

"I don't know why you don't get in naked," Missy chided her. "Who's going to see you?"

"I just don't feel comfortable that way," Victoria said quietly, looking away from Missy's large breasts floating on the surface of the bubbles.

"Wait a minute, what's with the piece of the rock?" Missy asked, pointing to Victoria's glistening five-karat engagement ring. Embarrassed, Victoria plunged her hand in the water. Bliss stared at her, right eyebrow arched, daring her to explain the circumstances to Missy. Victoria avoided her accusatory gaze by focusing on the sunlight's reflection in the dancing waters of the river outside. Missy looked from one sister to the other, trying to divine the source of the palpable tension.

"Are you going to tell her, or just wait for her to catch it on TV?" Bliss asked pointedly.

"Bliss!" Victoria cried with uncharacteristic sharpness. In her campaign to dissuade Victoria from a potentially disastrous union, Bliss had emailed her sister every three hours for the past two days. Her messages had been short, not so sweet, and to the point: "Don't do it!!!" "Just say no to marriage." "Say 'I don't.'" "Don't clean up Charlotte's porn scandal with a marriage."

"It's thick in here," Missy commented. "When did the Cold War start again? Girls, loosen up."

"I wanted to tell her in my own time, Bliss," Victoria chastened.

"Like she wasn't going to notice the portable skating rink on your finger. And if it's such great news, why are you keeping it to yourself?"

"Victoria, did you get engaged?" Missy asked wide-eyed. Victoria took a moment before bashfully answering, "Yes."

"But engagements are made to be broken," Bliss commented. "You can still get out of this."

"You were engaged to Manuel for nearly three years! You didn't break it."

"I was in love with him!! Can you honestly say you're in love with Dean?" Victoria turned her gaze to the view again, avoiding answering the question.

"So it's Dean you're marrying? I thought he was toast," Missy queried.

"He should be," Bliss commented.

"With all due respect, Bliss, it's not your place to say," Victoria snapped.

"You don't love him! Tell me you love him and I'll shut up forever, because that's worth the ride even if it's a train wreck like my marriage!"

"I've never loved any man!" Victoria shouted in a growl worthy of *The Exorcist.* She herself was shocked at its force. Both Missy and Bliss stared at her dumbfounded. Victoria adjusted her turban and regained her composure.

"I'm sorry," she offered. "Bliss, I've never felt what you felt for Manuel. For anyone. So, I can either sit around waiting for the rest of my life to be struck by a lightning bolt, or just buck up and get on with it."

"'Buck up and get on with it?' Listen to yourself. You sound like you're about to undergo basic training for the Army, not get married. I won't lie, the last years with Manuel were Hell, but the first few were Heaven. I want that for you!"

"Well, I'm not you! Maybe some of us can't feel what you feel and never will!" Victoria cried, her eyes moist with burgeoning tears. "Don't you think I've stayed up nights wondering what's wrong with me?"

Remorse and empathy filled Bliss's heart. She regretted every email and text message, she regretted the entire conversation. But she couldn't bring herself to believe that a woman as feeling as her sister, for all her reserve, could be exempt from the rapture of true, romantic love. Though she had given up on the thought of ever loving someone again as much as she had Manuel, she couldn't bear the thought of Victoria resigning herself to the emotional pragmatism of marrying "Mr. Good Enough."

"I'm sorry, Victoria, I never meant to hurt you," she said putting her arm around her sister's narrow, bony shoulder. Victoria wept in earnest, soon Missy was sobbing too.

"What's wrong?" Victoria asked gently, utterly forgetting her own sorrow.

"Nothing, I don't want to spoil your moment."

"What moment? Her sister making her miserable?" Bliss deadpanned.

"Girls, it's over. I'm getting a divorce," Missy blurted.

Bliss and Victoria flanked Missy, caressing her shoulders, Victoria tentatively so.

"Listen, I'm relieved. It's not a marriage, it's a rooming situation. What marriage isn't in the end?"

"There must be some," Bliss said, thinking of Jordan and his beautiful, brilliant Genevieve.

"What happened?" Victoria asked Missy, genuinely concerned.

"Nothing. Just one morning we looked at each other and he said, 'Muffin, the mares need reshoeing. What if we started divorce proceedings today?'"

"I'm so sorry," Victoria exclaimed, burying her perfect nose in Missy's fleshy neck.

"No, I'm okay, really. It's hard to live in a relationship that's dying."

"Even more so something that's DOA," Bliss commented pointedly.

"Bliss, stop it!" Victoria cried, her dark eyes flashing.

"Okay, had to try one last time."

"Bliss, marrying Dean will help our family name. Especially if that DVD gets out one day."

"It's not getting out. It's been quashed. And, what name? What are we, the *TV Guide* Windsors? And who the hell are the Windsors? A pack of inbred gluttons of privilege."

"Some of them are pretty nice," Missy corrected her. "What DVD?"

"Bliss, I'm marrying him. It will help make Mum happy," Victoria said, ignoring Missy.

"Do you need an old, washed-out matron of honor?" Missy offered.

"Absolutely," Victoria answered, smiling and massaging her old friend's neck.

"Don't stop!" Missy moaned gratefully. "That feels good. Most relief I've had in seventeen years," she laughed. "So what's the date? I want to know how long I have to drop these twenty pounds, one for nearly every year, and a half for each child."

"We haven't set it," Victoria answered, looking out at the Potomac again.

"There is a God," Bliss commented. Victoria shot her a cease-and-desist look.

"Too bad they don't serve liquor in this place," Missy commented, looking around at the pristine surroundings.

"They do at the bar downstairs. . . ." Victoria ventured, looking up at her with her enormous coal-black eyes.

"I say bottoms up," Bliss ventured, raising an imaginary glass. "To life, love, and—"

"Getting plastered!" Missy finished Bliss's sentence.

Bliss felt suddenly grateful for her situation. Though Missy would never have to worry about money, she'd clearly never known rapture. As painful as it was to amputate a limb, she was happy to have had one in the first place. It was true what they said: given the choice, one would always choose one's own misfortunes over other peoples. She just prayed Victoria had chosen her misery well.

chapter thirty

Bliss walked at a nervous clip down the fourth-floor corridor of Healy Hall. Jordan had summoned her to his office, a rare, even unprecedented, move that she feared presaged the worst: more cuts to the teaching-assistant staff in his Civil War class. If she lost that position, she'd have no source of income whatsoever and would have to resign herself to spending her dotage as a ward of her bickering parents. Perhaps it was time to submit that résumé to McDonald's. She kicked herself for being overeducated but devoid of any real marketable skills. Why hadn't she taken that juggling class at Yale?

As she made her way past students eight and ten years younger than she, she began to feel a special kinship with all the penniless yet genteel women who suffered through the canon of nineteenth-century novels from *Jane Eyre* through *The House of Mirth*. Her life had turned into the House of Mirthlessness, and unlike Lily Bart, she couldn't even end her days as a milliner because in all her years of schooling and fighting for the rights of those less fortunate, she'd never bothered to learn to sew.

Buck up, she told herself. *You're smart. You'll switch gears and go to law school and you'll work for the Legal Aid Society. Your apartment will be tiny, but at least it will be yours. I will not be a ward of 101 Windsor Lane. I will not be the vestal of 101 Windsor Lane. I will not end my days living with my mother and three thousand cats wondering what became of my life.*

Her fear of impending disaster was somewhat mitigated by the excitement of seeing Hottie Jordan, of an audience alone with him, his beautiful hands, and his musky cologne. The inklings of spring had brought on a touch of that season's fever. "Who am I kidding? I'm in a perpetual state of fever," she chided herself. A group of gradlings passed her, laughing. Were they mocking her? Paranoia was indeed setting in. This is how people went slowly mad. Even if the worst happened, she told herself, there was still plenty of time to turn the sinking ship of her life around. She was only thirty-three and half, well, three quarters, but no matter. The future awaited her.

She swung open the door to Jordan's reception area. There she found his assistant of the past twenty years, Myrtle Johnson, a diminutive busty woman who had served in the Kennedy administration, but, as she proudly proclaimed, not serviced. She wore trim suits with gold buttons every day and would never be caught dead without her lipstick. Myrtle was proffering her ever-present box of Kleenex to Dierdre Detweiler, the Valkyrie, who sobbed wildly. Bliss's heart beat faster. The Valkyrie had been placed on earth to make others cry. What had brought her to this vulnerable pass? Bliss wanted to turn on her heels and run. Maybe she could just grab Bella, move to Bora-Bora and live on scavenged nuts and fruits in rustic splendor for the remainder of their days. What did success in Western terms mean to her anyway?

The Valkyrie was so distraught, she didn't even see Bliss through the blur of her tears. She merely pushed past her as Jordan opened the door of his office, desperate to get away.

"Bliss, come in," Jordan said, in what Bliss took to be a funereal tone. She walked in and took a seat opposite his enormous Roosevelt-era flattop desk. A promotion gift from his late wife when he was named head of the department, it had some provenance of note that she could no longer recall. Why bother, she wouldn't need to know about such things anymore when she lived on an atoll in Bora-Bora.

"Thanks for coming on short notice," Jordan said earnestly. "I have important news I didn't want to share over the phone."

The bottom dropped out of Bliss's stomach. No one went to this trouble for innocuous news. She mentally began to pack up her TA cubicle. Perhaps she should just leave it, or in a final gesture of bitterness, burn it to the ground.

"So, you know they cut the funding for the fellowships down from three to two. Last week, they said they would only be granting one." Bliss rose from her seat, resigned to her pathetic fate.

"Where are you going?" Jordan asked.

"Sorry, I just can't hear it. I get what you're saying and I need to be an ostrich."

"But you're the one who got it."

"Got what?"

"The fellowship. You have a grant to go conduct your research in London and Paris and . . . Bordeaux, I think it was. For six months."

Bliss sat back down, stunned. She took a deep breath and closed and opened her eyes, then realized she must look like a complete madwoman.

"Bliss, you got it!" Jordan repeated. Bliss jumped up, hugged him, and covered his face with kisses. Suddenly, she pulled back, mortified at her spontaneous show of affection. Jordan smiled as he bashfully wiped her lipstick off his face.

"How did I get it?" she asked, attempting to recover her dignity.

"Your proposal was great, the area is fresh. It was down to you and Percival Linton but you beat him."

"How?"

"Cuthbert was deeply impressed by your oral exam, and liked your line of thinking. Somosa liked your line of thinking and your general lines. Barrows tried to bury you, but she couldn't. She was outnumbered," he said with a flirtatious wink. Bliss still sat dumbfounded. It had been so long since she'd received any good news or felt as though she'd done anything right that she didn't know how to respond. She was so used to fighting off pain that this moment of pure joy and vindication paralyzed her.

"Bliss," Jordan prodded her gently. "It's okay to go and celebrate."

"I will," she promised, getting up from her seat. "I have papers to grade, but—"

"Do it over wine," he suggested.

"I will," she said. "And thank you!"

She strode out of his office and down the hall, feeling for the first time in a long time that the world was hers. She and Bella would go spend six months living in Europe. Her sentence at Harcourt House was coming to an end.

chapter thirty-one

Bliss sat in a high-backed booth at the Pint and Horseshoe, reading through undergraduate term papers. The assignment was to imagine oneself as a character during the Battle of Gettysburg: a Union or Confederate soldier, a freed slave fighting for the North, or one of their loved ones or dependents back home awaiting news. One of Bliss's students has written a "conscientious objection" to the entire exercise.

"I cannot complete this assignment because I find it degrading both to the subjects I am being asked to impersonate and to myself as a twenty-first century woman." *Hmm,* Bliss mused to herself, *someone who didn't have time to get the assignment done and is hiding behind political correctness.* As an eighteen-year-old, she too might have found the assignment objectionable but she would have written the hell out of it, gotten an A, then gone to complain to the professor at the end of the course. She could see the young woman was setting the stage to bring this to an academic tribunal and eke out a passing grade without doing the coursework. The contemporary world was full of scammers.

Victoria arrived and interrupted her work. She handed her a box festooned with a satin bow. Bliss hugged her and opened it.

"It's a wallet for foreign currency," Victoria explained. "See, Euros, pounds."

Bliss laughed, "You're assuming I have currency in the first place."

"You're on your way," Victoria assured her, squeezing her hand.

"This fellowship is just the beginning, your life is turning around. You're getting it back." Bliss hoped Victoria was right. She did feel truly hopeful. For the first time in over a year, she thought of herself as a justified optimist rather than a loser in utter denial. She fingered the wallet, so representative of her sister in its immaculate lines and practicality.

"I got one for myself too, different color, for the trip to England," Victoria added.

"The jousting contest? They've roped you in?"

"It'll be fun," Victoria shrugged. "I haven't taken all my vacation days. They're doing some renovations at the Archives so I'd be kicked out of my office anyway. You know I'm no good with nothing to catalogue, so when Sue proposed it I said 'why not.' They're holding the next competitions at this beautiful medieval castle with a famous garden."

"I suppose Dean is going with you."

"No! He had to cancel!" Victoria said with a bit too much enthusiasm. She caught herself. "He has a trial coming up," she added with mischievous glee. Bliss stared her down but didn't dare comment since their contretemps in the hot tub the month before.

"Will you come?" Victoria asked.

"No, what am I going to do over there?"

"Have fun, go into London to start your research while we watch Bella. It might be the last vacation we take before I get . . ."

Again, Bliss refrained from commenting on Victoria's obvious misery at the prospect of taking her vows. Instead she chose to make light.

"Did we ever have a vacation alone?"

"Yes, the time we went to New York before you married Manuel."

Bliss had forgotten. She could see them now, twenty-three and twenty-five, clueless and running through Times Square.

"That was a lifetime ago," Bliss mused.

"So, this could be like that. I'll even come into London with you."

"You have to promise to flirt with someone."

"Me? What about you? If I were you, I'd go for Wyatt."

"Victoria!"

"Come on. You two have been flirting quite a bit, I saw the way he looked at you in Vienna."

"He looked but he didn't even *try* to touch," Bliss joked. She was now on day 495 of celibacy. Soon, the Guinness Book of World Records would want to feature her.

"He also told me to ask you," Victoria announced.

"No?" Bliss asked incredulous. Victoria nodded vigorously.

"Yes, he did."

"That settles it," Bliss declared, slapping a hand on the table. "Okay, I'll pack my good underwear. Actually, I no longer have any it's been so long."

"I'll take you shopping," Victoria offered happily. "I need to get a honeymoon trousseau myself . . ." she added more somberly. She looked up at Bliss who smiled sympathetically, but refrained from offering another escape plan. One couldn't save the people one loved most, that was the cardinal lesson of adulthood. Even if she couldn't rescue Victoria, she could make her laugh.

"Wyatt, no Wyatt, we'll have a blast," she vowed. "I'll even go bird-watching with you!"

"You hate bird-watching," Victoria chided.

"Yes, but I'll do it for you. I'll do anything for you," she assured her. Victoria took her hand, grateful for the support.

chapter thirty-two

Bliss sat in her window casement admiring the view of the Hever Castle grounds. She could understand her mother's adoration for the English countryside. With the sweet smell of fresh-cut grass filling her nostrils, and an expanse of green rolling hills as far as the eye could see, she could allow herself to be swept away to another place and time. For a moment, she was Dorothea Brooke in *Middlemarch,* or Elizabeth Bennet set to walk across the grassy fields to visit her ailing sister at Netherfield. She chose not to dwell on the fate of one of the castle's original inhabitants: Anne Boleyn of the lopped off head. Once again, the irony of celebrating the ultimate chivalric trial to win Diana's hand at the birthplace of a queen condemned to death by a greedy husband who wanted to dump her for another woman was lost on anyone from the network. A grating voice intruded upon Bliss's reverie.

On the gravel walk below, Sue Minors tromped along with bullish determination, barking into her ubiquitous cell phone. As usual, she was trailed by the long suffering Punch, who at this point probably wanted to earn her name and land one on her charmless, relentlessly rude boss.

"Why didn't anyone tell me Henry VIII's knights were practically midgets? We just had the fitting, and the armor looked like metal bras and garter stockings on these boys. All my suitors are six feet at least! Get the armor and get it fast, I don't care if you have to open an iron foundry to make it!!!! Punch!!!" she screamed as though the latter were leagues, instead of merely inches, away from her.

"I'm right here, Sue," Punch said in a voice that sought to soothe the savage network beast.

"Get me a latte, now!!!!" Sue screamed.

"They don't have lattes here," Punch explained timidly.

Sue stopped in her tracks, whipped around, and unleashed her full fury on the long-suffering creature.

"Then make one!!!!" She roared. Punch ran off in the direction of the castle kitchen. In a paroxysm of frustration, Sue stomped one of the shrubs lining the path until it was completely flattened. Bliss watched her in amazement. At the height of her divorce, she never destroyed other people's property. She had pummeled Manuel's chest, but this . . .

She heard a knock at the door. She opened it and there stood Wyatt, looking better than ever in a pair of faded jeans, an oxford shirt, and a sport coat.

"Hello, beautiful," he said, planting a kiss on her forehead. "May I come in?" A rush of delight made the color rise to Bliss's cheeks.

"Sure, " she said, stepping away from the door and ushering him in.

"Nice digs," he said, looking around. "A little morbid, especially when you think who lived and met her 'death mate' here, Anne," he drew a finger across his neck, "Boleyn."

Bliss smiled wide at the reference. Wyatt always got the joke, unlike the rest of the crew of *The Virgin*.

"So, where's the kid?"

"You mean Bella?" Bliss asked. She didn't particularly care for the term "kid," finding it cold and dismissive, but she inwardly chided herself for having inherited a touch of her mother's proper West Indian formality. What, after all, was in a name?

"Yes, Bella."

"She's with my mother. They're visiting the rose gardens. Forsythia is in her element here. It's a dream come true. She wants to instill the hunger for castles in her grandchild. This is her last chance. Unless of course, Diana chooses Alistair."

"That's not going to happen," Wyatt scoffed. His certitude took Bliss aback.

"How can you say that? You don't know. Or do you?"

"No, this is reality TV, remember? 'Unscripted,'" he said, miming quotation marks with his fingers.

"What are you saying?" Bliss asked warily.

"No, honestly, I don't know. Dario knows, but I don't. That guy would do anything to get a rating. Did you ever wonder how Beowulf learned to waltz? Never mind."

Bliss had the uncomfortable feeling he knew more than he was letting on.

"Was Dario involved in those DVDs?"

"I can't say. Please don't make me go there. I just don't think the chinless wonder with the double-barreled name is your sister's type. She looks like a girl who likes to get it on."

"No, she's not," Bliss objected. "She's the Virgin."

Wyatt rolled his eyes.

"In practice, not in her soul. But I didn't come here to talk about her," he said leaning in.

"I'm glad you didn't," Bliss snapped, put off by the crassness of his assessment.

"Just so you know, I don't get along with all my sisters, but I don't like other people dissing them," she warned.

"You're right. I'm being a jerk. I'm sorry. It's just that all this pomp and chivalry is really starting to get on my nerves. The real reason I came here is to ask if you would have dinner with me."

Bliss looked at him, stunned.

"Don't look so surprised. I wanted to take you out in Austria and the schedule got too crazy. Now, I have a second chance."

"I'd need to change."

"No, you look hot, as always," Wyatt said giving her an appreciative once-over. "You forget, I've seen you dance," he whispered in her ear. His warm breath and soft lips brushing her earlobe sent a shiver of desire down her spine. She decided to go for it. It was time to stop watching life from a window casement. Her mother and Victoria could babysit Bella. She grabbed his hand. It was large and a little rough.

"Let's go," she said. Wyatt beamed.

Downstairs, a burgundy Aston Martin sat in front of the castle door, its engine running. Wyatt opened the door and bowed.

"Step in," he invited her. Bliss eased in to the camel-color leather seat. Wyatt got in the driver's seat and the car took off.

"Where are we going?"

"To the end of the earth, to Heaven," he laughed. As the car sped over the gravel out the front gate down a winding road lined with oaks, the wind blew through Bliss's hair and she felt Wyatt might fulfill that promise yet.

chapter thirty-three

It was well past eleven when Wyatt brought Bliss back to Hever Castle. Over dinner at the local pub, he'd plied her with so many glasses of port—explaining the provenance of each one—that she'd forgotten the time and her mother waiting in her room. Her head was spinning as he walked her to the door of a suite. Suddenly getting her bearings she said, "This isn't my room."

"No, it's mine," he said in a voice that seemed to have grown deeper. He opened the door and pressed the small of her back. As she entered, his hand slipped to caress her deliciously ample bottom.

"You've got a Brazilian ass," he whispered in her ear as he cupped each cheek with a hand from behind. The words revolted her, but the moves aroused. She leaned back into him instinctively. His rock-hard shaft grazed her bottom. She started to reach for it but he grabbed her hand to stop her.

"Uh uh, let's take it slow," he said, turning her around to face him, grazing her lips with his, then working his way slowly and delicately down her neck toward her bosom, stopping just at the cleavage and casting his gaze up at her. His blue eyes were alive with desire, and mesmerizing. He walked her backward and laid her on the enormous canopy bed that creaked under their weights.

"It's going to be noisy," he joked, "but don't worry, I'll be gentle." Bliss's whole body went deliciously limp as she surrendered to his touch. Finally, on day 510 of captivity, her libido would be freed!!! A delicious, sensual reward, at the hands of someone who knew what he was doing, would be hers. As he slowly slipped her panties down over her buttocks, she thought to herself that this had been worth the wait. Whatever happened in the morning didn't matter. She was living for tonight. He slid himself down and looked up at her from between her thighs. Moist with anticipation, she closed her eyes. She waited, nothing happened. Suddenly she felt his warm tongue on her left thigh, inching its way upward, then switching sides and working its way down her right thigh. Wyatt was leading her in a hesitation dance, a tease. Here was a man who knew how to build desire stroke by stroke. She sank farther into the pillows, stretching her arms above her head. She felt his warm breath just above her mound. She bit her lower lip and there was a knock at the door. Wyatt sprang to his feet.

"Hold that thought," he said. Bliss sat up, hugging her knees to her chest. Wyatt crossed to the door, and opened it a crack, blocking any view of her.

"I need to talk to you," Dario's voice said, from the other side.

"Shit," Bliss cursed.

"You got someone in there?" Dario asked, in a voice of indignation. Bliss wanted to smack him. As if he didn't have some chippie warming his bed every night.

"It's not a good time," Wyatt explained.

"My ass it isn't! We need to talk now."

"Okay, okay. Give me a minute," Wyatt answered, annoyed. He shut the door and turned to Bliss.

"I am so sorry about this," he said in a tone of utter sincerity.

"So am I," she said, pulling up her panties.

"Look, let me get rid of him so you don't have to do the walk of shame."

"I'm not ashamed. At all." She gave him a full, ripe kiss that contained all the unspent desire of the last 510 days and thirty minutes. "To be continued," she promised.

She stepped out into the hall and yanked her dress back into place, head held high. She looked down the corridor and saw Dario raise his eyes to her with an expression of devastation. He bit his upper lip in frustration, and seemed to compose himself. For a moment, Bliss didn't dare move, then she turned to walk in the other direction, only to realize her room was on the other side. She did an about-face and with her chin defiantly in the air, prepared to walk right past Dario. As she approached, his eyes never left her. She had wanted to avoid even speaking but it would be too rude.

"Good night," she tossed off.

"Bliss," he said in a tone that stopped her in her tracks. It had a tinge of anger but also of true despair.

"That . . ." He seemed to stifle a thought. He composed himself and continued, "That . . . guy doesn't deserve you." For a moment the statement sank in, as Bliss tried to make sense of it. Then she remembered Wyatt's words, "Dario would do anything for ratings." Dario was casting aspersions on Wyatt to deflect anything Wyatt might have told her about him.

"I think he'd say the same about you, not that you'd ever want me anyway. Thank God." The last statement seemed to make Dario flinch, as though she'd stabbed him. She chalked it up to a massive ego that demanded that he be the object of lust of every woman in his path. Well, he could count her off the list. Life had just revealed a new sweet mystery to her, and she promised herself to unravel it farther.

chapter thirty-four

Promptly at five to six the following evening, as Bliss sat reading *The Wind in the Willows* to an enthralled Bella, there was a loud pounding on their door. Bliss hoped fervently that it was Wyatt whom she had only glanced from a distance that afternoon as he rehearsed his narration of the jousting competition that would take place the next day. Such sightings had only tantalized her further: consummation was so close, and yet so far. Perhaps tonight would prove to be *the* night. She rose from the bed eagerly and threw open the door. To her disappointment she found Forsythia, Diana, Victoria, and Charlotte, with Harold reluctantly bringing up the rear. They all wore their black-tie best, Forsythia's gown in particular a shimmering riot of silver paillettes and sequins, the whole crowned with an extravagant fascinator in rhinestone-studded feathers. Charlotte cut a particularly sullen figure in a high-necked pink polka-dot dress with an enormous bow at the collar, forbidding as a do-not-touch sign. Bliss surmised that this clownish and antisexual evening wear by Bozo was sartorial penance, imposed by their mother for Charlotte's video transgressions.

"Come along, my girl," Forsythia commanded. "We'll be late for the Troubadour or Bard Banquet and Competition!"

"We're ready," Bliss reassured her.

"That's what you're wearing?" Diana deadpanned as she surveyed Bliss's simple teal-blue cocktail dress. As usual, she herself looked beauty-pageant ready in an empire cut ice-blue chiffon gown, which, along with her updo and pearl-drop earrings, set off her swanlike neck to full advantage.

"I'm not on camera, remember. I get to be the family frump," Bliss joked self-deprecatingly.

"I'll say," Diana assented.

"I think perhaps your mother is bedecked and bedazzled enough for all of us," Harold suggested diplomatically.

"My new clothing line," Forsythia preened. "Eat your heart out, Tina Knowles. The House of Deréon, indeed. This is Forsythia's Formals. Elegant don't you think?" she said, swaying coquettishly from side to side.

"Remarkable," Harold commented.

"You flatter me."

"Not at all, my dear," he added sardonically.

"Onward, we don't want to be late," Forsythia insisted.

"Yes, come on, we're supposed to arrive as a clan of old," Diana explained as she turned and swept down the hall.

"Can I pleeeaase change?" Charlotte moaned, pushing down the bow that kept popping up in front of her mouth, obscuring her plump lips.

"We haven't time. And you look perfectly lovely, more importantly, decent," Forsythia decreed.

"Come along, Harcourts, march!" Forsythia bellowed. Her loyal troops fell in, Bella taking the command literally and doing her best to lift her braced leg in proper soldierly fashion.

"You don't have to do that," Bliss reassured her.

"But Glamma said 'march,'" Bella insisted.

As they arrived at the carved-oak double doors leading to the castle's State Dining Room, two pages blew their trumpets, nearly blasting their eardrums. The doors flew open and a very fey majordomo announced, "the House of Harcourt" halfheartedly. His entire expression telegraphed *Frankly, I'd rather be at Stratford-upon-Avon.* Bliss pitied this man, who might well be a graduate of the Royal Academy of Dramatic Arts but was reduced to greeting tourists with delusions of royalty. Bliss hung back with Bella while the others entered. When she heard Dario yell "Cut!" she walked in.

The double-height-ceilinged room had been set up for an elaborate banquet, its long rectangular table laden with golden plates, cut crystal goblets, and cornucopias disgorging fruit and nuts. The original Tudor tapestries adorning the walls depicted scenes of armored battle and royal hunts from centuries past. Bliss took it all in as she scanned the room for Wyatt. She spotted him standing in a discreet corner, adjusting his bow tie in a mirror. She considered rushing over, but told herself to stop behaving like a heifer in heat. Desperation didn't become her. If she could make it 511 days without sex, she could stand a few more hours.

Sue and Dario stood in another corner talking to one of the cameramen. Diana made a beeline for them.

"Okay, so which one is my camera?" she demanded. Before Dario could answer, Bella rushed over and threw her arms around his waist.

"Mr. Fuentes, where've you been? I missed you!" she cried to Bliss's mortification.

"Bella, sweetie, Mr. Fuentes is trying to work," Bliss cautioned, joining them.

"Yes, we are," Diana seconded.

"It's okay. She can hang with us for a moment," Dario reassured them locking eyes with Bliss. The intensity of his gaze unnerved her. She couldn't tell if his glare signaled anger, resentment, sorrow, or all three.

"Fine. Just for a moment," she tossed out, crossing away as Dario hoisted Bella up in his arms and began to explain.

"This is the lens adjustor. It helps zoom in or out. . . ."

Bliss walked by Punch, who perched on a stool awaiting orders from Sue. She stared at Victoria, blushing and smitten. The latter took no notice. Bliss felt a rough but warm hand on her arm. She turned to see Wyatt, grinning sheepishly, his beautiful baby blues gleaming with mischief. His lips, which once struck her as too thin, now evoked delicious memories of his artful kisses, and suggested talents she had yet to sample fully.

"So sorry about last night," he whispered in her ear, his mouth tantalizingly close to her neck. She longed to offer it up, like a maiden mesmerized by a vampire in a Dracula movie.

"Not your fault," she whispered in return, her own lips nearly brushing his earlobe.

"How about toni—"

The trumpets sounded again, interrupting his proposition and giving everyone a start. Bliss longed to say "Yes, tonight is perfect!" but Wyatt had already made his way toward the door.

"My word," Forsythia exclaimed.

"The House of Grant-Smyth," the majordomo announced with as little enthusiasm as ever. A couple of about Harold and Forsythia's age entered.

"Who are they?" Charlotte asked, peering.

"The Grant-Smyths, silly goose, Alistair's parents, of course. Very very distinguished." Forsythia explained in a stage whisper. "Isn't it thrilling to have them here? Real members of the peerage," she added, impressed.

"Hardly," her husband scoffed.

"Harold, he's an inventor."

"Of bologna made of soy. There's a contribution to mankind. Not since Jonas Salk," Harold joked. Forsythia poked him in the ribs to make him stop. As the pair approached, she stood up taller, prepared to meet these grandees properly. At five foot three, Lady Grant-Smyth was Forsythia's equal in height and girth. Both women ascribed to the same Holy Trinity of dressing principles: never wear a dress your own size when you can squeeze into the next size down; décolletage or die; and sparkle, sparkle, sparkle. Pale and blond, Lady Grant-Smyth had stuffed her plump person into a black bugle-beaded dress with a plunging neckline. The two women wore identical fascinators, only Lady Grant-Smyth's was black and Forsythia's silver.

Wyatt led the Grant-Smyths into the room.

"Harcourts, meet your future in-laws, possibly, the Grant-Smyths."

"How do you do?" Forsythia said solemnly, dipping into a near curtsy.

"How'd you do," Lady Grant-Smyth sniffed, her upturned nose high in the air. The reaction startled Forsythia but she was soon swept up in Sir Wallace Grant-Smyth's charms. He eagerly took her hand, bowed, and kissed it.

"Delighted, delighted," he said before vigorously shaking Harold's hand. With his bulging eyes and reddened cheeks, he looked like a demented, overgrown cherub who'd fallen into a vat of wine.

"And these must be your girls," he said devouring each Harcourt girl with his gaze. "Pretty family," he commented, licking his lips and leering.

"Bit dusky if you ask me," his bride muttered under her breath.

"I beg your pardon?" Forsythia answered, her lynx ears catching the dig. Dario yelled, "Places, please. It's time to roll. Take your seats for the banquet."

"Where can I sit where no one will see me?" Bliss asked.

"Who would want to?" her mother shot back.

"Plenty of people," Wyatt countered with an encouraging wink to Bliss. Dario approached her.

"We've arranged this table for you and Bella. It's not in any of the shots," he said, indicating a small table by the cameras. He pulled out a chair.

"Thank you," Bliss responded, surprised by this show of consideration.

"I'll sit with you," Victoria volunteered.

"Victoria, how can we be a clan with you marooned in a corner? Don't you want Dean to see you on television?" Forsythia objected. Victoria winced at the mention of her fiancé. Bliss gave her hand an encouraging squeeze.

"I'm fine out of sight, Mum," Victoria assured her.

"Let's get the contestants in," Dario asked.

"Why do they get the center table?" Lady Grant-Smyth asked her husband audibly in a nasal whine. Forsythia bristled.

"They're the stars, and they're an awfully comely bunch," he answered, leaning over the table and lifting a glass to Victoria who looked around for a place to hide.

"Sir Wallace puts me in mind of someone," Harold commented, studying the "peer." "Ah yes, Mr. Rumleigh, the butcher down the road when I was a boy. I can see him wielding a cleaver." Forsythia glared at Harold. Wyatt took his place in the center of the room.

"Harcourt clan, Grant-Smyth clan, we are gathered here tonight to watch the crusaders for the Virgin's heart vie in the penultimate contest: the Troubadour or Bard Competition. With us because we are on their home turf, is the Grant-Smyth clan, Sir Wallace Grant-Smyth, my lady."

Lady Grant-Smyth nodded imperiously.

"We're honored to have you here in this historic castle where the great love of Anne Boleyn and Henry VIII was born. Now, let's bring in the contestants. First up, your son and heir, Alistair."

Forsythia and Lady Grant-Smyth applauded vigorously as Alistair entered looking far better than usual in a custom-made tuxedo. He shook hands with Wyatt and offered a slight bow, an inclination of the head really, in Diana's direction.

"Alistair, buddy, time to level with the audience here. You didn't win the dream date and you didn't win the waltz competition. So far, you're behind in this contest. How are you feeling tonight?" Wyatt asked him.

"Confident," Alistair chirped brightly in his English toff tones. "Anything can happen. As Churchill said, "Never, ever, ever give up.""

"Great attitude. Love it. And I'm sure our maiden fair will too. Are you troubadour or bard tonight?"

"Bard," Alistair answered with a hearty nod and self-satisfied grin.

"Go for it. Lay some rhymes on us," Wyatt encouraged him, stepping out of the camera's view. Alistair planted himself directly in front of Diana, who looked at him from under her endlessly long lashes and flashed the jewel-encrusted watch he'd given her. Forsythia nodded her approval of the gesture to her daughter. Alistair commenced, chest and paunch puffed out.

"My lady, Diana, since no gem can woo thee, to possess thee truly, I've turned to Shakespeare, the bard himself, to plead my case. Ahem," he cleared his throat. Diana wriggled suggestively in her seat and simpered encouragingly. Garbling his words in a marbles-in-the-mouth monotone, he recited, "'When forty winters shall besiege thy brow/ And dig deep trenches in thy beauty's field,/ Thy youth's proud livery so gazed on now/ Will be a tattered weed of small worth held.'"

Diana, looking stunned, mouthed "Forty winters?" Bliss stifled a laugh. The bubble over her sister's head might have read "Furrows? Trenches? Me? No way! Botox, buddy." Diana fumed as Alistair warbled on, oblivious to the damaging effect of his chosen verses on his future prospects.

"'Then being asked, where all thy beauty lies/ Where all the treasure of thy lusty days/ To say within thine own deep-sunken eyes . . .' Um . . . ah . . . 'thine own deep-sunken eyes,'" he repeated, lost.

Everyone waited for him to resume his recitation, Lady Grant-Smyth beaming maternal encouragement, her eyes seeming to say *Come along, darling, you can do it.*

"I told you we should have gotten that dope cue cards," Sue complained sotto voce to Dario.

"That's cheating," he protested.

"Like that matters now," she countered. Bliss registered the exchange and looked at Dario questioningly. He ignored her. Alistair continued to stare up at the ceiling in search of the remaining lines of his sonnet. "Ah, I've got it now," he said at last in a triumphant tone.

"'If thou couldst answer "this fair child of mine/ Shall sum my count, and make my old excuse,"/ Proving his beauty by succession thine!/ This were to be new made when thou art old,/ And see thy blood warm when thou feel'st it cold.'/ In other words, 'Die single and thine image dies with thee,'" he added with a deep bow.

"That was uplifting," Bliss deadpanned to Victoria who didn't know what to make of Alistair's display. Diana sat, shocked and disgusted at Alistair's ineptitude. He looked at her for approval but she just stared back blankly.

"Bravo, bravo, darling," Lady Grant-Smyth said, applauding and rising to her feet.

"Hear, hear!!! Well and very prettily put," Forsythia concurred. "Are you listening girls? 'Die single and thine image dies with thee.'" Forsythia repeated, pointedly looking at Victoria, who closed her eyes and crossed herself, suppressing a groan. Charlotte sat gape mouthed, staring absently into space.

"Charlotte, shut your mouth. You'll catch flies. Did you understand?" Forsythia asked.

"Understand what?"

"The poem!"

"She's probably never heard of Shakespeare," Lady Grant-Smyth sneered.

"Of course she has," Forsythia bristled. "Haven't you, Charlotte?"

"Yeah, I have, they've done tons of movies of his scripts," Charlotte rebutted, most pleased. Lady Grant-Smyth let out a loud guffaw.

"What a ninny," she sniffed.

"Now look here—"

Forsythia stood up, prepared to lunge across the table and smack the self-satisfied smile off her face.

"Cut!" Dario yelled.

"Why cut? That was gold, a surprise catfight," Sue objected.

"We've got enough surprises going on," Dario insisted. Bliss felt he hid a greater secret.

"Let's bring in the next bard," Wyatt announced. Beowulf lumbered in, perspiration pouring down his face.

"Beowulf, how are you feeling?" Wyatt asked chummily.

"Nervous." Bliss wanted to give him a hug and warn him to run for his life. He'd clearly mistaken Diana's perfect beauty for goodness. He was the original fool in love.

"Are you troubadour or bard?"

"Bard."

"Take it."

Diana mustered a smile and sat up straighter to at least appear interested. She couldn't entirely dismiss a young man worth a cool billion.

"Diana," he declared, kneeling before her, "my feelings for you are limitless. Like the multiverse. I tried to distill it all in a Haiku I composed. It's called 'To Diana, My Sublime Geometry.'" He paused for a breath then stated sincerely, "'As pi rules circles/ You ring and sound my soul's/ Infinity. You.'"

He bowed his head for a few moments, then raised it again, desperately searching Diana's face for a sign of approval she refused to bestow. Flashing a perfunctory grin, she looked at him puzzled, the meaning of his poem and the profound emotions it expressed completely eluding her. He remained prostrate before her, hoping she'd grasp the depth of his feelings when from the musician's gallery above, the strumming of a lute was heard.

Everyone looked up as a clear, soulful tenor belted out, "'Alas my love you do me wrong,/ To cast me off discourteously/ For I have loved you well and long,/ Delighting in your company.'" Paul, dressed in full medieval-chain-mail regalia, peered down at them and placed one bulging tight-swathed thigh over the balcony. Diana preened and pushed her breasts out, as if saluting this virile apparition. Paul continued his plaintive song: "'Greensleeves was all my joy/ Greensleeves was my delight/ Greensleeves was my heart of gold/ And who but my lady Greensleeves.'" He leapt down from the gallery to the gasps of all assembled and landed catlike on his feet. He tossed aside the lute and launched into a rap, "Greensleeves, I gotta lay it on the line!"

From the sound system came the acoustic accompaniment of a throbbing bass line that made the tumblers on the table rattle. Charlotte in her clown ensemble began rocking out to the pulsating rhythm.

"Stop, you're making a spectacle of yourself," her mother admonished in a whisper.

"She's hardly the only one," Harold pointed out as he watched Paul's antics in bemusement.

"'Greensleeves, I gotta lay it on the line,'" Paul sang out as he pounced around the room with the ferocity and grace of a panther. Bliss couldn't decide if this was the most seductive or ridiculous performance she'd ever seen. "''Cause, Greensleeves, I gotta make you mine/ Can't let you be with Prince No Chin,'" he indicated Alistair, whose mother threw down her napkin in disgust. "'And even billions don't make up for a dude too thin,'" he pointed to a mortified Beowulf. "'No, princess, your man's Paul D./ 'Cause only he can give you ecstasy/ And one day soon, a whole country/ From sea to sea America'll hear me yell/ Step off, Barack, this is my Michelle.'" He ended on one knee, thumping a fist against his ample and well-built chest. Diana slowly rose from her center seat, leaned over the table, grabbed his head, and planted a kiss directly on Paul's lips. They stood locked in an embrace.

"My word, this is hardly maidenly," Forsythia exclaimed, embarrassed.

"Cool!" Charlotte exclaimed, pumping the air with her fist.

Sue rubbed her hands together delightedly. "This is going to make *such* a good promo," she chirped to Dario. Bliss watched waiting for his reaction, but he remained poker-faced and inscrutable.

As Diana and Paul disengaged from their embrace, Wyatt stepped forth, slapping Paul on the back, a bit hard, it seemed to Bliss.

"Well, it's clear to see who won this contest!" he commented.

"Yes, Paul definitely took the day," Diana concurred, "he was both troubadour and bard. A sure way to a maiden's heart," she said, resuming her air of coy diffidence.

"Well, Paul, this puts you in the lead as we go into the joust tomorrow. But beware, as one of the other suitors said, anything can happen."

"Mommy, does this mean Aunt Didi wants to marry the man in the ballet outfit?" Bella asked in a whisper.

"I don't know, sweetie," Bliss answered truly confused. Would her calculating sister really let her libido rule?

"Not happy about this," Forsythia complained to Harold. "You must drum some sense into the girl."

"I'm afraid it's too late now. The faluka sailed down the Nile long ago."

"Harold, this is her husband she's choosing."

"On national television. If we cared, we would never have let her participate in the first place."

Again, her father's abdication saddened Bliss. Perhaps there was something she could do.

chapter thirty-five

Later that evening, Bliss left Bella in her room with Victoria as she went in search of Diana. She felt it her last chance to spark the affirming flame of decency that the bald pursuit of fame and fortune had completely extinguished. She wondered to herself why she bothered, but at the end of the day, for all their differences, Diana was her baby sister. She hated to see her intelligence and abilities put to such misguided purposes. She spotted crew members milling outside the library and lights from within. She approached.

Dario put his finger to his lips to indicate silence. Diana sat opposite Wyatt, who was interviewing her.

"So, the moment of decision fast approaches, Virgin Diana. Who will gather ye rosebuds?" Bliss winced at the reference.

"I don't know," Diana demurred. "It's so hard. Right after dinner, it felt like Paul, but Beowulf is so . . . sweet and gentle, and Alistair has been so generous. I didn't care for his poem, well, actually, Shakespeare's, but he was trying."

"What inspired you to give Paul that kiss?"

"I just felt it, in the moment."

"Passion."

"Yes," she admitted, then looked down at her folded hands bashfully. "I haven't kissed a lot of guys." Bliss knew this to be a bald-faced lie. Though she knew her sister had never crossed the line to sleep with someone, she'd caught her more than once playing spin the bottle in their living room when she was a teen.

"Cut!" Dario yelled.

"Hey, it was just getting interesting," Wyatt objected.

"We've got enough. She should get some sleep," Dario insisted. Diana expertly raised her arm as a crew member removed her microphone.

"Night, night. See you all in the morning. And remember, tomorrow is another day," she said tauntingly. Wyatt smiled in response and watched her walk out, a touch of admiration in his gaze it seemed to Bliss. Then again, a man had to be blind not to appreciate Diana's perfect form, Bliss mused to herself. As Diana passed her in the corridor, she stopped her.

"Diana, can I see you a moment?"

"Sure, what is it?"

"Whatever you do tomorrow, please try to pick someone you have some feelings for, and if it's no one, pick no one. It's been done before on these reality shows," Bliss begged.

"What are you babbling about?"

"Marriage. It's not a joke or a game."

"You think I don't know about marriage?" Diana countered, sounding suddenly older and harder than her twenty-one years. "Do you know how many of my friends' dads have hit on me?" Bliss reacted stunned. "That never happened to you, huh? Lucky you," Diana continued. "The bottom line is, sooner or later every man ignores his wife, the same way Dad ignores and tolerates Mom. Well, I'm never going to let that happen to me because whatever my husband does, the world is going to love me." Bliss knew her sister's defiance was born of pain and disillusionment.

"Anything else?" Diana challenged.

"No, that was all, good luck tomorrow," Bliss offered gently.

"I'm not the one who needs luck," Diana tossed out before sauntering down the long, dark hall. Bliss peeked back into the library.

To her surprise, Dario and Wyatt huddled, deep in conversation. She withdrew her head. Wyatt hadn't noticed her and it was perhaps for the best. When she finally broke her run of celibacy, she wanted to take her time with her lover, not have him rush off to get a proper night's sleep before an early morning shoot. *Anticipation will only make the eventual release more exquisite,* she reasoned as she made her way back to her room.

chapter thirty-six

The sun shone brightly on the list field where the jousting tournament would begin in moments. Some three hundred spectators, dressed in pseudomedieval garb, like extras from a Robin Hood remake, had gathered in the stands under crenellated canopies. From the castle tower, a standard billowed in the breeze. Erected for the occasion, it was white, embroidered with a sequined rose and inscribed with the words *The Virgin* in an Elizabethan script. Bella and Bliss sat with Harold, Victoria, Charlotte, and Forsythia, whose wig formed a furry halo beneath her high-pointed medieval hat. One row behind them, Sue, dressed like a latter-day Maid Marian, chewed on a toothpick, legs akimbo under her long skirt. Charlotte's high-necked, shape-concealing gown made the previous night's polka-dot affair look like a disco dress. Victoria struck Bliss as the only one among them who managed not to look utterly ridiculous. With the white wimple framing her face, she cut as delicate and ethereal a figure as the Black Virgin of Guadalupe. Bliss caught sight of Dario, who was down on the field, having resumed his original line of work as sports cameraman for the occasion. He had taken on the most dangerous duty: close-ups on the horses and riders while they charged. Spotting Bliss, he stifled a laugh. She couldn't help but offer a wan smile in return. She did look like a frustrated actress moonlighting at a Renaissance fair theme park in suburban New Jersey and had the disgruntled attitude to match. A bugle sounded.

"It's about to begin," Forsythia cried, squeezing Harold's hand so hard he winced. She remained oblivious to his pain. The gesture seemed to Bliss a fitting metaphor for their entire marriage.

The three suitors trooped out onto the field on their mounts. Beowulf was red faced from the heat. Alistair, whose paunch strained the links of his armor, looked smug yet bewildered. Paul, ever the politician, remained the picture of cool composure. His confidence had only ballooned in the wake of the previous night's triumph. Like Victoria, his perfectly symmetrical bone structure made up for the ludicrousness of his costume. As Alistair trotted by, his mother and father waved enthusiastically. They sat at a remove from the Harcourts, Lady Grant-Smyth objecting to an association with this mixed-race family, yet unwilling to pass up another opportunity to shine in the television sun. Again Sir Wallace Grant-Smyth clearly didn't share his wife's distaste for the dusky of the earth. On the contrary, he seemed to have quite an eye for the brown ladies. Bliss caught him leering at a comely African girl sitting a few rows away from him as he took greedy gulps from the silver flask he'd tucked in the folds of his costume.

Wyatt spoke from a box erected above the field.

"Welcome to the ultimate contest to win the hand of the Virgin: the jousting tournament. Here to offer commentary and explain the rules is an expert in all things medieval, Sir William De Haliburton."

The crowd applauded politely.

"Thank you, ladies and gentlemen," Sir William mumbled in the half-garbled drawl of the upper-crust Englishman who's exceeded his day's allotment of Bombay gin.

"Today, on this historic plain, three knights will vie as of old for the love of a lady fair," Sir William announced.

"Would that she were fairer," Lady Grant-Smyth stated audibly. Forsythia stared at her, seething and ready to pounce. Harold restrained her.

"Let's not come to blows," he pleaded, "the jousters are on the field."

"She's insulting our child. Our beautiful, precious child."

"It's no matter, she's a half-witted parvenu," Harold said.

"The contest will be met in twos," Sir William continued. "The knights shall attempt to unhorse one another. The last two standing will then duel it out with swords. He who fells his opponent will win the hand of . . ." Sir William had clearly lost his train of thought. Expert actor that he was, Wyatt jumped in.

"The Virgin, so let's bring her out!" he yelled.

The trumpets sounded again and Diana appeared at the top of the stands, resplendent in the white chiffon dress she'd worn in her introductory video. The crowd gasped at her beauty. As she descended the stairs, aided by a page and followed by two buxom ladies in waiting holding her train, people reached out, eager to touch her hand or the hem of her garment.

"Look at her," Forsythia exclaimed, near tears, "she's a real princess. They adore her! Eat your heart out, Kate Middle-Class."

As the crowd began to chant "Vir-gin! Vir-gin!! Vir-gin!!!" Forsythia looked back triumphantly at Alistair's bigoted mother.

"I suppose Alistair will lighten up the children, and she is pretty," Lady Grant-Smyth conceded to her husband, who was still too consumed trying to catch the eye of his African cutie to care.

Bliss wondered if the ladies in waiting, who with their store-bought breasts and collagen-plumped lips looked more like they were about to execute a pole dance than carry the train of a lady pure, were Dario's leftovers from the night before. Was being extras their reward for a job well done? *Why am I even thinking of that?* she scolded herself, but she couldn't put the image of him and his pained expression two nights before out of her mind.

"No fair," Charlotte complained. "I shoulda been a lady in waiting, instead of being stuck here. Who's going to see me?"

"You'll have plenty of attention at the wedding," Forsythia admonished her.

Diana made her way through the adoring throng to the front of the stands and took her seat in a special box right in the middle.

"And now, the parading of the knights before the maiden's box," Sir William bellowed.

"Am I the only one catching the writer's double entendres?" Bliss wondered aloud to Victoria, who playfully smacked her arm. One by one, the suitors filed past Diana, each bowing on horseback when he reached her. Each man had been given a coat of arms for the occasion. Paul's shield bore a mule and a gavel in reference to his family's emancipation and career in law. Beowulf's bore an Xbox, his favorite gadget. Alistair wore the coat of arms his father had designed when he'd been knighted. It featured a wild boar, a fox, and a cornucopia beneath a coronet symbolizing strength, determination, and cleverness yielding fruits of glory.

"It should be a shopping cart filled with ham and eggs," Harold quipped. "After all they are 'in markets': supermarkets."

The trumpets blared again.

"And now, the order of battle will be determined by the toss of a coin," Sir William proclaimed.

Diana rose majestically and moved to the edge of her box.

"Heads or tails," she challenged Paul.

"Tails," he called out in his cocky tenor.

Diana tossed the coin expertly. Bliss surmised that other than beautifying herself, she must have spent the better part of the previous day practicing the toss and catch. Given her days as an expert baton twirler, she could have done it and added a pirouette.

"Heads," Diana cried.

"Knight Paul Daniels the Fourth of the Mule and Gavel, withdraw," William bellowed.

Sure enough, on the next toss, Diana did a spin. The crowd went wild. She shimmied with less-than-virginal gusto, then remembered the need for maidenly decorum.

"The battle is hereby joined between Knight Beowulf Jones of the Internet, and Knight Alistair Grant-Smyth of Penny Wise Foods and Soylogna," William declaimed the names with all the solemnity of one announcing the arrival of noble dignitaries at court.

Beowulf bowed low to Diana and cried out to her on the stands.

"I hope to win, my lady fair!" His sincerity touched Bliss. While she found the entire display ridiculous, Beowulf still struck her the most likeable and deserving.

"It should be noted that Beowulf Jones wears a hair shirt under his armor, his penance for breaking the vow of chastity required in the contest. He's worn it everywhere for the past months, except, he tells me, the shower," Wyatt announced to camera. "Now, over to you, Sir William, take it away." Wyatt descended the steps and moved off.

"Knights to your stations," William called. Beowulf and Alistair rode away from each other, taking up places on either side of a wooden rail. They each donned their helmets, and closed their visors, hiding their faces from view. Diana nodded to Sir William, who in turn nodded to the buglers to blow their horns. The crowd froze in anticipation. Alistair dug his heels into his horse's sides. Beowulf followed suit and they charged toward each other, lances pointing forward. Alistair's balance was uncertain and he looked ungainly on the horse. Beowulf, by contrast, had a newfound grace, moving in perfect unison with his steed. Galloping past Alistair, he unseated him handily. The crowd gasped at the fall, then roared its applause once they saw Alistair stagger to his feet.

"Man down," Sir William called. "The Knight of Penny Wise Foods and Soylogna is hereby eliminated."

Lady Grant-Smyth sank dejectedly into her seat.

Forsythia's lower lip quavered. "We've lost the baronet," she lamented.

"Good riddance," Harold grumbled. "Diana would have made mincemeat of the boy. Look at him."

"So now he lost and has to go home?" Bella asked her mother.

"Yes, it's curtains for him."

"Bye, bye," Bella waved.

Bliss found herself secretly rooting for the underdog, Beowulf.

"Now, we summon Knight Paul Daniels the Fourth of the Gavel and Mule to the field!"

Paul strode forth, clearly the best equestrian in the group. His horse responded to his every prompt like a pliant female. He rode right up to the box, stood up in his stirrups, and extended his hand to Diana. As she gave him hers, he bowed and kissed it. The crowd cheered and let out titillated cries of "Ooh." Diana raised the right side of her mouth in a slightly lascivious smile.

"Knights, to your places," Sir William commanded.

Paul and Beowulf each rode to their end of the field and donned their helmets. The bugle sounded and they charged, Paul digging his spurs into his mount and driving her to go faster and faster. He reached Beowulf before the latter had the chance to make it a third of the way toward the center. He aimed his lance at his arm, struck him, but failed to unseat him.

"That's cheating," Bliss cried. "He's supposed to strike him on the chest." She looked to Sir William, who scanned the countryside distractedly. *He'd probably taken the gig for the day in his capacity as local celebrity and to pay for a few tiles on the roof of his own stately yet crumbling home,* she thought to herself.

The riders charged toward each other again. With renewed determination, Beowulf drove his mount full tilt. He reached Paul, struck him right in the chest, and knocked him off his mare. Bliss jumped out of her seat and cheered. Others in the crowd followed suit. Forsythia looked less than pleased, and Diana sat frowning.

"Now for the sword fight," Sir William declared.

Beowulf was about to dismount when a knight all in black and wearing his visor galloped toward him from the middle of the field.

"Look, Mama, another knight!" Bella called out. People in the crowd began to ask, "Who's that?" Sir William pulled out a pair of binoculars.

"There appears to be a fourth unscheduled contestant," he commented. Forsythia looked to Sue, who shrugged. Diana sat up, preening as the horseman bowed to her. She nodded in return.

"Fair lady, do you accept this entrant?"

"I do," Diana said eagerly, leaning forward in her seat with renewed interest and hope.

"But who is he?" Forsythia asked. "We only had three, now we have four. Maybe he's richer than the rest!" she conjectured gleefully. "The network never told us about this."

"Papa, what's going on?" Bliss asked. "If this guy wins, does she really have to marry him without even knowing him? And who is he? This is insane."

"Why should anything surprise us?" Harold sighed.

The bugle sounded, the knights took their places, and charged toward each other. Beowulf, tired from the last two rounds, had a less steady seat. As he approached his opponent, Diana called out "Careful, Beowulf!!" He turned to look at the object of his adoration and in that moment, the Black Knight struck him full in the chest. He tumbled to the ground.

"Someone should make sure he's all right!" Bliss called out. She was relieved to see him struggle to his feet. He bowed low to Diana and unsheathed his sword. The Black Knight jumped off his gelding, and pulled out his weapon.

"And NOW for the sword fight!" Sir William declared. The Black Knight assumed the en garde position, one arm up behind him. Beowulf loomed over him and thrust his sword forward. The Black Knight parried with his blade and agilely jumped to the other side of Beowulf. The latter turned awkwardly, leaving his chest wide open. The Black Knight lunged, sticking his sword right in the center of Beowulf's armor and scratching an *X*. The crowd roared. Diana jumped up, applauding furiously.

"Touché!" Sir William called out, with a bit of a delay. "The Black Knight is the victor! And to the victor goes the Virgin!!!" All around Bliss, Victoria, Bella, and Harold, the spectators leapt to their feet, screaming, "Go Black Knight, go Black Knight!!!" Bliss wondered how they could cheer a perfect stranger who could be Satan himself for all they knew. Beowulf knelt before Diana's box and extended his sword to her. She took it half-heartedly and watched him as he dejectedly led his horse off the field. The Black Knight got back astride his horse and rode directly toward Diana. The crowd rustled with excitement.

"But who is he?" Forsythia screeched.

As he approached, the Black Knight recited without removing his helmet or lifting his visor: "'Come live with me and be my love,/ And we will all the pleasures prove,/ That hills and valleys, dale and field, and all the craggy mountains yields.'"

Diana's chest rose and fell in step with her quickening heartbeat. She stood up as he approached. Bliss tried to place the voice, as it sounded somewhat familiar though purposefully deepened.

"'The shepherd swains shall dance and sing/ For thy delight each May-morning:/ If these delights thy mind may move.'"

He stopped directly in front of Diana and added, "Then live with me and be my love."

In a swift gesture, he whipped off his helmet.

"It's Wyatt, the host!!!" Forsythia screamed. The audience gasped, applauded, and cheered. Victoria and Bliss sat frozen in shock. Sue Minors chomped away at her toothpick and tossed off a nonchalant, "Son of a gun."

"Mommy, isn't that the game show hoster?" Bella asked.

"Yes," Bliss managed to say, her mind running through the events of the previous nights and her near coitus with him. He had been prepared to bed her while planning to wed her sister.

"What's going on?" Victoria asked. Bliss had no answer and was certainly too embarrassed to share her misadventures.

"Ladies and gentlemen, it is most unusual, but not unprecedented for a knight to enter the fray belatedly. Sir, what are your intentions toward this lady fair?" Sir William announced.

"To make her my wife, if she'll have me."

"My lady?" Sir William asked.

"I will!" Something in Diana's tone of certainty stung Bliss. She and Wyatt had been plotting this for some time. She searched the field for

Dario. He had put down his steady cam and was directing the others, seemingly unperturbed by this supposedly unforeseen turn of events.

"You may exact a kiss from the lady fair," Sir William announced (prompted by Punch). As Wyatt leaned in for a deep kiss with Diana, the crowd erupted in another wild standing ovation. Forsythia jumped up and down with joy, as Harold stood stoically by. Victoria put her arm comfortingly around Bliss as the latter marveled at her deep empathy when she didn't even know the half of it.

"How can you let this happen?" Bliss challenged Sue. The latter shrugged.

"America will love it, so get over it. You think this is bad, you should watch *The Bachelor*. Twenty-five babes and one guy in a hot tub."

"They're in love!!!" Forsythia crowed. "I always liked him."

Victoria and Bliss looked at each other in horror. "In love?" they both asked flabbergasted.

"She doesn't know the meaning of the word," Victoria said sadly.

Bliss looked over at her father who applauded like an automaton, resigned yet again to the unfortunate unfolding of events beyond his control.

chapter thirty-seven

Bliss had passed the afternoon in a state of shock. She'd forced herself to focus on being in the moment with Bella who loved exploring what to her seemed a fairyland. Bliss didn't have the heart to explain the tragic fate of the castle's most famous occupant, Anne Boleyn. Life would teach her soon enough that love and marriage came at a price, hopefully one less dire. She tried to make sense of her own feelings. She could not claim to be in *love* with Wyatt. It was *like* and attraction. She suffered more than anything from a bruised ego and a sense of betrayal. It was depressing to her how duplicitous human beings could be. Starting with her sister, was she perpetrator or pawn? She'd known nothing of Bliss's flirtation with Wyatt, but had she participated in a plot? Was this what she had meant when she had said the world would love her? One thing about her was certain, in the words of Moss Hart, Diana would be with a man "through thick," then drop him like last year's platform shoes if the going ever got rough, or if a better opportunity came along.

With Bella ensconced in the library with her grandfather, Bliss combed the castle for the architect of the entire fiasco: Dario. After searching several rooms, and making her way down wood-paneled passages, passing five-hundred-year-old portraits of men and women whose eyes seemed to follow her, she finally found him outside on the tower. The sun was just setting on this rare rainless day, casting a golden glow on the expanse of rolling green hills below. She watched Dario instructing the cameramen on the precise angle at which to install equipment for the next day's shoot: sunrise on Hever Castle. It would no doubt be shown with accompanying pulse-quickening music and a voice-over by Wyatt, to be recorded later at a sound studio in Los Angeles, describing the scene. She could see the headlines now before this climactic episode aired: REVERSAL OF VIRGIN. Perhaps someone from the crew would sell the story in advance to *Star* or *The Enquirer.* Sue and Dario would have to keep an eye on crew members suddenly driving expensive new cars. Dario spotted Bliss and instructed the crew to take five. He strode directly toward her.

"Are you okay?" he asked.

Her disgust was complete. *What a rank hypocrite he is,* she thought to herself. Trying to contain her bile, she responded.

"So now you're an actor too? Are you going to take Wyatt's place as the host of the show?"

"What are you talking about?"

"Don't tell me you didn't know. How else would he have been so prepared with the costume. . . ."

Dario looked away.

"You did, didn't you?" she hectored.

"I can't answer that."

"You mean you won't."

"Why do you care so much, anyway? Paul, Beowulf, Alistair, Wyatt, they're all just stepping-stones for your sister."

"How dare you!" she said with utter indignation, though of course she knew he was absolutely right. Nonetheless, they were her family, hers to insult, not his.

"I apologize," he said. "But you're upset because he's not who you thought he was."

Again, he'd read her thoughts, but she was far too proud to admit it. She just looked at Dario, defiant in her stubborn refusal to admit the truth.

"And maybe you had plans of your own . . ." he added almost as though he was fishing.

"I had no plans!! And it's no business of yours if I did. But you helping to sell my sister into marriage for ratings is my business. Where do you draw the line? What's next, live executions?"

"I didn't do it for ratings!" he yelled, then realized he'd said too much.

"At least that's something of an admission," she said, crossing her arms with satisfaction.

"I'm not admitting or explaining anything. Especially to you. You've made it very clear you don't listen to what I say. There were reasons. And if you really want to know the truth, you may want to ask Wyatt and your baby sister. They deserve each other," he added, visibly pained.

Bliss regretted the strength of her attack. Like Manuel's secret affair and her divorce, these events had made her question her most basic instincts about people. She'd had misgivings about Wyatt all along, but had chosen to ignore them to her detriment. Was she now misinterpreting Dario? Before she had a chance to question him further, or to apologize for her accusations if indeed they were unfounded, he had walked back over to the parapet and was watching the sun sink behind purple and pink clouds. Silhouetted against the early evening sky, Dario struck her as beautiful and as an enigma.

chapter thirty-eight

Bliss made her way down the grand second-floor hallway that led to her room. As she looked up at the vaulted ceilings, she tried to make sense of Dario's irritatingly sphinxlike responses, his brimming anger, and the wounded look in his eyes. Clearly he had known about Wyatt's usurpation plot in advance. How could he have condoned it? Had it been his idea? Just as she approached the coffered door to her room and inserted the ancient iron key in its hole, she saw a slim, androgynous figure emerge from the room next door, Victoria's room. As the person stopped to tuck their shirttail in their pants, she recognized Punch and stopped in her tracks. Punch look flustered and cast nervous glances down the hall. She had the furtive air of someone who'd just committed a transgression and didn't want to be caught. Bliss checked the number of her room again. Yes, indeed, it was Hever 114 and she wasn't dreaming: there was a woman coming out of her sister's room, rearranging her disheveled clothes and hair. She was beginning to relate to Socrates's signature quotation: "All that I know is that I know nothing." What other surprises would the coming days yield? Would her mother run off with Alistair's jungle-fevered father and become Lady Smyth-Biscuit-Tin?

She snapped out of her shock to open her door, not wanting to embarrass Punch, but the latter turned to walk in her direction. An encounter was inevitable. Upon spotting Bliss, Punch flushed beet red and stopped, then resumed her progress, attempting to assume an air of casualness. She waved halfheartedly, then as she neared Bliss let out an awkward "How's it going?" and without waiting for an answer, scurried down the hall. Bliss had wanted to speak to Victoria anyway about her general confusion, but now she *had* to see her. She braced herself and knocked on the door. After a few long moments, Victoria's newly languid voice called "Come in."

Bliss entered to find her sister reclined on the bed, her blouse unbuttoned, looking dreamily out of the leaded-glass windows. Her slight state of undress confirmed what had happened. Bliss hesitated to broach the subject. It had occurred to her more than once over the years that her sister might indeed be gay. Her give-this-woman-a-suppository stiffness in the presence of even the most desirable men was palpable and sometimes painful to witness. Bliss had ultimately concluded that her sister belonged to that rarest of human breeds: the asexual woman. Now, though, seeing her sprawled on the bed like an odalisque in a Manet, or one of Boucher's naked *courtisanes,* she realized how wrong she'd been. Hers was the face of postcoital contentment, an expression Bliss had not worn for 512 interminable days and nights. She didn't dare take another step into the room, but waited for Victoria to speak. The latter turned to her at last.

"Now I know," Victoria said with the unshakable calm that comes from facing one's truth at last. Bliss gingerly sat at the edge of her bed, and took Victoria's hand. The latter smiled at her. Then all at once, large tears began to roll down Victoria's cheeks. She sat up and threw her arms around Bliss, quaking. Hers were not tears of sorrow, but of deep gratitude and relief. Bliss rocked her gently back and forth.

"What happened?" she asked softly.

"Punch came to help with my computer. I couldn't get a signal. Maybe I invited her on purpose. Did I? Anyway, she was so nice, and leaning over me, guiding my hand and moving the mouse. Then her hand traveled up my arm. And it was like an electric current went through me."

"I know that feeling," Bliss affirmed, longingly.

"I pulled away, so she stopped, but then, I leaned back into her. It was like she was waiting to see what I wanted. She could feel me get comfortable, and so she started caressing me again," Victoria said, reliving the moment as she ran her own hand over her arm. "Then she leaned down and kissed my neck." She stopped with eyes closed, savoring the memory.

"Then she got to my mouth, and she brushed her lips against mine, back and forth a few times, then she stopped and I opened my mouth. . . ." Victoria reopened her eyes. "It was Heaven."

"So you made love," Bliss added.

"No, that was the most beautiful part. We started to, but then, I realized I wanted Missy. I want Missy to be my first," Victoria stated simply.

"Missy? Five kids, ten horses, and three dogs Missy?" Bliss queried, stunned. Victoria nodded *Yes.*

"Does she have any idea you feel this way about her?" Bliss asked.

"No. We've always been just friends, but the truth is, I've always loved her."

"When are you going to tell her?"

"As soon as I get home, right after I break it off with Dean."

Bliss and Victoria sat on the bed, each lost in her own thoughts. Bliss remembered all too well the feeling of wanting to share one's whole self with someone for the first time, to merge with them body and soul. It was what she'd felt for Manuel, the first and only man she'd ever known. The sensation was overwhelming, grand, precious, and elusive. If not cherished, it would be dashed by life. As Bliss admitted to herself she might never feel it again, she rejoiced in Victoria's discovery of one of life's miracles. She also felt a pang of sadness that Victoria had had to suppress it for so long.

"Do you think you always knew?" she asked.

"Maybe, I was just so scared, and busy. I guess it took being engaged to admit to myself what I really want. What I've wanted all along.

But now, I'm done hiding, from life and love," she declared, standing up and walking to the window. She threw it open and drank in the night air like a coed on spring break downing a jug of beer.

"I love Missy," she said matter-of-factly. "I love Missy!" she shouted out into the night. Bliss ran to the window and shut it.

"Are you forgetting that Mom is right next door?"

"Oh," Victoria said, suddenly embarrassed.

"Don't get me wrong. I want you to tell her the truth, and the sooner the better. But I don't think you want her finding out this way."

"No," Victoria said. Her exhilaration turned to worry. "What will she say?" she asked, sounding like a panicked teen afraid to tell her parents she's pregnant. Bliss imagined Forsythia hearing the news. She would either faint on the spot or let out a bloodcurdling scream to rival the wildest of banshees, then catalog all the reasons Victoria couldn't, shouldn't, and wouldn't be gay if she had anything to do with it. She'd look up one of those deprogramming camps run by Christian fundamentalists that yielded lobotomized-looking graduates giving robotic testimonials about their newfound happiness. Oh, it would not be pretty.

"Let's think about that tomorrow," Bliss suggested. "She doesn't need to know till we get back to the States."

"Okay. You're right. Why ruin this trip?" Victoria wept anew, this time with apprehension and sadness. "I've tried all of my life to be perfect," she admitted.

"And you are," Bliss insisted, "just as you are. Papa will understand. And when you do tell Mum, I'll be right there beside you. Always."

"It's going to be okay," Victoria affirmed, more to muster her courage than out of real conviction.

She and Bliss hugged, each praying that it would be.

chapter thirty-nine

Victoria walked into the heat room at the Mandarin Oriental Hotel and to her relief saw Missy sitting alone in the whirlpool, slumbering. She allowed herself to take in the planes of her face; the beauty of her milky skin, beading with sweat; her delicate, rosy lips with a hint of plumpness at the center. She could imagine their softness against her neck. She knelt beside her, admiring the fall of her baby-fine hair. She raised a hand to brush the hair back and Missy opened her eyes and sat up, startled. Victoria sprang back up to her feet.

"Sorry, I didn't mean to scare you," she said, suddenly feeling embarrassed and caught. Almost as soon as she'd gotten back from England, she'd arranged this meeting to confess all to Missy but suddenly felt it was in incredibly poor taste. What if Missy reacted in utter disgust? On top of it all, for the first time, Victoria wasn't wearing her Speedo one-piece. Underneath her fluffy robin's-egg-blue robe, she was naked and newly waxed. Missy would feel utterly hijacked. Their years of acquaintanceship had inspired her to jump the gun. She had selected this spot because it was their usual hangout, not thinking how seductive an environment it was. She was mortified at her own clumsiness. She fastened her robe tighter.

"What are you doing?" Missy asked, laughing her guttural laugh, "Get in!" Victoria hesitated.

"What's wrong with you? I've seen it before," Missy teased. *No you haven't,* Victoria thought to herself. *Not like this.* She walked to the wall of hooks and with her back to Missy removed her robe.

"Going commando, I see. Finally," Missy commented, moving deeper into the pool.

Victoria slowly and deliberately walked in step by marble step. The water was warm and soothing. Her nipples were erect with anticipation. She hoped Missy wouldn't take notice. To her relief, she seemed oblivious to her arousal.

Victoria had never allowed herself to feel it, or let her mind fantasize about what she and Missy would do as lovers. Now that she'd admitted her longing to herself, every inch of Missy's person called to her, from her rounded shoulders, to her strong square hands. Yet, she reminded herself, the attraction was on her side. Once she told Missy the truth, she was likely to leap out of the whirlpool and hightail it to the dressing room, never to be seen again.

"What's up with you today?" Missy chided.

"I have a lot on my mind," Victoria explained, swallowing hard and thrilled she didn't have a penis that would give it all away in a four-star salute.

"Well, get in here and relax," Missy ordered, grabbing her by the hand. Victoria clutched her hand tightly. Missy looked at her in surprise. Victoria instantly let go.

"So, how are the wedding plans going?" Missy asked.

"Diana's almost all set. They're having it in Rome."

"I'm talking about yours."

"I broke it off with Dean."

"I'm sorry. No, actually, I'm not. He was a stiff. In the wrong ways. Sorry, hope I'm not offending you."

"It wasn't his fault," Victoria explained. "You see, I'm in love with someone else."

"Great! Who?" Missy asked, utterly unsuspecting. Victoria bit her lip and winced. She prayed she wouldn't lose her friend forever. She considered not telling her, but couldn't withhold the truth any longer.

Looking Missy directly in the eye, she softly said, "You." She instantly closed her eyes, dreading rejection. For moments that stretched on like an eternity, only a deafening silence greeted her. She dared to reopen her eyes. Missy sat slack-jawed with shock. *You fool,* Victoria told herself. *You've just lost everything, even the friendship. You should have kept your mouth shut, taken your secret to your grave. The woman has five children, why would she want you?*

"I'm sorry. Forgive me for saying anything," Victoria blurted, rising out of the tub, suddenly mortified at her nakedness and crouching to hide it.

"Stop," Missy commanded. "Come back," she requested more gently. Victoria slowly sat back down, not daring to look her in the eye, but staring at the wall straight ahead, straining to find a spot in the marble on which to focus.

"I need to get this straight, no pun intended, you think you're in love with me?"

"I know I am," Victoria admitted. "I always have been."

"Since when?" Missy asked, incredulous.

"Since the first day at Madeira, when I saw you get out of your parents' Volvo, laughing, with a saddle tossed over your arm. You were everything I wasn't: nonchalant, free. I was so stiff, so . . . terrified of everything. I think I knew then, but I just stuffed it down. And became your friend. I'm sorry to embarrass you," she said, looking up to face Missy at last. "And I'll understand if you can't go on being my friend."

"Now let's not get crazy. As your friend, you're stuck with me. As for the rest . . . I've never thought of it," she said, her voice trailing. Suddenly she turned to Victoria and said, "Kiss me."

"What?" Victoria asked, recoiling.

"Come on. That's what you came here for. Let's give it a try." Victoria sat frozen.

"Missy, not like this," she objected.

"Oh for goodness sake," Missy protested. Leaning over, she planted her lips on Victoria's. The latter opened her mouth to receive Missy's tongue, and ran her right hand down the length of Missy's hair. As she did so, Missy shuddered. The kiss continued, at first languorous, then hungrier and more insistent. At last, Missy pulled away for a moment and studied Victoria's face. They stared at each other, each processing her own arousal. Missy delicately traced the outline of Victoria's heart-shaped mouth with her index finger. Victoria lay her cheek in the palm of Missy's strong hand. She ran her finger down Missy's cheek. Missy's nostrils flared as she savored the pleasant sensation.

"Have you ever . . ." Missy hinted. Victoria shook her head *no.*

"Me neither. So we're both virgins." They chuckled.

Victoria looked at her hopefully and caressed her cheek again, this time with the palm of her hand. Suddenly instinct took over and she leaned in, brushing the inside of Missy's arm with her left hand. Missy flinched with arousal.

"What are they going to say at the farm?" she whispered, leaning in, fully prepared to surrender to the moment. Victoria moved closer, wrapping her legs around Missy's waist and inching her face toward hers. She brushed her nose against Missy's. They melted into each other in the warm waters of the hot tub.

chapter forty

The Harcourts had gathered for dinner at home. Diana sat sipping her cream of mushroom soup while reviewing sketches of potential wedding gowns.

"Too Kate Middleton," she said, tossing one rendering to the ground. "Too Grace Kelly," she said, discarding another. "Too Jacqueline Bouvier. I want one that screams 'ME!!!'" she cried impatiently.

Victoria entered through the front door.

"Sorry I'm late," she said, slipping into her usual seat. Bliss smiled at her encouragingly.

"You're just in time," Forsythia reassured her. "We're looking at wedding gowns," she added eagerly. Victoria shuddered, then composed herself.

"Where's Dean?" her mother asked.

"He couldn't make it," Victoria said abruptly. "Papa, could you fill my soup bowl please?" Bliss tried to catch her eye to offer more encouragement but Victoria did her best to avoid connecting with anyone. Forsythia returned to the subject at hand.

"I think you should change twice, and go with the designers who did Lady Diana's dress. That was splendid!"

Harold groaned.

"When's Daddy getting married?" Bella asked Bliss. An awkward silence followed as everyone around the table stared at Bliss, awaiting a response.

"Soon, I think, " Bliss answered hesitantly.

"Am I going?" Bella asked.

"I'm not sure, sweetheart," Bliss answered.

"Why not?" Bella asked. *Because I may have completely screwed it up for you,* Bliss thought to herself. She had yet to send an email of apology to Manuel, or to call. Other than his usual taped campaign bulletins, he hadn't phoned Bliss either since the dreadful scene in the garden. It was a relief to her not to deal with him, with hearing his voice and having to remain stoic, but she had to admit to herself that she was not helping her daughter. However, she could only deal with one family crisis at a time. At the moment, she had to help Victoria.

"Victoria, you don't have a bust so you should take this Kate Middleton style gown," Forsythia suggested. "Did you look over the list of venues I sent you? The show might still consider a double wedding if you would commit in time."

"There isn't going to be a wedding!" Victoria insisted vehemently. Everyone looked up from their soup bowl. If there'd been a family dog, he would certainly have pricked up his ears.

"What are you talking about, Queen Victoria Harcourt?" Forsythia demanded to know in her most imperious tone. Each daughter's first name was the title of nobility associated with her Windsor name, thus Diana was "Princess"; Charlotte "Queen Consort"; and Bliss, whose real name was Elizabeth, "Queen." Harold had acquiesced to this folly but would not stand to watch his wife steamroll their eldest today. He bided his time to jump in and defend her.

"I'm not getting married," Victoria repeated.

"I beg your pardon? And why ever not this time?"

"Because I don't love him!" Victoria cried.

"Since when is that a reason not to marry someone?" Forsythia asked, flabbergasted.

"Since I realized I love Missy!!! And she loves me. And we always have."

Everyone at the table sat stock-still. *When did you tell her,* Bliss wanted to ask, but it wasn't the moment to delve into the details. For the second time in Bliss's memory, her mother sat dumbfounded. Forsythia held her spoon poised above her soup bowl, immobilized by what she'd just heard. Diana broke the silence.

"So you're a lesbian?" she asked, in a tone of utter disgust. Forsythia stared down at her soup, not deigning to look at Victoria, and began furiously spooning it into her mouth. Harold, Charlotte, and Bliss awaited the response to Diana's question. Bella wanted to ask, *What's a lesbian?* but sensed from the tension in the room that she'd better refrain. Bliss looked at Victoria encouragingly. Squaring her shoulders, Victoria stood up.

"Yes, I'm a lesbian," she declared, holding her head high. Charlotte pumped her fist in the air in a sign of victory and cheered "Yes!" relieved that now the spotlight of opprobrium would no longer shine on her. There was a new black sheep in the family. Diana's face contorted into an expression of revulsion.

"Ugh, how could you?" she said, her voice dripping contempt. Victoria looked at her devastated, then stared at her mother, who continued to look down, into the depths of her soup bowl, refusing to acknowledge the revelation. Bliss surmised that she was using her ostrich tactic: Forsythia believed if she ignored something long enough, she could make it disappear. It was how she had handled the snide racial comments of her neighbors over the years. The strategy had served as an effective armor against prejudice, but was deadly to her daughters.

"It's not a choice, Didi," Bliss admonished her sister.

"Mother, aren't you going to say something?" Victoria dared to ask.

Forsythia wiped her mouth and, keeping her gaze fixed on the window and away from Victoria, spoke with deliberate calm.

"After supper, I will phone Sue Minors to tell her the good news that there will be two weddings in Rome. You will wear the Victorian-style

Kate Middleton dress. It suits your figure. You have no bust and it will look beautiful on you. You're much prettier than Kate Middleton is."

"Mother, I'm not getting married, not to Dean anyway. If I marry anyone it will be Missy," Victoria responded, gently but firmly.

"Can a lady marry another lady?" Bella inquired, confused.

"Fortunately not!!! It's against the laws of God and man. And no child of mine will ever commit such a sin against all morals and decency! I raised you better than that!" Forsythia yelled, her Jamaican lilt asserting itself full tilt in her fury.

"Then I am no child of yours," Victoria retorted. Her mother looked at her, wounded. Bliss could sense her shock and terror at the rebellion of her most compliant child.

"I love you, Mother, but this is who I am. All my life, I was afraid to even admit it to myself. But it's the truth. And it's like being black, you can't just make it go away," Victoria added.

"Don't you ever compare this, this . . . deviant behavior to our heritage! It's a choice!"

"Then it's my choice!"

"Get out of this house!" Forsythia screamed. Harold stood up and threw his napkin down in frustration.

"That is enough, Forsythia. This is my house too and you will not kick any child of ours out of here."

"If this is what she chooses, she is no longer my child."

Diana vigorously nodded her approval. Bliss wanted to throttle her, but decided not to waste her time.

"Mom, listen to yourself. You can't mean that," she urged.

"Forsythia, apologize to our daughter now!" Harold demanded.

"I will not!!!! She renounced me. Now, I renounce her."

"You can't!" he shot back.

"Stop, stop. I'm going," Victoria pleaded.

"Stay!" Bliss begged her.

"No. I don't belong here." Victoria rose from her seat and rushed to the door, followed by Bliss.

"Victoria, Mum says a lot of things she doesn't mean."

"She means that. That's why I never wanted her to know. I tried so hard. Why do you think I was so perfect at everything, because I knew one day . . . don't worry. I'll be okay." Victoria looked back toward the dining room. Forsythia stared up at her with the fury of one betrayed. Victoria threw open the front door and rushed out.

"Well, now she can't come to Italy, that's for sure. I've lost a bridesmaid," Diana commented.

"Missy can come too, lesbians are in," Charlotte suggested.

"Stop using that term!" Forsythia yelled then resumed her air of calm control and continued to eat her soup.

"You will excuse me," Harold stated, heading toward the door.

"Where are you going?" Forsythia demanded to know.

"Out to find my daughter and make certain she's all right." With that, he exited the house. Forsythia stared at the door. Neither Bliss nor Diana dared to interrupt her silent musings. Bella sat calmly eating her food, not wanting to disturb the adults. After a long pause, Forsythia picked up the portfolio of gowns and began furiously leafing through it.

"Let's find your wedding dress, Didi," Forsythia insisted as tears rolled down her cheeks. Bliss had been ready to attack her mother with both barrels until she saw her crying. Her mother's obvious pain helped temper her own fury at Forsythia's narrow-minded, conditional love. She told herself that she couldn't drag Forsythia screaming into enlightenment, or badger her into understanding the truth. Nor could she stand by idly.

"Mum," she said gently, not certain where her words would lead her. "Please try to think of the courage it took Victoria to come here tonight and admit this all to you."

"Courage? She's an ungrateful child," Forsythia said mournfully.

"She's anything but that. She loves you and she wants to please you, but she has to live her life."

"Fine then, she can live it on her own. And with that other . . . person. Never cared for that girl."

"That's not what she wants, and that's not what you want either. When you reject her, you might as well reject all of us."

"Oh, Jesus help me, are you a . . ." Forsythia couldn't even bring herself to utter the word, "one of *them* too?"

"No, Mum, you can relax. Of all my *failings*, that's not one. But that's my sister you just threw out of the house. It's not love when you love people only when they turn out the way you want them to," she cried. Charlotte nodded in agreement. Forsythia couldn't even look at Bliss. Bliss waited, hoping her mother would say something, anything at all but Forsythia just pursed her lips.

"Okay then," Bliss said, steeling herself. "I'll stop wasting my breath." She walked back into the dining room.

"Bella, let's finish your dinner in the kitchen," she suggested.

"Okay, Mama," Bella assented.

Bliss looked back at her mother once more, but Forsythia had buried her head in the bridal-gown sketches.

chapter forty-one

Bliss mounted the listing staircase, holding Bella's Cinderella cup, one of the rare concessions to the Disney empire she had allowed. There were no Amelia Earhart sippy cups so she had little choice. It was SpongeBob or a Princess. As she approached her room, she was surprised to hear her mother's voice, reading a story.

"Goodness! How I've changed! I hardly recognize myself!" Forsythia exclaimed in a baby voice.

Bliss entered the room and found her mother sitting on Bella's bed, holding a well-worn copy of Hans Christian Andersen fairy tales she recalled from her own childhood. Its frayed jacket was comfortingly familiar. Bella looked up at her bespectacled grandmother with wonder as she continued.

The entire tableau was novel to Bliss, because Forsythia rarely ventured into her private lair. She was touched, in spite of herself, at this rare attempt on her mother's part to connect with the grandchild who represented none of what he had hoped for in her offspring, especially in the wake of what had transpired that evening.

"'The flight of swans winged north again and glided on to the pond. . . . Now he swam majestically with his fellow swans. One day, he heard children on the riverbank exclaim: "Look at that young swan! He's the finest of them all!" And he almost burst with happiness.'"

"Yay!" Bella cheered. "But how did the ugly duckling become a swan?" she asked, puzzled.

"Because he was a swan all along," Forsythia answered with a wink.

"You used to read that to Victoria and me when we were little," Bliss said quietly, putting a hand on her mother's shoulder.

"Yes, I did," Forsythia said, shutting the book. The mention of Victoria had clearly touched a nerve. Turning to Bella, she added, "In life, don't let people tell you who you are. Always remember you are a swan inside."

"Yes, Grandmamma," Bella said obediently.

"That's very good advice," Bliss acknowledged. Forsythia turned to her with what looked almost like gratitude, but said nothing. Giving Bella a peck on the forehead, she turned off the light by her bedside. Bliss knelt by her bed and kissed her tenderly on the cheek.

"Good night, my little toughie," she said.

"'Night, Mommy."

"I'll leave you," Forsythia offered, hastening out of the room.

"Mum, wait," Bliss called, following her out into the hall. She closed the bedroom door behind and caught her mother by the arm.

"Mom, I know this is hard for you, about Victoria, but she's not doing this on purpose to hurt you. And she's not gay because you didn't force her to wear enough frilly dresses when she was young."

"You don't understand," Forsythia said in the eerily calm voice that precedes an emotional storm.

"I do, Mum, I disagree with your point of view, but I know why you're upset."

Forsythia turned to face Bliss, her usual histrionics replaced by a mask of stoic self-control. Her aplomb was unsettling to Bliss if only because it was so unusual. She could feel the emotions raging beneath its surface.

"Chocolate drop, black bird, tar baby," Forsythia recited flatly. Bliss stared back blankly.

"What are you talking about, Mom?"

"And you think you understand?" Forsythia said, bitterness in her tone. "Those are just some of the names they used to call me when I was a little girl." Bliss placed her hand gently on her mother's forearm. Her mother's deep-brown skin contrasted vividly with the pale cream of hers. All her life she'd asked her about her childhood and been waved off as her mother launched into a frivolous soliloquy on manners or her latest doily. Finally, she'd stopped asking. Now at last, Forsythia was ready to share. Bliss listened intently.

"Every day, I prayed to God to take me away, someplace far away, where I could fly. When I was nineteen, he answered my prayer and got me to America."

"You got yourself here," Bliss corrected.

"Then, after I married your father, I dreamed of having beautiful girls who would grow up to have everything I didn't."

"And we do, Mum," Bliss said reassuringly, desperate to ask more about her years in Jamaica, but not daring to, lest her mother slam the emotional door shut in her face as she had throughout her youth.

"You've thrown it all away!" Forsythia cried in a tortured tone that startled Bliss.

"Mum," she started to object, sympathetically.

"You more than any of the others!!!" This took Bliss utterly by surprise. She'd always thought of herself as her mother's least favorite child.

"You had everything and you threw it away."

"Mum, say what you will, I don't regret Manuel."

"I'm not talking about him," Forsythia insisted.

"Who are—"

"Chauncey Gardner!" Bliss couldn't believe her ears. Chauncey Gardner, the little rich boy whose family had moved to their neighborhood from Boston and purchased the largest house in the area. He'd had a crush on Bliss when they were both eleven and had followed her home from school one day. As her mother appeared on their front stoop, he'd snickered, "Why is your maid all dressed up?"

"That's my mother," Bliss had corrected him.

"No, it can't be. She's a nigger. You're not a nigger," he'd insisted. Bliss had decked him, yelling, "No one is a nigger! But if my mother is, then I am too!"

"Why did you have to tell that boy I was your mother?" Forsythia asked. Bliss couldn't believe her ears. She stared at her mother in utter disbelief. In all these years, they'd never discussed the incident. But she remembered her mother pulling her off of Chauncey while she pummeled him and insisting she apologize. Bliss had tried to explain what he had said, but her mother had given her no opportunity. Bliss had refused to apologize and been exiled to her room for dinner for three days.

"That boy called you a nigger," Bliss said, her voice quavering as her own pain brimmed to the surface.

"So what?" Forsythia challenged. "He didn't need to know you were mine!"

"So then what, Mum, we could have married ten years later and I could have lived whitely ever after?" Bliss asked, trying to follow her mother's twisted thinking.

"It wasn't just him. I knew then that one day you'd throw it all away."

"All what away?" Bliss asked baffled.

"All that beauty! All your advantages! You could have gone to college and forgotten about us. You were at Yale!!! You could have had anyone!"

"Why would I want to forget all of you?"

"Because that's what it takes! I would have come to visit, but as something else. Your old nanny. Do you think Merle Oberon would have become a star if everyone knew she was Indian? No! So her mother worked as her maid. I would have done that for you!"

Bliss struggled to process the revelation. All those years she'd thought her mother hated her for being too tomboyish, outspoken, and unfeminine. Instead she'd been brokenhearted because she had placed her highest hopes on her, and Bliss had dashed them at every step.

There was a strange relief in knowing that for all its sad, self-loathing logic, what motivated her mother was fierce, blind love. Forsythia loved her to the point of self-abasement. Bliss would never be able to make her understand her pride in her heritage since her own had been beaten out of her so many years before. She could now, as a grown woman, forgive her shortcomings and, unlike those who'd raised and warped her, accept her as she was: wig, prejudices, pretensions, and all. She stepped toward Forsythia and wrapped her arms around her. As her mother wept on her chest, Bliss whispered in her ear: “I'm sorry, Mum.”

chapter forty-two

Three of Forsythia's prize etiquette pupils, handpicked by her, stood in a line, backs ramrod straight, holding bouquets of silk flowers. Forsythia, clad in a oatmeal-colored tweed suit dotted with a confetti of pastel colors, stood on the other side of the room, a pavé-diamond whistle in her hand, poised to give them their marching orders. The cameras rolled on the scene, supervised by Dario and observed by Bella, who sat outside of the camera's range on her grandfather's lap. Forsythia blew her bedazzled whistle to bring the young ladies to attention.

"Now, flower girls, remember that you are the first members of the wedding party—other than me—that the congregation will see, therefore no slouching, no twitching, no pouting, and no running." She turned on a metronome, pressed a button on a boom box, and "Pachelbel's Canon" began to play.

"Forward, march!" she yelled, as though commanding an army, rather than preparing a bridal party for its progress down the aisle of a church.

"Smile!!!" she barked. "Make the people feel welcome. Don't look around, Bridget," she yelled at a towheaded six-year-old, "you're not searching the pews for a husband!"

"Grampa, I want to go to Aunt Didi's wedding," Bella said to Harold, who put his finger to his lips. "Pleeaase, why won't Mommy let me go?"

"You're ruining our shot!" Desiree, a pint-sized dead ringer for Diana, snapped at her. "You can't go anyway because you're handicapped!"

"I am not," Bella snapped back, sliding off her grandfather's lap to confront the child.

"Cut!" Dario yelled.

At that moment, Bliss entered the front door, carrying her habitual load of library books.

"Girls, stop it. Desiree, don't talk to my grandchild that way," Forsythia warned the diminutive beauty.

"I'm just telling the truth. She is handicapped," Desiree answered, feigning innocence.

"I put you in this procession, and I'll take you out. I could replace you with Bella, if her mother will let me," Forsythia cautioned the child, her eyes narrowing. At the threat of losing her coveted television spot, Desiree, a veteran of many local baby beauty pageants, fell in line. Daphne, the oldest of the girls, couldn't resist the opportunity to torment Bella, the odd-looking little thorn in her side.

"Where's your daddy, anyway?" she taunted. "How come he never comes to see you?"

Bliss almost lunged for the girl. It took all her reserves to restrain herself. Bella burst into tears. Bliss ran to her and held her in her arms.

"You apologize to my grandchild this instant or the only way you'll see this wedding is on television, in your parents' tacky living room!" Forsythia snapped. Stunned and terrified, Daphne complied, then ran out of the room with a teary "Excuse me, going to the bathroom."

"That will teach her," Forsythia declared. "Does anyone else have a comment?" she threatened. Desiree and the third flower girl silently shook their heads.

"Well done, my dear," Harold said sincerely. Bliss looked up at her mother with gratitude. She'd expected her to make a snide comment conceding that Bliss had been mistaken in her choice of husband. It was not the Hallmark moment one would hope to have with one's mother, but it was progress.

"Let's take five, everyone," Dario commanded. Dario knelt beside Bliss and spoke low to Bella.

"Listen, princess, these girls don't know what they're talking about. Your Daddy is the luckiest dad in the whole wide world. Sometimes, grown-ups just get very busy. It sure doesn't mean they're not thinking about you." Bella stared at him, blinking back tears.

"If I had a little girl like you, I'd be thinking about her all the time, even if I was a million miles away," Dario added reassuringly.

"Even if you were on the moon?" Bella asked.

"Especially if I were on the moon, if I were in a different galaxy, or universe. I'll bet he's thinking about you right now. If you close your eyes, you can probably feel it," he added.

Bella followed his suggestion.

"I feel him," Bella said with her eyes closed. She opened them wide and wrapped her chubby arms around Dario. Harold approached.

"Bella, let's you and I go and read some Beatrix Potter."

"Hunca Munca the mouse?" Bella asked brightening.

"The very rodent I had in mind. Shall we go to my study?" Harold offered, taking her hand.

"Go on, I'll meet you in there," Bliss added. Bella made her way down the hall with her grandfather.

"Thank you," Bliss said to Dario, once Bella was out of earshot. He merely nodded his head. They'd barely spoken since the trip to England. Bliss felt embarrassed at her behavior, but couldn't bring herself to apologize. She still didn't know what to make of this man. She did, however, accept his affection for her daughter as genuine.

"I understand your principles, but your daughter really wants to go to this wedding. I know it's none of my damn business, but I think maybe you should reconsider. It could take her mind off other things," Dario counseled.

"I hear you, but I have to do this my way."

"Your child, your call," he conceded.

"Can we get back to the shoot? We don't have these girls all day,"

Forsythia reminded Dario testily, blowing a stray strand of her bouffant wig out of her face.

He nodded and walked away.

Bliss headed upstairs, Dario's words dogging her every step. She didn't want to send Bella off to Italy without her, especially now that Victoria wasn't attending. And she would not participate in the carnival freak show herself. Even if her own marriage had failed, and she had foresworn the institution, she believed in its sanctity. It disturbed her to see her sister treat it as nothing more than an opportunity to gain product endorsements and land the cover of *People*.

Once in her room, she sat at her computer and opened the saved-drafts email file. She pulled up an unsent letter of apology to Manuel. She'd started it not quite three months before, right after the trip to Vienna. She'd feared if she sent it, he would interpret it as a ploy to see him again. Now, it no longer mattered what he thought. Though she had hoped he would make a greater effort to claim his place as Bella's father, she had clearly scared him away. The time had come to put aside all pride and invite him back. Under the subject heading: "Re: Sincere and profound apology," she began to type. She looked at the salutation: "Dear Manuel." She hesitated, then added, "and Cindy" and began to rewrite.

chapter forty-three

Bliss could not pry Bella away from the window of their bedroom. She had tried every inducement: a Dora computer game, a lollipop, even the umpteenth viewing of *Cinderella.* Nothing could tear the child away from the spectacle of Aunt Didi taking off for her wedding. Clad in a cream-colored skirt suit Elizabeth Taylor might have worn to board the Queen Mary in 1955, Diana stood beside an endless suite of matching Louis Vuitton luggage, emblazoned with candy-colored LVs. An enormous white Rolls-Royce sat curbside. Across the street, the usual crowd of gawkers had gathered to cheer the proceedings and hold up signs that read BYE, BYE, VIRGIN! They were on take number twelve of Diana's so-called candid farewell to her childhood home and neighbors. One shot had been ruined by a six-month-old who, instead of fulfilling her duty as adorable tyke, had thrown up all over Diana as she leaned in to kiss her. Diana had nearly smacked the child, leading Bliss to hope she and Wyatt would focus on making millions instead of babies. Other than that incident, nothing ruffled Diana. She played the scene with the same beauty-contestant grin each time.

"Why can't I go with them?" Bella kept asking. Bliss didn't dare answer. She wanted to give her hope but not too much lest her plan be dashed. She looked at her watch and tried to contain her nervousness.

Diana swept into the car yet again, waving a gloved hand. *Who travels wearing white gloves,* Bliss thought, *other than germaphobes?*

The car pulled away from the curb and a battered taxi pulled up in its place. Bliss's heart beat faster and she thanked God as she saw Manuel emerge from the vehicle. She heard Dario yell "Cut!"

Diana dropped all pretenses to femininity to bark "What now?" Bella sprang up from her pout.

"It's Daddy!!" she yelled as she waved wildly to get his attention. She pushed past Bliss and stumbled out of the room. Bliss joyously watched her go, and followed her down the stairs, barely keeping up.

At the foot of the stairs, Dario had caught Bella.

"Easy does it," he cautioned.

"My daddy's here, let me go . . . please," Bella said, wresting herself from his grasp. Dario looked up at Bliss as if for permission. She nodded her assent, touched by the concern he evinced.

From outside, Bliss could hear Diana yelling. "Damn you, Manuel, you ruin everything! That was the perfect take and you spoiled it! Sue, did you see the way I positioned my foot before pulling my leg into the car? It was genius. Louboutin would have loved it!"

"I think you'd better let us by so that you can continue with the shoot, or the Virgin is going to end up pummeling my ex with the heel of her designer pump. I don't think that's the kind of product placement you had in mind," Bliss warned Dario.

"Okay," he relented, puzzled. Bliss followed Bella to the entrance and pulled her Cinderella suitcase out of the hall closet. They walked outside and Bella threw herself into Manuel's arms. He enfolded her in his.

"Daddy!" Bella squealed.

Dario stepped out on the stoop and called "Take five everyone, let's give these people some privacy."

"We're burning daylight!" Diana snapped, walking toward the trailer parked at the end of the block. The crew dispersed.

"I came to surprise you, *mi amor.* I'm taking you away," Manuel explained to Bella.

"You are?" Bella asked, wide-eyed. "Where?"

"Back to my house, so you can see your new room, and meet my . . ." he looked to Bliss, hesitating to use the word. She nodded and he finished the thought "fiancée." Bliss winced only slightly, agony having given way to the dull ache of wistfulness.

"Mommy said she's very nice," Bella added innocently. Manuel chuckled.

"Did she?"

"I did," Bliss seconded with mock indignation. Manuel smiled at her with genuine gratitude. It was the first chuckle they'd shared since either of them could remember.

"Then Cindy and I are taking you to Disney World!" Bella screamed and threw her arms around her father's neck. She turned to face Bliss.

"Mama, I'm going to Disney World!"

"I know," Bliss answered, moved to tears by her daughter's unbounded glee.

"Bliss, I know you've got mixed feelings about the whole Disney thing, but I wanted to give her a dream come true," Manuel whispered in Bliss's ear. She looked into his caramel-brown eyes and recognized their familiar warmth. This was the way he used to look at her as they held hands across their tiny kitchen table after a long day. She knew a part of her would always belong to him, though they would never again be man and wife. Looking into his eyes, she knew the same was true for him. Rather than savor the memories, she reminded herself that this was no time to dwell on love lost. This day belonged to Bella, and the father she'd regained. Bliss looked around.

"Where's Cindy?" she asked.

"In the cab," Manuel answered. "I wasn't sure . . ." Bliss took Bella by the hand and proceeded toward the car. The moment had come to formally meet the woman she'd last seen with her legs wrapped around Manuel's torso as they made mad, passionate love on top of a desk. She would have to find a way to erase that mental image from her mind, for Bella's sake as well as her own.

A tall, lean blonde about twenty-eight years old stepped out of the taxi, looking tentative, but resigned. After giving her the bionic female once-over, in which she assessed her height to within an inch, weight to within an ounce, and age to within a minute, Bliss offered a half smile and said, "Hi, Cindy, I'm Bliss." Relieved to be greeted civilly, Cindy extended a hand. Bliss took it and they shook, awkwardly holding on a bit too long, neither quite knowing when to let go.

"And this is Bella," Bliss said, disengaging herself at last.

"Hi, Bella," Cindy said, kneeling on the pavement and smiling warmly. *She's risking running her stockings to greet my child. This is a good sign,* Bliss noted.

"Thank you for asking us to take her," Cindy said, looking up at Bliss from her kneeling position. "Thank you," she repeated.

After nearly two years of dread, Bliss found the enemy was a human being after all. A very skinny human being who probably never in life experienced a bad hair day, but not the manipulative weasel of her imaginings. She was neither cheap nor common, just somewhat ordinary. *Throw a quarter out of your window in an upscale Los Angeles suburb and you'd hit ten of her,* Bliss thought, but she couldn't write her off as some Twinkie. Strangely, it made it more bearable to have lost to a somewhat worthy opponent, rather than to the usual cliché of the bimbo du jour.

"It's so nice to finally meet you," Cindy said. "Your Daddy talks about you all the time. And he's shown me so many pictures of you." Bella beamed. Bliss hoped Cindy wasn't exaggerating. Manuel approached and placed a hand on Bliss's shoulder. She flinched at his touch, so he removed it immediately. The three adults stood in awkward silence, Bella looking up at them all, grinning.

"You really should be off," Bliss suggested at last. She handed Manuel an envelope. "Here's a list of instructions, what she likes to eat, snack on, how to take care of the brace. In the bag, she has some organic Cheerios. Make sure she drinks something when the plane takes off and lands, or her ears will clog."

"I've got it, Bliss," Manuel assured her.

"Yeah." Bliss kneeled beside Bella. "Have a great trip. You know Mommy's going away too, but she's only a phone call away. I'm going to see you in ten days. Have a great time."

"I will," Bella said, "I'm going to Disney World!"

"Great, just great." She stood up. "Well, you know where to reach me. Call me if there's anything . . . call me."

"Thank you," Manuel said. He gave her a quick peck on the cheek, and led Cindy and Bella to the car.

As Bliss watched the taxi drive off, she wondered if she was doing the right thing. Would Manuel be able to handle Bella? What if she was homesick? She realized she was deluding herself. No child would be homesick at Disney World. If she truly loved Bella, she had to let her go and learn not to be indispensable to her.

"Can we get back to my departure?" Diana yelled as she emerged from the trailer.

"It's all yours," Bliss said, going back into the house, oblivious to the fact that Dario had been watching her from the living room all along.

chapter forty-four

As Bliss emerged from her car, she saw the trailers being loaded up, the cameramen exiting the house. Finally, the cast and crew of *The Virgin* were exiting her home and her life, never to return. Instead of the relief she thought she'd feel, a pang of sadness gripped her. *Perhaps it was like Stockholm syndrome,* she thought to herself, *when the kidnapped fall in love with their captors.* She shrugged it off and Dario appeared in the doorway, directing the boom operator where to stow his equipment. He brightened upon seeing her and made a beeline for her.

"It's your lucky day, we're finally out of here," he said, mustering a smile. She didn't know what to say in response. Sensing her discomfort, he continued, awkwardly, she thought, especially for one so cocky.

"Bet you thought it would never come."

"I can't believe it's been seven months," she said at last. "Where does the time go?"

"Sorry you're not coming to the wedding," he offered.

"I'm not. Not a big fan of weddings these days. And there seem to be a lot of them."

"It was big of you to let Bella go with her dad," Dario said sincerely.

"I didn't really have a choice," Bliss responded, brushing off the compliment and not wanting to dwell on the subject.

"Yes, you did. A lot of women wouldn't have done that."

"Are you going to bash women again?" Bliss warned, with mock-sternness. Dario groaned.

"I'm kidding," Bliss rejoined. "These are the jokes, folks. Guess I need to work on them."

"So, when do you take off for Europe?" he asked with genuine interest.

"In two days, the day after you guys celebrate the big event."

"Paris, right?"

"Yes."

"Just you and what's the dude's name? The Chevalier Saint Ignatius—"

"Chevalier de Saint-Georges," she corrected. For all his good looks, and palpable sensuality, Dario was painfully ignorant, she reminded herself. She thrust her right hand forward.

"Well, it was nice knowing you," she said with forced politeness. He nodded and, in an uncharacteristically chivalrous gesture, bowed as he took her hand. She was about to tease him for taking the chivalry part of his show too seriously, but something in his manner prevented her from teasing him. She nodded in response, removed her hand, and began to walk toward the house.

"Bliss," he called, as she reached the steps. She turned around.

"I found something of yours," he pulled a shining object out of his pocket and ran back to her. He placed it in her hand; she looked down and recognized the Yale insignia ring she'd tossed to the ground in the garden the day Manuel announced his engagement.

"I know you were . . ." he searched for the appropriately diplomatic word, "discarding it, but thought you might want it back at some point. For Bella." Bliss stared at the ring, the symbol of Manuel's pledge to her. She had not gone looking for it in the garden, but she'd missed it. Though she would never wear it again, she was relieved beyond imagining to have it back. Once again, Dario had read her deepest wishes. His perceptiveness was uncanny.

"Don't throw away your past. It's part of what made you what you are," he added. She nodded in response, afraid that if she spoke, she might begin to cry. He took a step away from her.

"If I'm in town, may I come see Bella?" he asked, almost as an afterthought.

"Sure," Bliss answered offhandedly. "Why not?" Dario nodded in response, and turned to deal with the crew. Sue Minors stood in the doorway, ruminating her wad of Smoke No More.

"Okay, let's move it out," Dario cried as he climbed into one of the trailers and it drove off.

"You're a cold fish," Sue reproached Bliss.

"What are you talking about?" Bliss asked, thinking this was the ultimate example of the pot calling the kettle black.

"After all that guy did for your family, you just let him leave like that?"

Bliss felt sincerely baffled. Sue didn't know about the ring. She looked at her puzzled.

"What did he do for our family?" she asked.

"Who do you think stopped the circulation of your baby sister's sex tapes?"

"The network," Bliss answered with certainty.

"Dario! The network would have loved the leak. Sex, scandal, and smut sell. Dario paid out of his own pocket to have them stopped."

"But Wyatt—"

"Scumbag. He was going to leak the tapes himself. He just wanted to drive the ratings up and become a bigger star. He achieved that by marrying your baby sister. And now they'll live happily ever after."

"So Dario was trying to help us by letting them get together?"

"Yes."

"Why?"

"Duh? Why do you think? Never thought I'd see it, but he's fallen hard for you. Who do you think bought you that ball gown for Vienna?"

Bliss recalled the exquisite dress, identical in color to the party dress she'd worn the first time she danced with Dario. Only a man who'd truly observed her could have made such a selection. She'd chalked it up to Wyatt and a good wardrobe person, but it had been Dario all along.

"Why are you telling me all of this now?"

"He swore me to secrecy. Now that the show's over, all bets are off. So, are you going to call him? Never mind, probably too late," Sue opined. "See ya around."

Bliss stood on her stoop, looking out at the tree-lined street, now returned to its usual calm and quiet. Could she believe Sue or was she just playing mind games? She had implied that Dario cared for her. Something in his newly awkward manner in her presence told her that he did and yet logic told her that was absurd. He liked her as a friend and no more. She was the opposite of his type. And he for that matter—other than his magnificent body, face, and hair, and unflagging attention to her daughter—was the polar opposite of hers. He had never read French history. He didn't read, period. In the end, it didn't matter. Her immediate future did not lie with a man. She knew in her heart she'd find her salvation in her books. Day 570 of celibacy loomed and Bliss was just fine with it.

chapter forty-five

Bliss sat at the desk in her father's study, picking at the roast chicken she'd prepared and enjoying the sound of silence. She had not been alone in the house since she could remember, and though she missed Bella, she relished not having anyone to care for but herself for a few days. It astonished her how much clearer her sentences were when they weren't being written in between dinner, bath time, helping Bella find the right word for a game of Super Grover in the Nick of Rhyme. She'd finished an entire book that afternoon alone. She looked at the little brass clock with Roman numerals. The minute hand moved: two minutes to eight. She fingered the remote control. Did she dare turn it on? This was the night of her sister's wedding, broadcast live from Rome, Italy. The entire affair was being held in the middle of the night so that American viewers could see it in real time, a first for network television, as *TV Guide* and every commercial had blared. Just as she was about to opt for correcting her students' poorly written papers while bleaching her unwanted facial hair, the front door's familiar trumpet fanfare sounded.

Bliss opened the door to Victoria and Melissa, their arms around each other.

"Do you have it on?" Missy asked.

Bliss knew she meant the wedding match made in Hell and merchandising.

"I was debating," Bliss answered as the women strolled in.

"The debate is over," Victoria declared, "we *have* to watch." She and Missy laughed, then melted into a kiss, the sort of expression of lust, love, and affection that is the hallmark of a new and passionate union. Bliss remembered how irresistible it had been to kiss Manuel in the early going. Where were the snows of yesteryear? She laughed at her own nostalgia. *Note to self: don't become the wistful and wizened spinster of the family.*

They filed into the study and Missy plopped herself onto the overstuffed couch with its fraying velvet Harold forbade Forsythia to change. Victoria grabbed the remote and flicked the television on. A booming announcer's voice filled the room.

"The television event of the decade: the Virgin's wedding." Church bells clanged. A giant envelope filled the screen. The flap opened and a card emerged with script that read:

The honor of your presence is requested at
the wedding of
DIANA WINDSOR HARCOURT
to
WYATT MONTGOMERY EVERS
Eight o'clock in the evening (prime time)
At Trinità dei Monti,
Rome, Italy

The little naked, trumpet-wielding cherubs framing the invitation came to life, flying across the page. They blew their horns and the invitation burst open to reveal the church itself, a Baroque splendor at the top of the Spanish Steps.

"Diana Windsor? They're kidding right?" Missy carped.

"No, that's her middle name," Victoria explained.

"It's all our middle names," Bliss corrected. "Our royalist mother gave them to us hoping people would think we were really related to the British royals. We're the suburban Maryland branch of the family. Our crest is a Chevy Blazer."

The camera zoomed in on the doors as they flew open and panned down the nave to reveal the guests, i.e. paid Italian extras, plus here and there an American reality-television star Airbused in for the occasion. The Kept Women of New York occupied the front pew on the bride's side, the Kept Women of Los Angeles, all blond with store-bought breasts, occupied the front pew on the groom's. Everyone flashed their best Pepsodent smiles. A portly Italian priest with the florid complexion of the copious Chianti drinker stood before the elaborate carved altarpiece, ready to unite the happy pair. Wyatt—looking smarmily flawless in white tie and tails, a smug smile on his face, his hair an ad for hair mousse—stood to the right, awaiting his bride.

"The swine looks good," Missy snapped.

"I can almost forgive myself for nearly sleeping with him," Bliss said, "but he really does look like he's about to sell snake oil."

"I'd go for the other one, that Latino-Italian guy," Missy commented with a lustful smack of her lips.

"Dario," Victoria said, putting her hand on her heart, unmistakable longing in her voice.

"Do-me-oh, I say," Missy corrected.

Bliss felt a pang at the mention of the latter's name. She found herself searching the screen for him, knowing full well he'd remain in the shadows, but wishing that she could catch a glimpse of him.

"He was hot, hot, hot. That's what I call sex on legs. I wouldn't kick him out of bed. Hell, I'd do anything to get him into bed," Missy continued. Victoria laughed out loud, and kissed Missy full on the lips. Watching her sister, Bliss thought she seemed almost drunk and in fact, she was, on desire fulfilled.

"If I were you, Bliss, that's the one I would have gone for," Missy prodded. Bliss's cheeks flushed. Now that Dario was safely out of her life, she could admit to herself that she'd found him desirable from the moment she laid eyes on him. But she wasn't about to reveal that to anyone else.

"Could you two be quiet, the wedding's about to start," she admonished with mock-severity.

A full string orchestra began to play the staple of every American wedding aspiring to class and dignity: "Pachelbel's Canon." Forsythia appeared wearing a purple taffeta float.

"What do you think Mom was going for, Elizabeth the Second, the purple of royalty, or Elizabeth Taylor, the purple of Hollywood?" Victoria inquired.

"Taylor," Bliss assented.

The announcer, now speaking in the hushed tones of a golf tournament commentator, said, "Forsythia Harcourt makes her entrance on the arm of Wieland Evers, Wyatt's brother and best man. She wears the famous Peregrine Pearl from the estate of the late Elizabeth Taylor."

Victoria and Bliss high-fived. While trying to maintain an air of aristocratic dignity, Forsythia beamed brighter than a tarted-up Christmas tree. Once Wieland had deposited Forsythia in her seat, the flower girls began to make their way down the nave, each one dressed as a different flower with her bodice the stem and her skirt the petals. The pink rose, yellow tulip, and the violet walked solemnly down the aisle. Bridget, the Diana look-alike, however, was unable to resist waving at the cameras. There was one additional child, a Chinese flower girl whose dress suggested a lotus blossom. Behind her bouquet, she concealed a DSi game player from which she never looked up.

"That last girl must be Ming, Sue Minors's adopted daughter. She's already inherited her mother's rudeness and obsession with electronics," Bliss commented.

Forsythia started out of her pew, no doubt to strangle the child, after ripping the offending contraption from her hands. Harold, looking utterly miserable in his garroting white tie, restrained her and forced her back down into her seat.

"What's your dad doing sitting in the pew? Isn't he going to escort your sister?"

"No, he refused. He said she might as well be on the auction block," Bliss explained. "I'm hoping he'll object when the time comes."

"The floral court has assembled," the commentator said in his hushed voice. "Now the moment America and the world have been waiting for: the arrival of the Virgin in her wedding gown."

Trumpets blared and the organist played Mendelssohn's "Wedding March." Diana appeared in a blaze of blinding light at the door of the cathedral, wearing a dress with a skirt so ample it took up the entire width of the nave. The extras rose and let out gasps of awe on cue.

"This gown, the winner of an international competition that included entries from top wedding designers and even one from Galliano, the disgraced creative director of Christian Dior, in a desperate bid to rehabilitate himself, was inspired by the Virgin Queen, Queen Elizabeth the First herself. It is incrusted with over ten thousand cultured pearls from the famed house of Mikimoto."

Diana, breathtaking behind her Alençon lace veil, glided down the nave, her steely blue eyes cast upward, as if fixed on higher thoughts, when in truth she was angling for the cameras hidden in the frescoes on the ceiling. As she arrived in front of the altar, Wyatt stepped forth, one perfect glycerin tear rolling down his cheek.

"Oh, brother," Missy scoffed.

"Dearly beloved. We are a gathered here today to witness the wedding of dees a man and dees sainted virgin. Who a geeves dees woman to be wed?" the priest asked, in Italian-accented English worthy of a comedy sketch. The congregation waited for a response. Bliss willed her father to have courage.

"I said, who a geeves dees woman to be wed?" the priest repeated. Forsythia jabbed her elbow into Harold's side. He doubled over in pain.

"I do," he said, wincing. Forsythia jabbed him again. "Her mother and I do, but—" Forsythia jabbed a third time, this time evincing a muffled cry from her better half.

Victoria and Bliss reacted with sympathetic winces of their own with each thrust of their mother's elbow.

"Good. Please be a seated."

"Where did they get this priest? Sal's Pizza Mart? He sounds like he's about to break into a chorus of 'Shut Uppa You Face,'" Missy commented.

"I think Papa wanted to say more. I think he might just object," Bliss said hopefully.

"Mum will kill him if he does," Victoria warned.

"Before the ceremony, a special song," the announcer proclaimed.

All three women groaned.

"The hopera singer Cecilia Bartoli will do 'One Hand-a, One Heart.' From de musical, *Westa Side Story*."

"Oh, I love that song," Victoria said earnestly.

"Me too!" Missy assented. They began to sing along with the television set, as Bliss watched dumbfounded. What had happened to her uptight, reserved, terrified-to-be-noticed sister?

"'Even death won't part us now,'" Victoria and Missy belted out, ending with a soulful kiss. *They should be the ones whose love is broadcast for all to see*, Bliss thought. *It is genuine and pure.*

"Before we continue with the ceremony, I must ask, if there is anyone who objects, let him or her now a speak."

The music turned ominous as the camera panned faces in the crowd, ending on Harold. Was this Dario's Machiavellian revenge on Wyatt? Had he planned for Harold to sabotage the proceedings? Harold made a move to rise, clearing his throat.

"He's going to do it!!!" Bliss cheered.

Just as she said it, Harold shifted in his seat and pretended to cough. After a few more moments the priest continued.

"Since there isn't, we ken a continue. Wyatt do you take dees . . ."

Bliss sat back down, deflated.

"I can't watch anymore," Victoria said, disgusted. Missy grabbed the remote and clicked it off. The three sat staring solemnly into space.

"Why do I care?" Bliss asked at last. "This is who Diana's always been. Why does it matter?"

"She's still our sister," Victoria said quietly. "And it's sad to see human potential wasted."

"What potential?" Missy objected. "She was born to be a beauty contestant. Sorry, I'm an outlaw, I shouldn't say that."

"You're right," Bliss said. "And what are we doing sitting around here moping? Let's go out and celebrate, on me. We'll drink to true love: yours."

"We'd like to, but tonight, we're dropping in on my parents," Missy said, glowing. "They've always loved Victoria and they want to toast us." Bliss hugged Victoria. Though her own mother had rejected her, she had the enormous consolation of being welcomed by her in-laws.

"You're probably the only woman in America whose mother-in-law likes her," Bliss joked.

"I am," Victoria cheered. "She called me right away when she heard to say 'Welcome to the family.'"

"Now we just have to get all the kids on board," Missy added soberly. "My eldest, Nate, is not too happy with me right now. His last words were 'See you in Hell.'" Victoria put her arm around Missy's shoulder and fervently kissed her cheek.

"We just have to give him some time. He'll come around. Everyone will, maybe even my mother . . . someday," Victoria added, willing a smile through tears.

"We've got my girls and my youngest, my parents, and Bliss. That's not bad, for a start," Missy insisted, suppressing her own sadness.

"And my dad," Bliss suggested encouragingly.

"We're lucky," Missy insisted with stiff-upper-lip, onward-Christian-Soldier determination.

"So, don't just stand here," Bliss suggested. "Go, go, go!!"

"What are you going to do for the rest of the evening?" Victoria asked.

"Enjoy the silence!" Bliss exclaimed. "Do not worry about me. I am fine," she insisted, escorting them to the door. As she closed it behind them, the house's silence no longer soothed her. It reminded her she was very much alone. She picked up the cell phone she'd left charging on the desk and rifled through the contacts." Under *F* she found it: Dario Fuentes. She pressed the number to connect, then instantly canceled. Dario was not a man one called in a state of vulnerability and desperation. She resolved to follow her first instincts where he was concerned. In spite of occasional flashes of kindness, he was far too seductive to be trusted.

chapter forty-six

Bliss backed her battered divorcemobile into a spot in the Pint and Horseshoe's parking lot. She sat for a moment looking at the back door of the establishment, wondering what her precise purpose in being there was. Did she plan to say to Jordan: *Hey, I leave for Europe tomorrow. Want to help knock out the cobwebs and end my five hundred and seventy-second day of celibacy?* Somehow that didn't strike her as a seductive mating call. There was that other subtle approach: lifting her dress up over her head. Did she even want to sleep with him? If one had to ask, maybe one didn't. If she couldn't even remember how to flirt and seduce properly, would she remember what to do in bed? Yes, of that she had no doubt. It came so naturally to her, even if the lead-up didn't.

Was she there on the rebound? From whom? Certainly not from Dario, though she had spent the last hour searching for him on-screen and been rather disappointed to see nothing but his name when the credits rolled. Had hope or sheer, unadulterated desperation brought her here? No one could accuse a woman seeking the attentions of Jordan McIntosh of desperation. The man was an Adonis and brilliant to boot. Then she remembered the legions of women who had thrown themselves at him, white, black, and everything in between, students, fellow professors, cleaning women. He had politely but firmly rebuffed them all. She remembered her father's stories on the subject. But that was when his wife had been alive. In two years, he hadn't been with anyone else. Was it possible he'd endured even more days of celibacy than she? No, a man would explode. And if it was true, she wanted his secret. It might be frightening to be the first after such a dry spell. Together they'd create a veritable meltdown, or at least cause an earthquake.

She decided to stop this futile analysis paralysis. It was time to move on with her life. She was off to Paris in the morning. Tonight, she should throw caution to the wind and see where life took her. For a passionate person, she certainly did overthink and play it safe sometimes. She vowed to herself never to hold herself back that way again. Yes, she'd been crushed by love, bulldozed in fact. But she was alive to tell the tale. Onward!!! She flung open the car door. As she did so, a man staggered out of the kitchen door of the Pint and Horseshoe. Even with his back to her, she could tell it was Jordan. She was about to yell his name when she caught sight of the person he was backing away from: a pale, blowsy woman in her midforties with jet black roots contrasting the copper red of the rest of her bobbed hair. She wielded an iron skillet menacingly, the fat underneath her arms jiggling like fleshy hammocks each time she raised them.

"You son of a bitch!" she screamed in a coal-miner's-daughter twang. Bliss wondered for a moment if she should call for the police. This was technically the South, after all, and the scene before her had shades of white female rape hysteria. She watched Jordan place his large brown hands on the woman's doughy flesh to calm her. The woman knocked them off. The familiarity of both gestures made it clear: this was not the first time Jordan had touched her.

"Keep off me! You lyin' piece of shit!" the woman yelled, her fleshy face trembling with rage, tears streaking her cheeks black with cheap mascara. She looked like a circus clown in agony, Tammy Faye Bakker Agonistes.

"You LIIIIIEED to me!" she roared in a voice that came from an abyss of pain Bliss recognized. She instinctively clutched her own midsection protectively.

"Lana, I'm sorry." Jordan offered weakly.

"Lana," what an improbable name for this woman in shambles. Her mother must have been an old-movie buff like Forsythia, Bliss surmised. Jordan's apology only doused fuel on Lana's rage.

"Sorry?" she repeated. "Ten years of waitin' and all I get is 'sorry'!" She lifted the pan to strike him on the head, but Jordan caught her arm. They stood wrestling on the landing by the back door, her face contorted with rage, pain, and the determination to bop the son of a bitch on the head. Even fueled by all the furies of a woman scorned, she was no match for the sinewy Jordan, who within a few moments wrested the lethal skillet from her hand. She crumbled to the ground in a heap, buried her face in her fleshy hands, and sobbed. Jordan stood over her helplessly, shifting his weight from foot to foot.

"Hug her, you idiot!" Bliss found herself saying. Then covered her mouth. She felt she should drive off, but had to see the drama play out. Jordan McIntosh, the hero of her youth and adulthood, had been carrying on with a blowsy fry cook for the better part of his seemingly perfect marriage. More astonishingly, he'd managed to hide the fact from everyone, including the apparatchiks at gossip central, the Faculty. She couldn't decide what shocked her most: that he'd transgressed at all or the object of his lust. Only in risqué French films did men like him fall for someone who looked like the help. The fact that she was white only added to the cliché. Men so exacting in their standards for black women dropped them entirely to go with Trailer Park Tessy. His wife had been a great beauty, a debutante, and a brilliant PhD in her own right. It did occur to Bliss that the beautiful Genevieve had never struck her as sensual.

Perhaps intuiting Bliss's advice, Jordan knelt beside his sobbing paramour and tentatively put his arms around her. This time Lana didn't resist, but buried her face in his cashmere V-neck-sweater-clad chest, the spot she'd probably sought all along, Bliss surmised. *A woman in love has no pride,* she thought to herself, remembering all too well the feeling that the person who's wounded you the most is the only one who can take the pain away. Bliss averted her gaze, feeling she was intruding a bit too much. After a few long moments, she saw them both rise, and Jordan kiss Lana tenderly on the forehead.

"What do you want to do?" he asked quietly.

"I don't know. I just don't know," Lana answered in the hopeless tone of one who'd surrendered her heart long ago. She turned and walked back into the restaurant. Jordan watched her go, leaning back against the railing. At last he turned to face the parking lot. Bliss jumped to get into her car but it was too late, he'd spotted her.

"Bliss!" he called, a tremor of panic in his voice, as if he wanted to ask, "How long have you been standing there?"

"Hi!!" She waved with forced cheer. He leapt the railing and bounded over to the car as she fumbled to open the door.

"Where are you going?" he asked anxiously.

"Um . . ." she didn't want to lie and say she'd already been inside in case he hadn't spent his entire evening in the kitchen. "I changed my mind," she offered lamely. He placed his hand on hers and she looked up at him.

"You saw everything, didn't you?" he asked. She nodded in response, suddenly feeling like the gawky thirteen-year-old who used to wait for him to show up at the house, then pretend to be reading a book as he entered. Only now, she knew his full story and could no longer project all the wonders of maleness upon him.

"I shouldn't have, it was none of my business," she said, looking away.

"I can explain," he offered.

"You don't have to. You shouldn't."

"I want to, please," he insisted. Bliss paused.

"I loved Genevieve. I really did. And I respected her more than any other woman." Bliss was still enough of a romantic to feel that respect and cheating didn't quite go hand in hand. She considered saying so but thought, for once in her life, she'd listen instead of giving a piece of her mind.

"Genevieve was so many things to me. And we had a beautiful life together, not perfect, but wonderful."

"So, if it was so wonderful, why did you need Lana?" Bliss asked, her mind reeling. Jordan smiled, charmed by her naïveté.

"You're an idealist, Bliss. Life doesn't work that way. I loved Genevieve, but over time, marriage changes. It's hard for one person to fill every void."

"So you're a guy and you get to have it all?" Bliss challenged. Jordan looked at her, his eyes hollow and tired.

"I don't have Genevieve anymore. Like Itzhak Perlman said, when your violin has lost a string, you play with what's left. I'm playing with what's left." He turned to walk toward his car, looking less like the faculty Adonis than a man whom life had dealt a deathblow. Would he really be content to creep along with his Jeffersonian secret mistress on the side, Bliss wondered. She wanted to run after him and insist: "Don't give up! Don't give up on love." She stopped herself, realizing it was the height of arrogance. At thirty-three, she knew the agony of heartbreak but not the devastation of permanent loss after a lifelong union.

Jordan turned to go to his car, then without facing Bliss, he added: "Have a good trip to Paris, Bliss. It's a shame I couldn't have fallen in love with *you.*"

He climbed into his Mercedes convertible and drove away, the wind ruffling his salt-and-pepper curls. An unexpected wave of relief washed over Bliss. *It's no shame,* she thought to herself. She prayed that Lana would have the strength to stand up for herself as she had. She remembered the day she discovered Manuel's affair and declared, "It's her or me." He'd moved out that night, leading her to think she'd made a terrible mistake. In the year and a half they'd been apart, she'd played the what-if game in the back of her mind. Tonight, standing in the parking lot, she knew for well and good that she'd done right, and anything else would have cost too high a price. There was someone besides the man you loved who could remove the thorn from your heart: you.

chapter forty-seven

Bliss ran down the narrow rue du Cherche-Midi in the Sixth Arrondissement. It was only six in the morning and already a line had formed in front of Poilâne, the legendary *boulangerie* known for its sourdough loaves handmade with crystalline sea salt from Normandy. Neighborhood residents and map-wielding tourists patiently waited their turn to purchase the freshly baked bread. Its aroma wafted out into the street, whetting Bliss's already acute appetite. She had tasted this delight once before, as a teenager on a summer Eurail-pass trip, and had promised herself to return. On her first full morning in Paris, she kept that promise.

With her purchase under her arm, she made her way down the elegant boulevard Saint-Germain, which was bordered on each side by nineteenth-century apartment buildings with iron balconies and earlier vintage *hôtels particuliers* hidden behind high walls and tall doors painted blue or swamp green. She peered in the windows of the various shops, some of them expensive designer chains, others quintessentially French and unique, like the tiny umbrella store founded in 1865. She ripped off chunks of her bread as she strolled, sinking her teeth into the fresh crust and the warm, moist *mie* that delighted her more than any cake ever could.

She arrived at Les Deux Magots, the café where Simone de Beauvoir and Sartre had held court for three decades, and where Hemingway had debated literary styles with Fitzgerald. A cup of coffee there would probably cost her ten Euros, a budget-breaking amount for a graduate student trying to save up enough to move out of her parents' home, but she decided to splurge. She took a seat on the outside terrace, overlooking the medieval Saint-Germain-des-Prés church across the way. The sun shone on the marble tabletops. She ordered a *café crème,* rich, dark roast with warm whole milk, which, as its name implied, tasted like pure cream. Two tables away from her, a long, lean Frenchman with a mane of wavy hair sat reading his morning *Figaro.* He was about fifty, distinguished looking, with a square jaw, broad shoulders, and large hands. He peered at her over his reading glasses and nodded. She smiled back.

She had reached day 575 of celibacy. If there were any place on earth to throw caution to the wind, this was it. She was alone in the world's most romantic city other than Rome and she had her own hotel room. Okay, it was matchbook-size and not exactly at the Ritz, but who needed space? She was almost thirty-four, divorced, *truly* divorced, and very single. It was time to add another name to her list of lovers, which thus far consisted of one. She didn't have quite the gumption to walk over to this handsome specimen, but if he came to speak with her, she resolved to respond. In the meantime, she buried her nose in her guidebook *Historic Walks Through Paris.* Whose itinerary would she follow today? Jefferson's, Gertrude Stein's, or Josephine Baker's?

When her waiter arrived at the table with a fresh *café crème,* she panicked about how she would pay for it till she saw the Frenchman smiling broadly and lifting his cup as if to toast her. Now, she beamed and mouthed "*Merci.*" He threw some change on his table and strolled over to hers.

"*Vous permettez?*" he asked, indicating the empty seat beside her.

"*Bien sûr,*" she answered.

Noticing her book, he switched to elegantly accented English.

"I'm Bernard Harcourt."

"I'm Bliss Harcourt. We must be related," she laughed at the coincidence.

"I hope not," he said, giving her an appreciative glance.

"Did your family follow William the Conqueror to England?"

"No, they were peasants tilling the soil until the nineteenth century, when my great-grandfather started working for the railways. You are English?"

"Half. And my family didn't follow William the Conqueror either, my mother just likes to pretend they did."

"Where is your other half from?"

"Jamaica."

"*Métisse. Joli mélange.* Are you here on holiday with your boyfriend?"

"It's not a holiday. And there's no boyfriend. I'm here to research my PhD thesis on the Chevalier de Saint-Georges."

"*Le Mozart noir,*" Bernard said knowledgeably. Bliss brightened at the recognition. Here was the first person who hadn't honked "Whoooo?" when she mentioned her hero. She looked more closely at Bernard. He had penetrating hazel eyes, a lovely inviting lower lip and his hands were large and magnificent.

"You know about le Chevalier," she pursued.

"*Bien sûr.* My favorite biography is the Gabriel Banat."

"That's mine too," she gushed. "Although I still think there's room for improvement."

"I agree. It takes someone who understands what it is to live between two worlds," he said flatteringly. "So, you are on your way to the Archives Nationales?"

"Yes."

"And then at some point you'll go to Bordeaux, where he and his mother and father landed."

"Not this trip, but at some point, yes."

"You must let me know when. I have property there and a good many contacts."

"Thank you."

"And dinner, tonight, what are you doing?"

"I hadn't really figured it out. It's going to be whatever my stipend will cover, which may just be this loaf of Poilâne."

"Nonsense. Call me, " he said, scribbling a number on a Deux Magots napkin. Bliss took it and read it. She could tell from the 06 prefix that it was a cell phone number. She studied Bernard for a moment: cashmere sweater, elegant driving shoes, family-crest ring on his pinkie finger. This was the sort of man who would have a proper card. She rose and gathered her belongings.

"*À ce soir,* then," he said. She looked him dead in the eye.

"Just out of curiosity, are you married?" she asked.

He shrugged.

"Does it matter?" he answered.

"Not to me," Bliss said, "but it might to your wife. Thank you for the coffee," she handed him back the napkin.

"Mais, voyons, Bliss, soyons raisonnables," he protested.

"That's just it. I'm not remotely reasonable or rational. Good thing I found out now and not after we did the deed, or I might have stabbed you with the top of the wine bottle I would have smashed over your head," she said with a smile and flounced off.

As she reached the river and the sun danced on its rippling wavelets, she looked out at the Gothic splendor of Notre-Dame Cathedral. The bells tolled and she walked on, over the bridge and into the bustle of the rue de Rivoli and the Fourth Arrondissment. She arrived in front of the limestone portal of the Hôtel de Soubise, former stomping ground of the Chevalier. This was why she had come to Paris. As she made her way down the main marble walkway of the oval courtyard, she rejoiced at the thought of meeting her idol at last. The Chevalier was one man who would never disappoint her.

chapter forty-eight

It was a beautiful day, far too beautiful to be spent inside, and yet Bliss's heart beat with anticipation as she approached the thirty-foot doors of the *hôtel,* a former royal residence, which now served as headquarters of the French National Archives and the extant writings of her love, her ideal man. In addition to housing many documents pertaining to his life, the *hôtel* had been the site of many of his performances as a violinist and orchestra leader. Bliss felt the same anticipation she did as a young woman preparing for a date, and had dressed accordingly in a figure-flattering spring dress that showed off her décolletage.

She laughed at herself; she was like a disturbed character from an old Hitchcock film, having an imaginary affair, dressing for a nonexistent dinner partner. But the Chevalier had lived and she would help resurrect him. Before going to view the documents, she decided to walk the halls he had walked and absorb the atmosphere of his day.

After mounting the majestic marble double staircase, she stood in the middle of the light-filled music room, its oval shape and floor-to-ceiling windows soothing to the senses. As fanny-pack wearing tourists milled about her, staring up at the Nattier murals depicting Psyche, she stood in the middle of the room, imagining the café au lait complexioned virtuoso, his powerful thighs nearly bursting his knee britches, closing his eyes as he coaxed exquisite sounds from his violin. She closed her own eyes and could hear his "Concerto in A" in her head. Its rising and falling notes evoked the birth of passion. He had once said "I evoke my emotion and anger through my music," and indeed she could feel the fury in the scherzo. It was a fury she had felt as a stealth mulatto, an insider/outsider in front of whom people felt free to express their prejudices. She knew the disdain and hatred that lurked in the hearts of those who smiled at her, but accepted her only in part. At least she could help redeem his struggle by bringing it to life. She didn't want to leave the room, but forced herself out. She only had five hours to spend with the source materials.

A scrawny little man brought her the papers in a gorgeous wood-paneled study. The folio bulged with documents. She donned a pair of gloves and opened it. A cloud of dust burst forth. When it cleared, there it was, the long fluid handwriting, as elegant as he. Her hands trembled as she lifted the first letter, addressed to his patron and love, the Marquise de Montalembert.

"Chère Madame," it began. Though she had read the words online and reprinted in the few volumes devoted to his life, to see the original and feel the 230 years that separated them evaporate excited her beyond reason. This was why she had become a historian, to find the link that bound one generation to the next and held the key to redemption. She was absolutely where she belonged.

chapter forty-nine

Bliss emerged into the milky northern light that illuminates Paris till nine in the evening. She felt spent yet exhilarated by her day with the Chevalier. She could well understand the women who had fallen under his spell. She breathed in the balmy spring air, and looked up at the sky. As she exhaled, she spotted a muscular frame reclined against a motorcycle parked by the front entrance. Her heart stopped as Dario turned to face her, smiling warmly.

Bonsoir, I thought you'd never come out," Dario said, rising to give her a slight bow. Bliss stood motionless, unsure of what she felt or what to say. She opened her mouth but found no words. She shut it again, for fear of looking like a deranged guppy. As it began to sink in that Dario had purposely followed her to Paris, tracked her down, and waited outside the archives on the off chance of seeing her, disbelief turned to gratitude, and speechless joy.

"So, does this mean you're happy to see me? Or should I hop the next plane back to LA and drown my sorrows in a margarita?" Dario ventured tentatively.

Bliss rushed over and threw her arms around him. He wrapped his around her and they savored the embrace. Bliss's body melded perfectly into his. She squeezed him tighter.

"Easy," he said, "I'm not going anywhere, but we are." Bliss looked at him quizzically. He handed her a helmet.

"Hop on," he ordered as he climbed onto the front of the motorcycle.

Bliss hesitated, then realized she should obey though it was hardly her nature. He relieved her of the computer bag. As the engine revved up and the motorcycle sped off, she clutched his waist suffocatingly.

"Watch it," he laughed. "Don't kill the driver," and they took off down the rue des Francs-Bourgeois. She knew better than to ask where they were going. It was time to let Dario take the lead.

As they sped down the highway and the wind whipped past them, Bliss was grateful they had stopped at her fleabag hotel so she could change from a dress to jeans. Only the contact with Dario's massive torso kept her from turning blue with cold on the forty-five-minute journey out of Paris. Dario guided the Harley to an exit ramp, and they wove down a country road bordered by towering elm trees. Finally, Bliss raised her head, which for the better part of the ride, she'd buried in his broad and fragrant back. She recognized a red marble courtyard she'd seen in countless photographs, and in reproductions of seventeenth-century prints. They had arrived at the forecourt of the Palace of Versailles. Dario parked the bike and helped her alight. She looked around in complete wonderment. Louis XIV had built the palace to astonish and intimidate, and she felt its full effect. Dario swelled with delight at her appreciation of her surroundings.

An officious middle-aged French woman in an impeccable knobby tweed skirt suit clicked briskly across the cobbled pavement to greet them.

"Monsieur Fuentes, bienvenu!" she exclaimed as she shook his hand heartily.

"Aurélie, this is Bliss Harcourt," he said proudly. Bliss stopped surveying the splendor around her long enough to acknowledge the elegant lady.

"Madame, c'est un plaisir," the latter greeted Bliss with a nod.

"How do you know her?" Bliss asked in a whisper.

"I've been here before," he answered cockily, a Cheshire-cat grin on his face.

"Suivez-moi," Aurélie invited, as she led them past the entrance gate to the other side of the palace and the gardens overlooking the Fountain of Apollo. The majestic vista took Bliss's breath away. The terraced parterres led the eye to the fountain below, the Sun God's chariot rising out of the water, pulled by bronze horses that appeared as though they were galloping toward the viewer at full speed.

"I always dreamed of coming here," Bliss commented softly.

"Now you're here. And you have the run of the place," Dario rejoined.

"How did you know?" Bliss asked, awed.

"I do my research," Dario answered confidently. "I couldn't get you to Rome, my favorite city, so I came to one of yours."

Aurélie led them down the main graveled allée to the parterre closest to the fountain. There a small round table had been sumptuously set for dinner for two. Aurelie lit the eighteen-inch tapers in the ornate six-armed silver candelabra.

"Voilà!" she announced. *"Je vous laisse.* You have my number when you are ready to tour the inside, Monsieur Fuentes," she said with a bow to Dario as she walked back toward the main building at a clip. A valet in gold-and-burgundy livery arrived and placed a computer on the table. Dario pulled out the gilded bamboo chair in front of it and indicated to Bliss she should sit. She complied, still utterly awed by her surroundings and wondering if she would awaken from this dream, as she had from so many others, only to find she was still marooned on her rickety cot in her parents' home.

Dario towered over her, opened the computer, and turned it on. She leaned back into him, shutting her eyes. When she reopened them, she found to her delight that she was still indeed at Versailles. The strains of a violin concerto she recognized began to play: the Saint-Georges "Concerto in D." The Chevalier's image filled the computer screen, a beautiful pen-and-ink rendering by one of his contemporaries, which captured his soulful eyes and delicate features underneath his regulation eighteenth-century gentleman's powdered wig.

"What's this?" she asked Dario, stunned.

"Watch," he encouraged her.

The words *Welcome to the World of the Chevalier de Saint-Georges: Fencer, Violinist, Conductor, Gentleman,* appeared over the portrait. A home page popped up featuring different sections: *Biography, Compositions, Timeline, Significance.* Dario pointed to the latter.

"I'm going to need you to provide content for that segment," he explained.

"When did you have time to do all this?"

"I've been working on it for a little while. It's linked in to MBC and the show's website. Kind of a read-more-about-it on chivalry. The real thing. After all, you told me the Chevalier was 'the guy,' and from what I've been learning, he really was," Dario explained.

Now Bliss pinched herself to make certain she wasn't hallucinating. No matter what she tried though, there was no waking up. This was all really happening. She had always believed that leopards didn't change their spots, but Dario, a man she had dismissed as the missing link, had devoted time and effort to learning about one of her heroes. And he had brought her to the very palace in which Saint-Georges had conquered France's nobility with his talents.

"You've been reading about him?" she asked, incredulous.

"Yup. Not the whole biographies. I got a research assistant to, you know, condense them for me."

Bliss smiled at the admission. His candor was endearing and adorable.

"The show's website has been averaging five million hits a month. Five million people are going to be reading about your guy who'd never even heard of him before. So, the show may be, what did you call it? 'The leading cause of death for the American brain,' and I may be no better than 'a crack dealer.' But we both can serve a higher purpose," he added teasingly.

Bliss winced at the recollection of the insults she'd hurled at him from the first time she'd met him.

"I'm sorry I was so hard on you," she offered sincerely.

"Maybe I deserved it," he admitted.

"So does this mean you're going to stop producing shows about women trying to get married, virgins. . . ."

"I don't know, convince me," he challenged. "You'll have a few days, weeks, decades . . . if you want."

She stared, stunned and grateful, into the warm depths of his amber eyes.

"Why are you doing all of this?" she asked, not daring to believe what she knew to be true.

"Isn't it obvious?" he said softly.

"Why me?" she asked in a whisper. "You hate everything about me, my loudness, my smugness, my snap judgments."

"So true. And you hate everything about me, my machismo, my ignorance, my crassness," he concurred. "We'll have to find some points we have in common," he added, tenderly kissing the palm of her hand. He looked up at her. In his eyes she saw adoration and acceptance.

"Thank you for everything you did . . . for my family," she said, cupping his chin with her hand. He kissed it again and placed an index finger on her lips, silencing her gently.

"I did it for you. And I'd do it again."

He leaned in. Seamlessly, they inclined their heads, their lips met in a long, slow kiss. As they parted she whispered: "575."

"What?" he asked puzzled.

"Days I've been celibate," she admitted, slightly embarrassed.

"Oh, we have to fix that. And I know just the guy," he chided, leaning in to kiss her again.

In this single instant, Bliss understood the word *epiphany*, the sudden and miraculous recognition of having exactly what you want and need before you. Every single thing Dario had done from the moment he appeared at the gate of the Hôtel de Soubise had made her feel cherished, beyond reason and beyond measure. After months of searching, she had finally arrived where she belonged. She laughed in spite of herself at the ridiculous improbability of it all, at her own blindness in not recognizing him sooner. Though she loathed fairy tales, sitting in the garden at Versailles, experiencing the dawn of a great love for the second time, she dared to hope she might actually live happily every after.

acknowledgments

The acknowledgments in my last tome provided a soporifically long list of friends, supporters and inspirations. I shan't repeat the names here, but refer the curious to the back pages of *One Flight Up*. (And no, this is not a thinly veiled bid for more sales and royalties, though Heaven and my accountant know I could use both.) I echo all of the sentiments expressed then, and now single out for praise and thanks my editor, Greer Hendricks; Atria's leader, Judith Curr; my agent, the indefatigable Suzanne Gluck; Marina Rust Connor, who started me on the journey that brought me back to prose; Adriana Trigiani, who is friend, muse, guardian angel, and the person who told me I should write books (a few Amazon readers vehemently disagree, Adri, and you'll have to take it up with them).

On a practical level, my deepest thanks to Caroline Weber, who spent a beefy, red-wine-soaked dinner and several follow up conversations explaining the Byzantine world of academia. Once again, I'm beholden to the New York Public Library, in whose Performing Arts branch I sit as I compose these words. The library is a democratic haven for all us wandering creative souls. I'm honored to sit in its magnificent rooms, surrounded by the young and the old, the obscure and the "great." May these hallowed halls welcome many more generations of curious minds.

To all the great performers past and present whose work dances in my memory, enlivening empty hours, encouraging me to continue the creative journey. Notably, brava to Adèle, who has reminded the world what divine alchemy can come of a piano, a haunting song, and a voice that grabs the soul and won't let go. I dream one day of writing prose that shakes people to their foundations as your song does. Now and forever, praise to the dancers of Alvin Ailey and ABT (special thanks to my "second daughter" Misty Copeland), who demonstrate that human beings were indeed born to fly.

questions and topics for discussion

1. Take a closer look at the epigraphs for *Imperfect Bliss*. How does each relate to the novel? Do you think they are representing the point of view of a specific character?
2. On the surface, Harold and Forsythia are an unlikely couple. What do you think draws them together? Are there other unlikely couples in *Imperfect Bliss* that seem to work?
3. Do you think *Imperfect Bliss* takes a cynical or an optimistic point of view on love? What about marriage? Use examples from the novel during your discussion.
4. Bliss feels that history holds the keys to the present and the future. To what extent is this belief illustrated in the book? Do you agree with Bliss?
5. Discuss the ways that the novel addresses race. Would you say it is central to the plot? What about to the identities of the Harcourt daughters?
6. How do Bliss's opinions of her mother and father evolve as the novel progresses?
7. On p. 246, Victoria compares being gay to being black. Do you agree with this comparison? Why doesn't this seem to resonate with Forsythia?
8. Early in the novel, Bliss thinks, "Fairy tales were like candy: fine if you didn't make a steady diet of them" (p. 3). Despite this statement, do you think Bliss learns anything from fairy tales over the course of the novel?
9. "You think this is bad, you should watch *The Bachelor*. Twenty-five babes and one guy in a hot tub." Do you think that *The Virgin* is

better for women than a show like *The Bachelor* or the *The Bachelorette*? Or is it just the same in principle?

10. What do you think the "imperfect bliss" of the title is referring to—and what is the novel saying about bliss, more generally? Does perfect bliss exist?
11. Consider Bliss's love interests throughout the novel—Manuel, Wyatt, Jordan, and Dario. What do they have in common? What lessons does Bliss take away from each of them?
12. How is Fales-Hill using satire within the novel, and what point do you think she is making about reality television? Did reading this novel affect the way you think about (or view) any specific shows?

enhance your reading group

1. Consider the significance of the Chevalier de Saint-Georges in the novel. What does he represent to Bliss? As a group, do some research into the historical figure—you might even listen to some of his music.
2. If you haven't already, read Susan Fales-Hill's previous novel, *One Flight Up*, as a group, and compare and contrast the portrayal of marriage in each book.
3. Adriana Trigiani called *Imperfect Bliss* a "piquant comedy of manners," and author Susan Fales-Hill acknowledged that she wrote the novel with Jane Austen in mind—in particular, *Pride and Prejudice.* Can you identify the parallels between the Harcourts and the Bennets?
4. Imagine that you are casting the film version of *Imperfect Bliss.* Who would you pick to play each of the four sisters? How about Harold and Forsythia? Dario and Wyatt?